CHANGE OF LEADS

BOOK TWO

AFTERSHOCK

THE NAVARRE LINK CHRONICLES

CHANGE OF LEADS

BOOK TWO
AFTERSHOCK

A. K. BRAUNEIS

First Printing: 2020
Printed and bound in the USA
ISBN 978-1-7335920-1-7

Two Blazes Artworks
710 Terry Lane
Selah WA 98942
USA

www.twoblazesartworks.com

Cover art, interior illustrations and design by
A. K. Brauneis

Dedication

To my husband, Paul. Though often shaking his head at my chaotic creativity, he has always been there with his love and support throughout this whole process. Love you, Babe. You're the best thing to come into my life.

To Peter Deuel. Though gone from this Earth for many years, he was, back then, and still is now, my creative inspiration.

Acknowledgments

Where would I be without the westerns! Movies, TV, books, they were all my sanctuary, my private world where I could go anytime and disappear into a world filled with fun and adventure.

Jimmy Stewart, Audie Murphy, and Ben Johnson, to name only a few who kept my eyes glued to the screen. Wagon Train, Wanted Dead or Alive, High Chaparral, Lancer, and my all-time forever favorite, Alias Smith and Jones. Westerns were abundant when I was growing up, and I'm sure I watched every single movie and most of the TV series that were out there.

Charlie Russell! Oh my, what an influence he had, and still has, on my creative endeavors. Attending the Out West Art Show in Great Falls, Montana, has become one of the highlights of my year.

Max Brand was my favorite western author, and though I read books by others, his were the ones that kept me coming back.

Today, I watch most of the new western movies that hit the silver screen, giving my support to a genre that has lost its way but is struggling to make a comeback. At the very least, these more recent westerns have been entertaining, but there are a few that stand out as gems: Butch Cassidy and the Sundance Kid, Tombstone, Silverado, Dances With Wolves, Appaloosa, and yes, I did enjoy Cowboys and Aliens!

I thank all these creations, and the many people that helped in their production for giving me a love that has lasted a lifetime. Now here I am, writing my own western series, and enjoying every minute of it.

For those people in my life now who have helped me along the way I would like to thank:

Renee Slider, curator at the Wyoming Territorial Prison National Park, for all of her assistance in tracking down the details.

S. Whyment for her support and contributions toward character development.

Lisa Baird for the many hours she dedicated to proofreading this manuscript. And for her knowledge in legal procedures and terminology.

Eric Hotz for his technical support. For someone, like myself, who is computer illiterate, his advice and assistance has been invaluable.

Also, to the various on-line writing sites that offered me a safe place to get my literary feet wet and for helping me realize when it was time to move on.

And, of course, my writing critique group. This group has shown me so much support and encouragement, both in finetuning my manuscripts, and in weathering the stormy waters of self-publication. You're a great group of ladies!

Thank you!

Also available on Amazon

ICE: Prelude to the Navarre Link Chronicles
ISBN 987-1-387-86345-1

CHANGE OF LEADS: THE LOST SHOE
ISBN 978-1-7335920-0-0

CHANGE OF LEADS: AFTERSHOCK
ISBN 978-1-7335920-1-7

CHANGE OF LEADS: DANGEROUS GAMES
ISBN 978-1-7335920-4-8

CHANGE OF LEADS: DEPARTURES
ISBN 978-1-7335920-5-5

CHANGE OF LEADS: THE WAY OUT
ISBN 978-1-7335920-6-2

Previously

Napoleon Nash and Jackson Kiefer have been working undercover for the governor of Wyoming in the hopes of attaining a pardon for their previous lives of crime.

A chance meeting with Cameron Marsham brings the fellas back to that family for a happy reunion. But unknown to them, the stable hand, Sam Jefferies, is in the employ of a determined US Marshal who will stop at nothing in order to capture the two outlaws and bring them in to face justice.

During the ambush at the Marsham ranch, Jack Kiefer is seriously injured and Napoleon Nash is arrested and transported to Cheyenne to stand trial.

Jack remains at the Marsham ranch to recover from his injuries. During this time, Penny Marsham shows her love for Jack when she risks her own life to protect his.

Jack shows resistance. Though he likes Penny, he is hesitant to commit to anything serious. He does not know what his future holds and can only focus on what is happening to Leon and what will ultimately happen to himself.

In Cheyenne, Leon stands trial and is sentence to a crippling sentence in the US Penitentiary at Laramie city.

Jack struggles with this sentence. Not only because of the lack of support from the Wyoming Governor, but also because of what now may befall himself. Where one goes the other fallows.

Now, with Leon headed for a life sentence behind bars, Jack must face his own trial. He knows, with the secrets he has kept hidden for so many years, that even the support of his friends, he could be facing a fate worse than death.

Table of Contents

Dedications 5
Acknowledgements.................................7
Prelude 9
Table of Contents ....

Chapters

1) Attitude 13
2) The Bell Tolls.................................35
3) Meeting of the Minds.......................45
4) Friendship......................................61
5) Prison Life.....................................77
6) Learning the Ropes.........................103
7) Josephine......................................115
8) The Prosecution 129
9) The Surprise Witness 143
10) The Defense 157
11) The Gunfight 193
12) The Verdict 213
13) Survivors' Guilt.............................231
14) Severed Link................................241
15) The Letter....................................269
16) Dire Straits 285
17) Kenny Reece 301
18) The Wayward Son 317
19) Partners 337
20) Hindsight.....................................358
21) Revelations 379

List of Characters 392
List of Wyoming Governors...................395
Prelude 396
About the Author................................397

CHAPTER ONE
ATTITUDE

Rawlins, Wyoming
Summer 1885

Six days before the Napoleon Nash trial.

Jack was bored. Usually, when he found himself locked in a jail cell, he would lay back, pull his hat over his eyes, and go to sleep. Even Leon had marveled at his ability to accomplish this feat at any time of the day or night, and under just about any circumstances. Unfortunately, even his undeniable talent had met its match, when the long summer days began to blend into weeks.

When the posse, with their prisoner, had finally arrived in Rawlins, it had been a great relief to get off the stifling train and away from the curious looks of the other passengers. Even the children, with their pointing and giggling, had worn thin. Jack was ready for some solitude.

It was relatively cool inside the jailhouse, and once he had been placed in a cell and the shackles removed, Jack felt a certain amount of stress ease off his shoulders. He was still hurting, though, emotionally, and physically. Morrison pushing him up against the bars for a routine, but totally unnecessary search, had caused his head to spin, and his stomach to threaten unpleasantness.

"All right, Kiefer," Morrison said. "I hope you like your new lodgings, 'cause you're gonna be here for a while. Behave yourself and we'll get along just fine."

"Yeah, sure we will," Jack mumbled, his cheek bone still stinging and bruised from the last time he had tried to comply with the marshal's wishes.

Morrison ignored the outlaw's grumbling and left the cell. Finally

alone, Jack sat on the bunk and released a heavy sigh of despair.
cradled his right arm in his left and wished he could find some way to
ease the aching. Exhausted, he tucked his arm inside his shirt, to give
it some support, then lay down, covered his eyes with his hat, and hoped
to sleep.

Forty minutes later, still awake and hurting, Jack heard the cell
door open. He groaned at the prospect of another encounter with the
marshal.

"C'mon, Kiefer, wake up." Deputy Rick's voice was a welcome
alternative. "I've brought the doc here to see you."

This sounded promising. Jack removed his hat as he sat up and
found himself looking at what he would have normally considered a
typical "country doctor". Of course, having gotten used to David and
his ways, an ordinary doctor might be a little hard to adjust to.

"This is Doc Jones," Rick said. "I asked him to check you out. I
know you've been hurting."

"Yeah, thanks," Jack said. "Ah . . . Morrison agree to this?"

"Nope, probably not," Rick admitted. "Like they say, 'It's often
easer to ask forgiveness than seek permission'," he smiled. "So, we'll
just see if the doc can help you out for now and take it from there."

Doc Jones eyed the prisoner, then, deciding that it was safe to enter
the cell, he walked in and placed his bag on the bunk.

"Howdy, young man. I hear you're still experiencing pain from a
bullet wound."

Jack nodded, his shoulder throbbing, as he watched the doctor paw
through his worn-out satchel. Finally, the doctor returned his attention
to Jack and approached him with a determination to be helpful.

"Okay. Let's see what we can do about it."

An examination of his shoulder did not take long, but it felt like
eternity to Jack. He could not help but take note of the differences
between this doctor and David Gibson. Though Doctor Jones was much
older than David, his probing fingers didn't have the same intuitiveness
behind them. It was like comparing a country bumpkin in a shooting
competition, to the Kansas Kid in a serious showdown. You knew who
the artist was.

The doctor was capable of doing his job, though. He set Jack's arm
in a new sling and prescribed morphine to help with the pain. This is
what Jack had really been hoping for. While Doc Jones treated the cut
on Jack's cheekbone, the patient made some inquiries "Ah, the doc that

patched me up, said I ought ta start doin' some stretchin' ta help loosen up them muscles. Do you know anything about that?"

"Stretching?" Jones was skeptical. "What was he getting at?"

"He said it would help me get back the use a my shoulder."

"He told you that?" Jones sadly shook his head. "Sounds like a fool to me, or a coward. Just said that to make you feel better, I'm afraid."

"What do ya mean?"

Jones finished treating the cut and put a consoling hand on Jack's left shoulder.

"Son, I'm sorry," he said, "the doctor had no right to tell you such a thing. The way your shoulder has been tore up, you'll be lucky to be able to write your own name. That is, if you could write in the first place. No, you just keep your arm in a sling, until it heals up right, and take the morphine when you need it. I'm afraid, it's the best you can hope for."

He gave Jack's shoulder a couple of pats, and turned to Rick with a sad smile. "Shameful what some doctors will tell a fella just to make him feel better."

Rick glanced at Jack to see how he was taking this bit of news, before escorting the doctor out of the cell block.

Jack slumped on his bunk, staring into space; now he really was scared. The doctor he needed, and had come to trust, was no longer available to him. Instead, he was stuck in the care of an old fogey, who had no idea how to help him. He found himself tempted to break out of jail, just to get back to Arvada, back to Doctor David Gibson.

***

Taggard came to see Jack as often as he could, but with his own duties in Medicine Bow, Leon's trial in Cheyenne looming on the horizon, and Morrison insisting on keeping Jack in Rawlins, it was stretching their worthy friend a little thin. At least Taggard brought Jack news on how Leon was faring, and that they were both on the same track concerning their current situation.

Taggard didn't know the details, but from what he related of Leon's attitude, Jack surmised that his partner had also made some promise to Cameron, and now, all three of them were honor bound. Leon and Jack were holding up their end of the deal, but only time would tell if Cameron did the same. One thing Jack did ask Taggard to do, was to please send a telegram to David.

Taggard frowned. "Who?"

"David Gibson. The doctor in Arvada."

"Isn't the doctor here helping you?"

"More like hinderin', I'd say."

Another frown from Taggard.

Jack sighed. "The doctor here is tryin' ta help, but there's no comparison between the two men. I need David."

"Okay. I'll send him a telegram. What do you want it to say?"

Jack stared off into space for a moment, then his response was blunt. "Help."

"That's all? Just help?"

"He'll know what I mean."

***

Arvada, Colorado

"Help?"

"Yes."

"That's all? Just, help?"

"I know what he means."

"A man of few words, isn't he?"

"He can be," David smiled at his wife, "but he gets his message across."

"Are you planning to drop everything and go running to Wyoming?"

David groaned. Was this going to turn into another fight?

Tricia felt the tension growing as she stood in the office and watched her husband pack.

"It's all right, David," she said. "I know this is part of who you are, and since I married you for who you are, it would be silly of me to try and change that."

David smiled, relieved. He took his wife into his arms and held her tightly.

"Thank you. I love you, you know."

Tricia smiled. "I know."

"Why don't you stay at the Marshams' while I'm gone? Or at your folks' place? I shouldn't be more than five days, or so."

"No. I don't want to impose on them. Millie is right next door. We'll keep each other company."

"Well, all right." David returned to his packing. "If you're sure. I am concerned about you being here alone."

"I'm hardly alone," Tricia rolled her eyes. "It's not like I'm out on one of those ranches by myself. We're right here in town, and like I said, Millie and I can keep each other company."

David nodded. She was right.

"I'll swing by the Hamilton's place, on my way to the train station, and let them know I'll be out of town for a few days." David mumbled this more to himself than to Trish. She was aware that the Hamiltons' had handled all the medical concerns before David had arrived in town. They were always happy to fill in for him, whenever he had to go away for a while.

"All right," she answered him. "Have a safe trip."

***

Rawlins, Wyoming

It could never be said that Dr. David Gibson was a stupid man. He arrived in the town of Rawlins during the late afternoon and intentionally avoided the jailhouse until he was sure Marshal Morrison had gone home for supper. He checked into the hotel, got an early supper for himself, then took up a strategic position along the boardwalk, where he had a clear view of the front of the jailhouse. And there, he waited.

Close to 7:00 p.m., David spied Rick making his way to the jail and disappearing through the front door. Ten minutes later, Morrison himself, exited the same building and began the twenty-minute walk that would take him home. David waited until the marshal was well and truly out of sight, then headed for the jailhouse.

He entered the office to find Rick in the process of making coffee for himself and the lone prisoner. The deputy looked up in surprise, then added more water and coffee to the pot.

"What are you doing here, Doc?"

"I received an urgent request from our friend, in there," David nodded toward the cell block. "It seems he hasn't much faith in the local physician."

Rick barked a laugh. "Yeah, well that doesn't surprise me. I'll let you in. But if Morrison finds out about it, I'll deny all knowledge."

"Coward."

"You bet."

"Why are you doing guard duty?" David asked. "Don't you have a spread to look after?"

"Yeah, but this was part of the deal we made with Morrison. We'd stay on until the end. I've got good people looking after my place for me and, I have to admit, my share of the reward money on those two is going to be well worth it."

"Yes, I suppose." David was non-committal.

Rick sighed. "Now don't get all judgmental on me, Doc. It was a job, and not an easy one at that. Kiefer's not a bad sort, but it doesn't change the fact that he's an outlaw, and a gunfighter, and I've got no qualms about bringing him in."

"I suppose you're right," David sighed. "In the meantime, I feel like I'm fighting the odds, just keeping the two of them on their feet. Your boss isn't helping."

Rick nodded his understanding. Truth be known, he was tired of Morrison's bullying. The marshal, shooting that outlaw from the train, exceeded his authority. Rick wasn't going to admit as much to the doctor, but he was having strong doubts about working with him again.

As the coffee started to boil, Rick took down the keys and led David into the block.

"Hey, David—" Jack was off his bunk in an instant, a grin stretched across his features. "Finally. You won't believe what the town doc here has been tellin' me."

"You guys want some coffee when it's done?" Rick asked, as he let the doctor into the cell.

"Sure."

Rick nodded, then left the two men together.

"What happened to your face?" David scrutinized the bruising.

Jack's smile disappeared. "Morrison."

David nodded his understanding. "Well, it doesn't look too bad. It should heal up all right. So, what's so bad about the local doctor that you had to summon me from my warm hearth and warm wife?"

Jack groaned. "Oh, David. The guy hasn't got a clue. I don't think he even went to medical school. I asked him about doing stretches and all that stuff you were talking about, and he looked at me like I had been taken in by the biggest crackpot west of the Mississippi. Why is it everyone thinks you're an idiot?"

David laughed. "Because I have gone to school, and then some. If the local doctor is an old coot, who's been at it for forty years, then he's not going to like some young whippersnapper coming in and changing the rules on him."

Then Rick was back.

"Here you go fellas—fresh coffee," he handed the two cups through the bars.

David took them.

"Thanks," he said, then mumbled as an aside, "I do seem to be spending a lot of time in jail cells, lately."

Jack heard him as he took his cup. "Yeah, tell me about it."

David smiled. "Sorry. I know it's been a lot harder on you."

Jack nodded in silent agreement, and the two men sat down for a companionable drink of caffeine.

"How was your trip here?" David asked. "From the look of your face, I'd say it didn't go smoothly."

"You can say that again," Jack answered. "You were right about that marshal. I don't know what's the matter with him. He's mean for no reason. My old gang tried ta hold up the train, didn't even know we were on board." He hesitated a moment, sadness returning to him. "He shot a friend a mine right outta the saddle, right in front a me, just ta get their attention. Killed 'im, right there in front a me."

"Yeah," David sighed. "I'm sorry, Jack. That does seem to be Morrison's way. He subdues by intimidation." The good doctor couldn't think of anything else to say and certainly nothing that would help his friend feel better.

"He's just mean," Jack repeated. "You warned me to watch out for him, well now I'm warnin' you. You tend ta rub him the wrong way, and one a these days, you just might rub him too hard. I wouldn't want ta see anything happen to ya—at least, not until my shoulder is healed up."

"Ha. Right. Thank you." David laughed. "Now you tell me, after summoning me here behind his back."

"Cheers!" Jack responded and tapped his coffee cup to David's.

They both took one more drink, then David stood up, took Jack's cup from him and put them both on the floor, out of the way.

"Okay, let's get on with the business at hand," he said, and gently removed the sling that was supporting Jack's arm. He started unbuttoning the shirt. "How has it been feeling on the most part?"

"Aching."

"Deep?"

"Yeah."

"Okay," David began to poke and prod again, "that's to be expected."

Jack grimaced with the pain of the exam.

"Try to relax, Jack," David told him, "and don't forget to breathe."

"What do ya mean? How could I forget ta breathe?"

"You weren't breathing just then."

"Yes, I was."

"No, you weren't."

"I was."

"Jack. Just relax."

"I am relaxed. OW! Dammit, David—you always hurt me."

"And yet, you summoned me here."

"Yeah . . . well."

"Come on, let your arm relax. There, thank you. Breathe, Jack. I know it hurts, but it will release in a minute . . . there. How does that feel?"

"Oh." Jack was surprised. He moved his arm around and could feel that the muscle had loosened up. "Yeah, that's better."

"Good."

After that, David showed Jack some exercises he could do on his own, to help with the stretching and increase muscle strength. They seemed straightforward enough.

"So," David continued, "how much morphine are you taking?"

"Ah, well. Enough so's I can sleep," came Jack's ambiguous answer.

David picked up on the defensiveness and started to push.

"Enough so you can sleep," David repeated. "How much is enough?"

"Dr. Jones gave me a pouch full and told me to take it as I need it."

"And how much is that?"

"Enough so's I can sleep."

David sighed. "Okay. Just at night?"

"Well—sort of, sometimes—well, usually."

David looked at him, his eyes narrowing with suspicion. "Jack, are you still taking it twice a day, on a regular basis?"

"Well . . ."

David groaned with exasperation.

"It hurts, David!"

"Just because they call you 'Kid', doesn't mean I'll accept childish behavior from you!"

"Hey!"

"Where is this intimidating gunfighter I've heard so much about?" David demanded. "Fastest gun in the West—ha. Everybody's so afraid of you, and you can't even handle a little bit of pain."

"Well why do ya think I became the fastest gun the West?" Jack yelled back. "It kinda discourages people from hurtin' me!"

The two men glared at each other for a moment, and then both started to laugh.

Rick heard the shouting and came back to make sure the two men weren't at each other's throats. He stood there watching them, with a furrowed brow.

"What in the world are you two going on about?" he asked.

"Oh, it's all right, Deputy," David assured him as he recovered his composure, "just a minor disagreement."

"Really," Rick commented. "Let me know if you decide to kill each other and I'll be sure to clear the building."

David sat back down and both men settled in to a companionable silence. David picked up the coffee cups and handed Jack's back to him.

"I'm sorry," David finally said, then started to chuckle again. He coughed and stifled it. It was time to be serious. "I did warn you about the dangers of being on that drug for a prolonged period."

"Yeah, I know." Jack slumped. "I guess, it's that ole Doc Jones weren't too encouragin' with his opinion. Even though I didn't believe 'im, it did kinda scare me. The painkiller was available, and it was easy to keep on takin' it."

"Okay. I can understand that. But now you really do have to cut back. Even if Dr. Jones encourages you to take more, don't allow yourself to be persuaded. It really is important, Jack. You get addicted to morphine, and you'll experience a whole new level of misery, trying to get off it again. All right?"

"Yeah, okay David. I know you're right."

"Good. Now where is the pouch Jones gave you?"

21

"Why?"

"I just want to see how much you have."

"It's not much."

"Fine. Just let me see it."

"You don't need to . . ."

"Jack!"

"All right! All right," Jack conceded. He reached under the pillow and brought out the pouch.

"Thank you." David opened the pouch and peeked inside, then he sprinkled a little of the powder into the palm of his hand. "No more than that amount, at night only. Okay?"

"Aw, that's not very much."

David stared at him.

Jack sighed. "Yeah, okay."

"Promise?"

"Yes. No more than that amount, at night only."

"Right. Good." David returned the pouch to Jack and stood up. "I'll get going now. The next train back home doesn't leave until 10:00 tomorrow evening, so I'll try and get in to see you one more time. That is, if Morrison doesn't find out. If he does, I'm sure he'll find a way to block me."

"That's it then?"

"No. Once you get moved to Cheyenne, I'll have more access to you, and not have to be skirting around Morrison. In the meantime, just do the stretching and the exercises I showed you. That should keep things from getting worse, anyway. When you get to Cheyenne, I'll see you there, and we'll really get after it."

"Okay, Doc. Hopefully I'll see you tomorrow evening, anyway."

"Yes. I'll try. Goodnight."

"'Night."

***

David got in one more time to see Jack, before he had to head back home. Time dragged by, and the mornings had developed a chill, when Jack was informed that he would be transported to Cheyenne later that day. It was time to begin the preparations for his trial. He knew Leon would be starting his own, any day now, and Taggard was busy helping to get things organized.

Jack had been left much to himself, and he was feeling lonely and worried for his partner. He missed him and felt he should be with him at this time but knew Morrison would never allow that to happen. And knowing this made him resent the marshal even more.

Jack could hear them, in the front office, getting things in order, long before the cell block door opened. Rick and Alex came in and began the routine of getting the prisoner ready for transport. Jack never would have thought that standing in a cell, surrounded by officers of the law, and being frisked, would ever be mundane. But repetition can make anything become tedious.

"C'mon, Kiefer, on your feet," was Rick's greeting to him. "We're going to have to leave this sling behind, I'm afraid. If Morrison found out that we let you out of this cell without being cuffed, there would be hell to pay. You don't really need it anymore, do you?"

"Well . . ." Jack slumped, "it does help."

Rick thought about it for a minute. "Yeah, okay. We'll bring it along, so you'll still have it when we get to the other end. It's not going to be too long a train ride, anyway. Anything else you need?"

"Yeah, under the pillow," Jack told him. "The pouch with the medication Dr. Jones gave me."

"I'll get it," Alex offered.

"All right, let's go," Rick finished securing the prisoner, and headed him to the door. "We've got a train to catch."

"Morrison not joinin' us?" Jack asked, as he snatched up his hat.

"He's already there. Preparing to testify at your partner's trial."

***

Just as Rick promised, the train trip proved to be a lot shorter, as well as a lot less exciting, than the previous one had been. There were only a few other passengers in the car they rode in—and no children. Aside from a few curious glances at the man in shackles, they were left in peace.

They found themselves pulling in to Cheyenne without incident and in time for a late lunch. Unfortunately, Morrison was at the train station waiting for them, and that killed any appetite Jack might have had.

The prisoner was shuffled off the train and straight over to a small building down a side street, that apparently used to be the main jailhouse, but was now only used for overflow. Or, as in this instance—solitary confinement.

When the group of men entered the office, Sheriff Turner awaited them with the ever-present coffee pot simmering on the stove. Much to Jack's surprise, he found the interior to be light and airy, with an open floor plan. The three cells to the left, were not partitioned off behind a heavy door, but were an extension of the office. Of course, Jack had been in jails laid out like this before, but after spending the last few months in a more secured abode, this was a refreshing improvement.

"Howdy, folks," Turner greeted them as he snatched the keys from the desk top. "So, this is Mr. Kiefer, is it?"

"Yeah, this is him," Morrison confirmed. "You better keep your eyes on him. He's not quite as slippery as his partner, but I hear he's been awfully quiet lately, so I wouldn't trust him."

"I see." Turner, though not impressed with the marshal's attitude, still turned a cautionary eye to the prisoner. "That true, young fella? You busy makin' plans?"

Jack simply smiled. With Morrison around, he had given up all efforts to communicate.

Turner nodded, as he led the group over to the first cell. He understood the reason for the prisoner's stoic silence.

Morrison went into the cell with the prisoner and removed the shackles, then pushed Jack up against the bars to do the usual end-of-journey search. He finished it, finding nothing, as usual, then held Jack in place. This was also becoming old.

"Don't move, Kiefer, not until you hear the cell door close. You got that?"

"Yup."

Fifteen minutes later, all the paperwork was signed and filed away and the three visiting lawmen headed out to get supper and find rooms for the duration. The two remaining occupants of the jailhouse settled in to their respective corners. Everything quieted down for the evening, with Turner sipping coffee and reading the paper.

Jack stretched out on the cot, with his hat over his eyes, but he couldn't relax. He was worried, and finally, with a sigh, he sat up and looked at the lawman.

"Sheriff?"

Turner stood up and came over to the bars.

"So, you've got a voice after all. What can I do for you?"

"How's my partner?"

"His trial starts tomorrow. I gotta admit, that will be a relief for everyone. He don't take well to confinement, does he?"

"No," Jack answered. "It tends ta make 'im a little stir crazy."

"Yeah, I noticed. You had any supper?"

"No."

"You want any supper?"

"I suppose."

***

The rest of the evening went by uneventfully. A couple of the young deputies from the main jailhouse arrived to take over the night watch, and considering their previous experience with Napoleon Nash, they were understandably anxious about what his partner might get up to. Their worries were for naught. In fact, Jack put his sling back on, took the prescribed amount of morphine and slept through the night.

The next morning, two other deputies showed up with breakfast, so they were a welcomed sight. After that, the day settled into the usual routine of paperwork and dealing with minor disturbances around the town.

But as the day wore on, Jack became increasingly restless. He was tempted to take more of the morphine, but he knew, even from afar, David was watching and would give him another reaming out, if the pouch emptied faster than the doctor judged acceptable. Besides, he realized that David was right, and for his own good, he had to back off it.

He knew Leon was in court that day, and he felt frustrated at not being there with him. For some reason, he had always imagined them going on trial together, facing it together. Probably because that is what they had always done. They'd always backed each other up, always been there for the other one. Now Jack couldn't be there for his friend, and guilt formed a knot in his already stressed innards. He took up his partner's habit of pacing the cell.

Around mid-afternoon, Sheriff Turner showed up to relieve the two deputies, and relaxed into his chair to drink coffee and read the daily paper. Eventually, after about an hour of this, Turner put the paper down and, with a heavy sigh, frowned at the prisoner.

"Listen, young fella, why don't you settle down in there? You're beginning to get on my nerves."

"Sorry, Sheriff," Jack answered, honestly. "I'm worried about my partner, is all. Any idea how it's going?"

"Well, yeah, actually," the sheriff admitted. "I've been over there with them. The judge ended the proceedings early today, to give your partner a chance to . . ." Turner hesitated, not sure how much detail he wanted to pass on to the prisoner.

Jack stopped pacing. "A chance ta what?"

"Givin' testimony has been kind of hard on Mr. Nash," Turner explained. "I think the judge wanted to give him some time to collect himself and regroup."

"Why?" Jack pushed. "What happened?"

"I think it best you wait and talk to your lawyer, or one of your friends, about that. I expect they'll be over to see you after supper. They would have come by yesterday, but, for some reason, Marshal Morrison forgot to tell them you had arrived."

Jack nodded, frowning with skepticism. Yeah, Morrison 'forgot', all right.

***

A couple of hours later, Jack was nibbling on some stew and biscuits, when the front door to the office opened, and David, along with another gentleman, whom Jack didn't know, came in.

Turner got to his feet. "Ah. Figured you fellas would be showing up, sooner or later. He's right over there."

The prisoner stood up and approached the bars.

"Jack, how are you doing?"

"Good, David."

"Mr. Kiefer, I'm Steven Granger. I'm going to be your lawyer." Granger reached through the bars, and the two men shook hands.

"Mr. Granger," Jack acknowledged him. "How are things goin' for my partner?"

"It's not over yet, but it has been rough on him."

"This is the second time I've heard that, but nobody will tell me what's goin' on."

"I'll leave your friend here to fill you in, Mr. Kiefer. I just wanted to introduce myself. I'll be back over to see you later tomorrow. We can get started then, all right?"

"Yeah, fine," Jack answered him but was looking at David.

"Goodnight," the lawyer said, and left the two friends to talk.

David called to the sheriff. "Do you think you could let me into the cell? I'll need to exam his shoulder, anyway."

"I suppose so, Doc," Turner sighed, shaking his head. "You seem to be making a habit of taking over my jail cells. Don't you have nothin' better to do?"

"Not at the moment, no."

Turner unlocked the cell door, and David sat down beside the prisoner.

"How's your shoulder?"

"Not bad."

"Did you back off the morphine?"

"Yeah. Just takin' a little at night still. I'm tryin' ta back off a that, too."

"Good." David sighed, feeling the real topic weighing in the air and wondered where he was going to begin. "Jack, did you and Napoleon ever talk about what happened when you were kids—what happened to your folks?"

Jack tensed. He hadn't expected this.

"No," he finally answered.

"Never?"

"No, never." Then Jack looked away and down at his hands. "Come close once, but it was just . . ." He trailed off, not knowing how to finish that sentence.

"Did you know that Leon had a younger sister? Still a baby at the time?"

"Sure," Jack shrugged at this common knowledge. "Little Jenny. Yeah, I remember her. She died too, just like my sister . . .."

"Yes, I know," David said, so Jack wouldn't have to put that painful memory into words. "But at least you remember your sister. Napoleon had forgotten about his."

"What do you mean?" Jack asked. "He forgot that she died?"

"No. I mean, he forgot about her completely. He forgot he even had a younger sister. When he was asked about his siblings, he said he'd only had three. All of them older."

Jack looked at David, incredulous, his jaw dropping. "How could that be? How could he have forgotten he had a baby sister?"

David shrugged "It happens sometimes, when an event is so

traumatic, so terrible, that the mind can't deal with it, so it simply pushes it back, out of conscious memory. Just as though the event had never happened. There have been several cases like this chronicled since the war, although there are those in my profession who doubt its validity. From what I saw in that courtroom, today, I'd say there's some pretty strong evidence supporting the hypothesis."

Jack frowned. "What's a . . . hypothesis . . .?"

"Oh, sorry. It refers to an opinion or view that has not been proven yet."

"Oh. And Leon had one 'a these, hypothesis . . .?"

David smiled, taking Jack's query at face value. "Yes, I believe so."

"Really?" Jack was amazed. "I wish that could 'a happened for me."

"No, you don't," David shook his head. "Sooner or later, something will happen that triggers those memories, and when that occurs, it's devastating. That's what happened to Leon today, while he was on the stand and relating the events of that raid. It hit him hard, Jack; remembering it like that. Believe me, it's not something you would want to go through."

Both men became momentarily lost in their own thoughts.

"How is he?" Jack finally asked.

"Better now."

"He's not alone, is he?"

"No. Your friend, Sheriff Murphy is with him."

"Oh. Good."

"Cameron and Caroline are also here."

"Caroline is here?"

"Yes. Much to everyone's surprise," David smiled. "But that young lady did a lot to help Leon feel better. For that alone, I'm glad Cameron brought her along. She definitely has her own mind."

"Ohh ho!" Jack laughed. "David, you don't know the half of it. Like I said, she and Leon are a lot alike."

The front door of the office opened again and Jack visibly tensed.

Morrison glanced into the cell and, seeing David there, gave Turner a scowl.

"What the hell is he doing in there?"

"Oh, relax," Turner got to his feet. "They're just talking. And I'm right here, keeping an eye on them. Everything's fine."

Morrison did not look pleased, but seeing that Turner was not backing down, he changed tactics.

"Me and my deputies will be spending the night here, Sheriff, so you might as well head back to the main jailhouse or go on home. Whatever you usually do at this time."

Jack groaned under his breath. David could sympathize.

Turner nodded and stood up for a stretch. "Yup, I'll be heading over that way," he said, just as Rick walked in the front door. "You gentlemen have a good night. I'm sure you'll see the doctor out."

Morrison scowled again, but sat down in one of the chairs, with his own cup of coffee and the newspaper. Rick also relaxed, putting his feet up on the desk and pulling his hat over his eyes. Getting a snooze in while he could, seemed like a good idea.

No longer comfortable discussing Napoleon with Morrison there, David did a thorough exam of Jack's shoulder and seemed pleased with the result.

"You've been keeping up with the stretches," the doctor observed.

"Yeah, a course."

David smiled. "Good. Try getting through the night without the sling. Put it on again in the morning when you're up and about. But if you can sleep without it, all the better." He sighed and put a consoling hand on Jack's shoulder. "I hate to do this to you, but I should get over to check up on your partner, before it gets too late."

"Yeah, that's fine, David. I'm all right. Say 'hi' to Leon for me, okay?"

"Yes, I will. I'll see you tomorrow. Marshal, I'd better be going."

Morrison got up to let the doctor out of the cell, then saw him to the front door.

"You keep showin' up like a stray dog, don't ya, Doc?"

David ignored the comment. "I'll be around to see him again, tomorrow, Marshal. Hopefully his shoulder will continue to improve?"

"Time will tell."

***

Once David was gone, Morrison came back to the cell and approached the prisoner. Jack had become too complacent of late, and the marshal didn't trust this behavior with these two outlaws. It was time for another attitude adjustment.

"C'mon, Kiefer, on your feet. Up against the bars."

Jack groaned. Not another search.

Then Morrison grabbed him by his shirt. The marshal hauled him to his feet and slammed him, head first, into the bars.

Jack hit hard, grunted, and nearly went down.

Rick almost fell out of his chair, and then was on his feet in an instant.

"Dammit! C'mon Tom! There's no need for that. What are you doing?"

Morrison ignored him. He grabbed Jack again, pushed him up, face first, against the bars. With a hand between the prisoner's shoulder blades, he held him there to the point where Jack found it hard to breathe.

"When I tell you to move—you move," Morrison snarled in Jack's ear. "I'm not gonna put up with attitude from you. You got that?"

Jack fought to cover the pain in his shoulder and wasn't able to answer him fast enough. The marshal grabbed the back of his shirt, pulled him away from the bars and then plowed him back into them again.

"I said, you got that?"

"Yeah—"

"Good."

Morrison whacked Jack's arms up over his head, and proceeded to give him another search. He was none too gentle about it, either, and Jack sucked his teeth.

"Your shoulder seems to be doing much better," the marshal sneered. "I guess ole Doc Jones knows a thing or two about healin' after all, doesn't he? That Gibson is a crackpot, if I ever saw one."

Jack and Rick exchanged a quick glance, acknowledging their mutual opinion of the town doctor.

Morrison finished with the symbolic search, completely missing the silent communication that had taken place around him. He found nothing on Jack's person and nor had he expected to.

Pulling Jack around, he gave him a hard shove into his cot and left the cell, clanging the door closed and locking it.

Jack stayed where he landed. He shook from anger and shock, and the ice-cold glare he sent after the marshal had made smarter men than Morrison back off.

Rick was tight-lipped with anger and didn't mind voicing it.

"What the hell was that?"

"Stay out of it," Morrison shot back at him. "I know what I'm doing, and I don't need you second-guessing me."

"Yeah, but Tom, he wasn't doing anything."

"And now he knows he better not be doing anything," Morrison settled back down with his paper and a coffee. "It's all about attitude."

Rick and Jack exchanged looks again. It was going to be a long night.

CHAPTER TWO
THE BELL TOLLS

Jack felt numbed in both mind and body. He sat on his bunk, knees drawn up and held to his chest, his eyes staring blankly ahead at nothing.

Morrison had exploded into the office, crowing like a peacock and gleefully announcing the verdict to all those present.

"Twenty years. Ha! That's one 'great' outlaw we're never going to have to worry about again. Hear that Kiefer? Twenty years to life—that could not have gone better."

"That was harsh," Rick commented. "That means he won't even be eligible for parole for twenty years. I could understand it, if he'd actually murdered someone, but—"

"Oh, typical 'Napoleon Nash' arrogance," Morrison explained, "thought he could get away with being disrespectful to the court, just like he is with everything else. Well this time, his attitude turned around and bit him in the ass—hard. Maybe he'll learn some respect in prison, eh Kiefer? Ha, ha. This is great. I think I'll go celebrate."

Then, just as quickly and obtrusively as he'd entered the office, Morrison banged out through the front door and was gone to join the crowd at the saloon, who were also in a celebratory mood.

Rick remained seated at the desk, but his eyes were on the prisoner. He'd never, in all his life, felt as sorry for another man as he did at that moment.

Silence prevailed.

Jack couldn't believe it. Twenty years to life? How could that be? How disrespectful could Leon have been to warrant such an unforgiving sentence? This wasn't how it was supposed to end. Five years of living on the edge, of dodging posses and bounty hunters, and other outlaws wanting to turn them in for the reward.

Damn. We tried to do the right thing, live by the book. We didn't always manage it, but dammit, we tried. This was supposed to have a happy ending. How could this be?'

Jack felt his throat tighten. He fought the impulse; he wasn't going to lose it, not here, not now. He bit into his lower lip, hands into fists, as he fought against the threatening tears. It was a silent battle, fought to keep him from drowning in fear and self-pity—and anger.

What kind of lawyer was this Granger, anyway? What good did he do? Leon would 'a done better, defendin' himself, with that kind of legal aid. The man must be a complete imbecile. And now this same lawyer is gonna be defending me? Damn, what hope do I have? Where one goes, the other follows. How could this be? How could this have happened?

Jack was so focused on his own inner turmoil, he wasn't even aware of the deputy's eyes upon him. But ever since that day at the Marshams' ranch, when Kiefer, pumped to the gills with morphine, had still managed that insane escape attempt, Rick had felt a grudging respect for the outlaw.

As the days of guarding him had turned into weeks, and now months, there was no longer any grudging about it. The deputy still didn't have any qualms about bringing the man in to justice, but he now hoped that somehow, Kiefer would find a way to escape the same judgment that had befallen his partner.

Obviously, Rick never had the chance to get to know Napoleon Nash. The strongest memory he had of the man, was of an enraged and manacled outlaw attacking three armed officers in a battle he couldn't hope to win.

Rick sighed as he thought back to that incident. In hindsight, he could understand why Nash had reacted in such a feral manner. His partner lay stricken and near death, their futures hanging by a thread, and Kiefer and Nash were well known for their loyalty to one another. Indeed, Morrison had banked on it.

Rick also believed, that a lot could be told about a man by the company he keeps. The supporters at Nash's trial had consisted of law-abiding, honorable people. Would Nash and Kiefer have such people standing by them at a time like this, if they were not honorable themselves? Or at least, putting in the effort to try and be?

Another frustrated sigh. He glanced at the prisoner and noted that he, too, was lost in his own thoughts. The deputy stood up and went to the stove to replenish his coffee. Not that he needed any more coffee, but he did need something to do.

He turned back to gaze into the cell, knowing that Jack Kiefer must be going through a hard time. Obviously, this is not a clear case of black vs. white, good vs. evil, or even, lawfulness vs. anarchy. There is so much more going on here. And what about that rumor of a pardon? Rick frowned, as he returned to his chair at the desk. Kiefer hadn't noticed, and Rick carried on with his own musings. Sheriff Murphy had certainly hinted that the outlaws had been offered something along that line, without coming right out and saying it. But if that were the case, then why hadn't the governor come forward? Too politically volatile? Hmm, that might make sense. The president could oust him out of office in a heartbeat, if he made the wrong decision there.

And what was with Morrison? I've worked with him on other cases and hadn't felt this sickened by the man's behavior. Or was that just because I've never actually gotten to know the previous prisoners?

On this occasion, Rick not only came to know, but had come to like and respect the man whom he was guarding. So, what did that say about Rick, himself?

The tables were turned. Rick had become so contemplative of his own thoughts he hadn't noticed the other man's shift of focus. Now the outlaw gazed upon him.

Rick sighed and came back to the present. The two men's eyes locked and held.

Eventually, Rick got to his feet, and opening the drawer of the desk, pulled out the whiskey bottle and two shot glasses. He filled the glasses and went over to the cell.

Jack sat on the bunk, his knees drawn up, and despondently watched the deputy.

"C'mon, Kiefer," Rick suggested. "Come over and have a drink."

"In celebration?" he asked, with a hint of sarcasm.

"No. In commiseration."

Jack hesitated a moment, then with a complacent sigh, got up and went to the bars. Rick handed him a drink and they tapped glasses out of a growing, mutual respect. Each downed his shot in one swig and instantly felt better for it.

Rick took Jack's glass and returned to his desk, intending to give the daily paper perusal. He barely got settled when the front door burst open and a flurry of skirts and blonde hair came flying into the office and made a beeline, straight toward the prisoner.

Rick came to his feet in an instant and made a run back to the cell, just in time to block Caroline from reaching her destination.

"Hold on, young lady. Just where do you think you're going?"

"Deputy Layton?" Caroline was indignant. "I just want to see my friend. You know he won't hurt me."

"It's not him hurting you I'm worried about," Rick admitted. Caroline sent him a confused look, so Rick continued. "Didn't I hear a suggestion that it was you who slipped Nash a lock pick, way back when? You wouldn't happen to be considering a similar tactic here and now, would you?"

Caroline blushed.

Jack smiled So much for her interest in becoming an undercover detective, seeing as how she just admitted her own guilt under very light interrogation.

Cameron chuckled as he and David entered the office at a more sedate pace.

"You see, Caroline," her father said, "there are always consequences."

"Yes, Papa." Caroline hung her head and looked contrite. "I wasn't going to do anything, Deputy. I just want to see my friend."

"And besides, Deputy," Jack put in. "Nash is the only one who can pull off that trick. Givin' me a lock pick would be a waste a time."

"Fine. You have your visit," Rick consented, but gave Caroline a stern look and wagged his finger at her. "But I'm going to be keeping my eye on you, so no funny business."

He headed back to his desk, sending a conspirator's smile to Cameron and David. Indeed, the only one who took Rick's threat seriously was Caroline.

Caroline approached the bars and greeted her friend.

"Hello Mathew."

"Hello Caroline," he answered her, and put his hand through the bars to stroke her hair. He gave her an affectionate kiss on the forehead. She looked like she might start crying again, but she kept a stiff upper lip and stayed dry.

"Hello, Mathew," Cameron greeted him. "I guess you heard the verdict?"

"Yeah. Why so harsh?"

"I think he would have done okay on the sympathy pleas, but then the defense attorney asked him a question that he refused to answer,"

Cameron explained. "I guess this judge won't tolerate that, and slammed him for it. Granger had warned Leon that it could go that way, but Leon wouldn't back down."

"Aww, no," Jack responded. "What was the question?"

"Something about a confidence game you two pulled that was not legally sanctioned," Cameron continued. "Mr. DeFord asked for the names of your accomplices, and Leon refused."

Jack looked confused. "What confidence game?" he asked. "What names?"

"A Nigel Snodgrass brought forward the accusation," Cameron informed him.

The light dawned. Jack closed his eyes and groaned. Then he got angry.

"This was supposed ta be about us!" he growled. "About me and Leon, earnin' our freedom. Not about us turning in our friends in exchange for it!"

Nobody said anything for a few minutes, giving Jack the time he needed to digest this bit of information, and to calm down.

"How is he?" Jack finally asked. "How is Leon takin' this?"

Cameron and David exchanged looks.

"Not good," David admitted. "Not good at all. And Turner won't let any civilians back in to see him. Sheriff Murphy has gone back there now, to try and calm him down."

Jack nodded. "Well, if anybody can to it, Taggard can. Leon must be fit to be tied, right now."

"We all went and had a little conference with Mr. Granger," Cameron told him. "We're going to put in a plan of action to force the governor to honor his promise to you two. I don't know how long it's going to take, but we'll keep after him until we get results. Caroline already has a full head of steam, and once she and Penny decide to do something—well, look out, governor."

Jack laughed. "Ohh ho! I feel better, already."

"So, don't give up, Mathew, okay?" Caroline said. "Promise?"

Jack smiled at her. "Okay, Caroline. I promise. I won't give up."

Caroline smiled back.

"We'll be heading home for a while," Cameron told him, "But we'll be back for your trial date. Mr. Granger ought to be coming over soon, to discuss strategy with you."

"Hmm," was Jack's only response.

"Don't hold what happened to Leon against him," Cameron said. "He's young, but he knows his business, and he's doing everything he can."

"He's really nice," Caroline added, with a shy smile.

Jack raised his brows and sent a questioning look to Cameron.

That parental figure rolled his eyes.

Jack tried to stifle the grin, but he wasn't too successful.

"We better be going," Cameron said, and he reached through the bars and shook hands with his friend. "Take it easy, Mathew. We'll see you in a few weeks."

"Yeah, okay," Jack answered, feeling disappointed that they were leaving.

"I'll be along in a few minutes, Cameron," David told him. "I'll see you back at the hotel."

Cameron nodded, and he and his daughter left the office.

David turned back to Jack, just as Rick came up with the keys and unlocked the cell before anybody even asked him to.

David appreciated it.

"I won't be long," he assured the deputy.

"Uh huh."

"What's going on there?" Jack asked his friend, as they returned to the bunk. "Don't tell me, Caroline is fallin' for the lawyer."

"Well, I didn't notice anything happening, but apparently Cameron did," David thought about it. "And the way Caroline acts whenever Mr. Granger is mentioned, makes me think that, just maybe . . ."

"Ohh, ho, ho," Jack laughed despite his worries. "I bet Cameron is just thrilled about that."

"Oh, it comes to us all," David prophesied. "So, the same old question, Jack. How's your shoulder? And why do you have a new bruise on your face?"

Jack rolled his eyes, "Shoulder's feelin' really good, but my face? Morrison seemed ta think I needed an attitude adjustment, and the bars of the cell were too convenient an opportunity ta pass up."

David gritted his teeth. "That son-of-a . . . there is something seriously wrong with that man."

"Yeah, maybe. Unfortunately, he ain't the only lawman out there who's like that," Jack told him. "Actually, it seems to be the rule rather than the exception."

"It worries me, leaving you here with him," David admitted. "I'll be staying on a few more days, at least until they move you over to the main jailhouse. There are more people over there, so he won't have as free a reign as he does here."

Jack lowered his voice. "Don't worry about it, David. I think Rick is gettin' fed up with his boss' attitude as well and will step in if things get outta hand."

"I hope you're right. Okay, how much morphine do you have, and how much are you still using?"

Jack pulled the pouch out from under his pillow and handed it over. David peeked inside and nodded.

"Good. You're backing off it."

"Yeah."

"Try to back off it even more. If you have trouble sleeping, we can always try some laudanum."

"Laudanum doesn't help at all."

"That's because your system is too used to the morphine. Just give it a chance."

"Yeah, okay." But Jack didn't look too pleased about it.

"Good. Let's get to it here." David stood up and faced his patient. "Unbutton your shirt."

Jack absentmindedly used his right hand to undo the buttons. It was only after he saw David smiling, when he realized what he had accomplished.

"Oh. I undid the buttons!"

"Yes, you did. Good dexterity. We'll get you back to almost good as new before you know it."

"Almost?"

"Let's not push it, Jack."

"Yeah, all right."

It only took about twenty minutes to get through their massage and stretches, but Jack was tired at the end of it. Another benefit, was that by the time David was ready to leave, a lot of the stress had been worked out of Jack, and he was feeling quite a bit calmer.

The doctor took his leave and Jack returned to his bunk. He lay down and taking his hat, put it over his eyes. He tried to relax. He didn't think he was going to fall asleep; he wasn't even trying to. He just needed to be alone with his thoughts for a while. He hoped Leon was doing okay. Thoughts of his partner, and what he must be going through, took over his mind, and a veil of sadness settled over him.

Until, finally, he did in fact drift off to asleep.

***

Two days later, Morrison entered the jailhouse with Alex and two of the regular deputies following in his wake. They all looked like they were on a mission. Rick got up from where he had been snoozing and reached for the keys to the cell.

"Is it time then?" he asked Morrison.

"Yup. Nash should be well on his way by now, so let's get this piece of dung off our hands."

Jack, who could not help but overhear this conversation, got on his feet and prepared himself for the usual, pointless search. Sure enough, as soon as Rick had the cell door open, Morrison came in, pushed Jack against the bars and quickly patted him down. The belt was cinched around his waist and his hands locked into the cuffs.

This whole routine had become a bore. Is this what the rest of his life was going to be like?

Again, his heart and thoughts went out to his partner; Will Leon be able to handle this? Will I be able to handle this? Jack sighed as they led him out of the cell.

They mainly kept to the side streets to avoid curious onlookers, as they made their way by foot, to the main jailhouse. About half a block away from their destination, the group of men came out onto the main street, crossed the road and went straight onto the boardwalk and toward the front office.

Jack wasn't paying much attention to the people they passed, other than to recognize the fact that most of them recognized him. But then, they walked by a gentleman sitting in a chair in front of his store, reading the daily paper.

Jack couldn't help but notice the headline on the front page of the opened newspaper, and he did a double-take.

NAPOLEON NASH RAILROADED?

What was that? Jack didn't have time to read anything more of the article, but maybe he would be able to convince Rick, or David, or somebody, to get him a copy of that paper.

In the meantime, Morrison had also noticed the headline and

hurried Jack along before he had time to really digest what he had read. The marshal didn't want any trouble. Morrison was so focused on getting his prisoner into the jailhouse, he didn't notice that the prison wagon was still pulled up, out of the way and to the side of the building. Or the people grouped around it.

Then, just as they approached the office, Morrison saw Mike standing, head and shoulders, above a group of men walking across the street from the back lane.

The group around the prison coach also noticed the lawmen coming from the side street and rushed them, waving their arms and shouting out questions.

Mike reacted aggressively toward them, and Morrison wondered at the reason, until he saw it for himself. He spotted Sheriff Turner in the group and then—dammit. Nash! What was he still doing here? They were supposed to have been gone an hour ago.

Too late, Morrison realized he wasn't the only one attracted by the commotion. He opened the door to the office, hoping to get his prisoner secured indoors, before Jack could react to seeing his partner again.

Jack ignored the other people around the coach, just wanting to get into the office and away from Morrison. But the sudden rush toward the other lawmen caught Jack's eye. Mike was so obvious in that group, that Jack couldn't help but focus on him.

Mike was a powerhouse. He pushed people away, even sending some of them sprawling into the dirt, and Jack wondered why the deputy was behaving so aggressively. But then, as the mob of reporters and pushy citizens was dispersed, Jack understood.

"Leon!"

Leon had been just about to step into the back of the wagon, when his head snapped up and he spun around.

"Jack? . . . Jack!"

Not thinking, just elated at seeing his partner again, Jack broke away from Rick and started toward his friend.

Morrison wasn't going to allow that to happen. Before Jack had gone two steps, the marshal was on him. The rifle butt came up in a flash and landed a staggering blow to Jack's right shoulder.

Jack heard the crack of a bone breaking inside, and then the pain of it exploded and assaulted his brain, causing him to pass out—but only for a heartbeat. He blacked out just long enough to come to and find himself on the ground within an eruption of pandemonium.

Feet ran past him, over him, and around him. Men yelled curses, and he heard Leon's name called out in anger, more than once. Then someone had him by the underarms and dragged him through the door and into the office, where he was unceremoniously dumped and left to lay there, writhing in pain. He heard the office door slam shut, and still, people running and yelling, and someone—Morrison?—shouting . . .

"Get me a doctor; that bastard broke my nose. But not that damned Gibson idiot. Get me a real doctor. Get Dr. Taff in here."

More running, the office door opened again and slammed shut again.

And then Jack passed out—again.

***

Leon grinned at seeing his friend, not only up and walking around, but having his arm free of the sling. Such an improvement, since the last time they had seen each other, was an incredible relief. Then Leon's grin disappeared, as he witnessed Morrison's assault upon his partner. Anger rose in him and became fueled by a long-standing hatred.

Suddenly, it was the right time for retribution, after all.

As soon as Leon turned at the sound of Jack calling his name, Mike grabbed hold of his arm, to pull him back around.

Already angry, Leon's rage exploded. He launched himself off the bottom step of the wagon and came straight up like a rocket, the top of his head slamming into the bottom of Mike's chin.

There was a resounding crack, and Mike staggered backward, blood spewing from his mouth, where he had bitten into his own tongue.

Leon charged. Head down, shoulders forward, he headed for Morrison like a runaway longhorn and plowed into the back of the marshal before the lawman had an inkling of bringing his rifle around to bear.

Leon hit him so hard, Morrison catapulted forward and went, head first, into the edge of the open office door. He went down in a crash, amongst yells and curses, but was on his feet again in an instant. Blood poured from an obviously broken nose, and there were the beginnings of an ugly red welt, reaching all the way from his brow to his chin.

Morrison was purple with rage and had murder in his heart as he went after the fallen Nash, yelling curses at him. Then everyone was on the move.

Deputy Alex pulled the injured Jack into the office, as Rick, and several of the other deputies, got between Leon and the marshal. In all the confusion, they were able to divert Morrison back toward the building.

Mike, who was miraculously still on his feet, grabbed Leon where he lay and hauled him, by his shirt collar and the manacle belt, back to the wagon.

Leon was in a daze from the double impact and was only vaguely aware of being grabbed and dragged, then tossed through the air as though he weighed no more than a small child. He landed in a heap on the ground by the back steps of the prison wagon.

Mike was on him again, grabbed him in the same manner, hauled him up and threw him into the enclosed vehicle. Leon hit hard, banging into the bench that ran along the inside of the wagon. He lay on the floor, shaking his head as he tried to clear away the buzzing.

Mike climbed into the wagon with him. He grabbed Leon by a manacled arm and hauled him up to sit on the bench. The big deputy shook the prisoner and gave him a couple of sharp slaps on his cheek.

"Hey, Nash," Mike's speech was slurred, due to his injuries and the blood he constantly spit out. "Nash, you awake? Can you hear me?"

Leon's eyes opened wide, though they still had a dazed look to them. He shook his head to further clear his brain.

"Yeah, Mike. Yeah, I can hear ya."

"Good."

Then Leon got a clear view of Mike's huge paw of a fist coming down, like a pile-driver, straight toward his left eye. Leon had barely an instant to think; Oh crap. This is going to hurt. Then the blow hit home, and he was swimming in a whirlpool of stars, followed by total blackness

CHAPTER THREE
A MEETING OF MINDS

The deputy-in-training ran into Dr. Taff's office. He was so flustered and out of breath, he had to take a moment to calm down enough to deliver his message.

Dr. Taff gave him a cup of water and a pat on the shoulder, along with the advice to take slow, deep, breaths, until the young man could finally speak clearly.

"We need ya at the sheriff's office—right now."

"Calm down, Deputy. Tell me what happened."

"The sheriff's been injured."

"Sheriff Turner?"

"No, no. The other one, ahh . . . Morrison. And one of the deputies, too."

"Morrison is a marshal, young man. You best learn how to tell the difference if you want to continue in this line of work."

"Oh." The deputy gulped, confusion flitting across his face. "Okay. But they need help, now."

"Were they shot?" he asked as he scurried around his office, grabbing items as he went.

"No," the deputy answered, finally getting his breath back to normal, "just beat up some. They're both bleedin' bad, though. I think the sheriff, I mean the marshal, has a broken nose."

Taff frowned. Marshal Morrison, though not a tall man, was built like a draft horse, so it would have been quite a feat for someone to break his nose. "What happened?"

"Umm, I think they were tryin' ta break up a fight between two prisoners."

"Were either of the prisoners injured?"

"Ahh, oh." The deputy had to think about that. "I tripped over one of 'em layin' on the floor, so I guess he was injured. The other one is on his way to the prison, so I guess he's okay.

"So, three injured men altogether?"

"Yeah, I guess."

"You're doing an awful lot of guessing here, Deputy."

"Well, everything happened so fast. They told me to get over here and get ya."

"All right, Deputy, that's fine," the doctor assured him. "You know where my assistant lives?"

"Yeah. That's Clive Hamlin, ain't it?"

"Yes, that's right. Go get him. Tell him what's happened and that I need him at the sheriff's office."

"Yeah. Yeah okay."

"All right. Off you go."

"Right. I'll go get Clive."

***

As soon as the doctor entered the sheriff's office, he understood why the deputy had tripped over Jack, because Taff did much the same thing. The shackled man was conscious and obviously in pain, so Taff knelt to assess him, but was distracted by a shout from the back office.

"Hey, Doc. Never mind about him. You gotta tend to the lawmen first."

Taff realized the prone man wasn't in any immediate danger, so he got up and headed into the back office. One look and he had to admit that it resembled a war zone.

Both injured lawmen were bleeding and in foul tempers. Just as the first deputy had surmised, the marshal did appear to have a broken nose, along with a couple of very impressive black eyes. The other injured lawman wasn't showing any bruising, but the blood around his mouth and the look in his eyes indicated a serious enough injury.

They all heard the front door open, followed by sudden curses coming from Clive as he also tripped over Jack sprawled on the floor.

"Oh. Sorry Clive," they heard the deputy respond. "I shoulda told ya about him."

"Yeah, Billy. That might have been a good idea. "Clive," Taff called. "Get in here. I'm going to need your assistance."

"What about this fella on the floor?"

"He's not bleeding. He can wait. Get in here."

Clive showed up at the door to the back office and looked around. "Oh, damn. Some prisoners gang up on you fellas, or something?"

"Actually, it was just one," Rick muttered.

"Just one?" asked Clive, then jerked a thumb over his shoulder as he headed over to assess Mike's injuries. "That one, out there?"

"Nope," Rick slurred his answer. "He actually didn't do anything too serious, just forgot where he was for an instant."

"Layton. Keep your mouth shut," Morrison growled at him through his blood-soaked handkerchief. "Kiefer tried to break custody and he paid the price."

"Oh, c'mon! That's not—

"Don't argue with me. That's what happened."

"Fine," Rick relented, with a resigned sigh. "At least let me go get Doc Gibson to tend to him."

"No!" Morrison grimaced with the pain the expletive caused. Then, to make things worse, Taff pushed the handkerchief away and stuffed padding up his nose to stop the bleeding. "Keep that idiot away from here."

"Somebody's got to tend to him," Rick mumbled. "We can't just leave him lying on the floor."

"I'm almost done here," Taff informed the marshal. "Clive, how is your patient doing?"

"He's going to need some stitches in his tongue," the assistant stated, "and, it's hard to tell through the blood, but he may have broken some teeth as well. We'll probably have to pull out what's left of those."

"Okay," said Taff. "I'll do that in my office. It'll be easier over there. In the meantime, Clive, you can look at the prisoner."

"Right." Clive gave Mike a smile and a pat on the shoulder. He then returned to the front office.

Mike looked surly.

***

Jack still lay where he had been dumped and then tripped over several times, when Clive came out and approached him. Jack's eyes were closed, but they opened halfway, when the assistant knelt and put a hand on his arm. The prisoner groaned.

"Your right shoulder looks a little awkward," Clive commented. "I'm just going to take a look at it."

Jack gave a barely perceptible nod, and Clive went about his business. He knitted his brow when he saw the freshly healed bullet wound, then returned his attention to the current injury. It didn't take him long to reach his conclusion. He smiled and nodded at Jack, then got up and returned to the back office.

"His collarbone is broken. Looks like a clean break though, so it should heal up fine."

Taff nodded his acknowledgment. "Are you okay to set it yourself?"

"If one of the deputies will help me."

"I'll help," Rick offered.

Morrison grumbled something rude, but the morphine Taff had given him was taking effect, so his blusterings weren't up to their usual standard.

Rick ignored him, and he and Clive were about to leave the office when Taff stopped them.

"You better give him some morphine before you set it, or it will hurt like hell."

Rick looked dubious. "Oh, I don't think that's—"

"Don't be tellin' the doc his business," Morrison muffled through the padding.

"But Gibson's trying to—"

"Layton, shut your mouth. The doc knows best."

Clive had already picked up the supply of morphine Taff had left on the table and was in the process of mixing a full dose into a cup of water.

Rick's jaw tightened as he looked at his boss. The look that was sent back to him was bleary, but adamant about what would happen if Rick interfered.

"Can I, at least, get the keys to those cuffs, so I can unlock him?" Rick's tone was quiet, barely concealing his anger.

Morrison started doing a quick, but wobbly search of his own pockets, and then withdrew the keys from their hiding place. He shakily held them out for Rick to take.

"Thanks," Rick snatched them from his boss. He turned and followed Clive to the front office.

"Okay, Marshal," Taff said. "I don't want you being on your own for at least twenty-four hours, so why don't you lie down on that cot over there and get some sleep. I'll check up on you later, today."

"Fine, Doc," Morrison mumbled, and carefully got to his feet.

Turner offered a hand, but Morrison waved him away. He weaved his way over to the cot and collapsed onto it.

"Well, Deputy," Taff said to Mike, "it looks like you're next in line. I'll get you stitched up, over at my office."

Mike didn't look pleased about that prospect, but nodded agreement. He stood up and followed the doctor out.

"That must have been one, big, mean outlaw, to have caused this much damage all on his own," Taff commented.

Mike rolled his eyes and declined to answer.

***

A couple of hours later, Jack was in a cell and passed out on the cot in morphine-induced unconsciousness.

Rick and Clive hadn't had any problems setting the broken bone, and the right arm had, again, been bound and wrapped snuggly against the patient's torso. Rick had been left standing outside the cell door for some time, watching the man sleep. He was worried about what Dr. Gibson was going to say about all this.

He debated back and forth about informing the doctor of this new event, or just hanging back, and letting Gibson find out about it on his own. After all, the damage had already been done, and telling Gibson about it now wouldn't change that.

Not knowing anything about drugs in general, it never occurred to him that Jack might have been given an overdose. Still, Rick felt obligated to say something, but also knew that by doing so, he would be going against his boss' orders.

What the hell. Knowing Gibson, he's going to be over to check up on his 'special patient' any time now, anyway. Might as well leave it alone.

Rick pushed himself off the bars and headed out of the cell block. Jack Kiefer was no longer his problem. He had been legally signed over to the custody of the Cheyenne Sheriff's Department and was now Turner's responsibility.

Still, if Mike had stayed on to watch Nash, Rick may be asked to do the same thing with Kiefer, especially since his friend, Sheriff Murphy, had already left for Medicine Bow. Maybe the prisoner will start getting an hour a day out of his cell, too.

Well, no harm in thinking about it a bit more, over a glass of beer and a sandwich.

***

Once the cell block was empty of lawmen, the two prisoners on either side of Jack's cell, got up and leaned against their respective bars.

"Well, George, what do ya think?" one of them asked the other.

"I dunno, Fred. He looks harmless enough."

"That's 'cause he's unconscious, you idiot. Nash was harmless too, when he'd had a snoot full."

"They can't both of 'em be that ornery," Fred reasoned. "They'd a kilt each other by now."

"I suppose," George shrugged. "That is the Kansas Kid, ain't it?"

"That's what they's sayin'."

"Well, ain't he supposed ta be the mean one?"

Fred shrugged. "That's always been my idee."

Both men lapsed into silent, looking down at the sleeping gunman, trying to imagine how anyone could be more cantankerous than the previous occupant of that cell.

***

Later in the afternoon, Rick returned to the jailhouse to find David Gibson and Steven Granger in the cell with the unconscious Jack, discussing the situation.

David sat on the cot, beside his patient, checking his vital signs. He seemed content that Jack wasn't going to expire, then and there, but he was still barely keeping his anger under control.

Granger was also tight-lipped with this new development.

"So much for going over strategy today," the lawyer grumbled. "But at least the judge has agreed to the hour a day recreation, for now anyway. Maybe we can get him out tomorrow if he's feeling up to it."

"We'll see," David commented, then noticed Rick by the cell door. "Why didn't you let me know this had happened?"

Granger was confused for a moment. Then he realized the doctor wasn't speaking to him, and he turned to see Rick standing behind him.

"Morrison refused to let me come and get you," Rick said, "and, last I looked, he was still my boss. I tried to tell them not to give him any more morphine, but they wouldn't listen."

"I think I'm going to have a word with your 'boss' about this, very soon."

"I'd watch my step if I were you, Doc," Rick warned him. "After what Nash did to him, he is in a foul temper."

"Why? What did Nash do to him?"

"Broke his nose, for starters."

David never thought anything Rick could say would put a smile on his face. But that bit of information did it.

"How come he went down so hard, Doc?" Rick gestured to Jack. "Hell, I've broken my collarbone before and I didn't pass out."

"It's cumulative," David explained. "His system is still dealing with the first injury, and then it gets hit with a second one in the same area. It may just be a simple break, but it was the shock of it that knocked the stuffing out of him. I suppose, putting him to sleep for a while, is probably the best medicine, right now. I just wish, he hadn't given him morphine." David sighed and stood up. "Oh well, we'll see what tomorrow brings."

***

Midmorning of the next day, David returned to the jailhouse to check up on the patient.

Turner took him back and opened the cell door for him. David stepped through and smiled a greeting to the occupant.

Jack was awake but subdued. He sat on the cot, leaning against the back wall with his knees drawn up. He cradled in injured arm, looking like he had just been through the wars. He was in a quiet, but smoldering mood over this latest injury.

Though not saying a word, his blue eyes were dark as the weight of disappointment lingered in the cell block. The two inmates on either side of the notorious gunman, kept their distance, yet watched him with the intentness of prey keeping tabs on the hunter.

The doctor ignored them.

"Well, Jack, how are you feeling, today?"

Jack flicked his eyes to meet David's. He sighed, but his lips held onto their tight line. "I was certain it was all just a bad dream. I woke up to find my arm all bundled up again, and I thought I was trapped in a nightmare."

David nodded and sat down beside his friend. He gave him a conciliatory pat on the knee.

"I know. But it's not too bad. It'll delay your recuperation a bit, but shouldn't have any other effect. One piece of good news though; Granger has arranged for you to get out of here for an hour every day, just like Napoleon did. So, you have that to look forward to. Granger will probably be by this evening to see you."

"I dunno how much good I'm gonna be ta him today, David. My brain feels like oatmeal."

"I know. That's why I told him to hold off until this evening. Give you a bit more time to get that morphine out of your system."

"Oh, yeah." Jack groaned. "I'm sorry, David. I tried ta tell that doctor, not ta give me any, but he had it down my throat before I could stop 'im. You guys are real good at that sort 'a thing."

David chuckled. "Yeah, I know. It comes with the territory. Don't worry about it, we'll just start over."

"How's Leon?"

David frowned. "I don't know. I never saw him. He's probably at . . . well, at the . . ."

"At the prison by now," Jack finished for him.

"Yes."

Jack nodded, and both men remained silent for a moment.

Then the sound of Morrison's gruff voice came from the front office.

David growled. "Take it easy, Jack," he said, as he got to his feet. "I need to have a word with the good marshal."

"Ohh, you be careful, David."

"Always. Deputy, I'm ready to leave now!"

***

David went into the office, and was met by Morrison's black and blue face, rounding on him.

"What the hell is he doing here?" Morrison demanded, in a voice that fought its way through a wet blanket.

"I could ask you the same thing," David countered, before Turner had a chance to respond. "Jack is no longer your prisoner, but he is still my patient. Why wasn't I informed of this new injury?"

"The local doctor took care of it. Your services weren't required. Why don't you just go home, where you belong?"

"Apparently, I belong here. You knew I was trying to get him off the morphine. Why did you let that doctor give him a full dose of it?"

"I figured the doc knew what he was doing."

"But he didn't know Jack has already been on morphine for months and is still taking it. It was dangerous to give him more. You could have killed him." Then David went quiet, as a thought occurred to him. "Or, is that what you were hoping would happen?"

Morrison's temper erupted. He threw aside a chair and lunged at the medical man. In an instant, Morrison had David backed up against the wall, his hands around the doctor's throat and squeezing with murderous intent.

Turner was taken by surprise, but two beats later, he was on the two men, trying to get the marshal to release his hold.

"Come on, Morrison, back off him," Turner yelled as he grabbed the lawman's hands and tried to get him to let go.

David fought for his life. Morrison had a stranglehold on his throat and wasn't showing any signs of letting go. David felt the blood rushing to his head, his ears buzzing as he started to punch the marshal on his broken nose, in a frantic effort to get him off.

The two deputies, Chuck and Larry, who were in the back office, heard the scuffle and ran in to help. Finally, between the three lawmen, they pulled Morrison off his victim and dragged him over to the other side of the room.

David slid to the floor, clutching his throat and gasping for air. He was shaking from the assault—he couldn't believe the man had attacked him. As the buzzing in his ears started to dissipate, he heard Jack shouting from inside the cell block, but David was in no condition yet to respond. He remained seated on the floor, fighting to get air into his lungs.

***

Inside his cell, Jack was on his feet the instant he heard what sounded like a chair crashing into a wall. The sounds that followed got his heart pounding, and he charged at the bars. He grabbed the door with his left hand, frantically yanking at it in the hopes that maybe, Deputy Larry hadn't closed it properly when David left.

No such luck. The cell door was closed and locked, and wasn't budging. Jack started to yell, still yanking at the door. He began hitting the bars in his frustration.

George and Fred exchanged looks across the cells, then each man retreated to his own farthest corner. They wanted to put as much distance as possible between themselves and yet another explosive madman, who had been plunked into their midst.

Finally, the block door opened, and David poked his head in, still holding his throat. Jack thought he looked pale.

"It's all right, Jack," David croaked and then coughed. "Everything's okay."

"Damn it, David. You sure?"

"Yeah, it's all right."

David disappeared, and the door closed.

Jack sighed with relief and turned to go back to his cot, his knees still shaking. He caught the expression on George's face, as that man tried to disappear into a corner of his cell. Jack then looked over at Fred and was met with the same expression from that corner.

Jack shook his head and smiled.

"It's okay, fellas," he assured them. "I ain't gonna self-destruct on ya."

***

In the office, Turner was in the process of pouring out five shots of brandy, while Morrison and David continued to glare at each other.

"I think everyone just needs to calm down," Turner stated, as he handed the shot glasses around. "Tempers seem to be a little high right now. Cheers."

Everyone downed their drink, and it did help to break the tension.

David found that the alcohol burned his throat on the way down, and it went straight to Morrison's already throbbing face, but everyone else seemed to enjoy it.

"You two need to find a way to get along," Turner suggested, as he poured out two more shots. "Why don't you take these drinks, go into the back office, and try to talk this out."

The suggestion was met with silent hostility. David didn't want to be anywhere near the marshal, and Morrison wished the doctor would simply go away.

"Are either of you intending to leave town soon?" Turner asked them.

"No," came the unified retort.

"Well then," Turner shrugged. "Better work it out."

He handed them each another drink and gestured toward the back office.

Feeling like boys who had just been caught fighting in the schoolyard, the two men took the offered drinks. They cautiously made their way into the other office, with David making sure that Morrison stayed in front of him, every step of the way.

They sat on opposite sides of the desk and solemnly glared at each other.

"All right," Morrison finally broke the silence. "Let's face it, Doc; I don't like you, and you don't like me."

"Nothing to disagree with, yet," David mumbled.

"I think you're a namby-pamby, lily-livered, sorry excuse for a real doctor, and you think I'm a sadistic bastard, who likes to inflict pain for no reason."

David glared at him.

"The Territory of Wyoming asked me to capture Kiefer and Nash, and get them to trial. Why they asked me, is for one reason, and one reason only. They knew I could do it. My ways are harsh, but those two outlaws have been running wild for over ten years, and nobody has been able to hold onto them. It was time to get tough."

"Getting tough is one thing," David answered him. "But you go beyond that. You're right; I do think you're sadistic. I think you really do enjoy hurting people."

"I don't enjoy it, Doc. I just don't mind doing it. Not if I know it will get the job done. I studied those two men. I figured out their strongest abilities, and that's where I hit them. If you go after where a man is strongest, then you have to hit hard, or he'll run right over you.

"Look what happened with Nash. I had him right where I wanted him. One look from me and he'd back off and keep his mouth shut. Then, all hell broke loose as soon as I handed him over to these idiots, here. This is supposed to be the most secure jail in the whole territory, but Nash damn near walked out the front door. It was just by chance he was stopped. That would not have happened if he'd still been in my custody."

"So, the whole idea was to break him?" David asked with a sneer.

"Break him? No," Morrison shook his head then instantly regretted it. "I just needed Nash to know he wasn't going to get away with pulling his crap on me. And he did know it. I didn't come anywhere near breaking him. If I had, I wouldn't be sporting a broken nose and two black eyes. No, it's going to take prison to break Napoleon Nash."

"And you're pleased about that?"

"Nope," Morrison said. "Couldn't care less, either way. My job is done as far as he's concerned. I arrested him, and I got him to trial. What the judge decided to do with him after that, was up to him. I admit, I'm glad he didn't get off. The man's an outlaw, through and through. I don't care about his past; a lot of us had a hard time, growing up—so what? Now, maybe the things that happened did make him who he is, but that's still who he is, and if he'd gotten a pardon, he would have gone back to being who he is—an outlaw."

"But, Marshal, they have been trying to go straight," David pointed out. "They had an agreement with the governor of this territory."

"Yeah?" Morrison asked. "If they had an agreement with the governor, then why did the governor hire me to bring them in? That's just a fairy tale, Doc. One they concocted between themselves to protect their own backsides."

"But they have friends, who vouch for them. A sheriff who supports what they're doing and has hinted at that very agreement. How can you deny it?"

"Yeah, right," Morrison smirked. "A sheriff who's been a friend of theirs for years and was once an outlaw himself. Nash is a master at manipulation. It's what he does, and it's what he did. I think those friends that he duped into believing that pardon story, got a bit of an eye-opener at Nash's trial, don't you? It seems, he wasn't staying quite as straight as his friends thought."

"I think there is more to it than that," David insisted.

"Well, then maybe he should have explained himself in court," Morrison countered. "But he didn't, did he? Because he couldn't explain it. He couldn't justify it. He got caught, and that's all there is to it."

"He couldn't explain it, because it would have meant implicating other people," David pointed out. "Seems to me, he was protecting someone else."

"Yeah," Morrison agreed. "Other thieves. This just goes to show that he's still thick with them. Still working with them. He's a cardsharp, a conman, and a thief, himself. Nothing has changed."

David decided to let that one go. Morrison had one opinion, and David had another. As far as the doctor was concerned, Leon had good people willing to stand by him, and that should carry some influence in judging the man. But Morrison was adamant, so there was no point.

Besides, Leon's situation was moot now, since the man had already been sentenced, convicted, and was probably getting his first taste of prison life.

David changed tack and brought up another situation that he felt had exceeded the call of duty.

"There was no need to shoot that man from the train. If you had wanted to get the attention of those outlaws, all you had to do was fire your gun in the air."

"Yup, that's true."

"Well then—why?"

"Because I didn't do it to get Shaffer's attention. I did it to get Kiefer's attention."

"But Jack said, you told—"

"I told Shaffer that I did it to get his attention, just to make him feel like he was important, like he actually had some say in the negotiations. But Kiefer was the one who was going to make things happen. He was the one who had to take control of his gang and make them do his bidding. I had to let Kiefer know—right now—what would happen if he didn't cooperate."

"So, you killed a man, just to get Jack to go along with you, something he probably would have done anyway."

"I didn't kill a man," Morrison sneered. "I killed an outlaw, and a two-bit one at that. And there was no time for 'probably'. I needed that situation defused instantly, like I said—right then. I did what I had to do, to make it happen."

David was silent, but he still didn't look convinced.

Morrison shook his head.

"You are so concerned over the death of one, low-life outlaw, that you're not seeing the whole picture. What do you think would have happened, if that gang had boarded the train and come across their boss in custody? Do you really expect they would have just walked away from that? They outnumbered us, three to one. They would have tried to take Kiefer by force, and who knows how many people could have been killed. Women and children, Doc, they would have been right in the middle of it. You should be thanking me."

David hated to admit it, but the marshal made sense. If a full-blown gunfight had broken out on that train, the results could have been disastrous.

"But still," David wasn't ready to give up, yet, "this most recent incident. From what Rick tells me, Jack wasn't trying to break away. There was no need to use that kind of force. Indeed, it was you, reacting that way, that set Napoleon off."

Morrison shook his head again, like he had to explain logic to a child.

"I said, right from the get-go, 'Don't let those two get together.'". I didn't want those two seeing one another, or even hearing anything about one another. Unfortunately, I couldn't stop their 'friends' from passing information back and forth, so that part couldn't be helped. But they've proven, repeatedly, that together, they're dangerous. Keep them apart, and you keep them off balance.

"Dammit! Nash was supposed to have been gone a good hour before I brought Kiefer over. And the prison coach was supposed to be on the side street. I don't know what the hell Turner was thinking. Now, maybe I did overreact a bit there, but I was mad. I'd had Kiefer's attitude right where I wanted it—and then he saw Nash. God dammit. So yeah, I hit him hard. Now, maybe in your mind, it was too hard, but I disagree. I don't want those outlaws to like me, I don't even want them to respect me. I just want them to know their place, and to stay there."

Morrison stopped talking for a minute and took a drink. David remained quiet, staring off into space.

The marshal sighed and continued.

"I've seen the way you are with those two, treating them like regular folk, calling them by their first names. I hear you talking to Kiefer, the two of you laughing, like you're old buddies. But I tell you Doc, the only people they're loyal to, are each other. They're linked together, like two dogs in harness; they don't care about anybody else.

"Look what happened to Mike. He treated Leon with a lot more leniency than I ever would have. Those damn, weekly poker games— what the hell was he thinking? But did Nash respect that? No. As soon as Mike got in his way—POW! Now, Mike's gonna be eating soup for a month."

Morrison's lips tightened and he shook his head. "And I don't know what's going on with Layton. He was my best right-hand man. But now," Morrison shook his head again. "I don't know. Anyway, those two outlaws have simply been putting up with you because you're helping them. And right now, it's Kiefer. Everything he is, is tied up with being a gunman, and he was scared to death he was going to lose that. Now, here you are, a young, up-and-coming doctor, all 'back-East trained', and full of ideas. And you're going to make him better again. He's just using you, 'cause that's what they do; they use people to get what they want and to take what they want.

"You mark my words, Doc; if there ever comes a time when you get in between the Kansas Kid and something he wants, you are going to find yourself face to face with a different breed of man. How do you think he got that reputation in the first place? By being the nice guy? You just might end up regretting helping him get his shooting arm back in shape."

A chill went through David, as he recognized the same sentiment coming from the marshal as had come from his wife concerning the outlaw's recovery. He still didn't feel that he wanted to agree with it, but it was unnerving, all the same.

Morrison finished his brandy and stood up.

"That's it for me. You chew on that for a while, Doc. If you've got anything more to say, I'll see you in the morning. Right now, I'm heading back to the hotel to get some more sleep."

The marshal plunked the empty shot glass down on the table and took his leave.

David sat there for a few more minutes, staring into space, his drink still untouched. He felt heartsick. Was his friendship with Jack just a ruse on the outlaw's part, in order to use him? He didn't want to believe it, but the marshal had put forth a convincing argument, and David wasn't sure what the truth was, anymore.

Finally, he downed his drink in one go and stood up to leave. He decided to check up on Jack one more time, before heading to the hotel himself. Perhaps he was feeling the need to re-connect with the man and to validate his own convictions.

Unfortunately, when he went up to the cell, it was to find Jack sound asleep. David sighed in disappointment, but wasn't about to wake him up, just for this. He'd see him tomorrow. He was just about to turn around and leave, when George came up to the bars to talk.

"Hey, Doc," he said, quietly, "you've spent time with the Kid. Is he just as mean and unpredictable as his partner?"

David looked at him, a cloud of sadness settling over him.

"I'm sorry. I don't know. I don't think I know him well enough."

CHAPTER FOUR
FRIENDSHIPS

Arvada, Colorado

Cameron lay in bed staring blindly at the ceiling. His left arm cradled his head, which worked overtime in a hopeless effort to sort things out. His right arm encircled his wife, who snuggled up against him, apparently asleep. He hadn't moved or made a sound, since they had settled into bed an hour ago, but, as usual, his effort to deceive his wife was about to end in failure.

Without moving or opening her eyes, Jean finally gave a resigned sigh, and Cameron heard a muffled "What's the matter?" coming from the vicinity of his armpit.

"Why does something have to be the matter?" He feigned innocence although he knew it was hopeless.

Jean pushed herself up on an elbow and looked down at her husband through the darkness.

"You and Caroline returned home from Cheyenne this afternoon, and other than the detached announcement that poor Peter was on his way to prison, neither one of you have said a word about how it went. Though I wouldn't be surprised if Caroline is busy filling Penny in on all the details, while we're speaking." She stopped and waited for some response. When none came forth, she gave him a gentle shake.

Finally, he sighed and pulled a 'Napoleon Nash' by running his left hand through his hair.

Jean knew she had him.

"Do you think I am a weak-minded, or indecisive person?" Cameron asked.

"What?" Jean was flabbergasted. This was the last thing she expected. "Why, in the world, would you think that?"

"All throughout Napoleon's trial, the ongoing theme seemed to be what an excellent conman he is. How easily he can manipulate people into believing anything he wants them to believe. Even to the point of disguising his own true character."

"And you think Peter has been manipulating us and the girls?"

"I don't know. I just keep remembering back to when they spent that winter living with us. I knew there was something odd about their story—there was no good reason for two men to be out in a storm like that, and we weren't so far out from a town that they wouldn't have known a storm was brewing before leaving. They wouldn't have left, unless they had been forced to.

"But I believed them, I took their word. I let them into our home, possibly endangering my family—the girls. I had no way of knowing what kind of men they were, and yet I trusted them. Why?"

"We didn't have much of a choice," Jean said. "Good heavens, Cameron, it was Christmas, and they were near frozen to death. Even their horses were done in. We couldn't turn them away. It would have been a death sentence."

"I know. And by the time that Sheriff Ericson and his deputies showed up, they were so much like family, I found it hard to believe they were who the sheriff said they were." He sighed at the memory. "Not until they ran. I would never, in my life, have thought I'd take the side of a pair of outlaws over the law, but I did. Even knowing for sure, then who they were, I was glad they escaped those lawmen. I hadn't had any intentions of doing it, but suddenly, I found myself making excuses for them, and even covering for them.

"We could have told the town sheriff that they had given us that money. But we didn't say anything." He stopped there, thinking back to that day, and Jean waited patiently for him to gather his thoughts. It didn't take him long. "In hindsight, I can see how Leon did it, playing on the girls' affections for him and Mathew. Making themselves indispensable to me in our situation. I simply couldn't turn them in, even knowing then, who they were. I couldn't do it."

Jean settled back down and nestled against her husband. Now that the floodgate had been opened, she knew she was in for a long dialogue.

"They were desperate," she said. "They found a haven with us, and Peter used a technique he knew would work, in order to maintain that safety."

"Yes. Manipulation."

"Do you regret now, promising to help them?"

"Oh, I don't know. Listening to Napoleon recount the events of his childhood, was heart-wrenching. What those boys went through was terrible—and that was just Leon's account. Mathew has yet to give his, and I find myself dreading it. I know they have led very desperate lives. When David and I were getting Leon cleaned up, the day they were arrested, we saw so many scars on him, most of them were minor injuries, but there were a few . . .."

"I know," Jean whispered. "Tricia and I found the same thing, while we were looking after Mathew. It's a miracle they're both still alive. But I think that explains, even more, the skills they had to develop, to stay safe in an extremely hostile environment."

"True. But now, I wonder if those skills have become so ingrained in their behavior, that neither one of them can ever truly be trusted."

"Cameron," Jean was saddened by her husband's concern, "they have always been true to us, you know that."

"Do I?"

"They're both honorable men. I know it, in my heart, that they are. Look at how good they are with the girls. Mathew could easily take advantage of Penny's youth and inexperience, but he doesn't. He's very protective of her."

"He knows I'd kill him if he ever did anything improper," Cameron said, but there was a hint of a tease in his tone.

Jean laughed. "That would be quite the sight; watching you try to outdraw the Kansas Kid."

"Oh, I don't know. If I get to him before his shoulder completely heals up, I might have a chance."

They both laughed.

Then Jean became reflective again. "And the way Mathew has taken to Eli; he's so gentle with him, and so patient. They've had a rough start and have developed some questionable skills, but they both want to change. They just need someone to show them how."

Cameron groaned, and he ran a hand over his eyes.

"What?" Jean asked.

"Something about Leon that made me wonder before, but now, it suddenly makes sense."

"What?"

"You were talking about how Mathew has taken to Eli. It reminded me, how, in contrast, Leon tended to avoid him."

"Yes, I'd noticed that. It's odd. Peter is obviously drawn to Eli, and yet it seems, deliberately stayed away from him, pushing him onto Mathew, instead."

"Yeah," Cameron sighed. "I wasn't going to say anything about this yet, but Napoleon had a younger sister, a baby. He even said to me in the court, '. . . not much older than Eli.' That baby died in the raid on their farm, and Leon blames himself for it.

"It was something he had forgotten about or didn't want to remember. So now, it suddenly makes sense, him not wanting to get close to Eli. The whole situation probably scared him, bringing him too close to emotions that had been buried so deeply, and for so long, that he dared not even look in that direction."

Silence settled over them again, while both contemplated the tragedy that had been so instrumental in shaping the lives of their two friends.

"I lied in court," Cameron finally admitted. "Not only about losing contact with them, but I also said that I truly believed Leon was capable of reforming, and all he needed was a chance to turn his life around. But even then, after hearing those testimonies of the things he had done, I was already having my doubts. And yet, I lied again. All the rumors and stories, we have heard about him, things we had come to believe were extreme exaggerations, I now realize were barely scratching the surface. We really don't know that man at all. Did you realize, he is half Shoshone Indian?"

Jean tensed. "What?"

"Yes. That's another thing that came out in court."

Jean was quiet for a moment, letting this news sink in.

"But he doesn't even look . . ." She stopped and re-thought her response. "Well, does it really matter? His heritage doesn't change the man we know. He's still Peter."

"True," Cameron agreed. "But my point is, he hid it very well. Again, manipulating the truth to create his own reality, and I wonder if I have done the right thing in promising to stand by him."

"I don't wonder about it at all," Jean said. "And I can understand him hiding his lineage. My goodness, they were treated badly enough, as it was. It must have been awful for him, at the orphanage . . .. No. I don't blame him at all for keeping that hidden. I don't care who his parents were, or what he has done in his past. He wants to change, to turn his life around, and I believe he is a good enough man to deserve our support. I also know you well enough; you will see it as a point of honor, to stand by your promise to him, even if you are having doubts about it now."

"Yes, you're right," Cameron said. "I even assured him of that again, the last time I spoke with him. He looked so scared and vulnerable; I couldn't turn my back on him." Then he laughed. "And Caroline, she has no doubts at all. She had a hard time, hearing some of those truths about her friend, but it was a good lesson, too; that loving someone doesn't necessarily mean they're going to be what you want them to be. You have to decide if you are willing to accept who they really are, and stand by them, or not accept it and walk away."

Cameron laughed again, a little ironically. "So, I guess our daughter has shown the way. Leon is part of this family, and even though he has done a lot of things I would never approve of, I have given him my word, and on my honor, I will stand by it. I just hope there is enough honor and strength in him to do the same."

With having worked his way around to this decision, Cameron became settled and relaxed in his mind. He hugged his wife, kissed her on the forehead, and still snuggled together, they drifted off to sleep.

***

Breakfast was, again, an animated affair. Caroline had filled Penny in on all the details. Not only of the trial, but of the strategy suggested by Mr. Granger to force some action.

"We already got in touch with the newspaper in Cheyenne, before we left, and gave them our point of view. They promised they would get it printed, as soon as they could," Caroline told her mother, "and then, Steven said we—"

"Caroline," her father interrupted. "Remember what we discussed."

"Oh, yes. Sorry Papa." Caroline continued with a slight change. "Then, Mr. Granger said we can start sending actual letters to people, once he gets the contact information from Mathew. And to start sending letters to the governor. The actual governor—can you believe it? Stev ... Mr. Granger even gave me the address to send it to, and everything."

"That sounds like you have quite an undertaking, there," Jean said as she spread preserves on her toast. "Do you think you can manage all this from home?"

"Oh, yes, Mama. We already have plenty of people we can contact, right now, and if they can contact people, and then everybody can send letters to the governor . . . we'll have his office swamped in no time."

"You're awfully quiet, Penny," Jean observed, "is this something you want to help your sister with?"

"Yes, Mama," Penny smiled. "I was just planning my strategy."

Cameron and Jean exchanged a glance over the oatmeal. This could get interesting.

"And how do you intend to pay for all these telegrams and letters you need to send?" Jean asked.

"Stev . . . Mr. Granger said he would wire us money to cover that cost, whenever we need it."

"I think we can take care of those ourselves, "Cameron commented, "considering I'm one of the people paying Mr. Granger, in the first place."

The two young ladies beamed smiles at their parents. The fact that they could finally do something to help, gave them both energy and high hopes for the coming months. Surely now, both their friends would be coming home for Christmas.

"Papa?" Penny began, hopefully.

"Yes?"

"Now that we are going to be working with Mr. Granger, and helping Mathew and Peter, can I come to Mathew's trial, next month?"

Strained silence settled over the breakfast table. This was the very question that had been plaguing Cameron all the way home from Cheyenne. He knew Penny would want to join them for the second trial, especially since Caroline would be sure to fill her in on what happened at Leon's. Was she old enough to deal with it? Mathew was someone she had quite the crush on, but it could become a "crush" of another kind, if what she heard at his trial ended up breaking her heart.

Napoleon's trial had been bad enough, but even though Caroline had found it hard to listen to initially, she rallied quickly. Finally knowing the truth about her friend had only inspired her to want to help him more. Would Penny respond the same way, or would she fall apart, and not be able to deal with it?

For a man who was head of the household and could usually make the tough decisions, Cameron now often found himself looking to his wife for her input. Two daughters, who had grown up right before his eyes, and demanding, by rite of passage, more and more respect and independence, were causing their father many a sleepless night.

"We'll see," Cameron finally answered her. "Your mother and I will discuss it."

***

Cheyenne, Wyoming

Betsy smiled sweetly at the blond outlaw sitting at the table and ordering supper. Steven Granger, she already knew, and the other man who wore a deputy's badge, and had been referred to as Rick, did not interest her at all. But Mr. Kiefer was a different matter altogether.

He had one arm tightly bandaged, and in a sling—poor dear—but in a way, this only made him more interesting. And the curls, along with those brilliant blue eyes that smiled back at her, melted her heart. She couldn't decide which of the two outlaws, whom she had met in this café, was the more handsome.

Even though Mr. Nash had been gorgeous to look upon, and the dimpled smile he used to flash at her took her breath away, he hadn't really been looking at her. He had just been going through the motions of acknowledging another human being.

But Mr. Kiefer, when he smiled and looked at her, he really looked at her, to the point where she felt embarrassed and wanted to cover up, even though she was fully dressed. But he wasn't leering; he was sweet, and very appreciative.

The other two men at the table sat back and watched this exchange with some measure of amusement. Where Taggard had been irritated by Leon's ability to flirt successfully, without even realizing he was flirting, Steven Granger and Rick Layton could appreciate an artist at work.

Betsy was oblivious to the fact that she was being observed.

"Would you like some coffee with your supper, Mr. Kiefer?"

"Oh, yes ma'am—ah, Miss," Jack smiled back, "some good coffee would be real welcome after the swill I've been drinkin'."

"Jailhouse coffee isn't that bad." Rick had to put one in for the team.

Jack snorted his opinion. "I hear even Leon couldn't drink it. It's gotta be bad, if he complains."

"We're serving steak and potatoes for supper, tonight," Betsy informed them, "and apple pie for dessert."

"That'll be fine, Betsy," Granger answered, "thank you."

Betsy disappeared, but soon returned with the three coffees on a tray, and she handed them out with another shy smile at the blue-eyed prisoner.

Rick reached over and unlocked the bracelet encircling Jack's left wrist, so he could eat his supper with some measure of freedom. The deputy still left the right bracelet intact, and the cuff dangling, for quick access. Rick had gotten over his scare that Jack would try to make a break for it again; he knew the time for that had passed, but he wanted those cuffs handy, just in case Morrison showed up. The mood marshal was in these days, it didn't pay to be sloppy.

Mr. Granger had been apprehensive about one of Morrison's deputies coming along on what was supposed to be a confidential discussion between himself and his client, but Jack put him at ease. The prisoner was not concerned about it and assured the lawyer that Rick was not likely to go running to the prosecution with any overheard information.

So, when Jack indicated that he was feeling better and would appreciate a decent meal instead of the steady diet of jailhouse food, it had been agreed that the café was as good a place as any to have a meeting.

Once the coffee arrived, Granger couldn't help but notice that Jack's appreciation of the beverage very closely mirrored his partner's actions. The two men were very different in many ways, and then something would happen, like the coffee, and the link between them would be so apparent, it was almost eerie.

Jack closed his eyes and savored his first mouthful—it had been so long since he'd had real coffee, he allowed his senses to be inundated with it. He finally swallowed and sighed with appreciation, then took another sip. He opened his eyes and found the other two men staring at him.

How could anybody make drinking a cup of coffee seem like such an erotic experience? Both men looked at their own coffees, wishing they could have some of what Jack had. It was all the same coffee, but still . . ..

The suppers arrived, and the three plates were distributed, but the plate placed down in front of Jack already had the steak and potatoes conveniently cut up into bite-size pieces.

Jack smiled. With his one arm in the sling, he wondered how he was going to manage that, and now, here it was all nicely taken care of for him. He needed to get out of that jail cell more often.

"Well, Mr. Kiefer," Granger began, between mouthfuls, "what are your thoughts about your upcoming trial? I know, it looks bleak, after what happened with Mr. Nash, but it would be dangerous for you to assume that the same verdict will automatically come to you."

Jack sent a skeptical look to Granger.

"I don't see how it can go different, Mr. Granger," he answered, after he'd swallowed his first mouthful. "All the prosecutin' attorney has ta do is ask me the same question he asked Leon, and the trial will be over."

"I take it you would also refuse to answer that question, if it were put to you?"

"Yeah," Jack answered, as though it should be obvious.

Granger sat back for a moment, considering the options.

"Well. We do have the right to keep you from testifying, thereby avoiding the question altogether. But it wouldn't look good, and it would also deny us what could possibly be our best defense, the sympathy plea. But again, it would be dangerous to assume that your trial will take the same direction as your partner's. Once we get the list of witnesses from Mr. DeFord, we might have a better idea of the type of defense we need to develop."

"What other kind of defense could there be?" Jack asked. "Leon and I are partners; we were both involved with the same crimes."

"Yes," Granger nodded agreement, "but the prosecution tended to focus on your partner's ability as a confidence player—a con man. It's highly unlikely they're going to try and use the same strategy with you. For one thing, Mr. DeFord knows we would be expecting that."

"Well then, what?"

"You tell me, Mr. Kiefer," Granger put to him. "What were your particular abilities that made you so good at what you did?"

"I backed Leon up," Jack said. "He came up with the plans, the schemes, and I backed 'im up."

"With your gun," Granger added.

"Well, yeah. But I never actually had ta shoot anyone during a robbery. That was the whole point of buildin' a reputation; people would automatically submit, once they heard my name."

"Hmm," Granger thought about this. "DeFord could go with that.

You are a gunman, but then again, as you say, you never had to use it during one of your robberies, so it would be hard for him to build a case on that alone." Granger stopped and considered other options while he chewed a piece of steak. "It's already been stated that Nash was a master of tactics. We could put to the court that you were influenced by him. He's your uncle, and you were accustomed to following his lead ever since you were children, so—"

"No." Jack was adamant. "I ain't puttin' that onta Leon. He didn't 'manipulate' me into anything. We were—we are, equal partners. We're in it together."

Granger sighed. "Your partner is already in prison, Mr. Kiefer. There is no need for you to feel that you have to protect him now."

"I don't care where he is," Jack's temper flared. "I'm not gonna say things about 'im that ain't true, just ta save my own neck."

"All right. We won't pursue that line." Granger sat back and considered his client. "I'm just throwing out suggestions, Mr. Kiefer. If you're not comfortable with them, I won't force them onto you."

"Oh. Okay, fine." Jack relaxed and went back to his supper.

"I received a telegram from Maxwell Coburn the other day," Granger said. "He was outspoken in his opinion of the legal system, after Mr. Nash's verdict was announced. He is, apparently, all set to launch an attack on the governor's office, in protest of the whole situation." He smiled, as a thought occurred to him. "Perhaps I should get the Marsham ladies in touch with him. That could be interesting."

Jack smiled. "Good ole Max. He's the last person we would have expected ta come ta our rescue."

"Just out of curiosity," Granger inquired, "How is it that you came to know a man like Mr. Coburn? He has a high opinion of you and Mr. Nash and appears protective of you. Is he a distant relative? And if he is, why didn't he take you in when you were orphaned?"

Jack almost choked on his potatoes.

"Ahh, I'm sorry, Mr. Granger," he said, trying to hide his amusement. "Max ain't quite as supportive as he appears. He told the local sheriff that we were related just as a cover story. He wanted ta keep us around ta do jobs he didn't want his sons doin'. Too dangerous, ya know? Anyway, when the sheriff started gettin' suspicious of us, Max told him we was all family. And old Max, he liked ta play it for all it was worth, I'll tell ya. He ain't a rich rancher for nothin'."

"Oh. I see," Granger nodded. "So, is he really on your side?"

Jack turned serious again. "Yeah, I guess so. Max coulda turned us in, more 'n once, and he didn't. Threatened to often enough, though."

"If he's that powerful a person, he just might be what we need," Granger surmised. "Even though he's not residing in this territory, a rich rancher like him could have far-reaching influence."

"You never said a truer word, Mr. Granger."

Betsy showed up with more coffee and cleared away the plates. It appeared that everyone enjoyed the steaks. She re-filled the cups and with a friendly smile to Jack, disappeared into the kitchen.

Jack watched her walking away, when, out of the blue, another thought occurred to him.

"Oh. Is there any way I could get a copy of the daily papers from the last couple 'a days? I'd like ta read up on what they're sayin' about Leon."

Mr. Granger was at a loss; he knew he didn't have any copies.

"Yeah," Rick put in. "We've got at least a week's worth, over at the jail. I know the one you'd be interested in is there, as long as Morrison didn't see it and throw it away. I'll look when we get back. Hour's almost up, anyway."

Then the apple pie arrived.

Jack smiled at Rick. "Time for dessert?"

Rick eyed the pastries. "Always time for dessert."

***

A few hours later, Jack sat on his cot, reading the newspaper articles from the last few days. He had to admit, the stories were convincing, and he could recognize Caroline's handiwork in the phrasings and sentiment. This could get interesting.

As he read one of the last articles about his partner, Jack heard the block door unlock and open. He looked up to see Sheriff Turner and David coming into the block. He smiled, happy to see his friend again, as it had been nagging in the back of his mind that the doctor had not been around lately, and that wasn't usual. When David was in town, he always came by to check up on Jack in the early evening, so for him to not show up, was cause for concern.

Turner unlocked the cell door, let David enter, clanged it shut behind him, and left, leaving the two men alone, as usual.

David lingered by the door and leaned back against the bars, looking at the prisoner.

Jack felt uncomfortable with the scrutiny, not quite sure what was going on.

"What?" he finally asked.

"Nothing."

"No, not nothin'," Jack countered, reminiscent of discussions with his partner. "Somethin's wrong. What is it?"

"It's just something Morrison said," David muttered. "It doesn't matter."

"Yeah? Well, don't believe 'im."

"What do you mean? You don't even know what he said."

"Yeah. But I know what he said has upset ya, and that man has no right ta run anybody else down, that's for sure."

David smiled. "Yes, I suppose you're right. Still, I'm thinking I might head home on the afternoon train, tomorrow. I'm feeling a little superfluous, here."

"Sir—what?"

"Ahh, redundant," David explained, "not really needed."

"Well, why don't ya just say that, then?" Jack complained. "Don't go turnin' into another Leon, on me. He's always usin' words I ain't never heard before. It's unsettlin'."

"Sorry. We can't do any exercises with your shoulder now, not until the collar bone heals. You don't need me here for that, so I thought I would just head home."

"Oh." Jack fidgeted. "I was kinda hopin' you would stay."

"Why?" David asked. "I'll leave you enough morphine to see you through, so long as you go easy on it. And Dr. Taff can help you out with anything else you may need. There's no reason for me to be here."

"Yeah, but . . ." Jack hesitated, setting the newspapers aside, "both Taggard and Cameron have gone home. I was hopin' you'd stay, is all."

"I'm sure you'll be kept busy with Mr. Granger, and you have Rick here. They'll stand by you."

"But they're hardly my friends, David," Jack pointed out. "Granger is my lawyer, and Rick is, well, a friendly official is the best way ta describe him."

"And I'm just your friendly doctor."

Jack sat quietly for a moment, feeling hurt.

"I thought we were more than . . ." he began but felt awkward. "I just thought . . . well . . ." then realization dawned. "Is that what

Morrison said to you?"

"What?"

"That you're just my doctor, and nothin' more?"

"Well . . ."

"Ahh no, David." Jack gave the innocent newspaper a slap. "Don't listen ta that blowhard, he ain't never had a real friend in his life."

David smiled, surprised at how relieved he felt.

"Yeah, I suppose you're right. I guess I could stay a little longer. Still, I really should get home for a while, and then if you want, I can come back with Cameron for your trial. It'll be interesting to see if the girls convince him to bring both of them along, this time."

Jack smiled with the beginnings of this sentence, but the smile dropped from his face as David completed his thought. The latter part wasn't funny, as far as he was concerned.

"Ohh, David. I don't think the girls should come. Please, tell Cameron I don't want the girls ta come."

"Why not?" David asked him. "Caroline handled things all right with Napoleon's trial."

"Yeah, but Granger keeps insinuatin' he's gonna put me on the stand, and, well . . . if I have ta go back ta that day, I just think those girls are too young ta hear about that."

"Could it possibly be any worse than what Napoleon described?"

"I dunno." Jack shrugged. "I dunno what Napoleon described. I just don't think that little girls should hear this stuff."

David sighed and smiled at his friend. "You seem to be making the same mistake that Cameron makes. Cameron, I can understand; he's their father. But you? Surely you can see they are not little girls, anymore. Two of Caroline's friends are married and have started families of their own. A friend of Penelope's is betrothed and will be getting married next spring. They are both young women; adults in their own right."

"Oh, David," Jack groaned. "You have no idea how dangerous it is for me ta think a Penny as a young woman. She has got ta remain a little girl, in my mind."

"But why?" David asked, confused. "She's about as grown up as . . .." Then he noticed Jack looking embarrassed, and signs of a guilty conscience began to show themselves. "Ohhh."

"David. Wipe that grin off your face. This ain't funny!"

"Well, what's wrong?" David asked, still grinning. "Penny is an attractive, young woman. And she is obviously very fond of you."

"'Young' is the key word, David. She's too young. It's terrifyin'."

"Yes," David nodded. "Love can be terrifying."

"Don't say that word." Jack was off the cot now, and very agitated. How could one possibly sit still during this conversation?

"Oh, Jack, come on," David tried to get serious, but had a hard time with it. "Many men take wives who are much younger than they are. Cameron and Jean are a prime example of that and look what a good marriage they have."

"That's different."

"Why?"

"Cameron had somethin' ta offer," Jack said. "What can I give ta Penny as a husband and a father?" Jack turned pale as he realized what he had just said. "Oh my god. A father? Oh no, no, no. No, she can do a lot better than me. I have nothin' ta offer her. Besides, I'm goin' ta prison. Yes! Twenty years, more than likely. What kind of a marriage is that? No. She'll find someone else, someone more worthy of her.

"On top a that, Cameron would skin me alive if anything happened. And, ya know, I need ta watch Leon's back. He can't stay outta trouble when he's left on his own, especially in prison; I can see him gettin' inta all sorts of problems without me there ta watch out for 'im. See? Penny don't need me. A pretty girl like her will find someone else in no time. I bet there's already some young fellas wantin' ta come courtin'."

David continued to lean against the bars, watching his friend pace back and forth, becoming more and more agitated as he argued, vehemently, with himself.

Finally, Jack realized he was the only one talking, and he stopped pacing to look at the man leaning against the bars. Unfortunately, the doctor was still smiling, apparently not taking the outlaw too seriously.

Jack sighed, and his shoulders slumped.

"Just tell Cameron, I would prefer it if he didn't bring the girls to the trial. At least, not to that part of it. Okay?"

David nodded, finally acknowledging his friend's concern.

"Yes, okay, Jack. I'll tell him."

***

Jack hardly had time to settle onto the cot again when Mr. Granger entered the jailhouse.

Sheriff Turner rolled his eyes. "This is turnin' into Grand Central Station. What's up now?"

"I need to speak with my client, Sheriff. In private, if you please."

"Yeah, yeah, I know. It's always in private. Well, go on then. I'll stay out here and read the paper. Again."

The lawyer cocked a brow.

Turner shook his head. "That's the most privacy you're gonna get. I'm sure not leaving him unguarded."

Granger sighed, realizing he'd hit a brick wall.

"All right, Sheriff. Just make sure it's an interesting article."

"Hmm."

By the time Granger approached the jail cell, Jack was already up to the bars.

"Mr. Granger. Something come up?"

"Yes. And I admit, I'm a bit perturbed. A new charge as been brought forth against you, and it is a serious one. I'm wondering why you did not bring this to my attention sooner."

Jack frowned, hiding the shiver of fear that tickled his spin. "Bring what to your attention?"

"Manslaughter, Mr. Kiefer. You have been accused of killing someone in a gunfight. Are you saying this is false?"

"Oh." Jack slumped. "Ahh . . ."

Granger actually growled. "What do you think? That this is a game we're playing?"

"No," was Jack's meek reply.

"The whole cornerstone of our defense is that you've never killed anyone!"

"During a robbery!" Jack pointed out, his ire rising in his own defense.

"A very fine line, Mr. Kiefer. Mr. Marsham is paying good money for me to defend you, but how can I develop a good defense, if you won't give me full disclosure?"

"I wasn't charged with anything at the time!" Jack insisted. "It was self-defense. Even the sheriff in that town thought so."

"Didn't you think it would help us, if we could have had him here to testify to that?"

"It was years ago," Jack pointed out. "I don't even remember his name."

"Given time, we can find him." Granger growled in frustration. He took a couple of deep breaths and convinced himself to calm down. Yelling at his client relieved tension, but it wasn't going to help their case. "Do you at least remember the town where this happened?"

"Yeah. It was in Brown Creek, Wyoming. I ain't likely ta ever forget that place."

Granger sighed. "And when was it?"

"Oh damn. Ahh, it was the same year we run into the Marshams. So, I guess that would'a been in '82."

"That's not too long ago. Even if that sheriff isn't still in office, there will be people there who remember him. This new charge is going to delay the trial for a few days, so I can still enquire after this sheriff. It's worth a try

CHAPTER FIVE
PRISON LIFE

As Napoleon Nash regained consciousness, his first awareness was the jolting of the prison coach as painful thumping radiated from behind his left eye. The second thing was that the very same eye was so swollen and puffy, he couldn't even open it. He didn't want to consider what it must look like from the other side. Even the top of his head hurt. What was that from? Oh yeah, the bottom of Mike's chin.

As the memory of what happened returned to him, so did a sense of guilt. He knew he'd hurt Mike, and the deputy hadn't deserved that. Leon had over-reacted again, and he didn't blame Mike for the subsequential retaliation. He hoped the fellow would be okay and not hold a grudge for too long. It's not good to have someone that big be mad at you.

Leon didn't want to open his eyes, and indeed, had not moved a muscle since awareness had returned to him. He knew he was sitting in the prison coach, leaning against the front and side paneling, his hands and ankles shackled by chains running through a metal ring imbedded in the floor. His body ached, and the jolting vibration of the wagon briskly making its way toward Laramie wasn't doing anything to help his situation.

He stayed quiet, in this position, for some time, not wanting to deal with the reality that was waiting out there, just beyond his closed eyelids. Please, let's stay inside for a while longer. Just a little while longer. Then someone coughed, someone quite close to him, and it startled him into opening his one good eye, and reality stared him in the face. Still not moving, he looked over and met the gaze of a guard, sitting directly across from him. The man had a rifle placed strategically across his lap. A small half smirk played across his lips.

"It looks like our new resident is finally awake."

"Good," responded a voice to Leon's left, coming from the back of the coach. "We're getting close to the stagecoach station, and I wasn't looking forward to dragging him in. What the hell. Probably just leave 'im where he is. We're only stoppin' long enough ta change horses anyway."

The first guard's half smirk developed into a full smile.

Leon finally shifted, gradually becoming aware of the stiffness in his back and shoulders from having been in the one, awkward position for too long. He pushed himself up straighter and sent a glance down to the second guard. He was much like the first.

Leon tried to produce a semblance of a smile.

"Gentlemen," he murmured, by way of greeting.

"Howdy, Nash," the first guard responded. "Enjoy your little beauty nap? That's some shiner ya got there—you oughta fit into prison life real well."

Leon meekly responded with a subtle nod, and then, giving up all effort at communication, closed his eye and awaited the inevitable.

In some ways, this trip was surreal to the convicted man. But in other ways, it almost seemed pre-destined. As though, no matter what he did, or how hard he tried to avoid it, he was going to end up in prison. The harder he fought against it, the faster he raced toward it. And here he was, chained, hand and foot, inside the barred and armored prison coach, with two large guards to keep him company. He crossed over the threshold between freedom and misery, silently cursing the promises made that had led him to this fate.

After three stops along the way to change horses, Leon finally, but way too soon, heard the driver of the coach call out to the horses to "whoa", and the vehicle came to a halt. Within seconds he heard a key in the lock of the rear door, and then that same door swung open.

The guard sitting across from Leon got up and released the chains from the ring in the floor.

"On your feet." He grabbed Leon by the arm and pulled him up then shuffled him toward the exit. The second guard had already stepped down, out of the coach and had turned to await the prisoner.

Leon's one good eye blinked as the late afternoon sun hit him. He hesitated as he gazed out the back of the coach, trying to get his bearings. There were two other guards out there, all waiting for him to disembark. He wondered what it was they thought he was going to do, trussed up the way he was. Still, it would probably be worth their jobs if a prisoner of his caliber got loose on them. They were all making sure that Napoleon Nash didn't get a chance to go anywhere he wasn't supposed to go.

With his feet still in the leg irons, Leon couldn't step down, out of the coach, and he hesitated, not sure of his footing.

"Jump," one of the guards on the ground waved him forward.

This, combined with a push from behind, made the decision for him. He jumped down to the step, then two of the guards grabbed him and brought him down the second jump to the ground. He was then hustled off toward the front door of the imposing building.

Leon looked around as best he could at his new residence, and even in the bright sunshine, he couldn't remember a drearier looking place.

Or maybe that was just his mood seeping through.

Fortunately, there was only one low step for him to navigate to the front door. He hesitated a moment, then felt the guard behind him give him a push. His shackled feet stumbled up the step, and his eyes peered up at the tan and red brick building towering above him.

He didn't have time to think about bolting for cover before he was pulled away from this view and ushered through the doorway of the prison. As that heavy door closed behind him, Leon felt his heart and his soul sinking deeper and deeper into oblivion. Even the atmosphere, the very air he breathed, was filled with oppression.

He found himself in a short, carpeted hallway that terminated at a closed and presumably locked door. There were some pictures on the walls, mostly depicting previous wardens or group shots of uniformed guards. Nothing that left a favorable impression with Leon.

There was a door on each side of the hallway and Leon felt a sense of panic hit him. This was the last place on earth he wanted to be. His heart rate quickened, and his knees went weak. An overpowering impulse to turn and run back out the front door hit him, and, despite the hopelessness of success, he would have done it too, if not for the guard behind him, giving him a shove in the opposite direction.

Leon stumbled forward, then was thrust into the room on his left.

The room was an office, but there was no one in it. Leon was positioned to stand in front of the desk, and there he waited, with an armed guard on either side of him.

Ten minutes went by, and Leon found his mind wandering. His gaze followed the various pieces of furniture around the room, taking note of more photographs on the walls and the general décor of a typical office. Aside from the main desk that faced the front door, there was a roll-top desk, and side tables that could be moved around as needed when the warden was entertaining official visitors.

He also took note of a stuffed pheasant on display by the window, and two mounted pronghorn heads on the wall bracketing the main desk. He gazed upon those glass eyes, feeling a kinship with the fate of these hunted spirits. He too, had been hunted relentlessly until he had finally been brought to ground. Now, here he was, stuffed and put on display as a prized trophy to be mounted on the wall and shown off.

His musings were interrupted as the second door to the right opened and allowed an official looking gentleman to enter the room.

By the man's attire, Leon assumed this was the warden. Unlike the other employees, he wore a suit rather than a uniform, and he had an air of superior authority about him, as he strode in and took his seat behind the desk.

Mason Mitchell was a middle-aged man, who took pride in his professional appearance. He kept his dark hair short and slicked back, while the handlebar moustache was always kept neatly trimmed. He had quite a high opinion of himself, even though he came from poor beginnings. But he had worked his way up the professional ladder, and achieving the appointment of warden for the prison was just another rung on his way to governor. He had grand ideas of how the territory in general, and the prison, in particular, should be run.

The warden viewed the receiving of Napoleon Nash into his keeping as a feather in his cap, even though he, personally, had nothing whatsoever to do with it. He took it on as his personal responsibility to ensure that the new inmate came to regret his chosen path in life, and Mitchell was willing to go to any length to achieve this end. His only regret was that Jack Kiefer had not yet arrived to receive the same education. Surely, time would soon remedy this omission.

The warden ignored the men in his audience. He browsed through the folder of loose pages that had been set there for him and was completely engrossed in them. The "guests" remained standing, awaiting the warden's attention.

Another ten minutes ticked by, and Leon sighed with the frustration of standing there, waiting for—whatever—to start happening.

Instantly, a rifle butt clipped the back of his right knee, and his leg neatly collapsed from under him. He went down in a sudden, disheveled heap. He stayed where he had landed, surprised by the suddenness of the retribution, until hands grabbed him and pulled him to his feet.

Leon expected some type of explanation, such as, "That was your first lesson, etc.", but nothing was forthcoming. The guards continued to stand placidly around him, and the man sitting at the desk didn't even look up.

Another fifteen minutes dragged by, with the only sounds being the ticking of the grandfather clock in the corner, and the paper rustling whenever the "suit" turned over another page. Leon stood silently, not making a sound, not moving a muscle. His eye hurt and his head pounded. He started to feel cold, but he didn't move. He would play the game until he figured out the rules.

The "suit" finished reading the documents, shuffled them into a neat pile, then stood up and looked the prisoner directly in the eye.

"So, Mr. Nash, I'm Warden Mitchell." He smiled and Leon's skin crawled. "I was beginning to think we would never be honored with your presence here, in Laramie. That's quite a shiner you have there, but I strongly advise you to cease the behavior that caused you to earn it. That will not be tolerated here, and you will find that punishment for breaking the rules will be far more unpleasant than a mere black eye."

"Well, I'll certainly . . ."

Another quick clip, this time behind the left knee, and Leon went down again. This was already getting old. Hands grabbed him, hauling him to his feet. He stood there, trying not to let his irritation show through, as he might just end up getting clipped for that, too.

"You'll learn the rules quickly enough," the warden continued, without skipping a beat. "For what's left of today, we'll just let you get settled in, then tomorrow, you can start your duties. Welcome to the U.S. Penitentiary at Laramie City, Mr. Nash."

***

Leon was shuffled through the same door the warden had entered from. He found himself in another hallway, this one was cold and bleak, and there were certainly no carpets, or photographs on the walls. All he saw there were two signs, indicating cell blocks, one to the left and another to the right. A quick glance to both ends of this hallway showed more barred doors, but only the one to the right was shut and locked.

Leon was then ushered to the right. They passed by the boiler room and then another barred door that led back into the entrance hallway, but Leon was forced past this door, then past the kitchen, where he heard pots and pans rattling. He caught a glimpse of striped-clad trustee darting around, helping to prepare the evening meal. His stomach knotted at the thought of food, but they weren't going in there anyway.

The leading guard opened another door next to the entrance hall, and Leon was escorted inside. This was a larger room than the office and a quick glance around indicated that this was the processing room. Aside from different writing desks and worktables, a chair with cuffs attached to the arms sat in the corner, and there was a camera lined up to face it. The inside wall had floor to ceiling shelving with blankets, linens and folded striped material that looked suspiciously like clothing.

There was a second door along the right wall, and Leon presumed that was the same one that opened onto the front hallway, right across from the warden's office. It occurred to him that if he ever entered either of these offices again, it would be through the back hallway, not through the main entrance.

Another man stepped into the room behind them and cursed when he nearly walked into one of the guards.

"Dammit. Haven't you got 'im ready yet? Get on with it, I ain't got all day."

"Take it easy, Doc," Officer Murray growled back. "We just got in here ourselves. For some reason Mitchell wanted a private audience with this one."

The newcomer snorted. "That prick. Gotta strut around like a cock in the henhouse, when some of us have ta work for a livin'."

"Don't go takin' your sour mood out on us," Pearson grumbled. "It ain't our fault Orson's gone ta visit his daughter, and you got stuck with his duty. I mean, c'mon, just how much effort does it take ta shave a man's head?"

"It ain't the effort, it's the idea." The doctor plunked his satchel down on the desktop. "Anyone a you yahoos could'a done this. But that bastard had ta give me the job, didn't he? Fuckin' asshole . . ."

This was Leon's introduction to Dr. Walter Palin. He also wore civilian clothes rather than a uniform, but this was the only similarity between him and the warden. Palin was uncouth in his manner and his dress, and Leon wondered how he managed to hold onto his job.

The second guard, Pearson, knelt and unlocked Leon's leg irons while Murray tugged at the belt buckle in the small of Leon's back. Once the belt was loosened, Murray stepped around in front and unlocked the cuffs.

Leon sighed with relief at the removal of those bindings. The leg irons, particularly, had begun to chafe his ankles, and it was a small mercy to finally be rid of them.

But he didn't remain unfettered for long. As soon as the shackles were stripped away Pearson pushed him into the chair and promptly snapped those cuffs onto his wrists.

Leon felt his irritation rise again at this power-play. All the guards needed to do was tell him what they wanted, and he would be happy to comply; there was no need for this manhandling. But he had already learned one lesson well; keep your irritation to yourself.

Dr. Palin set his satchel on the table close to them, and Leon felt a moment of panic over what was being planned for him.

They don't—gulp—castrate new inmates, do they?

His anxiety increased as the doctor laid out a sharp straight edge, and he felt a sudden urge to cross his legs. This was followed by instant relief, as Palin stepped behind him and began cutting his hair with a pair of sheers.

Okay, this makes sense. I've seen fellas newly released from prison, and they all had shaved heads. I can deal with this.

Still, he was surprised at the heartbreak he felt as he watched the floor around him become littered with his thick, dark locks. He hadn't realized how much he identified with his mane of hair, or with how naked and exposed he now felt as it all ended up on the floor.

Once his hair was down to a long stubble, Palin took the straight edge and started to scrape the rest of it clean.

All went well until the blade rasped across the bruise left by Mike's chin. He flinched and Palin pulled back.

"What the hell? Why has he got a bruise on the top of his head? And don't think I didn't notice the black eye, either. You fellas figured you'd get a head start in beating the rules into 'im?"

"Don't go blamin' us, Doc," Pearson griped. "He came here already packin' those bruises." He cocked a smile. "Seems like we got us a fighter here."

Even though Leon couldn't see the doctor, he heard the man roll his eyes.

"Any excuse, eh, Pearson?"

Pearson simply snorted, and the Doc got on with his job.

Once done, Palin collected his belongings and left without a word.

Leon then found himself staring into the lens of a camera. It sat on a tripod about five feet in front of him, and Murray stood behind it, fiddling around with the knobs. Obviously, they were getting ready to take his picture.

Leon, again, felt a sense of predestiny at this minor undertaking.

Though he and Jack had done little to hide their identities from their victims, they did go to great lengths to avoid their likenesses being captured by a photographer's camera. One of the main reasons he and his nephew had stayed free for as long as they did, is because the law did not have a photograph of them.

They'd even gone out of their way and paid a young lad good money for a sketch he had done of them as they'd ridden into a town. The boy had an uncanny talent, and the likenesses he'd captured were too close to the subjects to be allowed into circulation.

This is ridiculous, Leon mused, as bitterness merged with his already sour mood. *So much for a deal with the governor's office. Here I am, sentenced to twenty years in this place because of some damn confidence game everyone decided was illegal. Dammit, it should be Snodgrass sitting here. He's more of a conman than I'll ever be.* He almost laughed out loud as another thought resurfaced, but instead, he allowed a subtle shake of his head at the absurdity of his situation. *How ironic. The various governors sent us out on assignments that were far more illegitimate and devious than any job Jack and I pulled during our outlawing years.*

And as for naming names, we'd have been shot if we'd revealed any of the people the governor had us doing jobs for. Our ability to keep our mouths shut was one of the qualities the governors had all appreciated. Heavy sigh, and he noticed a quick glance from Pearson. Leon's lips pursed; he already hated this place.

He sent a glance toward Murray. *Look at him. After years of ensuring that no photographs were ever taken of us, here I sit, cuffed to this damn chair, while this fool casually snaps away to get my likeness in print as though it'll make any kind of a difference now.*

He sighed at the irony of it all.

Pearson sat at the roll-top desk, writing something down on a card. He hadn't noticed Leon's rule breach, but he did frown and send a glance his way.

"How tall do ya think he is?"

Murray shrugged. "Wanted posters say five-eleven. That's close enough."

Pearson nodded and wrote that down.

"His weight? Hmm, he's tall but kinda skinny. 150?"

"160," Leon said.

Both guards glared at him.

Oh crap. Leon bit his lip and dropped his gaze. *Am I going to get hit for that now?*

The tension lingered in the air only for a second, then Murray allowed his gaze to soften.

"I'll let you have that one for free, Nash, since you're new. But you better learn to keep your trap shut. You understand?"

"Yessir," Leon murmured, but didn't look up.

Murray didn't say anything but twitched a smile. Some of these inmates were quick to pick up the rules.

Pearson went back to filling out the card.

"Okay. Height, weight, ah, eye color: brown. Hair . . . hmm." He looked at the remnants on the floor around the chair. "Black or, no, dark brown, I guess. Ha! Gettin' rid a your Indian roots, eh, Nash? Okay, let's see here, birthdate: February 24th, yadda, yadda. Ahh, aliases. My, but you've had a few, ain't ya Nash? We know about Josh Harden, Charlie Smith, Hersial Hamilton, and Peter Black. Any more you wanna add?"

"No sir."

"Yeah, a course not. Hey, I got an idea. What about your Injun name? Your ma must a called ya somethin' other than 'Lil Papoose'. Ha, ha."

Leon's jaw set tight. That one wasn't even original.

Murray and Pearson smirked at each other, then Pearson snickered. "Yeah, right. Okay, I'm done here. Your new name is Prisoner number 312. I suggest ya remember that."

Leon frowned. *What's that supposed to mean?*

Murray unlocked the cuffs and pulled Leon to his feet, then turned him to face the row of shelves.

Murray grabbed a thin pillow, a blanket, a set of long johns, two pairs of socks and two sets of the striped prison garb, and handed them to the inmate.

"Are you literate, 312?"

The question took Leon by surprise. "What?"

Murray sighed. "Are you literate? Can ya read and write?"

"Oh. Yes."

Pearson brought over a small box containing writing paper, two pencils, three candles, five pieces of candy and a packet of tobacco with rolling paper.

He noticed Leon glance at the tobacco and guessed its meaning. "If ya don't smoke, you can use it to trade for somethin' ya do want."

Pearson plunked the box on top of the other items Leon held, then Murray added a pair of shoes to the pile.

Leon shifted it for a better hold. He didn't even want to consider what would happen if he dropped anything.

"Okay, Convict, follow me."

With Murray leading the way and Pearson following, they took him out to the back hallway again, and led him to the left.

Murray pushed the heavy barred door open further and carried on through.

Leon felt a moment of panic as he got his first look at South Block, and his spine contracted as Pearson clanged the barred door shut.

The sight before him was daunting. Three tiers of cells with steel and concrete stairways led up to each level. It was cold and dreary, and even with fireplaces set into the walls at each end of all the aisles, Leon felt a chill run through him.

The guards hurried him along. They ushered him to the right and carried on past the stairway, then took a left, passing the rows of cells along the back side. There were three windows facing the enclosed prison yard, and Leon's eyes drifted to the daylight streaming in through the heavily barred glass. It was nice to see the setting sun, but he was still in a cage.

They entered a room at the far end of cell block. There were latrines in here, and bathtubs, but Leon was escorted past these and into a small room with a drain in the middle of the floor.

Murray motioned to a bench along the side wall. "Put your things over there. Strip, then fold your clothes neatly and set them on the bench as well."

Leon accomplished this without any hesitation. He remembered back, feeling embarrassed when David had insisted on giving him a sponge bath, but here, there was no room for that. His mind blocked out those emotions as having no place in this new life. The old life he had known was gone, and he was going to have to re-invent himself, re-establish the ground rules.

"Stand over there, under the shower."

Leon glanced up at the ceiling and noticed the shower head directly above the drain. He stood under it.

Pearson pumped the leaver on the wall pipe, and cold water gushed out of the head and cascaded over the naked body of the new inmate.

"Here," Murray tossed him a bar of rough soap. "Scrub down from top to bottom."

Leon completed this task without complaint, and then he was doused again with more cold water, until all the soap had been rinsed away. Murray tossed him a rough towel, and he quickly dried himself off in the hopes that he might warm up. He didn't.

Hugging his torso and shivering, he stood, waiting for his next instruction.

"Get dressed," Murray said.

Leon reached for his own clothing.

"Not those!" Murray stopped him and indicated the striped material. "Those."

Leon didn't hesitate. Then another piece of his heart chipped and broke away when he noticed the number 312 sewn to the front of his new tunic.

It doesn't matter, he told himself. *It's just a number, it's not who I am.*

He pulled on the long johns first and felt himself warming up, thank goodness. With his shivering abating, he donned the remainder of the prison duds and waited for further instructions.

He was led out to the cell block again and stopped there. A few minutes later, another guard appeared from what Leon would later come to know as the laundry room, and approached the three men.

"Is he done?"

"Yessir, Officer Reece."

Officer Kenny Reece nodded then turned his steely gray eyes to the inmate.

Leon wasn't sure how he felt with this scrutiny. The guard was older than Leon, but younger than the doctor, and he carried himself with an air of authority, but not arrogance. Those eyes were hard and meant business, but there was intelligence there, and Leon decided to hold off on judgment until he got to know the man better.

"There is a small library, as such, in the common room," Reece informed the new inmate. "After supper, you can choose one book. When you have finished that one, you can choose another. Any infringement of the rules, and this privilege will be taken away. Do you understand?"

"Yessir."

"You will not speak to any of the other inmates, unless you are giving or receiving instruction. You will only speak to a guard if you are asked a direct question. Do you understand?"

Leon had already figured this one out. "Yessir."

"The guards are always right."

Leon hesitated, then he looked this guard directly in the eye.

"Eyes down!" Reece's tone held an edge, daring the inmate to challenge him. "The guards are always right. Do you understand?"

Leon dropped his gaze and stared at the floor.

Pick your battles.

"Yessir."

Officer Reece was satisfied with this answer and nodded to the guards to carry on with their duties.

Leon felt the tug on his arm, and he knew it was time to move on. They directed him back to the stairway, at least he assumed it was the same one. He had lost all sense of direction in this cold, bleak place where every corridor looked the same, and every door led to more misery. He was in a daze and gave up trying to understand the layout of the cell block, trusting that with time, it would become as familiar as the Elk Mountain hideout.

***

Leon's first introduction to his cell was terrifying.

They escorted him up the steel and concrete stairway, where the only thing between him and a drop down to the main level, was a thin metal railing. Not usually afraid of heights, this stark structure left him feeling unnerved, and he kept himself as close to the wall side of the stairway as possible. The cells were all in a line along the aisleway, but this was where any resemblance between these cells and the open barred ones in a jailhouse, ended.

These cells were completely closed in on three sides, so even though you had neighbors, you would not be able to see or communicate with them. The front of the cell was made up of the door, and the door was cross barred, so, even though the inmate could see out to the corridor, it was only through small square openings which allowed a very limited view.

Leon felt claustrophobic even before he was pushed inside one of those shoe boxes, and the sound of the door clanking shut behind him almost sent him into a panic. It was so small. He stood where he was for a full ten minutes, feeling that if he dared to move, he'd explode.

Deep breaths, deep breaths. Calm down. If this is going to be home, better to embrace it.

"Supper will be in an hour," he heard Murray inform him. "Follow the other inmates to the community hall. I'm sure you can figure out what you need to do. Just keep your mouth shut while doing it."

Then the two guards were gone.

***

He forced himself to relax and then to take in what little there was to offer in this 'cozy' accommodation. A small cot was to his right, and he noted how thin the mattress was. There was also a small table, and a bench to accompany it. The cell wouldn't have been able to accommodate any more than this, and he realized that pacing was going to be a challenge. He also spotted a wooden bucket under the table; this, he assumed, was the chamber pot.

He sighed. Finally, he moved to the cot and sat down, still holding the supplies the guard had given him. He stared ahead, into space, or was it just a solid wall? He felt every shred of happiness sink away and disappear out of sight. Jack, Cameron, Jean, and the girls were gone. Taggard was gone. They slid, further and further away, as though they belonged to another dimension, another life—another Napoleon Nash. He, this being who sat on the cot in a cell in the Laramie Penitentiary, was alone.

***

The first couple of weeks were difficult. Leon fell into the routine of doing everything with a group. Everyone got up at the same time, everyone went to meals together, and everyone went to work together.

The only deviation from this, was that the inmates could have their meals in the large common room that did triple duty as dining hall, chapel, and library, or on their own, in their cells. After supper, they could spend the evenings doing what they wished, so long as they didn't make any noise and didn't break any of the rules.

The jobs he was given to do were menial. Once he was taught the principles of "how to make a broom", it became a basic motor skill, and most of his time during the day was spent daydreaming and trying not to go mad with boredom. The hardest thing for him to accept was the "no talking" rule. How can human beings work and eat together, day in and day out, and not have conversation?

His tongue was sore from all the times he'd had to bite it in order to stay quiet.

Then the day came when his mood was foul enough to take over his common sense.

He was busy at a workstation, binding the coarse straw to the wooden broom handle when the twine broke, causing the straw to come apart and scatter to the floor.

"Dammit."

The curse was under his breath, but the young guard standing near him still heard it.

"Shut your trap. Get more twine and then clean this mess up."

Leon flashed him a glare. "You clean it up!"

The young man's eyes widened in surprise, and he was at a loss on how to deal with this uppity inmate.

Then Leon got hit from behind. A blow to his kidney then a swipe at his knees brought him to the floor. His temper flared and, with another curse, he scrambled up.

A boot kicked him in the midriff and, gasping for air, he dropped to the floor again. This time, before he could regroup, the business end of a billy club pushed against his throat, pinning him where he lay.

"What's the matter with you, Nash?" came Reece's voice. "You know the rules. You might have been somebody out there, but you're nobody in here. Remember that."

Leon snarled. He could barely breathe, but he still managed a strangled rebut.

"Go to hell."

He heard a heavy sigh, then the pressure on his neck released just as Reece grabbed his shirt and hauled him to his feet.

"Murray!"

"Yessir." Murray grinned; he knew what was coming.

"Nash can be a guest of the dark cell until tomorrow morning. Give him a taste of what hell might be like."

Murray gladly stepped forward. He grabbed Leon and pushed him toward the exit.

"Get movin'. One more sound outta you, and you'll be spendin' time in the infirmary, after you've done your punishment."

Reece watched them leave, then turned to the recruit still standing beside him.

"You're new here, Wilson, I know that. But you cannot let these inmates get the upper hand. Nash challenged you, and you stepped back. Don't ever do that again."

"Yessir. I'm sorry, sir. He just took me by surprise, is all."

"Every time you engage with these inmates, there's the chance that something will happen. Always be ready. There are tools in here that any one of them could use as a weapon. Being inattentive can get you killed. You understand?"

Wilson hung his head, embarrassed by the reprimand, especially because he knew he deserved it.

"Yessir. It won't happen again."

"Good. Carry on."

***

"Move it." Murray shoved Leon again to quicken his pace across the yard. "Draggin' your heels ain't gonna change anything." Another shove. "Move."

Leon fought the urge to turn on the guard. Every fiber of his being wanted to spin and attack, but he knew that would only make things worse. He glanced up at the watch-tower and noted the armed guard up there, observing them. Now was not the time nor the place for retaliation.

They crossed the yard and stopped at the door leading into the prison cell block. Murray pushed Leon face first up against the wall.

"Stand there and don't move."

Leon heard the jangling of keys, then the click of the door lock.

Murray grabbed Leon, pulled him off the wall, and then pushed him through the open doorway.

"Move. Around to the front."

Leon felt his legs tremble, as fear built up in his chest. The dark cell was the last cell on the ground floor, but it differed from any of the other cells in one, important aspect. It was completely closed in. Even the door was solid steel, and once placed inside, the inmate lost all contact with the outside world.

Leon had passed it many times on his way to other duties, but he always avoided looking at it. The mere idea of being locked up in that black box sent dread to his heart, and now he was heading there for just that purpose. He could see no way out of it.

Murray stopped him in front of the solid door. He grabbed the lever to unlock it, then swung it open.

"Get in. Be thankful it's a short sentence. Mr. Reece is being kind."

Leon stood, staring into the dark enclosure, his legs refusing to move.

Murray sighed, stepped behind the inmate and gave him a full body shove across the threshold that catapulted him against the far wall.

In a full panic, Leon pushed off the wall and made a run for the door.

"No—"

But the door slammed shut in his face and he heard the lever slide over, locking him in.

Fourteen hours in the dark cell stretched into an eternity of night fears. The darkness weighed heavy upon him, as every worry, every problem, every phobia that had ever haunted one's dreams, came calling. During those long, silent hours, huddled in a corner in the pitch black, everything that couldn't be seen brought terror to the heart and despair to the soul.

Leon lost sight of who he was in the dark cell. Images of rats scurrying around him, and snakes slithering by, made him jump and tremble at the slightest mind rustle of fantasy. He tried again to control where his mind took him. He closed his eyes and willed himself to relax, to push away the terrors as simple imaginings that had nothing to do with the reality of what was in the cell with him.

Nothing was in the cell with him. He was alone, just him. Then he would hear a scurrying or feel a light brushing against his leg, and the terrors would overwhelm him again. Spiders, he came to realize, were for sure in there because the itchy bites he acquired while in the cell could not be caused by mere imaginings. He feared falling asleep, thinking about what would be crawling over him in the dark. He often pushed himself to his feet and walked just to prevent his mind from free-falling into the abyss.

If he'd been a man of lesser intelligence and imagination, he probably could have handled this punishment a little easier. But Leon could not turn his mind off, and in this situation, he couldn't even slow it down. In the silent darkness, time and structure disappeared. The only thing he had to help him hold onto that awareness of "self", was his mind, and it was running him ragged.

When finally released into the light of day, all he could remember about the dark cell was that it was the worst experience he'd ever been through. So much so, that the second time his bullheadedness sent him there, he fought the guards and had to be beaten nearly to unconsciousness, before they could subdue him and drag him inside.

One of the hardest things Leon had to endure, not only while in prison, but throughout the whole of his life, was the dark cell. The terrors of that punishment never left Napoleon Nash, and he continued to experience nightmares of that unholy place up until the day he died.

***

On the evening of the following day, when Leon returned to his cell, he was surprised to realize his change in attitude. The tiny room that had at first filled him with such panic, now became his haven. It was the only place where he did not have to be constantly on the alert.

He settled onto his bunk and sighed with relief.

He'd rather have his reading privileges taken away than to spend one more minute in the dark cell. But he also realized that he had asked for it. He knew the rules by now, but he had allowed his own stubbornness to over-ride his common sense. He had to be careful not to let that happen again.

Used to being the man in charge, submitting to the guards on every level was the hardest rule for him to learn.

And the hardest part about learning the rules, other than the few Officer Reece had mentioned to him upon his arrival, is that no one told him what they were. The only way to find out what was accepted and what wasn't, was to break what was, apparently, a rule, and then be punished for it. Seeing as how reading was very important to Leon and was the only thing that helped him to stay sane, he had incentive to learn the rules quickly, and on the most part, he did.

By the end of his third week, he had read the few books that had held any interest for him, and desperation forced him to consider reading others, with which he was already familiar. Soon, overwhelming boredom forced him to consider other avenues to obtain reading material.

He remembered that day, a lifetime ago, when he had first met David Gibson, and how impressed he had been with the man's knowledge and abilities. Indeed, Leon was convinced that no other doctor in the West could have saved Jack's life, and for that, Leon would be forever in the debt of the medical man. But Leon also remembered the intense curiosity he had felt, over the doctor's technique, and how it had lit a spark in his mind to learn more about it.

That spark had become dormant, what with all the other stresses he'd had to deal with since that day. But now, his thoughts returned to it. The question was, "how to get hold of medical journals?". He hadn't seen any in the library, and he wasn't allowed to ask, so how would he be able to find out? The next day, at work, the answer came to him.

Leon stood at his work station, his mind transported into another dimension, when the dull knife he used to cut the dense straw for the brooms, slipped and embedded in his left palm.

He hissed in pain, dropped the knife and clutched the wrist of his injured hand.

Murray rolled his eyes. "Done it to yourself now, haven't ya? Wait here and try not ta bleed all over the floor."

Leon stood where he was, cradling his injured hand, until Murray returned along with Officer Reece.

"Let's see it." Reece held out his hand, expecting to be obeyed.

Leon cautiously obliged, hoping this injury wouldn't be used to inflict more pain.

Reece took the hand, but all he did was spread the wound open to see how bad it was. More blood surfaced and dripped to the floor.

"Yeah, that's going to need stitches. Carry on with your duties, Mr. Murray. I'll take him to the infirmary."

"Yessir."

Officer Reece escorted Leon out of the warehouse, across the yard and into the cell block, then up to the second floor, where the infirmary was located. It wasn't an impressive, or large facility, which also doubled as a dental office, but it was functional, and it served Leon's purpose completely.

Reece led Leon into the room, where they found Dr. Walter Palin sitting at his desk, busy writing up his reports for the morning.

He glanced up when the men entered and the first thing he noticed was the blood dripping from the inmate's hand. He let his paperwork lay, and with a mild curse under his breath, he went to the supply cabinet to pull out a needle and some suturing thread.

He motioned to Leon to have a seat on one of the beds and wheeled over a small table for Leon to support his injured hand. The doctor placed a towel underneath Leon's arm, then turned the hand over, palm up, so he could give it a closer examination.

"Hmm," was his only comment. It seemed that every new inmate found a way to injure himself one way or another, and Palin suspected it was a feeble attempt to avoid work. It wouldn't make any difference though, because the guards would simply find them something else to do, until the injury healed.

Leon sat quietly, as the doctor worked, and conducted his own examination which was more informative than the one he had been able to conduct upon their first meeting.

The doctor was an older man, sixty if he was a day. His white, scruffy hair barely concealed his spotty scalp. and his craggy chin was covered with a perpetual five o'clock shadow. He was of average build and height, but flabby, and he used suspenders to hold up his loose trousers and keep a rumpled shirt in place. A thread bare and stained undershirt peeked out around his neck and along hairy arms. His fingers were short and stubby, but they knew their business and were quick and agile while treating the wound.

Leon frowned as the doctor settled in close to him. He was sure he got a whiff of alcohol coming off the medical man. And not the kind used for disinfecting, either. Apparently, it wasn't just the inmates who found this place oppressive.

The doctor returned to his cabinet, grabbed some more supplies, and came back to his patient. He lifted the injured hand and placed a bowl beneath it. Pulling the stopper out of a bottle of clear liquid, he poured some of it over the open wound.

Leon just about hit the ceiling.

"Damn it, Doc! A little warning would have been nice." Then quickly flicked a glance at the guard, expecting a reprimand for daring to speak out of line.

Reece showed little concern over the blatant disregard, and everyone carried on with the matter at hand.

"Hmm," was again all the learned gent had to say.

Leon frowned. This was turning into a strange experience. If the doctor remembered him from their first encounter, he wasn't letting on.

Palin sprinkled some powder on the wound and Leon felt his hand start to go numb. The doctor prepared to stitch the cut together.

Meanwhile, Leon distracted himself with a quick scrutiny of the room to see if there might be some medical books lying around. He was disappointed to find that there were none to be found. He decided to go for broke. Reece hadn't done anything with Leon's first breech of protocol, so perhaps that rule didn't apply in the doctor's office.

"Say, Doc, you wouldn't happen to have any medical journals or books, lying around, would you?"

"Hmm," came the usual response as the doctor began stitching. Then, to Leon's surprise and relief, he elaborated. "Got plenty in the other room. Why? You think I don't know what the hell I'm doin'?"

"Oh. No, no, no," Leon was quick to deny, despite his surprise at the blatant profanity. Still, it was a prison and even the personnel here were hardly going to be cultured individuals. "No. I was just wondering if you would loan me a few to read. I find it fascinating, especially resuscitation techniques and the like. I want to learn more about it."

"You'd probably find the medical journals a little beyond you." The doctor sniffed and scratched at his beard stubble. "Why don't you check out the library? There are plenty of dime novels over there."

Leon smiled, feeling frustrated. "Ahh, well . . .."

"This is Napoleon Nash, Doc," Reece informed him.

Leon looked at him in surprise. He hadn't expected assistance from any of the guards.

The Doc looked up at Leon, his brows raised in recognition. "Ohh. Well, dammit! Why the hell, didn't you say so?" He scratched his gray stubble again, as he reflected on his stash of books. "In that case, I'm sure we can find something over there to get you started. Resuscitation techniques, eh?"

Leon smiled, his dimples appearing for the first time in weeks. "Yeah. To begin with."

"Okay. I can think of a couple, off-hand, you can borrow. When you're done with them, bring them back and I'll give you some others. You just make sure you do bring 'em back. I know what you bastards are like—ya get a hold a somethin', then, all of a sudden, it's yours."

"No, no, I'll bring them back. That'd be great, Doc, thanks." He hesitated, as another thought occurred to him. "But, how do I get back in here? I don't really feel inclined to be slicing myself, every time I need a new book."

Doc finished with stitching and was wrapping the hand in gauze, as he looked at the guard.

"How about it, Ken? You think, if Nash here, let you know he wanted to see me, you could find a way to bring him in?"

"Sure," Reece agreed. "I don't think that will be a problem."

Leon glanced at the guard. He knew he'd seen something of a decent man in those eyes. Leon hoped, maybe, he had himself an ally in this godforsaken place.

Heading up the stairs toward his cell, his left hand neatly stitched and wrapped in gauze, and his arms supporting a stack of new reading material, Leon appeared pleased with himself.

Ken Reece watched him, the corners of his mouth tipping up just a bit.

"Why do I get the feeling that slicing your hand open wasn't an accident."

Leon discerned that this was not a direct question and declined to answer.

***

As the weeks passed, Leon became more familiar with the various guards. The social dynamics inside the prison walls weren't that different from any other cloistered group. It was easy to find the full range of the human condition, from the most arrogant individuals all the way down to the cowardly. Unfortunately, both extremes encouraged abusive behavior.

For some time, Leon was under the impression that Kenny Reece was the senior guard, but this assumption turned out to be incorrect. Reece was third in command, under the warden and a bull of a man named Floyd Carson.

Once Leon had Carson identified, he did his best to avoid him. He knew the type, having had to deal with them during his outlawing years. Their love for cruelty set them apart from polite society, and they found their niche as lawmen or outlaws. But they were the worst kind of man, no matter which profession they turned to.

Now Carson, he truly did take perverse pleasure in setting an inmate up to fail, then punish him for trying to comply in the first place. Standing up to him, in any way, often resulted in a severe beating or a day in the dark cell, and Leon wasn't sure which one was worse.

He also knew that Carson had his eye on him, just waiting for the opportunity to establish dominance and control over the infamous inmate. Leon watched his step, but he knew that a confrontation with the senior guard was inevitable.

Below Carson in the pecking order were a couple of his cronies. Men who liked to be in control of others but didn't have Carson's leadership abilities to be in charge. They were happy to follow their boss's lead, and to back him if any of the inmates got too uppity. On their own, they were easy enough to handle, but get them coming at you in a group, and look out.

Corporal punishment was considered the normal form of discipline. The billy club was used most often for quick and ruthless retaliation. Used properly, that club could knock the wind out of a man's lungs or bring him to his knees in an instant. Of course, the dark cell was an ever-present threat for misconduct along with a removal of privileges, such as reading and writing materials, or time spent outside.

For severe misbehavior, the lash, or a heavy iron ankle bracelet were brought into play.

Another form of punishment was the devilish contraption called the Oregon Boot. Made of heavy iron, a four-inch-wide band was strapped around an inmate's ankle with an iron support strap bolted to the heel of the shoe. It weighted close to 30 lbs., and was extremely effective in inhibiting the inmate's mobility.

When the boot was first designed, inmates were forced to wear them at all times to prevent escape attempts, and it was very successful. But the damage this contraption did to the ankle was extensive and permanent, causing such painful injury to skin and bone that even after release, an ex-con would be left crippled for life.

Public outcry put a stop to the barbaric use of the boot as a deterrent and it could only be used as punishment, and certainly not for prolonged periods of time.

All these tactics were known and approved by the warden, but it was up to the discretion of the guards to what extend they delved out these punishments. Warden Mitchell was not above harsh discipline, so

Carson knew that as senior guard, he had full rein. If he decided he didn't like you, then you could expect to be in for a rough time.

As for most of the guards, they just needed a good, steady job. They came to work, put in their shifts, and then went home if they had one, or to the guards' dormitory adjacent to the common room. And, hopefully, at the end of the day, nobody got hurt.

At first, Leon put Kenny Reece in this category, but again, Leon's assumptions about this guard proved to be false. The longer Leon was there, and the more he was able to differentiate between the guards, the more Kenny Reece stood out as a man apart.

It's not that he was a saint, or anything remotely similar. He knew his job and what was expected of him. You didn't cross him, that was for sure, and as Leon had discovered, his retaliation and punishment would be doled out just as swiftly and severely as anything Carson could deliver.

But, whereas Carson did it for pleasure, Reece did it for discipline, and he was fair about it. If Kenny Reece got you with the billy club or sent you for a day in the dark cell, chances are you deserved it.

Kenny also kept his word. When Leon finished the first two books the Doc had loaned him, all it took was a raised eyebrow and a subtle nod. The guard showed up at Leon's cell after supper that evening and escorted him to the infirmary.

The first few visits were easy to cover, as the Doc wanted to see the inmate anyway, in order to remove stitches and check on healing. He was also keeping tabs on the injured eye. It didn't take long for the swelling and bruising to fade, but even after all else had healed, the evidence of broken blood vessels remained apparent for a long time to come. Still, it made for a convenient excuse to visit the infirmary.

After that, it became a bit trickier, but somehow Kenny always managed to get Leon over there with no questions asked, and Leon was getting an extensive education.

***

When it came to the other inmates, there was just as strong a pecking order among them as there was among the guards and it didn't take long to work out who the alpha was.

The warehouse was very much akin to a large pen containing a pack of wolves, and if the guards weren't there to keep things civil, it's a sure bet that dog fights would be breaking out all over the place.

Speaking, of course, was not allowed. But it was amazing how much communication could be conveyed through simple body language. It was a true art form and very effective.

Hank Boeman was the alpha wolf amongst the inmates, and he looked every bit the part. He wasn't exceptionally big, but he had a meanness to him that was apparent. One look from him at any of the underlings, and they'd scamper out of his way, double-time.

Reece and Carson were the only guards who would stand up to him on their own, the others made sure they had backup, first. Boeman truly thought he was in a position of power, choosing to ignore the fact that he was still a prisoner and had spent many a day in the dark cell, himself.

Boeman's first encounter with Leon was anticlimactic. Despite the fact no talking was permitted, the information still found a way to get around that the new inmate was indeed, Napoleon Nash. As was to be expected, Leon's reputation came right along with him. Hank Bowman assumed that he and the outlaw leader would be locking horns over the alpha position, before much time had elapsed.

Much to Boeman's surprise and probable disappointment, Leon had no interest in being the alpha wolf over this sorry pack of miscreants, and he declined all Boeman's challenges. Leon's body language and eye contact, or lack thereof, did not so much indicate submission, as it did condescension, and this attitude ticked Boeman off more than anything else. Leon was saying that what Boeman had wasn't worth the great outlaw's acknowledgment or desire, and, therefore, Boeman was permitted to carry on as before.

Boeman silently blustered and strutted, trying to set up a confrontation. But his mind was nowhere near as devious as his adversary's, and Leon saw the bushwhack coming, long before the trap was sprung. He simply avoided it, and carried on with his duties or retired to his cell to read. Not surprisingly, he had made himself an enemy.

***

Time slowly ticked by and always, in the back of Leon's mind, was the worry over his nephew's upcoming trial. Most of his conscious mind hoped that Jack would get off somehow. That maybe the court would view Leon as the leader and instigator, and Jack simply followed along. There was a chance that Jack would still get his pardon. But another part of Leon missed his partner, and though he wouldn't wish this place on his worst enemy, he was ashamed to say, he did wish it upon his best friend.

Leon felt so alone here, so unprotected. If Jack got the same sentence, then at least they would be together and could watch each other's backs. Together, maybe they could make it through, maybe even get early parole. Why not? Stranger things have happened.

Then Leon felt ashamed of himself for wanting his friend here for purely selfish reasons, and he would push those thoughts down and out of sight.

If Jack got off, he would work tirelessly to get Leon out of here. So really, logically, it would be better all-around if Jack remained on the outside. Out there, he would have a lot more power and a lot more influence than if he ended up stuck behind these bars.

Then fear and loneliness would clutch at Leon's heart as he lay on his cot at night and stared up at a ceiling he couldn't see—and he'd worry. He didn't think he could do this alone. He tried to find a way to settle in, but he already felt strangled by the enforced confinement. He was suffocating. He remembered what Cameron said, about it only being that way because he told himself it was.

Change your way of thinking, you can change your life. Repeatedly telling yourself you're going to die in this place, and chances are you will.

Leon sighed. *How can I change the way my mind works? I've been trying to do this most of my life; trying to get it to shut down, to turn off, just so I can sleep. But it doesn't listen to me. My mind has a mind of its own.* He smirked at his little inward joke, then sighed. *If I can't even do that, how am I supposed to get my mind to change its view of my whole world?*

Leon rolled onto his side and hugged his knees to his chest. He stared into the blackness.

During the day, he had the medical journals to keep his mind occupied. Learning something new, something more challenging than how to make a broom, gave him hope for a future, even being stuck in this miserable place.

But at night, when the prison sank into darkness, his hope faded and all he saw was despair

CHAPTER SIX
LEARNING THE ROPES

Fortunately, not all was darkness and misery at the prison. The weekends did offer some reprieve from the mundane and tedious work days. Saturdays, visitors could come calling. New inmates weren't allowed visitors for the first three months, the reason given was that they needed time to settle in. More likely, it was to give the bruises sustained while learning the rules, time to heal up. No need to get friends and loved-ones upset over nothing. Still, it was something for Leon to look forward to, and he hoped that someone—anyone—would come to visit.

Mail call was also on Saturdays. Mail got sorted, inspected, and then placed in the cell of the recipient during the afternoon of that day. Again, dominance prevailed. Often, if an inmate received something of value, like a warm jacket, or a pair of socks, one of the guards would help himself to it before it even came close to a prisoner's cell. It was times like this that having a guard who was willing to watch out for you, came in handy. But stolen property aside, receiving a letter from the outside often was the lifeline that kept an inmate holding on from one week to the next. It gave hope.

Leon never forgot the leap his heart took, when one Saturday afternoon, he returned to his cell after dinner to find a letter on his cot addressed to him. It was originally addressed to Peter Black, then that name had been crossed out and Napoleon Nash took its place. The letter itself, however, began with "Dearest Peter . . .".

He settled onto his bed and, as he drank in this letter along with his after-supper cup of coffee.

"Caroline here. Oh Peter, we all feel terrible about what happened to you. I can't even imagine you being

locked up in that place. Even

though I have no idea what it is like there, I am sure it's not much fun.

We are doing everything we can to get the governor to act upon this, especially with Mathew's trial looming ahead of us. Once we stop this awful thing from happening to him too, then we will focus completely on getting you a pardon.

I'm sure you remember your lawyer, Mr. Granger. Well, he is helping us to launch a campaign to protest your sentence. I am sure we will be successful.

Hang on and don't give up. Okay?"

Here, the handwriting changed from Caroline's flowing script to Penny's short and to the point style.

"Hello Peter. We are so angry over what happened to you. It just isn't fair. Mr. Granger is helping us to write letters and telegrams to whomever we can think of who might influence your sentence, and Mathew's trial.

Oh, it's Penny here, in case you couldn't tell. We are all heartsick, over this, especially Papa, as he feels it's his fault; that he pressured you into standing trial.

I am so worried about what will happen to Mathew. If you had gotten off, I wouldn't be so concerned, but the way things are . . . oh, I don't know. I'm just so scared . . . But be brave, okay? We will get you out of that place. We love you, Peter. You're family, and don't you forget it.

Bye for now. We'll write again soon."

The script changed again, and Leon smiled.

"Hello Peter. This is Jean . . .."

A warmth seeped around Leon's heart. He cared about the girls, and hearing from them meant a lot. But Jean was special. She was a warm home on a cold night. She was apple pie and cinnamon, she was chicken prepared in so many different and tasty ways, that you forgot it was all there was to eat until the spring thaw. She was a shoulder to cry on, and simply seeing her name made him feel safe.

> *"I know the girls have already told you," The letter continued, "but I wish to emphasize the importance of their words. We care about you. We are not going to simply sit back and forget about you. I don't know how long it will take, but you know what our girls are like. Once they get an idea in their heads, there is no stopping them. We will all continue to fight for your release. Know that we love you and that you are never far from our thoughts and prayers.*
>
> *Cameron sends his regards, but you know what men are like when it comes to letter writing.*
>
> *Goodbye for now, but we will stay in touch.*
>
> *Jean."*

Leon set the letter aside as his thoughts turned inward. He felt a combination of self-pity and hope. But most of all, he felt relieved. Maybe he could hang on and endure after all.

He began looking forward to Saturdays.

***

There was also the Sunday service in the common room. Leon was not a churchgoing man. Even with his chosen lifestyle making attending services impossible, he resented the hypocrisy of the pious view.

As a child, religion had been a confusing issue for him. His father put great importance on going to services every Sunday, and his mother supported him, insisting the children go as well. But Napoleon knew his mother struggled with it. The spiritual views of her own people conflicted with those of the white man's god, although many Indians on the reservations were being converted to Christianity.

This seemed to be a good thing for them, but young Huittsuu-a could not bring herself to forsake her ancestors in this way. To be accepted into her white husband's tribe, she had gone along with his religion. Even accepting her Christian name, Hannah, to show sincerity in her efforts to fit in. But in secret, she taught Netuá the ways of his Shoshone roots.

As a child, Napoleon took his mother's teachings to heart. Even when the magical tales faded along with his memories of family life, he hadn't been one to believe in the Hell and Brimstone threats that were divvied out for misconduct. Therefore, this type of sermon did little to catch his attention. Then, when the religious teachings at Blessed Heart Orphanage and the Residential School tried to hammer home the same brutal message, young Napoleon rebelled against it even more.

This animosity took a firm hold as he grew into an adult, and his anger would flare at anyone who dared preach to him about God's love and forgiveness. God's love had never done him or Jack any good.

Now, at this prison, his hackles rose at the suggestion that he attend services. It wasn't every Sunday that a preacher blessed the prison with their presence, but when one did, everyone was expected to attend. When it was made clear to him that he either attend, or spent that time in the dark cell, he still baulked at it.

Then Kenny Reece made an offer he couldn't refuse.

"You can sit in the back if you find the situation that revolting to your sense of decency. You're good at disappearing into your own head, and Warden Mitchell insists that all inmates attend for the first few months, at least in the physical. Where your mind goes is up to you."

Leon sighed, judging that with Kenny, he could get away with this mild form of protest. And he did, but he still attended services.

After breakfast on Sunday morning, he made sure to sit as far back from the makeshift pulpit as possible. He could hide there and shut out the holier-than-thou sermon that he knew was coming, even if it was of the fire and brimstone variety.

Damn, I wish I could have brought one of my books with me. He sent a resentful glance to the guard on the floor and another to the one up in the barred look-out and knew there would have been no way to hide that indiscretion. Another sigh. *Oh well . . .*

His heart sank further when the attending preacher turned out to be exactly what he expected.

Dressed in somber black, Reverend Simmons sent daggers out upon the spectators from under stern and gray caterpillar eyebrows.

Some of the inmates squirmed under the accusing scrutiny, but Leon simply sighed. *Here we go. I wonder how long we have to sit and listen to this blow hard.*

The squared shoulders of the preacher arched back as he drew in a trough-full of air then spewed it out with a loud and gravelly "Damnation to all who do not repent!"

This was all Leon heard. His mind shut and bolted the door, and he immersed himself in his own studies.

I wonder how you save someone who's been shot in the throat. Would it be possible to? I remember that fella, oh geesh, what was his name? Iverson, or something like that. He took that hit in the throat. We tried to help him, but he drowned in his own blood. Leon shuddered. *That's not a thing I want to witness again. Dammit. I bet David could have saved him. There must be a way . . ..*

***

Once a week, usually on a Saturday, or a Sunday after services, the inmates who were on good behavior were allowed a certain amount of casual time outside. Leon, along with the other prisoners, greatly anticipated this privilege and it was added incentive to stay out of trouble as the weekend approached.

Even though the days were getting colder, Leon took as much time outside as he could and kept warm by briskly walking the perimeter of the yard with arms swinging in vigorous motion. Guards were still in attendance during these outings, and four were stationed, high up, in the corner towers where they could oversee everything and everyone. Even so, it became the only time during the week when Leon felt the claustrophobia ease off his spirit, even if just for a short time. These outings became precious to him.

But one Sunday, something happened that marred the experience. After that day, walking outside in the cold sunshine, with the sound of crunching frost-rimmed leaves under his feet, would bring with it a sadness that lingered long after he was back inside and warm again.

On this Sunday, it was such a day in early autumn. The leaves that had fallen inside the yard had been raked into piles and left in the shadow of the tall prison walls. They had frozen overnight and had not defrosted throughout the day. Even by mid-afternoon, they were still crunching underfoot.

Leon did his usual brisk walk, blowing on his hands to warm them up, when he heard hurrying footsteps rustling up behind him. He spun, expecting Hank Boeman to be launching an attack, but instead, he was met with the young, exuberant countenance of Harvey Konachy.

Harvey couldn't have been more than twenty years old, and he was an open-faced, pleasant looking, young fella, who'd simply had the misfortune of falling onto hard times.

Leon noticed him being depressed and, if Leon thought about it in the four weeks he'd been here, he had never really seen Harvey smile. He went through his days in a trance, had his meals, which he picked at, and then returned to his cell to brood. His eyes were dull and his manner hopeless, as though he had given up.

So, it was with some surprise that when Leon turned to see Harvey, he was met with a sparkle in the young man's eyes, and a broad grin upon his face.

"Hey, Nash," Harvey greeted him, "I've just discovered something. You gotta watch this, okay?"

Leon tensed and did a scan of the numerous guards to see if any of them had overheard Harvey speaking to him. Even outside, talking was not permitted. But nothing changed; nobody noticed. Still, Leon didn't want Harvey to push his luck, and he tried to motion the young man to quiet down.

"No, listen, Nash." Harvey's eyes danced. "I've found a way outta here."

"What?" Leon couldn't help himself, though he did keep his voice to a whisper. "What do you mean? How?"

"Just watch me. I'll show you the way out."

Much to Leon's astonishment, Harvey turned and bounded across the yard like a young buck in rut, and then plowed, full force, into the back of Officer Carson. The guard plunged forward, a long line of curses trailing after him, before his natural agility saved him from falling headfirst onto the frozen ground. He regained his footing and turned, bringing his rifle around with him, but by that time nobody was there.

Harvey continued running, making a beeline toward the far perimeter fence that surrounded the compound.

Leon stood for a moment, transfixed with shock. Then, deaf to the guards shouting out their warning, he ran forward. He wasn't sure what exactly he could do, but certain there must be something.

Everyone in the yard was alerted to the young man's run as he continued his dash. He reached the pile of leaves, then made a wild leap up against the high wooden fence, and somehow, miraculously, found something to cling onto.

Leon never forgot the sight of that lad, almost spread eagle, clinging onto the side of the twelve-foot-high fence. Then, the sound of rifles, like a Gatling gun, sent a barrage of bullets into Harvey's back.

Harvey hung there on the wall for what seemed like forever but could only have been a couple of seconds. The bullet holes that punctured him were too numerous to count. In slow motion, bright red blood flowed out of the wounds and spread across his shirt, and then he fell back and landed, with a crunchy thud, into the crisp autumn leaves.

Leon stood still, his mind spinning with the shock. Suddenly, he was in a bubble again and Jack was in his arms, and there was blood everywhere. Leon couldn't stop the bleeding, and Jack held onto him, with desperation in his eyes. *I'm sorry, Leon . . . I'm sorry . . ..*

Then, Leon got shoved from behind and the bubble burst. One of the guards used his rifle to push him forward, toward the door that led back into the cell block.

Everyone was yelling, and Leon heard more than one rifle report, as the guards sought to regain order and control. The convicts were hustled back into the corridors and up the stairs to the appropriate levels, then into their cells.

The whole prison went into lockdown.

Leon paced what little room there was in his cell. He was agitated, his mind still reeling.

What was that? How could Harvey have had any hope of getting over that fence?

But at the same time, Leon knew that Harvey hadn't planned on getting over the fence, he just planned on getting out—the only way he knew how.

***

The following morning, the entire place was in subdued spirits. Leon didn't even know what Harvey had been in for, or how much longer he had to go on his sentence. It kind of seemed irrelevant now, but still, it nagged at him, and he was down in the dumps over the whole situation. The workday dragged even more than usual, and after supper, Leon simply returned to his cell to focus on reading, until he was tired enough to get some sleep.

He wasn't long at his book when he felt the presence of someone at the open door of his cell. He looked up and saw Carson. When their eyes met, the guard beckoned him over, and Leon, feeling like this was the last person he wanted to deal with, none the less closed his book and approached. He stood quietly, avoiding direct eye contact, and he waited for whatever Carson had up his sleeve.

"Evenin', Nash," Carson greeted him. "I hear your partner's not going to be joining you here, after all."

Leon was startled into locking eyes with the guard. His heart leapt. *Does this mean Jack got his pardon? Is he a free man? Is he going to join the fight now, to get me out of here?*

"Yes siree," Carson was obviously enjoying himself. "They done found the Kansas Kid guilty of cold-blooded murder, and at 11:00 this morning, the law went and hanged him by the neck until he was dead. Hanged him, Nash, like the filthy, thieving, murdering, gunslinger that he was."

Carson started laughing; a loud, raucous laughter that followed him as he disappeared from the doorway and continued his way down the aisle.

Leon's body turned to ice. He gasped and staggered backward as though Carson had just punched him in the stomach. He stood there for a full thirty seconds, his eyes staring straight ahead at nothing, until his knees gave way beneath him. He went down hard, landing on his rump, upon the cold floor. But he didn't feel a thing. Suddenly, his whole body heaved, and he made a desperate grab for the wooden bucket as he began to retch.

***

Leon didn't sleep a wink that night.

It never occurred to him that Jack might end up facing a murder charge and possibly be hanged. Jack would have been charged with the same crimes that Leon was. They were partners, after all. Leon assumed Jack would either be joining him in prison or getting his pardon and be freed.

But, the death penalty? For what?

A slight chill tingled his spine as he stared at the dark ceiling.

Could this be about Bartlett? Did DeFord find out about that and twist the truth to make it look like cold-blooded murder? Leon snorted. *Yeah, I wouldn't put that past him. Anything to get a conviction.*

But the death penalty? No, that can't be right.

110

As time dragged on, the shock of Carson's words wore off, and Leon realized the guard could just be playing a sadistic game with him. But still, the seed of doubt had been planted. Leon remained cold with fear throughout the long night, and despite the logical workings of his mind telling him not to panic, it was all he could do to stay calm and focused.

He lay there, staring up into nothing, as he worried and stressed, and thought about all those things he couldn't change and couldn't stop, and berated himself for being so powerless. Those events had happened anyway, despite his apparent genius, his brazen self-confidence, and his downright audaciousness. The fates still had control.

He thought about his sister, how he had left her to die a terrible death and had not even tried to save her. He hadn't even done her the honor of remembering her. Instead, he hid her away, pushed her out of mind and memory. He buried her and covered her up with an over-compensation of self-righteousness and arrogance.

She'd be what? Twenty-four now, twenty-five? But she's gone, like the rest of my folks. I'm the only surviving member of the Nash family. Those bastards who live back East don't count. They denied me when I needed them the most. They were no longer kin.

Then a deeper sadness entered his heart. His last visit to his mother's people, during the time when he and Jack were apart, had made it clear that where the child had been welcome, the adult was not. Leon was a white man and did not fit in with the Shoshone way of life. He could never return there.

His mother had sacrificed everything to be with her white husband, and her son was her only offspring. She had willingly given her own life to offer him a chance at survival, and what had he done with it? He had become an outlaw, a convict—a loser. His mother would be so ashamed of him. So disappointed.

Still, there was Mukua; Ata-i, his mother's brother. But he was in the same situation as Leon and could never return to Crowheart Butte. They were both outcasts.

Now, he was trapped again, subject to forces beyond his control. His closest friend, his nephew, his only true Nash family link, had faced another life and death battle on his own. Again, Leon had been powerless to help him.

Maybe Carson is telling the truth, and Jack is already dead.

But surely, I would have felt something. I would have known if Jack

111

had died yesterday. Wouldn't I know?

Somewhere, in the bowels of that cold prison, the bone-chilling screams of one of the inmates in the throes of a nightmare, rose and echoed through the cell block.

A tingling of fear shivered down Leon's spine.

There, but for the grace of God, go I.

But Leon knew that the grace of God had never been present in his life, and soon it could be him, screaming into the night and slowly going mad.

The sound of banging reached his ears, as the night guard whacked the billy club against the offender's cell door.

"Shut up, Johnston. You'll have the whole place in an uproar. Wake up!"

Then, there was only silence.

***

The chilly morning finally dawned. A row of windows set high on the walls, on the far side of the concrete gully, allowed muted rays to seep through, bringing a gradual lightening within the depths of the prison. Then, the loud clanging of the bell, and the harsh mechanical clunking of all the cell doors unlocking in unison confirmed the beginning of a new day.

Everyone had to be up and standing at the door of their cell for roll call, to make sure nobody had died during the night. Then, the silent procession to the wash basins at the end of the aisle, then down for breakfast; usually oatmeal and, really, do you call that coffee? Leon tried to eat, but his stomach was in a knot. This was not going to be a good day.

***

Halfway through the morning, Leon was trying to focus on the finer art of making a broom, when he felt the presence of one of the guards standing beside him. He tensed, not sure who it was, but knowing he dared not look up.

"Don't listen to what Carson says to you," Leon heard Kenny's quiet voice. "He likes to play mind games with the new prisoners. Wait until you know officially. Personally, I have yet to hear the outcome of

Kiefer's trial."

Once again, Leon was surprised into breaking protocol, and his gaze snapped up to meet Kenny's grey eyes. Then he jumped, startled, as Kenny's billy club whacked down on the table, barely an inch from where Leon's hand rested.

"Why are you looking at me, Convict?" Officer Reece demanded. "Eyes down. Back to work."

Leon instantly dropped his gaze, and Kenny moved on to continue with his rounds.

Leon found himself shaking, partly from shock and partly from relief. Even though he had already been telling himself that very thing, Kenny's validation of his unease over the source, did a great deal to alleviate the inmate's concerns. He would wait, before he let despair eat him alive—wait, until he heard something official.

CHAPTER SEVEN
JOSEPHINE

Cheyenne, Wyoming
Autumn, 1885

It was close to 10:00 p.m. as Steven Granger went over some last-minute paperwork in preparation for the trial due to begin the following morning.

It was a starless night, with a definite chill in the air, and he knew that he should call it quits and head for home. His tummy made it clear that it was past supper time.

Tomorrow was going to be a busy day, and if Nash's trial was any indication, it would be a stressful one, as well.

He was tidying up his desk, when a quiet knocking was heard at his door. He sighed in disappointment. Who in the world would come calling now? He walked to the door, took hold of the lock, and then hesitated. He was involved in two highly controversial trials, and this late at night, he couldn't be too careful.

"Who is it?" he asked.

"I need to speak with you," came a quiet, but urgent, feminine voice.

Opening the door, Mr. Granger was surprised to find himself looking into the dark brown eyes of a petite, and pretty, woman. At first, he took her to be quite young, but when a nervous yet determined smile greeted him, the light from the streetlamp revealed creases around the eyes and lips that suggested more years than she probably wished to admit to.

"Good evening. May I help you?"

"Oh, yes." Even her voice came across as a young maiden's. "I was told you are the attorney handling Jack Kiefer's trial."

"Yes, that's correct. But isn't it a bit late for this? Can you come back in the morning?"

"No!" and she did a quick scan of the boardwalk. "Please, let me in. I have some information that might be of interest to you."

Granger nodded and opened the door wider to allow her access.

"Have a seat, Miss . . . Mrs. . . .?"

"Miss," she informed him, and smiled as she sat down. "Miss Josephine Jansen."

"Miss Jansen," Granger greeted her and returned to his chair. "Are you familiar with my client?"

"Oh yes," Josey answered, as she attempted to tidy her elaborate chignon. "I've known both Jack and Leon for years. They're dear friends—both of them."

"Indeed?" Granger was cautious. "What's the information you have, Miss Jansen?"

"Well . . ." Josey hesitated, clearly nervous and unsure of herself, "I feel terrible about what happened to Napoleon. I should have been here. If I had, none of this would have happened. But they insisted, if they were ever captured and brought to trial, I was to stay away—that it was too dangerous for me to be associated with them."

"Dangerous?" Granger asked. "In what way?"

Josey swallowed and chewed her lower lip.

Funny, Granger thought, on her, it looked cute.

Josey noticed the lawyer noticing her and got down to business. "Is anything I say to you considered confidential?"

Granger leaned back and scrutinized his visitor. This could get interesting.

"Yes. If that is what you wish."

"Yes, I do."

Granger nodded, encouraging her.

"Well," she shifted, hopping her chair a little closer to the desk, "as I said, I've known both for years, and . . . well, I have harbored them from the law, on more than one occasion."

"You've harbored known outlaws from the law?" Granger cocked a brow. "That is a serious offence, Miss Jansen. You could go to prison."

"Well, I know!" Josey sent him a look of irritation. "That's why I asked for confidentiality. But you must understand, we grew up together. You see, my parents were killed in an accident, so I was at the

116

Blessed Heart Orphanage with them. They were always looking out for me. I had such a crush on Napoleon, even then, but he only saw me as a younger sister. It was very frustrating."

"I'm sure it was."

"So, naturally, I would be there for them when they needed me." Josey wrung her hands, uncertain about how much she should reveal. "But now, well, I feel terrible. You see, it was my fault, what happened to Leon. And if I can prevent the same thing from happening to Jack, then, I had to come and try. And maybe, it will help Leon, too."

"How is what happened to Mr. Nash, your fault?"

"The name that Leon wouldn't give, the reason he was found in Contempt of Court . . ." Josey stopped, tears beginning to slide down her face. She dabbed at them.

"Yes?"

"It was my name, Mr. Granger."

"Oh. I see."

"If I had been there for Leon's trial, I would have stood up and told the court that it was me," Josey then frowned and shook her head, causing strands of dark hair to fall loose from their binding. "It's just like Napoleon to refuse to give me up. I could punch him sometimes. Always acting like my big brother. It irritates the fire out of me."

"Yes, I'm sure," Granger repeated. "Well, you doing that, might have helped to reduce his sentence, but it wouldn't have prevented his conviction, in any case."

"But, why not?" Josey puffed up, all indignant. "They did it to help me."

"Yes," Granger nodded. "Mr. Nash did go so far as to admit he did it to help a friend. But the thing is, Miss Jansen, it's not why he did it, it's the fact that he did it in the first place. By his own admission, it was an illegal act, perpetrated at a time when he and his partner were claiming to be law-abiding. I'm afraid, Mr. Nash was going to prison either way. Nothing you could have said would have changed that."

"But they didn't want to do it, Mr. Granger." Josey leaned forward in her determination. "I, well, I blackmailed them into it."

"You blackmailed them?"

"Yes," she admitted. "They didn't want to, but I was desperate. My employer needed their help, and I knew that Leon was a good enough conman to pull it off. It wasn't for personal gain, Mr. Granger. A very nasty man was blackmailing my employer, who was a sweet, loving

117

woman, but he was threatening to let certain names out to the press; names of people who would be ruined if it got out . . . well, she had to pay him, or her own reputation would have been ruined, along with those of her . . . clientele. But either way, her business was going to be ruined, and I simply would not accept that. I needed Jack and Leon to get the money back from that man. It just wasn't right."

"Don't tell me," Granger put in, "this nasty man, was his name Nigel Snodgrass?"

"Yes!" Josey was worked up into a dither. "That lying, thieving, no good—" She stopped and took a deep breath. "Mr. Snodgrass started out as a client of my employer, and all the while, as she was entertaining him, he was collecting information to use to blackmail her. I had to get Leon and Jack to help me get my money back . . . I mean, her money."

Granger smiled at the little slip. He was getting the idea of where this was going but needed to clarify. "Why didn't you simply go to the authorities?"

Josey pursed her lips. "Well, because . . . my employer's business was not—"

"You were running a house of ill-repute?"

"No!" Josey was indignant. "I'll have you know; I only work at the highest level. I have been wined and dined by the most influential men . . . well, enough said about that. But I do not run a dirty, low-class bawdy house. It is of the finest quality. Still, you can understand, I'm sure, the need for the utmost discretion. My clients are all wealthy men, and many of them are, shall we say, otherwise attached."

"You mean, married."

"Well yes. If you must be so vulgar. So, you see, I could not go to the authorities, because that would mean divulging my client list, and that would have been just as bad as allowing Mr. Snodgrass to do it. Besides, the law has never been my friend—well, except with a few exceptions, but we needn't discuss that."

"Yes, all right," Granger nodded his understanding. "So, how is it that you blackmailed Mr. Nash into helping you?"

Josey looked sheepish. "They told me about their deal with the governor. At first, I didn't believe them, because the governor never said anything to me about—well, anyway, I thought it was most unusual; that it was simply Leon playing his games. But then, Johnny confirmed it, so—"

"Johnny?"

"Governor Hoyt."

"Oh. I see."

"So, when this situation came up, well, I had to be very careful, you understand. I knew that Leon and Jack wouldn't willingly jeopardize their pardons over something like this. They didn't approve of my profession anyway, which seems hypocritical to me, since they both patronized other establishments in my line of work. But that was Leon for you; still acting like my big brother. But a lady must make a living somehow. Anyway, I'm afraid, I threatened to tell certain people in Leon's previous line of work, about his deal with the governor. So . . ."

"You threatened to blow their cover?"

"Yes," Josey whispered.

"And you consider yourself to be their friend?" The comment slipped out before Granger could stop it, then he regretted it when the woman in front of him broke down into desolate weeping. "I'm sorry, Miss Jansen, I shouldn't have said that." He stood up and poured her a glass of water.

"Thank you," she accepted it through her sniffles. "That's all right, Mr. Granger," she continued, once she had her tears under control. "It's really nothing more than what I've already been saying to myself. But I was desperate. Now, I wish the whole thing had never happened."

They sat quietly for a few minutes.

Granger slowly sifted through the new information and tried to think of how it could be used to assist his client. Nothing significant came to him.

"I'm afraid this information is coming too late for Mr. Nash. He has already been found guilty of fraud and running a confidence game, as well as Contempt of Court. His trial is over, and he was convicted and sentenced. As for Mr. Kiefer, this information may not be relevant."

"What do you mean, not relevant?"

"I have the prosecuting attorney's list of witnesses for Mr. Kiefer's trial," Granger explained, "and Mr. Snodgrass is not on it."

"So?"

"So, that strongly suggests that Mr. DeFord is not going to be building a case against Mr. Kiefer based on that information. He is planning a different strategy. The incident involving Mr. Snodgrass is probably not even going to come up.

"You mean, I've come forward for nothing?" Josey couldn't believe it.

"Possibly."

"Perhaps I could be a character witness for Jack," Josey offered, desperate to be able to help in some way.

Granger steepled his fingers under his chin. "I highly doubt that, given your profession."

"But I could tell the court that I knew about the deal they had with the governor," Josey insisted. "They don't have to know how I knew."

"Perhaps," Granger remained skeptical. "Unfortunately, it's late in the game now for me to submit your name as a witness, although, if I push, it still might be accepted. However, the court and Mr. DeFord would have to approve it. Also, Mr. Kiefer would have some say. If he is adamant about you not testifying, then I wouldn't be able to call you."

Josey's expression fell.

"Oh dear. They both are so protective of me. They are afraid, I will get into trouble for helping them. Can I see him? Maybe I can convince him to let me help."

"Yes, of course. If he agrees." He glanced at his pocket watch. "It's late, but perhaps we can head over to the jailhouse now. I doubt he's sleeping, and I don't think there will be time in the morning."

"Yes," Josey agreed, and she began to dab at her eyes and tidy up her hair. "Let's go, right now. Yes."

***

Jack Kiefer sat on the cot with his back against the wall and his legs drawn up. His arms rested upon his knees, as he blankly stared straight ahead at nothing.

The other cells around him were empty. Fred and George had long since departed along with countless others who had come and gone, during the past month. Those who had shared the accommodations with the outlaw, had been surprised to find him an amiable enough roommate. Chatter and checkers had come easily, and both helped to pass the time.

But the other cells were empty now; one of those unexplained lulls in the flow of time, when everything turned quiet and nothing happened.

David had returned, as promised, and was pleased to find Jack's collar bone well healed. It wasn't ready for much stress or exercise yet, but it was doing fine.

Most maddening, as far as Jack was concerned, is that David had refused to give him more morphine. The doctor left him a dose of laudanum, to help him sleep, but Jack was skeptical of its success.

Taggard was back in town to lend his support, and to testify on behalf of the defense. He would be coming by, first thing in the morning, to get the prisoner out for breakfast and a shave. He needed to be looking presentable in court, and four months in various jail cells hadn't helped him much.

Finally, Cameron had also returned to do his part. When he dropped by to visit the prisoner that afternoon, he was alone, and Jack felt relief that the girls weren't with him. That relief was short-lived when Cameron confessed to having left both young ladies at the hotel, despite their protests of not being allowed to visit Mathew.

"Why did you bring them?" Jack asked with disappointment in his tone. "Didn't David tell you how I felt about this?"

"Yes, he did. But there is more going on here than just your comfort."

"They shouldn't have to hear this," Jack persisted.

"But, maybe, they need to," Cameron countered. "Penny has stronger feelings toward you than as just a friend, or brother. You can deny it all you want to, but we both know the truth of it. Now, whether you reciprocate those feelings or not, is going to be up to you. But Penny needs to know the truth about the person who holds her heart, before it goes any further."

Jack sighed and leaned his forehead against the bars of the cell. "But that's why," he said, his voice muffled. He looked up and met Cameron's gaze, anguish in his eyes. "What I have to say could break her heart."

"Better now than later."

***

So now, Jack Kiefer sat, alone and quietly tormented about what he might have to divulge to the court, and what effect it could have on his friendships.

The furthest concern from his mind was what the next day might bring to him, personally. He was beyond caring; his best friend, his partner, his uncle, was gone. Serving what may as well be a life sentence, because knowing Leon, he wouldn't be able to survive ten years behind bars, let alone twenty. And the thing that irked Jack the most was the certainty that the judge knew damn well the truth of this, and sentenced Leon to it, anyway.

Jack didn't know what the best outcome of his trial would be. If he was pardoned, he could focus on putting pressure on the governor. He knew Caroline and Penny were already getting their campaign up and in full swing. They were busy getting letters and telegrams sent out to anyone they could think of who would join in the fight.

He could go places and get in touch with people that two, young, maiden ladies could not properly go near. Adding his efforts to theirs might be all it would take to make the difference.

On the other hand, if he were sentenced and sent to the Penitentiary, then, at least, he could be with Leon. They'd be together, watching each other's back, supporting each other through the hard times. Just like they'd always done. Jack would keep Leon going until the girls, along with Cameron, Taggard, David, and any of their other friends, who could be rallied to the cause, convinced the governor to pardon them.

He sighed. Which way would be the best outcome? And how many of those friends would he have left, after giving testimony? He frowned, chewing his lip. Still, they had stood by Leon, despite all the misconduct they'd heard about them committing during those years they'd lived outside the law.

But Jack had a few dark little secrets that even Leon knew nothing about. Leon was aware that something had happened during the years they'd spent apart, but he never asked what, and Jack never told him.

Truth be known, it had never occurred to Jack that the things he had done before he and Leon had partnered up again, might now resurface. But when he and Granger looked over the prosecutor's list of witnesses, not only were several expected names not there, they had been replaced by ones that Jack didn't recognize.

Granger had been concerned about what DeFord's strategy was going to be, so they could build a defense against it. But with Jack not recognizing the names, this proved to be difficult.

It was then that the cold chill of realization hit Jack. Like a vulture in his mind, circling and waiting all those years, until past deeds resurfaced, and it could finally glide down to feast upon them.

He hoped and prayed Mr. DeFord had not gotten wind of those deeds, because if he had, Jackson Kiefer might not get out of this alive.

These were thoughts going through Jack's mind, when Steven Granger entered the block and stopped outside the cell. Jack snapped to the present, surprised to see his lawyer back so late in the evening.

"Mr. Granger. Was there something more we needed to discuss?"

"That depends on you," Granger said. "A woman has come forward, wishing to be a character witness on your behalf. She is concerned you will not permit her to do so. I am concerned that it may cause more problems than it solves. Still, the decision is yours."

Jack's confusion increased. "Who is it?"

"A lady by the name of Josephine Jansen."

"What?" Jack was off the cot and over to the bars. "Josey is—" He covered his mouth and sent a furtive glance toward the office, then whispered, "Josey is here? Now?"

"Yes," Granger confirmed. "She's in the office, waiting for you to agree to see her."

"Aw no, what is she thinkin'?" Jack complained. "She shouldn't be here. What if . . . well . . ." Jack hesitated; not sure how much Granger knew of Josey's involvement in all this.

"Miss Jansen has informed me of her profession, and of her actions in Mr. Nash's case," Granger assured his client. "She also informed me that she is, indeed, the person whom your partner refused to name in his trial."

Jack started to pace, hands gesturing as he shook his head and mumbled a stream of incoherent words concerning Miss Jansen, and her sense of timing.

Mr. Granger waited a few moments for this to subside, then decided it was time to push the matter, or they would be here all night.

"Mr. Kiefer, shall I invite her to join us?"

Jack stopped and stared at his lawyer for a minute, then ran a hand through his curls and groaned. "It'll be up to me, if she testifies?"

"Yes."

"And everything she says here, between us, will be confidential?"

"Yes."

"Arrgg." He threw his hands up in defeat. "May as well; she'll never give up, otherwise."

Mr. Granger returned to the front office, and instantly, the door banged open again, and Josephine charged into the block and over to the cell.

"Jack! Oh, Jack. I'm so sorry about what happened. I couldn't believe it, when I heard. What was Leon thinking? I'm so sorry, I'm so sorry."

She grabbed Jack by his lapel, pulled him up to the bars, and planted such a kiss upon his mouth as would make a convict blush.

Mr. Granger and Sheriff Turner exchanged shocked looks over top the young woman's head, and then watched, in amazement, this uninhibited display of affection.

"No . . . Josey . . . stop . . ." Jack tried to push her away, but as the kiss continued, his protesting hands became caressing. Then he was hugging her through the bars and returning the kiss with more passion than was comfortable for the other men to watch.

"All right. Break it up." Turner took hold of Josephine's arm and pulled her away from the prisoner. "That's enough of that, young lady," and he sent Jack a reproving look. "I said you could come back here to talk with him, but not . . . what . . . you were doing."

"Oh yes, I'm sorry, Sheriff," Josey was breathless as she straightened out her hair and then her blouse. "It's been so long since I have seen my friend, and so much has happened."

"Uh huh," Turner commented. "Well, just you stay away from the bars, Miss, or you won't be having any conversation at all. Do you understand?"

"Of course, Sheriff. Again, I apologize."

"Fine," Turner then looked to the lawyer. "Mr. Granger, I'll let you folks have your little confidential chat back here, but she's to stay away from the prisoner. You understand?"

"Yes, Sheriff. I'll make sure of it."

Turner nodded and headed back to his office, closing the door behind him.

"Josey, what are you doing here?" Jack demanded. "It's too risky, having you here. We told you to stay away."

"I know, Jack, but I just couldn't sit back and let what happened to Leon happen to you too. Not if I could do something about it."

"There ain't nothin' you can do for Leon now, and he wouldn't want ya to, anyway," Jack continued. "If you admit ta your part in that scam now, then you'll be in trouble too, and Leon would 'a gone ta prison for nothin'."

124

She grabbed Jack by his lapel, pulled him up to the bars, and planted such a kiss upon his mouth as would make a convict blush.

"But I could explain to them what happened, and that I was desperate," Josey leaned closer to the bars, pushing her point. "I can say that I asked you to help, and you did it because of an obligation to me."

"That won't make it any less illegal." Granger said as he pulled her back. "You'd just be setting yourself up to be charged, not only with conspiracy to commit blackmail against Mr. Snodgrass, but also in threatening to divulge confidential information obtained by nefarious means. And if the authorities find out about your client list, then you'd be in even more trouble. The kind of trouble you were trying to avoid in the first place. All of this is exactly why I don't think it's a good idea for you to take the stand."

"But I don't have to say anything about having that information," Josey said. "The deal between the governor's office and my friends could remain a secret."

"But Mr. DeFord will want to know why Mr. Nash and Mr. Kiefer were so willing to put their pardons at risk. I'm afraid simply feeling obligated won't do it. He will want to know why, and he will dig for it. It's not a good idea."

"But . . ."

"And you're forgettin' one other thing, Josey," Jack reminded her. "DeFord knew we had two accomplices on that job, and he was insistin' on both names. How do ya think "Fingers" would handle prison, Josey?"

"Oh dear. I had forgotten about that," Josey admitted, then brightened up. "I just won't give Mr. DeFord the name."

"And end up in the same situation that found Mr. Nash in Contempt of Court," Granger explained. "It's too risky. Mr. Kiefer, I strongly advise you not to allow your friend to take the stand."

"I think I will take your advice, Mr. Granger."

Josey pouted and stamped her foot. "But I—"

"No," Jack insisted, "it's too risky."

"Fine." she crossed her arms, her brows knotted into a frown. Then she wagged a finger in Jack's face. "But I'm not leaving town. I'll be in that courtroom tomorrow for the trial, and if that no-good, scheming, Snodgrass shows up, unannounced, and causes trouble, then I will stand. And there's nothing either one of you can do about it."

"I think that about does it for tonight," Jack commented. "Mr. Granger, would you mind escorting my friend back to the hotel?"

"But—"

"I would be happy to, Mr. Kiefer," Granger assured his client. "I

126

will see you tomorrow. Try to get some sleep, if you can."

Mr. Granger took hold of Josey's elbow and steered her toward the exit.

"No. But . . . Jack—"

"Goodnight, Josephine."

"Well, I never," Josey protested. "This is ridiculous. I think I can walk on my own, Mr. Granger. Of all the . . ." and she continued to protest, as her voice faded further and further away, until they had passed through the office and disappeared out the front door.

Jack rolled his eyes, and then released an exasperated, but relieved, sigh. He was in the process of turning away from the bars when the sheriff and Deputy Larry came into the block and up to his cell.

"Hold it, Kiefer," Turner ordered him. "Put your hands through the bars, right now."

"Aww." Jack slumped in disappointment but did as instructed. He had been through this enough times with Morrison, so he knew what was coming next.

The handcuffs were snapped into place, and the two lawmen entered the cell. They gave the small room a thorough search, and then Turner came up behind Jack and gave him the same treatment.

"Just had to make sure, Kiefer," Turner explained. "That young lady got a little too close to you for comfort—my comfort."

Once he was released from the bars, and the lawmen had left, Jack lay down on his back and rested his right arm across his chest. His shoulder was aching again. He knew, between the pain he was in, and the worry on his mind, that laudanum alone was not going to help him sleep. This night, of all nights, he needed to sleep.

He sighed and, sitting up, reached under his pillow and pulled out the pouch of morphine the town's doctor had supplied him with. He felt guilty about not telling David that the local medical man had been supplying him with the drug, but not guilty enough to refrain from using it. Once the trial was over, he would stop. Hell, if he was convicted and sent to prison, he wouldn't be able to continue taking it, anyway.

So, either way, after the trial, he would stop.

CHAPTER EIGHT
THE PROSECUTION

The next morning found a familiar scene in the courtroom. Some of the key players had changed, of course. Instead of Mr. Granger and Leon sitting at the table reserved for the defense, now it was Jack. Taggard Murphy, Sheriff Turner and Rick were back in their original places right behind the bar. The faces of the jury had changed, but Mr. DeFord was seated in his usual spot, looking well prepared and smug.

Yet again, Mr. Granger was struck by the extreme differences between his two clients. Whereas Nash had been agitated and nervous to the point of shaking, Mr. Kiefer appeared calm and relaxed, apparently unconcerned about the proceedings around him.

Taggard knew better though. It was simply the different ways his two friends dealt with stress. Maybe it was Jack's special abilities developed as a gunman, that allowed him to camouflage his nervous energy and present it to the outside world as calm, self-assurance. Or, maybe Jack had already possessed this ability, and that is what made him such an extraordinary gunman.

Taggard didn't know which came first, but he did know that Jack Kiefer was extremely nervous, and he stayed close to give whatever assurances his presence would lend. It was going to be a tough day.

Jack had been surprised to walk in on a packed courtroom that was filled to capacity, leaving standing room only. The loud murmurings instantly quieted when the party entered the room, creating an ominous, but expectant atmosphere that was hard to ignore. The defendant did not attempt to look around at who might be present; he had a good idea of the important ones, and he knew where they were. That was all that mattered to him.

Once the Honorable Judge John W. Lacey had assumed the bench, and the usual proceedings attended to, everyone settled in to witness the trial of The Territory of Wyoming vs. Jackson Kiefer. The charges against the defendant included, but were not limited to, Armed Robbery, Assault with a Deadly Weapon, and Manslaughter. The overly optimistic plea of Not Guilty had already been entered during the arraignment., and the trial was ready to get underway.

Mr. DeFord stood and the first witness he called forth was Richard Layton.

"Deputy Layton," Mr. DeFord began once the necessitates had been dealt with, "it is my understanding that you were part of the posse that arrested Mr. Kiefer and his partner. Is that correct?"

"Yes, that's correct."

"You're not a regular, full-time law officer, are you, Deputy Layton?"

"No, I'm not. I own a spread here, in Wyoming, and work it most of the time. I only pin on a badge when Marshal Morrison requires my services."

"And what might those services be that a regular deputy could not fulfill them?"

"I'm a sharpshooter with a rifle."

"So, Marshal Morrison felt that there might be a need for a man who is an expert with a rifle?" DeFord asked, "just in case?"

"No, sir. There was no 'just in case' about it. The plan was to hit the outlaws by ambush and take Jackson Kiefer out of the equation before either of them had an inkling of what was happening."

"That's rather drastic, isn't it?" DeFord asked, "for two men, who are known for their 'non-violent' policy during the commission of their crimes? Why would you feel it necessary to shoot one of them through ambush, rather than simply take them by surprise and arrest them?"

Rick looked out upon the spectators. "I think everyone in this courtroom is familiar with Mr. Kiefer's reputation as a gunman," he said. "He is the fastest, most accurate shooter I've ever heard of. Just because he has never killed during a robbery, doesn't mean he has never killed—"

"Objection, Your Honor," Mr. Granger was quick to his feet. "This is hearsay. It has never been shown that Mr. Kiefer has killed anyone, under any circumstances. The witness' comment gives an inaccurate impression."

"Agreed," Judge Lacey stated. "The jury will ignore the witness' last comment."

DeFord accepted the rebut. "Perhaps you can re-phrase you comment, Deputy Layton."

"Fine. Just because he has never killed during a robbery doesn't mean he's not capable of doing so. We couldn't take the chance of him reacting on instinct and going for his gun. He's too damn good."

"Indeed," DeFord commented. "So, in your mind, Mr. Kiefer is a dangerous man?"

Rick hesitated in answering this question. He looked at the defendant, feeling that whatever answer he gave, it would not encompass the truth. Four months ago, he would have had no doubt of his opinion, but now . . ..

"If you go by reputation, then, yes, Jack Kiefer has the reputation of being a dangerous man," Rick agreed to this much. "But if—"

"Thank you, Deputy Layton. You've answered my question. It has also come to my attention that Mr. Kiefer attempted, on two separate occasions, to break legal custody. Don't you think that is odd behavior for a man claiming to be going straight, even to the point of anticipating a pardon from the governor?"

"Not when you take into consideration the circumstances surrounding them," Rick countered. "The first time Mr. Kiefer tried to run, he was badly injured and being treated with a strong dose of morphine. He wasn't in his right mind and had no clear idea of what he was doing or where he was going. As for the second attempt, I don't feel he was trying to escape. He was surprised at seeing his partner and had simply reacted to it. There was no malicious intent."

"No malicious intent," DeFord repeated, "and yet you shot him from ambush. Do you regret that, now?"

"No. As I stated, he's too good with that six-shooter. We couldn't take the chance."

"Thank you, Deputy. Your witness, Mr. Granger."

In the back of the courtroom, Morrison rolled his eyes. What's gotten into Layton? He never used to be so wishy-washy about the outlaws they'd brought to justice. Instead of being a solid witness for the prosecution, all he did was muddy up the waters.

Mr. Granger addressed the witness. "Deputy Layton, it seems to me Mr. DeFord interrupted you earlier, so I will put the question to you, again. Do you feel that Jack Kiefer is a dangerous man? In your opinion, Deputy, not according to his reputation."

Rick, again, looked to the defendant and organized his thoughts.

"I have spent the last four months in the company of Mr. Kiefer. I have seen him fighting for his life. I have seen him running scared. I have seen him angry, frustrated, and depressed. I have also seen him excited, exuberant, gentle, and compassionate. Only once did I see him 'dangerous', and then it was fleeting, and he defused it, himself. He can also be tenacious, once he puts his mind to it."

Jack felt, rather than heard, Taggard give a soft chuckle, adding the barely audible comment: "You have no idea."

Mr. Granger remained focused on his witness and continued, "So, do you feel the defendant is worthy of a pardon?"

Rick sighed and considered the question. He felt torn over this.

"No," he finally had to admit. "He's a criminal, there's no doubt about that. He has done things that need retribution. However, I do think that their efforts to go straight should be taken into consideration."

"All right. Thank you, Deputy," Mr. Granger concluded. "No further questions, Your Honor."

"Fine. Deputy Layton, you may step down. Mr. DeFord, your next witness. And I hope, for your sake, he or she is more supportive of your case than this one has been."

"I'm sure he will be, Your Honor." At which point, Mr. DeFord flashed a smile to Mr. Granger. "I would like to call Mr. Edward Jaxton to the stand."

Jack looked around as the witness made his way to the front of the courtroom.

When Granger had shown him the list of witnesses, this name had seemed familiar, but in a distant sort of way. He hadn't been able to put his finger on it, and he hoped that a look at the man might help. Again, something about him tugged at Jack's memory, but it wasn't giving him any recollections.

Taggard looked the question to him, but Jack could only shrug and shake his head.

Mr. Jaxton was a young man, much younger than Jack. He seemed to be both nervous and excited at being called to testify. He was animated, as though this were a great adventure, and he was determined to make the most of it.

"Mr. Jaxton," DeFord began, "are you familiar with the defendant?"

"Oh, yes sir," Jaxton nodded, all eager to please. "I've seen 'im a couple a times now—though, I have ta admit, I didn't know who he was until I saw the article in the newspaper. The one about Nash and Kiefer being captured, and there was a picture of him. Then I thought, Whooee. Imagine that! I guess that kinda makes sense. Then I knew, I had ta come forward ta tell you folks what I know."

Jack felt a slight dread in the pit of his stomach. He still couldn't place this young man, but he was getting close and it didn't bode well.

"That's fine, Mr. Jaxton." DeFord tried to keep his young witness focused and coherent. "Perhaps you can tell the court how it is you first became acquainted with Mr. Kiefer."

"Sure," Jaxton agreed. "It was a little over four years ago that I seen him down Brown Creek way. A course, he was goin' by Mathew White then, but I seen 'im, sure enough—in the fastest gunfight I never thought I would live to witness."

Ohh no. That's where I've seen that youngster before.

Not in Brown Creek, but three years ago, in some town he couldn't remember the name of now. He'd been waiting for Leon to show up, and that excitable kid had accosted him in the saloon about meeting the man who had shot Quincy Bartlett. Damn it. This could be trouble, and the trial has only just begun.

Taggard was going to be in for another unwelcome surprise.

"Indeed," DeFord feigned ignorance. "By all means, fill us in on the details."

"Sure. As I recall, Mr. Bartlett was a real slick businessman. He showed up in Brown Creek, and right away, bought up the best gamblin' house the town had ta offer. He didn't put up with no nonsense, neither. You get some fellas in there with a little too much ta drink, and they start losin' at the tables an' stuff, well, some of 'em don't want ta leave it at that, and they start ta fightin'. Well, Mr. Bartlett, he'd put them in their place, right away. Finally, one of them fellas, who was losin', regularly, well, he made the mistake of challengin' Mr. Bartlett to a gunfight. Right in the middle of the street, too. Well, I swear, I ain't never seen anybody draw a gun that fast. Mr. Bartlett, he done put that cowboy down so quick, he probably never knowed what hit him."

"Are you saying that this Mr. Bartlett killed the man?" DeFord asked.

"Sure as shootin'," Jaxton stated. "Deader than a fly in honey."

"And the sheriff in the town, he didn't think the incident worth investigating?"

"The sheriff witnessed it, and he felt it was fair. It was the cowboy what was itchin' for a fight, not Bartlett. Mr. Bartlett was just defendin' himself."

"So, I take it, the cowboy drew first."

"Yessir, sure did. But Bartlett, he still beat 'im, and beat 'im easy."

"I see," DeFord commented. "So, what happened next, Mr. Jaxton?"

"Well, I think it was the next day," Jaxton continued. "Mr. White there . . . I mean, Mr. Kiefer, he and his friend were outside the livery stable, gettin' their horses ready for travel. I guess, they were plannin' on leavin' town.

"Now, Mr. Bartlett, he comes out of the gamblin' house, and he's callin' to Mr. Kiefer, like accusin' him a somethin'. 'A course, this starts ta get people's attention, especially after what had happened the day before, so everybody's kinda watchin' ta see what's gonna happen.

"So, Mr. Kiefer, he steps out from between them two horses, and he faces off against Mr. Bartlett, but they just keep on talkin'. I couldn't make out what they were sayin', but it still sounded like Mr. Bartlett was accusin' Mr. Kiefer of somethin'. But boy! You could just feel the tension buildin', even out there, in the street—you just knowed there's gonna be a showdown.

"Now, you could tell that Mr. Kiefer was ready for a fight, but he stayed real calm, and wouldn't make the first move, though you could tell that Bartlett was tryin' ta push 'im. Then, what happened next, I still can't believe it. I never seen nothin' that fast. Well, I can't even say that I saw it this time. And I was watchin' 'em. I had my eyes glued onto Mr. Kiefer, because I had seen Mr. Bartlett draw the day before, and I knowed how fast he was, and that there ain't nobody faster than that.

"So, I was watchin' Mr. Kiefer, 'cause, well . . . I ain't never seen a man die before. And I was sure Mr. Kiefer was gonna die, right there on that street, and I wanted to see that."

There was a quiet murmur of disapproval from the spectators , and Jaxton had the sense to look ashamed of himself.

"Well, you see, I'd missed it the day before," he explained. "I'd been watchin' Mr. Bartlett, 'cause he looked like a gunfighter, and I wanted ta see how fast he was. And boy, was he fast. Anyway, Mr. Kiefer now, he didn't look anything like a gunfighter, other than that he wore his gun tied down, so I figured it was gonna be a repeat of what happened the day before. Not knowin', ya see, that Mr. White was actually the Kansas Kid. Well, I tell ya—like I said—I had my eyes glued onto Mr. Kiefer, 'cause I thought for sure he was a dead man. And then it happened, so fast. I swear, I didn't even see it, and I was lookin' right at 'im."

"Yes, Mr. Jaxton. If you could please get to the point."

"Well sure. That's what I'm doin'. Like I said, they'd been talkin', then, I guess, Mr. Kiefer, he got tired of the game, and he turned, like he was gonna walk away, and then . . ." Jaxton stopped and sat there, with his mouth hanging open, shaking his head in disbelief.

Mr. DeFord tried not to roll his eyes. "Yes, Mr. Jaxton," he prompted the witness, "and then what happened?"

"Well, I just . . ." Jaxton wasn't sure how to put it into words. "I was starin' right at 'im, and I didn't see it. One instant, Mr. Kiefer had turned ta walk away, and the next, there was a loud report, and the gun was in his hand, with smoke coming from the muzzle. It was unbelievable. And I'm not the only one who thought so—everyone who saw it—or maybe, didn't see it, if ya know what I mean. Everyone was just standin' there, amazed. I think Mr. Bartlett was just as shocked as everyone else, before he died that is. And I missed it, again."

"Yes. How unfortunate for you," DeFord commented. "So, what happened after that Mr. Jaxton?"

"Everyone sorta just mulled around for a while," Jaxton continued. "Quite a few went over to Mr. Bartlett's body, just ta make sure, I suppose. Then the sheriff was talkin' ta Mr. White, I mean, Mr. Kiefer, and I suppose his friend was Mr. Nash there, they talked together for a bit, and then Mr. Kiefer and Mr. Nash rode outta town."

"The sheriff simply let them leave?"

"Well, yeah," Jaxton shrugged. "I guess, Mr. Bartlett was the one who drew first, and he was dead. So, that was the end of it."

Mr. DeFord nodded. "Well, this does bring up an interesting point," the prosecuting attorney addressed the jury. "Here, Mr. Kiefer has been insisting, all this time, that he's never killed anyone, and yet, we have a very clear, eye-witness account of him doing just that. Not only doing it but doing it during the time when he was supposedly working toward a pardon. Interesting, don't you think? I have no more questions."

"Thank you, Mr. DeFord," the judge replied. "Mr. Granger, your witness."

All the time that Jaxton was talking, Jack could feel Taggard tensing. This wasn't good. It had been a fair gunfight; even the town sheriff had thought so, but under their current circumstances, it made the defendant look bad. There was going to be hell to pay from Taggard during the lunch break. First Leon, and now Jack, had done questionable things that could threaten their bid for a pardon, and they had not informed their benefactor. And, as Jack had surmised earlier, the trial was just beginning.

"Mr. Jaxton," Mr. Granger addressed the witness, "as you say you observed this whole episode right from the start. In your own opinion, which of the two adversaries was the antagonist?"

"Umm, what do ya mean?"

"Who started it?" Granger explained. "Which of the two men was pushing for the fight?"

"Oh. Mr. Bartlett, for sure. A course, I don't know what happened ta get him riled like that, but he was, for sure, the one pushin' for the fight."

"And you said Mr. Kiefer tried to walk away; that he didn't want to fight."

"Well, maybe," Jaxton hesitated. "Mr. Kiefer did turn away, a bit. I can't say for sure that he was plannin' on leavin'. It looked more ta me like he was tryin' ta fake a move, to goad Mr. Bartlett inta drawin' first."

"Can you say what his intentions were?"

"Well, no. I don't suppose so."

"And the town sheriff did not feel that Mr. Kiefer was at fault. Is that correct?"

"Well, yeah. But he didn't know that Mr. White was actually the Kansas Kid."

"Under the circumstances, Mr. Kiefer's identity is irrelevant," Mr. Granger pointed out. "He was either the one at fault or he wasn't. Who did the sheriff decide was at fault?"

"Mr. Bartlett, I suppose." Jaxton shrugged, as he considered that altercation. "It was Mr. Bartlett who was pushin' for a fight, and he sure weren't gonna let Mr. Kiefer leave town. No siree."

"Thank you, Mr. Jaxton," Mr. Granger said. "No more questions, Your Honor."

"Fine. You may step down, Mr. Jaxton. Mr. DeFord, call your next

136

witness, please."

"I'd like to call Mrs. Julia Stanton to the stand."

A young woman came to the front, also looking nervous at being put on the spot, but determined to have her say.

Jack sighed with frustration. All these people coming to testify against him, and he didn't have a clue who they were. His only hope was that the witnesses they had lined up for the defense were going to be just as effective.

"Mrs. Stanton," DeFord began, after she had been sworn in, "would you please tell the court where you live?"

"Of course," she answered, quietly. "My husband and I live in Hannibal, Missouri."

"Are you acquainted with the defendant, Mr. Kiefer?"

The young woman, though keeping her head lowered, locked eyes with Jack. She knew him and hated him, and Jack had an inkling that he knew why.

"Yes, I am acquainted with him," her voice hardened, "though I doubt he recognizes me."

"Would you please tell the court how you are acquainted with him?" DeFord prompted her.

"He murdered my father!" she sobbed, bringing her hand up to her mouth as tears began to fall. "He rode onto our farm and shot my father down in cold blood, right in front of me." She sobbed again and grabbed her handkerchief from her purse.

There was a loud, sympathetic murmuring from the spectators, while Jack, just like Leon before him, wished he could disappear.

In the back of the courtroom, Cameron already regretted bringing his daughters. Those two young ladies clutched each other's hands in mutual support, as they each bit into their lower lips to maintain control.

As for David, his thoughts could not be read.

Judge Lacey brought the gavel down in three successive raps.

"Order! Order in the courtroom!" The spectators quieted. "Mrs. Stanton, you may step down."

She gaped at the judge, not quite believing his words. "But I'm not finished yet." She pointed an accusing finger at Jack. "He killed my father and want to see—"

The gavel banged. "Mrs. Stanton, step down. You will be recalled at a later time."

"Oh, yes . . .."

Judge Lacey's hard gaze encompassed the two attorneys. "Mr. Granger, Mr. DeFord, approach the bench."

The two men came forward, passing Mrs. Stanton as she meekly returned to her seat.

Lacey glared at Mr. DeFord. "What the hell are you doing? If you had a witness making such a claim, then charges should have been laid before these proceedings began. The worst crime that Mr. Kiefer is being tried for Manslaughter, not Murder."

"I apologize, Your Honor," DeFord said. "She presented herself as a character witness. I had no idea she was going to make such an accusation. However, now that it's been made—"

Lacey stared him into silence. Once this had been accomplished, he turned to Mr. Granger. "Did your client not inform you of this? You had the list of witnesses; he must have realized what was coming."

"No sir, he did not reveal any such event. When I asked him about the witnesses, he claimed no knowledge of them."

"You know what you need to do, Mr. Granger. I will give you until tomorrow morning to decide how we will proceed."

"Yes, Your Honor."

Mr. Granger sent his opponent a sharp glance as the two attorneys returned to their places.

Sheriff Turner and Rick were quick to get Jack on his feet and headed toward the side door before anyone could intercept them.

Sure enough, there were many who rushed to the front, with hopes of getting a word in with the defendant, but they weren't fast enough.

Josephine, amongst others, got there just in time to have the door shut in her face, with no admittance allowed.

***

Jack sat on his cot, feeling dejected. His lunch was on the floor, untouched.

Taggard and Steven Granger stood on the other side of the bars, making it clear that neither of them were happy with the morning's revelations.

Taggard looked almost as dejected as Jack. He resigned himself to the fact that both of his friends found it necessary to omit certain decisions and actions they had taken during the past five years.

Mr. Granger struggled to keep his temper under control.

A.K. Brauneis

"First Manslaughter and now Capital Murder. Is Mrs. Stanton correct? Did you kill her father?"

Jack looked down, guilt hitting his heart. "I might have."

Taggard groaned.

Jack looked at him, knowing, that just like Leon, he had let their friend down. He wished, and not for the first time in his life, that he could undo the things he had done.

"I'm sorry, Taggard. It was so many years ago. I was young and stupid, and full of anger. The need for vengeance outweighed whatever common sense I might have had."

Taggard looked Jack in the eye. "Was he one of the men who attacked your family?"

"Yes."

"Are you sure of that?"

"Yes," Jack repeated. "I'll never forget the look of fear that came into his eyes when he realized who I was. I'll never forget it, Taggard. It wasn't until after I shot him that I heard a child scream and I saw a little girl by the barn door. She was staring at me and screaming. It broke my heart. I realized I had just done ta her, what her pa had done ta me." He stopped and shook his head, full of regret. "I looked at her for a minute, but I couldn't think of nothin' ta say, so I took off—fast as the horse could run. I damn near ran that poor beast into the ground. I lost my taste for revenge after that. Since then, it's only been Bartlett, and that was self-defense!" He directed the last sentence pointedly at Granger.

The block door opened, and Cameron came in to join the three men at the bars.

Jack found it hard to meet his eyes. He felt both guilty and angry at the same time. He knew what had been said in court would have disappointed those two young ladies, who held him in such high esteem. But he had warned Cameron not to bring them, and he had brought them, so there was nothing more to be done about it.

"Mathew."

"Hello Cameron."

"I suppose I should start calling you Jack now, shouldn't I?"

"Mathew is fine."

"Not according to the judge," Cameron stated. "He made that quite clear at Napoleon's trial."

"The way things are goin', you may not have ta worry about what

139

ta call me," Jack mumbled. "Just whatever's on the headstone."

"Don't talk like that, Jack," Taggard told him. "It's not over yet and there's no way to tell which way it's gonna go."

"Yeah." Jack didn't sound convinced. He made himself look at Cameron and meet his eyes. "How are the girls?"

"They're understandably upset," Cameron said, "but more out of fear for you, than disappointment in you. I must admit, they are both holding up better than I thought they would. They wanted to come see you, but I didn't think that was a good idea, so they're at the café. David is keeping an eye on them."

Jack nodded. "How is David?"

"Quiet."

"Ohh, I know what that means," Jack stated. "Same thing as when Leon goes quiet: he's worried, and he's thinkin'." He sighed and headed to his bunk. "I guess I can't blame him for that." He plunked himself down onto the mattress.

"Why don't you eat some lunch, Jack?" Taggard suggested. "Maybe you'll feel better."

"I'm not hungry."

"How about I get us both a cup of coffee, then?"

"Yeah, okay."

The three men left the cell block. Two of them headed to the café, to go over testimony for the afternoon's proceedings, while Taggard got the coffee. He returned to his friend and kept him company throughout the rest of the afternoon.

***

Mr. Granger returned to the cell block shortly after suppertime. His expression gave the bad news before his words were uttered.

"That was a dead end, I'm afraid. Sheriff MacAfee died of influenza last year."

This news was met with two sets of groans.

"What about other witnesses?" Jack asked. "There must be someone who overheard us."

Granger shook his head. "Of the few people who responded to my enquiry, none support what you say. They agree that Bartlett drew first and Jaxton already stated this. No one recalls the conversation the Sheriff had with you concerning fault. Only the fact that you and your partner left town afterward. Again, we already have Jaxton's testimony for that."

"Okay," Jack said. "So, what do we do?"

"If you know of any other witnesses to either of these killings, I would move to dismiss the current charges without prejudice, which would allow us to start over again. New trial, new jury. And a chance for us to build a case against the murder charge."

"Yeah, but there ain't no other witnesses." Jack ran a hand through his curls. "Sheriff MacAfee is dead, and Mrs. Stanton was the only witness for that incident. And she sure ain't in our favor. Besides, how long would it take ta get another trial set up?"

Granger shrugged. "It would depend on how fast we could build a case. Probably a few months."

Jack groaned. "Aw no, there's gotta be another way. I wanna get this over with, one way or another."

"Are you sure there is nobody else we could call upon? Even a witness who could verify that Mr. Wissen was part of the raiding party that hit your farms."

Jack shrugged. "Even if I knew of anyone, would they be willin' ta come forward?"

"It's worth a try. I just need time to dig."

Jack stayed silent; he didn't want things delayed that long.

Mr. Granger felt the need to unlock his client's position. "The judge has given me a few days to decide how we will proceed. Surely you can wait that long on the chance that I can find a witness."

"A couple a days?"

"Yes."

Jack sighed. "Okay."

CHAPTER NINE
THE SURPRISE WITNESS

Steven Granger sat back in his office chair and rubbed his eyes.

Why do people insist on showing up in the middle of the night?

The banging on his front door repeated. He groaned and stretched, then blinked bleary eyes at the grandfather clock just on the verge of striking eleven p.m.

Well, maybe not quite the middle of the night.

More banging.

"Yes! I'm coming. Just a moment."

He pushed himself out of the chair, stumbled to the front door, nearly tripping over the corner of the carpet. He caught himself, then hesitated again, not sure who his late-night caller might be.

"I'm closed for the day. Come back in the morning."

"I need to speak with you now, Mr. Granger. It has to do with Julia Stanton."

Steven was so tired that this information didn't sink in right away. He stood, blinking his itchy eyes and thought about his next move.

"It's important, Mr. Granger," came the muffled voice from outside. "I would have come earlier, but Mrs. Stanton was watching me."

Steven cocked both brows. He unlocked the door and opened it to reveal his night visitor.

He was an older man. The light from the street lantern shone on a face carved with the wrinkles and lines from a lifetime of hardship. Long strands of gray hair poked out around a bowler hat, and the suit appeared just as worn and hard-done-by as its owner.

The dark eyes brightened as the light from the hall hit them.

"Mr. Granger, sur. Thank you. I realize it's late, but it wasn't safe for me to come before dark."

Steven was taken aback. The smooth southern accent didn't fit this apparent vagabond. He recovered quickly and, opening the door further, he gestured the man into his office. "Yes. Well, come in. Please sit. Mister . . .?"

"Collier, sur. Mr. John Collier."

Mr. Collier removed his bowler hat and absently fingered the rim as he sat in the plush chair. His hands and face were red with the night's chill.

"Would you like a drink?" Steven offered. "A brandy, or I believe there is still coffee on the stove."

Mr. Collier smiled, revealing a row of crooked teeth. "Brandy in coffee would be most welcome, sir."

Steven nodded and stepped to the stove to prepare the beverage. He poured himself a coffee as well, forgoing the brandy. He had a feeling he would need all his wits about him before the evening was done.

He returned to his desk and offered the cup which was quickly accepted by hands eager for the warmth just as much as the content.

Steven returned to his chair. "So, Mr. Collier, what can I do for you tonight?"

Furtive eyes darted around the well-lit room. The cup pressed against lips and a healthy swig of hot coffee and brandy brought comfort and courage to the visitor.

"I'll tell ya, but you must promise ta keep me hidden until you need me in court."

Steven frowned. "Keep you hidden? Whatever for?"

"I can tell you things about Cal Wissen that'll make your toes curl, but his shrew of a daughter will do anything ta stop me."

"Please, Mr. Collier, show some restraint. I'm sure Mrs. Stanton is simply overwrought with—"

"Ha! Overwrought. That's a good one. Her and that limp dick of a husband of hers will do anything ta hide the sins of her father. That's why I couldn't come to you any sooner. They were watchin' me. They even tried ta waylay me on my journey here. I know it was them." He laughed, but there was an edge to it that send a shiver down Steven's back. More coffee and brandy went south and a ruffled coat sleeve darted over the damp lips. "When I heard that bastard got himself killed, I went out and celebrated. Ain't nobody on this God's earth that deserved it more. So, when I heard that his daughter was gonna do everything she could ta get that gentleman who killed him hanged, well, I knew I had ta come forward."

"Indeed?" Steven was suddenly awake, his own coffee forgotten. "You knew Mr. Wissen during the war?"

"You bet I did." Collier waved a finger at papers on the desk. "Now you get yourself out a fresh sheet a paper and fill your pen, because I got a story ta tell."

***

The Following Morning

Judge Lacey leaned forward, his elbows resting on his large, mahogany desk as his steepled fingers supported a strong chin. His eyes were skeptical as they squinted at Mr. Granger.

"You wish to include this charge in the current trial, Mr. Granger? Considering the seriousness of this accusation, would it not be wiser to set a new trial date to deal with it alone? That would give you time to build a case against this charge. It could mean the difference between time in prison or a death sentence for your client."

"I'm well aware of that, Your Honor, but my client is adamant to get this done and off his conscience. As for preparation, I've had a new witness present himself for the defense against this murder charge. He could make all the difference."

"A new witness?" DeFord snorted. "Mrs. Stanton just made the accusation. How could you possibly have found a witness to counter it?"

"I did not find him, Mr. DeFord, he found me. He was already in town for the trial and when your witness declared herself, apparently without your knowledge of her intentions, he felt it was his duty to step up."

Mr. DeFord tutted, shaking his head. "You cannot bring a new witness in at this late a date. But I suppose you're still too wet behind the ears to know this."

Long-suffering looks were sent to Mr. DeFord from both Mr. Granger and Judge Lacey.

"You need to be careful where you point your indignation, Mr. DeFord," Judge Lacey cautioned him. "It was your witness who accused Mr. Kiefer of murder right in the middle of these proceedings.

If you were going to conduct such a drastic maneuver, then you can hardly be surprised if your opposition takes necessary steps to counter you."

Mr. DeFord huffed his insult. "As I said, I had no idea that Mrs. Stanton was going to—"

"Yes, yes, yes," Judge Lacey waved away the protest. He sighed as he surveyed the two lawyers standing before him. "This is a most unusual development. Are you sure, Mr. Granger, that you wish these proceedings to continue as they are? What is it this person has to offer in the way of evidence?"

"He claims to be a witness to the attack on the Kiefer homestead."

"A witness or an accessory?"

"Well," Mr. Granger looked the judge straight in the eye, "an accessory, Your Honor. He has requested immunity in exchange for testifying. He has also requested protection as he is concerned about his safety."

"Safety? If we grant him immunity there will be no retribution for his testimony."

"Not protection from the court," Mr. Granger pointed out, "but from the Stantons. His testimony is damning toward them. I suspect Mr. DeFord will want to recall Mrs. Stanton to answer to them."

"Oh, come now," Mr. DeFord said, sending a look to the judge to suggest how ridiculous this all was. "You don't even know what Mrs. Stanton will reveal in her testimony. There may be no need for your witness at all."

"I already know she has accused my client of murder. We have the right to bring in a defense. The sooner the better."

The judge considered the options. "You are that certain of your witness, Mr. Granger?"

"Yes, Your Honor, I am."

Judge Lacey leaned back and snorted through his lips. "All right, fine. Court will stand adjourned until 9:00 a.m. We will reconvene tomorrow morning where we left off yesterday with Mrs. Stanton's testimony. And I hope, Mr. Granger, for the sake of your client, that your new witness does not disappoint."

"Likewise, Your Honor. Thank you."

Both lawyers turned to leave the judge's chamber.

***

"You may carry on with your testimony, Mrs. Stanton," the judge said. "And keep in mind you are still under oath."

"Yes, Your Honor. This has been hanging over me for so long, I need to get this over with. It's very difficult."

"I'm sure it is. If you feel you need a break at any time, just say so."

"Thank you, Your Honor."

DeFord smiled encouragingly at her. "How long ago did this event happen, Mrs. Stanton? Do you recall?"

"Oh yes. I could hardly forget. It was thirteen years ago. I was seven years old, and I saw that man ride onto our farm and shoot my father down where he stood. I'll never forget it." She sent another set of visual daggers in Jack's direction.

"Thank you, Mrs. Stanton," Mr. DeFord said. "I have no more questions."

"Mr. Granger, your witness."

"Yes, Your Honor." Mr. Granger approached the stand. "Mrs. Stanton, I realize this is difficult for you, but a man's life could hang on your testimony here. You were very young at the time of this shooting, and it was many years ago. How can you be sure that the defendant is the same man who came onto your farm that day?"

"I realize it was a long time ago," Mrs. Stanton answered, "and Mr. Kiefer was much younger, then, himself. But it was him—I'm sure of it. I'll never forget those eyes."

"Yes, ma'am," Granger accepted that. He hesitated, collecting his thoughts.

Over in his corner, DeFord smiled, feeling that he had this trial all wrapped up; it was just a matter of going through the motions.

Granger continued. "The war was a devastating event for many people, especially those living in Missouri and Kansas. Men did things during those times, that they would never dream of doing during peace. Do you know in what capacity your father participated in the war, Mrs. Stanton?"

Mrs. Stanton drew herself up, sensing that the defense attorney was suggesting something shameful.

"My father was an honorable man," she insisted. "He fought bravely in the war and rode proudly with the Missouri Militia."

Another murmur started to rise from the spectators but quieted quickly as the whole courtroom listened in anticipation.

"The Missouri Militia," Granger repeated. "Fighting along the Missouri-Kansas border?"

"I'm not really sure where he fought," Mrs. Stanton admitted. "What difference does that make?"

"As I stated earlier, many terrible things happened, not only during the war, but in the months leading up to it; things men would never dream of doing during peacetime." Mr. Granger felt his way along, trying to be gentle, but needing to make the point, none the less. "The defendant's family lived in Kansas, close to the border, and they were murdered by raiders. Could it be possible that your father—?"

"No!" Mrs. Stanton drew herself up, sensing an attack. "My father was an honorable man. He would never butcher a family—women and children. How can you even suggest that?" She began sobbing uncontrollably.

Mr. Granger stood for a moment, watching her cry, and realized there was no point in continuing until after his own witness had his say. He met the gaze of the judge, and both decided, through silent agreement, that the witness was done for the day.

"I have no more questions for this witness," Mr. Granger conceded.

"You may step down, Mrs. Stanton," the judge directed.

Mrs. Stanton nodded through her sobs and left the stand.

A young man, presumably Mr. Stanton, rushed forward to embrace her and assist her back to her seat. A heavy silence settled over the courtroom.

Jack felt sick. These little secrets he had successfully buried, so that even Leon didn't know about them, were starting to surface. He had no defense against these charges because he knew he was guilty, and no witness would change that. He felt shame for the things he had done to ease a young man's anger and need for vengeance. All he had succeeded in doing was hurting other people and damning himself.

"Mr. DeFord," the judge continued, "your next witness, if you please."

"Yes, Your Honor. I call Mr. Brian Charles to the stand."

At least Mr. Charles was someone Jack knew. Hopefully, there wouldn't be too many surprises here.

"Good day, Mr. Charles," DeFord greeted him. "Welcome back."

"Yes. Thank you."

"Could you please give a brief account of how you know the

148

defendant and his partner?"

"Of course. Well, as I stated at Mr. Nash's trial, I also suffered the loss of my family during those border raids and was sent to the Blessed Heart Orphanage. I was there for a year or so before Leon and Jack showed up, and as I also stated before, they made their presence known, quickly."

"Yes, Mr. Charles," DeFord said. "You gave a clear description of Napoleon Nash's behavior during that time. If you can be as forthcoming concerning Jack Kiefer, that would be most helpful. What are your memories of his behavior, Mr. Charles?"

"Well, as I stated before, Jack was kind of a sweet kid. Quiet and polite. But he was small and scrawny for his age, so he got picked on quite a bit by the older boys. We learned, early on, to watch out for Leon, because if he got wind of us picking on Jack, there would be hell to pay.

"But Jack had a willful pride, and he often wouldn't tell Leon if he got beat up—only if the bruises showed, because then there could be no denying it." Mr. Charles hesitated, then smiled. "Oh, but Jack could be quite the little bobcat, too, once he got riled. It'd take quite a bit of doing, to push Jack over the edge, but once you did—look out!

"And he'd always go for the biggest boy in the group. It wouldn't matter how many were picking on him, either; he'd zero in on the biggest, and go for him. It was funny actually, to watch him." Mr. Charles laughed, oblivious of the fact that no one else in the courtroom thought this was funny. "Seeing this little kid, going after a boy a foot taller and twice his weight. Ha. Boy, yeah! That was something. He'd have no chance of winning the fight, but he wouldn't back off; just like a little wolverine. He'd end up bruised and bloody during one of those encounters, but it usually took the Matron, or Leon to break it up."

"Really?" Mr. DeFord cocked a brow. "And yet, you say that he was a 'sweet' kid. Kind of hard to mesh the two extremes, Mr. Charles. How do you explain that?"

"Like I said; Jack would take a lot of bullying before he was pushed to that state. But once the older boys discovered what it was that could wind him up, well, they'd use it more and more, just to watch him explode."

"There was a trigger?" Mr. DeFord asked.

"A trigger?"

DeFord covered his sigh. He had forgotten how easily Mr. Charles could be confused.

"Yes," he explained. "One thing, specifically, that would upset him."

"Oh yeah. Yeah—his ma. Boy, you say anything against Jack's ma, and he'd go to pieces. I tell ya, it was fun just to watch."

Mr. Charles continued to be oblivious to the discomfort his testimony was creating in the courtroom. Nobody else thought this was funny. Bad-mouthing a young boy's deceased mother; that was just plain cruel.

Jack, himself, was having a difficult time maintaining his calm exterior, with the memories of that harassment coming back home to haunt him. The fact that ole "Bratty" Brian still got a laugh out of it, made Jack want to rip the man's heart out. Fortunately, he had learned a lot about self-control since those days, and he kept his temper in check.

Still, his whole body was tense, and Taggard noticed his fists, clenching and unclenching, with the strain of keeping himself contained.

"Take it easy, Jack," Taggard whispered to him, "he's cutting his own throat."

Jack glanced back at Taggard, and the anguish the sheriff saw in his friend's eyes was enough to make him forget the anger caused by the previous revelations.

Again, this trial was turning into another emotional bucking bronco ride for everyone involved, and there was no telling in which direction events were going to take them.

"So, in your opinion, Mr. Charles," DeFord got things going in the right direction, "did Mr. Kiefer display an explosive temper, even as a child?"

"Oh, for sure," Mr. Charles agreed. "Especially after Leon left. Leave him alone, and he was a sweet kid, but push him too far, and look out!" Mr. Charles' smile faded, and he furrowed his brow. "Then, one day, things kind of changed."

"How do you mean 'changed'?"

"Well, I don't really know how it came about. I guess, one day, Jack got tired of being bullied, and with Leon gone, he realized he had to stick up for himself. The older boys found another opportunity to pick on him, only this time, when they insulted his ma, the reaction was different."

150

"Different? In what way?"

"It was opposite to what we expected. Instead of exploding and attacking, Jack went real quiet. It was eerie and, I hate to admit, it scared the tar out of us."

"It scared you? How so?"

"He just stood there, calm as could be," Mr. Charles chewed his lip, uneasy with the memory. "Suddenly, you could feel a chill in the air. Suddenly, he was dangerous."

The spectators went quiet.

"Dangerous?" DeFord asked.

"Yes. It was his eyes. Something in his eyes." Mr. Charles shuddered. "Suddenly, they were like—death turned to ice." He looked at Jack, looked into those blue eyes, again. A chill went through him, and he quickly looked away.

The silence in the courtroom was suffocating, as though the chill had settled over the whole assembly.

"Then what happened?" Mr. DeFord tried to break the ice. He needed to keep things moving.

"Ah . . ." Mr. Charles collected his thoughts, "everyone kind of backed off him. Even Gerald, who was the biggest bully of them all, knew there was something wrong. He tried to cover it up, but we all knew he was scared, too. I don't know what would have happened if one of the Sisters hadn't shown up. She was one of the nicer ones, and she tended to look out for Jack. Well, she got into Jack's line of sight, and that broke it up." He sighed, a reflective look on his face. "Nobody ever bothered Jack again, after that."

"In your opinion, Mr. Charles," Mr. DeFord asked, "do you believe that at this point, Jack Kiefer was capable of murder?"

Granger came to his feet. "Objection. Mr. DeFord is leading the witness."

The judge nodded. "Sustained. Mr. DeFord, please allow your witness to testify in his own words."

"Yes, Your Honor." DeFord turned his attention back to the witness. "Ignore my last question, Mr. Charles. In your opinion, based on your knowledge of Mr. Kiefer, does anything being discussed in this courtroom surprise you?"

"No sir," Mr. Charles answered. "He was just a little kid, no more than ten or eleven years old, I'd say, but after that day, none of the stories I was to hear about the Kansas Kid ever surprised me. I saw it.

I saw it that day—what he was. A killer."

Granger again came to his feet. "Objection again, Your Honor," he protested, but his words were drowned out by the sudden upheaval of voices coming from behind him. He raised his voice and repeated his demand.

The spectators continued with their vociferous conjectures, until a loud staccato from the judge's gavel brought them to order.

"Quiet!" came the order from the bench. "My but you are an unruly group today. This is a court of law, not a gambling establishment. Show respect for this court."

Sheepish looks were passed amongst the spectators, and people took their seats or returned to their spot along the walls.

Mr. Granger breathed a sigh of relief. "I object, Your Honor. The witness is surmising. Mr. Kiefer has not been found guilty of murder. Nor have any of the testimonies suggesting this been proven beyond a doubt."

Judge Lacey sighed. "Mr. Granger, Mr. DeFord, please approach the bench."

The two attorneys snatched a glance at each other, then joined the judge for a whispered conference.

"Mr. DeFord," the judge growled. "We discussed this in my chambers this morning. Did you not instruct your witnesses on courtroom procedures? They are to state only the facts as they recall them, not surmise on possible future events."

"Yes, Your Honor, I did inform them of this."

"And yet, you continue to ask leading questions and encourage them to extrapolate. If it happens again, your witness will be excused, and his or her testimony will be stricken from the record. Do we understand one another?"

"Yes, Your Honor."

"Fine. Please continue."

Jack had turned cold with fear when the courtroom erupted behind him. His initial thought that Charles's testimony would be easier, because it was known, couldn't have been further from the truth. It hit home—like a knife.

Taggard put a hand on his shoulder, afraid that he was going to have a collapse of some sort, like Leon. But Jack shook his head. He was all right. It was just having all those memories coming to the forefront again; it was hard to deal with.

Mr. Granger returned to his seat, hoping that Mr. Collier would indeed be a strong enough witness to counter the damage to his client's reputation.

Mr. DeFord approached his witness. "Again, Mr. Charles. Please stick to the facts as you know them."

"Fine. Then I'll simply say no, I am not surprised by anything that the other witnesses have said."

"Thank you, Mr. Charles," Mr. DeFord said. "No more questions."

"Mr. Granger, your witness."

Granger nodded, and he stood up to approach the witness.

"Mr. Charles," he began, "I find it interesting that you and the other boys at Blessed Heart, found it 'fun to watch' a young boy being bullied to the point of losing control and 'exploding', as you put it."

Mr. Charles squirmed in his chair as he felt some of the heat being directed back onto him.

Mr. Granger continued to push. "You knew that the young Jack Kiefer had witnessed the brutal murders of his family—including his mother, and yet, you saw nothing wrong in using those memories as a tool, to 'wind him up' as you said; to get a reaction?"

"Well, we were all just boys," Mr. Charles defended himself. "We'd all been through similar experiences and had learned to deal with them. If Jack was going to allow it to eat at him, then he kind of had to expect to be picked on."

"So, a ten-year-old boy was expected to have the fortitude to withstand that kind of bullying?"

"Like I said," Mr. Charles reiterated. "We all had been through similar experiences. Boys will be boys, after all. Any boy who shows weakness like that, is going to get picked on. It's the natural order of things."

"The natural order," Mr. Granger emphasized. "Yes, I suppose you're right, Mr. Charles. Unfortunately, there will always be bullies. So, the rest of us must either stand up to them or accept being tormented by them."

"Well—yeah."

"Yet, when Mr. Kiefer did finally stand up to you, you accuse him of being 'dangerous' . . . a killer, even," Mr. Granger pointed out. "Could it not be that he simply got tired of being picked on?"

"Objection!" DeFord was quick in his retaliation. "That part of Mr. Charles's testimony has been retracted. Mr. Granger is leading the witness."

"Objection sustained." The judge rolled his eyes and sighed. "Mr. Granger, you will stop leading the witness. As you, yourself, insisted on pointing out, Mr. Kiefer has not been proven to be a killer."

"Yes, Your Honor." Granger turned back to the witness. "My apologies, Mr. Charles. I will rephrase the question. When Mr. Kiefer finally stood up to you, you accuse him of being dangerous. Could it be that he simply got tired of being picked on?"

"No," Mr. Charles was adamant in his response. He looked at Jack Kiefer and shook his head. "No, Mr. Granger. You weren't there, you didn't see it. After that day, we didn't go near Jack. Not unless one of the Sisters was with him. There was no room, anymore, to push him. You look at him sideways, and he'd come at you. And it wasn't just to bloody your nose or bruise your face; he'd come prepared to gouge your eyes or strangle the life out of you." Charles shivered. "No, Mr. Granger, I will not retract what I said. Jack Kiefer did not turn mean, he turned dangerous. I'm positive, if it wasn't for Napoleon Nash keeping him in check, he would have hung from the gallows years ago."

"Mr. Charles," Judge Lacey interjected. "Again, you are surmising. We only know what is, not what might have been."

Mr. Charles scowled. As far as he was concerned, he knew what he knew, and he was tired of all these interruptions. At least he was smart enough to know the judge had final word, and he refrained from complaining aloud.

Mr. Granger continued. "So, the fact that Mr. Kiefer has been staying out of trouble for the past five years, doesn't hold any weight with you, I take it?"

"No sir. And from the testimonies I've heard here today, he hasn't been staying out of trouble. That poor woman losing her father so violently shows what he is capable of, and the testimony about that Bartlett fellow further proves it. I am not surmising here; these are eyewitnesses. And no, I am not surprised to hear them. I dread to think what would happen if he's granted a pardon, with Leon not around to keep him under control. I dread to think."

"All right, Mr. Charles, thank you. I have no more questions, Your Honor."

Mr. Granger returned to his client, feeling frustrated. It had been easy to turn Mr. Charles' opinion around during Nash's trial. But in this situation, he stubbornly stood his ground. There was no point in trying to push it further.

"You may step down, Mr. Charles," the judge instructed. "I think we all need some time to settle our tempers. The court will recess for lunch and reconvene at 1:00 p.m.

The gavel came down and the courtroom began to buzz.

CHAPTER TEN
THE DEFENSE

"Mr. Granger. Please call your first witness."

"Yes, Your Honor. I call Sheriff Taggard Murphy to the stand."

Again, Taggard placed a reassuring hand on Jack's shoulder and came forward. He settled into the witness box and was duly sworn in.

"Sheriff Murphy, if you could please inform the court how it is that you are acquainted with the defendant."

Taggard nodded. "As I stated before, I came to know Napoleon Nash first, and rode with him, on and off, for about two years before I met Jack. I was aware that Leon had run with Jack before we met up, but didn't know their history until later, since Leon never talked about him. We heard rumors about the Kansas Kid; that he was buildin' a reputation as a gunman, and, as far as I was concerned, that was reason enough ta stay away from him.

"After one of our usual separations, I heard that Leon was with the Elk Mountain gang, and I decided to join up with him again. Elk Mountain was a haven for the winter, and there was always a group of us fellas who would migrate that way when the weather turned cold. When I got there, I discovered that Jack had the same idea, and he and Leon had buddied up again, so I considered movin' on."

"Really?" Granger asked. "You had a safe haven. Why would you risk being caught in the mountains when the snows hit?"

Taggard shifted, as he considered his answer. "I didn't like gunmen." he stated. "The ones I'd come across were generally mean-spirited and unpredictable. I saw no reason to believe that Jack Kiefer would be any different. But, you're right, Mr. Granger. By the time I got there, it was late in the season and snow was startin' ta fly. So, considerin' I had a stake with me ta contribute to the winter supplies, and that I had always got on with the fellas, I was encouraged to stay.

"Leon wanted me to stay as well and assured me that Jack would be okay with it. So," Taggard shrugged. "I did. I figured I could keep out of Jack's way until spring, and then see how things were.

"As you can imagine, it's kind a hard to stay away from someone when you're all in the same bunkhouse together. So, whether I liked it or not, I was forced inta Jack's company.

"I can see how tensions could rise," Granger said. "Is it safe to say that nothing untoward happened while you were snowed in?"

"I object," DeFord came to his feet. "The defense is leading the witness."

"I agree." Judge Lacey turned a dark eye to Mr. Granger. "If Mr. DeFord had not protested, I would have. Please allow the witness to state the situation in his own words."

Granger nodded. "Yes, Your Honor. Sheriff Murphy, please continue. In your own words."

"Thank you." Taggard's comment came out curt, so he drew in a breath to calm himself then continued with his narrative. "After a few weeks, I found myself likin' Jack Kiefer, and I realized he wasn't anything like what I had assumed. I found him ta be a quiet, well-mannered fella, and though he garnered respect for his abilities with a handgun, he wasn't arrogant or pushy about gettin' his own way. I never saw any display of an unpredictable, or dangerous temper durin' that time, and I still find it hard ta understand how he would have warranted that reputation.

Taggard hesitated as his mind's eye took him back to those days. Then he nodded and continued. "It became apparent over that winter, that he and Leon were close friends, and had grown up together. They had quite an intense history. I also discovered they were family as well as friends. The bond between 'em was obvious. So much so, I wondered why they had separated in the first place. But I never asked about it. If there had been a fallin' out between 'em, it was obviously settled, and they partnered-up again.

"I stayed on with the gang for a couple of years, but then I started doin' a lot of soul searchin' and had decided outlawin' was a dead end. I knew I should try and get out of it and get my life straight while I still could. So, before the cold weather set in, and despite Leon tryin' ta talk me out of it, I packed up and left Elk Mountain.

"As I have previously stated, I approached a friend who was a lawman, and he brokered the amnesty for me. It was then that I began workin' for him, as a deputy."

"Really?" Granger asked. "That was taking an awful chance, was it not? How do you know this sheriff wouldn't turn on you?"

"It was a risk I was willin' ta take. We'd stood by each other durin' the war. We owed each other plenty. I didn't think he would turn on me, and he didn't."

"So, you became a deputy," Granger clarified, "and then a sheriff."

"Yes."

So, how did it come about that the same offer was given to Mr. Nash and Mr. Kiefer?"

"Well, a few years later, Governor Hoyt approached me to offer a similar opportunity to Leon and Jack, I felt I should, at least, inform them of it. Unfortunately, things haven't gone as smoothly for them, as they had for me."

"No, obviously not," Mr. Granger agreed. "So, despite what you heard throughout Mr. Nash's trial, and what you have heard here, this morning, do you still feel Mr. Kiefer is deserving of a pardon?"

Taggard sighed and glanced at Jack.

Jack sat quietly, not sure what his friend was going to say.

"People make foolish choices when they're young," Taggard surmised. "I know that from personal experience. Leon and Jack made some bad decisions, which they both now regret. But I also know from their histories, they were carryin' a lot of hurt, and were actin' out in response to that hurt, and the anger created by it.

"No disrespect intended, but I believe the sentence handed down to Napoleon Nash was unfair and should be appealed. I also believe, despite some backslidin', that both Leon and Jack are sincere in their desire to straighten out their lives and should be given an opportunity to do so."

Jack smiled and nodded a thank you to his friend. He didn't know if Taggard's statement was going to help him in the long run, but at least he now knew that Taggard was still his friend and was going to stand by him.

"Thank you, Sheriff Murphy," Mr. Granger said. "No more questions."

"Mr. DeFord, your witness."

DeFord approached the witness, shaking his head in bewilderment.

Taggard thought that the prosecuting attorney had missed his calling and would have done well on the stage.

"I'm sorry, Sheriff Murphy, but I find myself completely befuddled," Mr. DeFord admitted. "You feel that Mr. Kiefer is deserving of an opportunity to straighten out his life, even after hearing testimony from two different sources, that he is a killer—in fact, a cold-blooded murderer. We have also heard from another source, that he does, indeed, have an explosive temper, and that he is dangerous. So much so, that as adults, Napoleon Nash is the only one who can control him. How do you justify giving this man a pardon?"

"Taking into consideration the treatment Jack Kiefer received from Mr. Charles and others, at Blessed Heart, I don't think it's surprisin' that he would eventually fight back," Taggard answered. "I would say it is to his credit that he put up with it for as long as he did.

"I also recall Deputy Layton, who was with Jack continuously, over an extended period of time, statin' that he never encountered an "explosive" temper, and, what might have been considered "threatenin' behavior" from him, was brief and self-defused.

"As to the accusations of murder, we have only heard one side of it, on each account. I, for one, am willin' to hold judgement until more information can be brought ta light."

"Well, of course," Mr. DeFord smiled, "you are his friend, after all. Still, considering that Mr. Nash so successfully hoodwinked you, I think you would be a bit more cautious in dealing with his partner."

Taggard felt his ire rising and told himself to stay calm. Mr. DeFord was deliberately trying to get tempers high, and the worst mistake was to allow him to succeed.

"As I stated earlier; I believe Mr. Nash's sentence was extreme and should be appealed. As for deceivin' me, he did what he had to do to help a friend. His refusal to name that person, is more to his credit than his detriment."

Jack held his breath, hoping he wouldn't hear Josephine's voice rising out from the spectators, indignantly demanding the right to be heard.

Fortunately, all was quiet in that quarter, and Jack sighed with relief. Still, he would feel a lot better if the line of questioning would move away from this subject.

The judge intervened, seeing the danger of the trial heading in the wrong direction.

"Mr. DeFord," Judge Lacey commented, "I would appreciate you returning to the trial of Mr. Kiefer. Mr. Nash has had his day in court;

there is no need to keep referring to it."

"Of course, Your Honor," DeFord backed off. "I have no more questions."

"Your next witness, Mr. Granger."

"I call Mr. Cameron Marsham."

Cameron made his way to the front of the courtroom and was sworn in.

"Mr. Marsham," Mr. Granger began, "you have known the defendant for some time now, is that correct?"

"Yes," Cameron admitted. "I've known both Mr. Kiefer and Mr. Nash for four years."

"And you have never been concerned about Mr. Kiefer being in the company of your family, even after learning his true identity?'

"That's correct," Cameron agreed. "Neither of those men have ever given me any reason to be concerned for the safety of my family. Indeed, both are very protective of the girls."

"Have you ever known Mr. Kiefer to display a violent temper?"

"No. Never."

"Have you, or your family, ever felt threatened by Mr. Kiefer, considering his prowess with a handgun?"

"No. Never."

"Thank you, Mr. Marsham," Mr. Granger finished up. "Your witness, Mr. DeFord."

"Mr. Marsham," Mr. DeFord approached the witness, "I realize that when you first became acquainted with Mr. Kiefer and his partner, you were unaware of their true identities. Is this correct?"

"Yes, that's correct," Cameron agreed, but felt frustrated at the redundancy of this question.

"And you had no clue that these two men were anyone other than who they claimed to be?"

"No. We had no reason to doubt them."

"No reason? I would have thought their aliases alone would have made you cautious. I mean, Mr. Black and Mr. White. How more obvious can you be?"

"Yes, I realize that, and I did question them about it," Cameron admitted. "But they laughed about that obviousness. They made a joke about it, commenting on how often those names gave them problems with people thinking they must be aliases. Let's face it, who in their right minds would choose Black and White, if they wished to remain discreet?"

"And yet, they did," DeFord pointed out. "Dumb like a fox, wouldn't you agree?"

"Yes," Cameron conceded. "I suppose so."

"Still, you were unaware, or perhaps didn't even care who they really were. Therefore, I assume you were also unaware that no more than six months prior to Nash and Kiefer arriving at your ranch four years ago, Mr. Kiefer had, in fact, in the middle of the day, in the middle of town, and in the middle of a crowded street, did willfully shoot down and kill another man. In cold blood, Mr. Marsham. With women and children there to witness it. He did willfully, shoot down and kill another man. Bang! Just like that."

Mr. DeFord paused to allow his dramatics to sink it. The rising murmurs from the spectators suggested that he had produced the desired effect.

He continued, "If you had been aware of this fact, Mr. Marsham, would you have welcomed those men onto your property and into your house?"

Cameron hesitated. He could see the trap being laid, but could not see how to avoid it, other than to lie outright, and that would be too obvious. He looked at Jack, and the two men locked gazes.

Jack knew his friend had no solid way out of answering that question, so he simply nodded and sent him a quiet smile to let him know that it was all right.

"Mr. Marsham?"

Cameron returned his focus to the lawyer. "No," he admitted. "If I had been aware of these facts at that time, I would not have allowed them into my home. But that—"

"Thank you, Mr. Marsham. No more questions."

Cameron was angry. He came off the stand with a tightened jaw and a hard expression.

He couldn't look at the defendant but walked straight back to his seat to face the disappointed eyes of his daughters. He sat down and heard David sigh beside him.

Both men were afraid of the direction this trial was going. Cameron, especially, knew he would never be able to forgive himself if Jack Kiefer was found guilty of murder and executed because he was the one who had pressured both Jack and Napoleon to face trial.

Now, Napoleon was living a life in prison, and if Jack died . . .

well, things couldn't get any worse. How could he go home and face his wife if that happened? How could he face his daughters—or himself? He felt sick. He needed a drink; a stiff one.

He felt a gentle hand touch his arm, and he looked into the forgiving eyes of his eldest daughter.

She gave him a sweet smile, and he couldn't help but smile back at her.

He gave her hand a pat, then held onto it with both of his and didn't let it go.

***

"Have you any more witnesses, Mr. Granger?"

"Yes. Your Honor."

"Fine. Call your next witness."

"I call Mr. Maxwell Coburn to the stand."

There was a commotion along a row of seats, as a tall, broad man stood up and, like a man-o-war in amongst row boats, he pushed his way to the aisle and strode up to take the stand.

Jack was surprised when Granger informed him Max had announced his intentions of coming to Cheyenne to have his say. Max liked his home and hearth, and it took a lot to get him dislodged from it.

Still, as Jack well knew, once Maxwell Coburn decided he was going to do something, well dagnabbit—he was going to do it.

Max sat down, squeezing himself into the chair, and then waited, with his arms crossed and a challenging expression upon his sun-blasted, chiseled face.

Jack couldn't help but smile.

Mr. Granger approached his witness with some trepidation.

"Mr. Coburn, you please tell the court when and how you came to know the defendant?"

"Sure," Max's sandpaper voice sounded like a rasping growl. "About five years ago, those two fellas came into my town of Red Sand, Texas. They were in my saloon when I came in with one of my men to have a drink. There was a bit of a confrontation and then, well, all three of them being young roosters, they got to huffin' and puffin', and the next thing I know, my man was challenging Mr. White there, to a gunfight. Damn, you shoulda seen the look of surprise on his face, when that dusty saddle tramp shot the gun right outta its holster, before my man even had a chance to draw. Yessir, I knew right then that those two boys might come in useful for some work I needed done. And they did."

"So, you were not aware of who they were at that time?" Mr. Granger asked.

"Nope. Didn't know and didn't care. It wasn't until after they completed the job for me, and left town, that the sheriff called me into his office and showed me those silly wanted posters. Damn, those posters could have been describing anybody, but with the talents those two fellas exhibited, I knew the sheriff was right.

"Now, a good businessman knows when to take valuable information and store it away for future use, so I told that sheriff, he was mistaken. That Mathew and Peter were friends of my son's, so therefore, they couldn't be Nash and Kiefer."

"And the sheriff believed you?"

Max's eyebrows bristled. "Of course, he believed me," he bellowed. "I own the town!"

Mr. Granger took an involuntary step backward.

Jack tried hard not to laugh. Max's testimony may or may not help him, but it sure was entertaining to watch.

Mr. Granger regrouped. "Yes, of course. So, you found that Mr. Kiefer and his partner were ah . . . reliable at pulling off . . . or, I should say, completing the jobs you hired them to do?"

"Of course, they were," Max answered, as he shuffled in his chair; this line of questioning already irritated him. "I wouldn't have kept on hiring them, if they weren't."

"No, no of course not," Mr. Granger agreed. "So, did you ever feel threatened by Mr. Kiefer at any time?"

"Threatened by my son's friend?" Max glared at the lawyer as though he were an idiot.

"He's not reall—"

"Well, I've come to think of him as such. They're like family. Both of 'em. Dammit, they're more like sons to me than my own natural born. All this damn nonsense about Mathew being a dangerous killer and having an explosive temper. He has no more of a temper than I have! Sweetest mannered man I ever knew."

"Mr. Coburn," the judge intervened, "I insist you refer to the defendant and his partner by their legal names."

"Why? I know who I'm talking about, and so do you."

"Mr. Coburn. Show some respect for this court," the judge insisted.

"Why?" Max repeated, "After what this court did to poor Peter? Best damn poker player I ever met—and an honest one, too. You don't find that combination very often. No. I owe those men a lot. More than I can say. And since my letter, apparently, didn't hold much water, I decided I better get over here and set things right. It's the least I could do."

"Why do you owe them, Mr. Coburn?" Mr. Granger asked him. "Did you not pay them for the jobs they completed for you?"

"Of course, I paid them," Coburn's tone becoming more gravelly as his indignation grew. "You think, I would try to swindle them out of their pay? When someone does a job for me, I pay them." He calmed down and softened his manner. "No, I am referring to a private matter. I owe them a debt of gratitude that I can never pay back."

"And what was that private matter?" Mr. Granger asked.

"Well it's private! That's why it's called a private matter."

"Mr. Coburn, please . . ." Mr. Granger pleaded with him.

"Fine! If you must know," Max agreed. "Well, Black, now he—he arranged a marriage between me and Senior Sandoval's sister."

A wave of chuckling came up from the spectators, everyone trying to imagine this bear of a man having a wife.

"That's important," Max insisted. "It doesn't matter how much money you have if you've got no one to share it with. Yes, sir. I owe Peter a huge debt. And Mathew too; they both had a hand in it. Then you go and send that boy off to prison for twenty years. That's not right. So, I knew I had to get here to make sure you didn't go and do the same thing to Mathew. Neither of them deserves that."

"Thank you, Mr. Coburn," Mr. Granger said. "I have no more questions."

Steven Granger strode back to his seat, feeling a wave of relief hitting him in the knees as he gratefully sat down beside his client.

Jack leaned over to him and whispered; "Ya did good."

Granger rolled his eyes and let out a huge sigh.

"Mr. DeFord, your witness."

Mr. DeFord looked pallid as he approached the stand.

"Mr. Coburn, you mentioned that the sheriff in your town informed you of their true identities, and you did nothing about it?"

"Of course, I did something," Max answered. "I told the sheriff he

165

was wrong."

"But, Mr. Coburn, you must have realized that what you did was illegal," Mr. DeFord bravely continued. "You assisted two known outlaws to avoid arrest. That is considered 'Aiding and Abetting', and it is a crime."

"So what? This courtroom is full of people who aided and abetted. I don't see any of them being arrested."

"Yes, well . . ."

"And I'd like to see you try," Max puffed his chest out like an old rooster, himself.

"Yes, well . . . moving on," DeFord wisely decided. "The jobs you hired Mr. Nash and Mr. Kiefer for, what were they?"

"Oh, I was having a bit of a border dispute with one of my neighbors, is all," Max explained. "Black and White, well, they helped to get it sorted out."

"So, they were successful, I take it?" Mr. DeFord asked.

"Of course, they were successful," Max frowned at him. "That neighbor is now family, so I would say, they were successful."

Outright laughter followed this announcement, and the gavel went to work to quiet the spectators down.

"Was there anything illegal involved?" Mr. DeFord asked. "Can I assume, the border you are speaking of is the international border between the U.S. and Mexico?"

"Sure is," Max agreed, "but there was nothing illegal about it. It was dangerous, that's all. I needed a couple of men who didn't scare easy. And I found them."

"And what did that job entail?"

"Simply to retrieve some cattle belonging to me, that had ended up in Mexico."

"So, to cross the international border with the intention of stealing livestock then returning with them to the States?"

"Not steal," Max growled. "They were my property. Why should I lose 2,000 head of my property just because the damn beasts learned how to swim?"

"Are you still in possession of this 'unstolen' property?" Mr. DeFord asked.

"Well, no, as a matter of fact," Max admitted. "Senor Sandoval bought the whole herd from me, fair and square. To seal the deal, it was agreed that I take his sister to wife. I admit, at first neither me nor Sinora

166

Sandoval were keen on the idea, my own wife being very recently deceased. My sons weren't too happy about it neither. But business is business, and it all worked out in the end. I have a fine woman for my wife and she's warmed to the idea, too, so everyone's happy."

"Except that Mr. Nash and Mr. Kiefer crossed over an international border—twice—illegally."

"So what?" Max sneered his distain. "People are doing that every day. Nothing new there."

"You don't seem to have much regard for the laws of this land, Mr. Coburn. Why is that?"

"Why should I?" Max asked. "I built up my dynasty with the sweat of my own brow. I took risks, made gambles; sometimes I lost, but most times, I won. There was no law in Texas back then. I held onto what was mine by taking care of the law myself. Nobody crossed me. If Chisum is New Mexico, then I'm Texas, and I make my own law. One thing about being rich, is you learn fast that laws can be bent. They're fluid; you can make them go any way you want them to."

"Really?" DeFord commented. "Mr. Nash didn't find them very fluid."

"That's not over yet," Max stated.

"As far as I am aware, Mr. Nash's trial is over."

"You think that because his trial is over, that it's over?" Max challenged, his voice becoming low and dangerous. "I'm telling you right now, it's not over." He looked to the judge, who was staring back at him with raised eyebrows. "No offence, Your Honor. I'm used to being the man in charge; having my own way. You understand. No offense meant."

"Indeed," commented Judge Lacey. "This line of questioning is getting us nowhere, Mr. DeFord. I suggest you wrap it up."

"Yes, Your Honor," DeFord answered. "Actually, I have no more questions for Mr. Coburn."

"Thank you," said the judge, emphatically. "You may step down, Mr. Coburn."

Max nodded and stomped back to his seat, sending Jack a quick smile and a nod, as he went.

Jack smiled back.

Taggard looked at him, slack jawed. "So, that's Max Coburn?"

"Yup."

"Geesh."

"Yup."

"The court stands adjourned. We will reconvene tomorrow 9:00 a.m."

The gavel came down and everyone relaxed.

Soft murmurings filled the room as spectators rose from the seats and made plans to meet and discuss the day's proceedings. And Jack, as usual, was escorted from the court.

***

The Next Day. 9:15 a.m.

"Mr. Granger, your witness."

"Yes, Your Honor. I would like to call Mr. John Collier to the stand. Mr. Collier did not feel safe being present throughout these proceedings, and requested protection. If the court will indulge a minor delay while the bailiff escorts Mr. Collier to the witness box."

"Fine, Mr. Granger. But be quick about it."

Murmurs rose from the spectators, but stayed muted just below crossing the line.

Those who cared to seek out Mrs. Stanton and her husband would have noted looks of both surprise and anger flash between them. Gone was the weeping willow, dabbing her eyes with a frilly hanky, to be replaced with a tight-lipped oak, her branches stiff with indignation.

She snatched her hand away from her consoling husband and sat fuming with this turn of events.

The side door opened and the bailiff entered, escorting a more presentable Mr. Collier to the witness box. His eyes darted around the spectators, seeking the Stantons. He couldn't find them, but he knew they were there, watching him. He gulped, then his attention was diverted by the bible that appeared under his right hand.

***

Mr. Granger approached the box. "Mr. Collier, will you please state your full name and your place of birth."

"Yes sur." Collier shuffled in his seat and straightened his bow tie. "My full name is Jonathan William Collier the Third."

Chuckling from the spectators prompted the first gavel banging of the day.

"Quiet!" Judge Lacey stormed as he glared out upon a courtroom bursting at the seams. "This is not a carnival show, though goodness knows, it's trying to turn into one. Respect this court or you will be found in contempt and removed."

Sheepish glances and soft murmurs followed this reprimand but, again, the spectators quieted, as none of them wished to miss the conclusion to this entertaining trial.

"Mr. Collier," Judge Lacey acknowledged the witness. "Continue."

"Yes sur. I was born in 1841 on a plantation in Lexington, Missouri."

"And what is your background there?" Mr. Granger took over.

"Wul, I wasn't aware of it, a course, but we were affluent. As a child, if I thought a it at all, I assumed everyone had large holdings and kept slaves. Why, some 'a them nigra children were my friends. We spent hours playin' in the fields and didn't think nothin' of it.

"A course, as I got older, I realized that such friendships were not appropriate so I ended them."

"Did you?" Mr. Granger asked. "How did you feel about that?"

Mr. Collier shrugged. "There was nothin' to feel. That's just the way it was. A white man can't be hangin' around with the Negros. It wasn't proper."

"No, I suppose it wasn't," Mr. Granger conceded. "Please tell the court how you became acquainted with Mr. Wissen."

"He was a friend a my father's. He often visited our home."

"Indeed. Is that how you became acquainted with Mrs. Stanton?"

"Oh, no sur." Mr. Collier snorted. "She weren't even born yet. I became acquainted with the Stantons some years later, after the war. She knew though, that our fathers had been friends and that we rode together durin' that time. And before it."

"Before it?"

"Well, durin' the Border War, a 'course."

"So, you and Mr. Wissen were involved in the Border War?"

"Yes sur. There was a lot of anger even b'fore the Border War erupted. Well, that was why the Border War erupted, in't it? Those anti-slavers were out ta ruin us. John Brown an' his raiders only added more fuel to an already hot fire."

"So, you were involved in the raids along the Kansas/Missouri border?"

"Objection!" Mr. DeFord stood and waved a dismissive hand at his opposition. "Mr. Granger is leading his witness."

"Sustained. Mr. Granger, allow your witness to tell his own story. He doesn't need any suggestions from you."

"Yes, Your Honor. My apologies. Mr. Collier, please, continue."

"Yes sur. Well, those anti-slavers were hurtin' us deep. They threatened our whole way 'a life, so a 'course we're gonna retaliate. There were a lot 'a skirmishes back 'n forth across that river. Some of 'im got pretty bloody."

"Which river are you referring to?"

Mr. Collier frowned at the absurdity of the question. "Why, the Missouri River, a course. Ain't no other river borderin' them two territories."

"Of course, Mr. Collier. I simply need you to be specific."

"Humph. Now, where was I? Oh yeah, those damn anti-slavers. They were ruinin' us. But even then, I didn't hold much with killin' women and children, no sur. It weren't their doin', they were just followin' their men. We were all for a bit 'a plunderin' and burin' their fields, because well, it's what they were doing to us. But we didn't attack just anybody. We'd pick our targets; we weren't out to hurt the common folks.

"But Mr. Wissen now, he and his gang didn't care about sparin' the women and children. I swear, witnessin' some of the things they did, about made me sick."

"Yes, I'm sure. Do you recall the Kiefer homestead in particular, Mr. Collier?"

"I sure do. Mainly because it happened late. Things had calmed down along the border by '58, kind of a calm before the storm, you know. But even though there weren't any raiders comin' across inta Missouri, them folks was still causin' us distress."

"What way could they harm you if they weren't attacking your homes?"

"In helpin' our slaves!" Mr. Collier's neck turned red with his rising anger. "Why, between '58 and '61, I can recall six of our best slaves that escaped inta Kansas and got help ta head north. We never did see them again. And our neighbors also suffered similar losses. The Jefferson Plantation lost plenty, as did the Mitchell Estates. Why, Mr. Wissen himself lost ten slaves. Three of 'em drowned in the river, and two were shot, but that's beside the point. They're still lost property.

"Now, we knew for a fact, that the Nashs and the Kiefers were behind it all. At least in our area. There were others, but we got them shut down. But those two families wouldn't take the hint. They had connections, you see. Connections that would move those slaves out of our reach. That was stolen property, and we had a right ta put a stop to it."

"By attacking women and children?" Mr. Granger wondered if he had made a mistake letting Mr. Collier testify. He could feel hostility building behind him among the spectators.

Mr. Collier came down a notch. "Wull, no. Like I said, I didn't hold with goin' that far. But Wissen, now, there was somethin' wrong with him. He was a brutal man. I hear tell he beat his own wife ta death—"

"That's a lie!" came the indignant yell from the spectators. Julia Stanton rose to her feet, shaking her fist at the witness. "You're lying! My mother ran off with some no-good thespian. My father was a good man!"

The gavel beat out a staccato. "Quiet in this courtroom! Mrs. Stanton, you will refrain from making such outbursts. You will have your chance to respond in due course."

Julia Stanton sat down, her anger dissolving in a whirl of anxiety. Why would she be recalled to the stand when she had already given her testimony? Real fear hit her gut at what this surprise testimony might reveal.

The judge turned back to the witness. "Mr. Collier, please continue."

Now that Mr. Collier knew where the Stantons were sitting, he kept a leery eye on them. But with the prompting of the judge, he nodded and focused again on Mr. Granger.

"Like I was sayin', Cal Wissen was a brutal man. He didn't need an excuse to attack the homesteads; he enjoyed it. He burned them farmers out, even if they weren't helpin' our slaves.

"But things had quieted along the border in '58. We were told ta' stand down and let things settle. And we did. But by 1860, things started heatin' up again. Wissen, he zeroed in on those two homesteads in particular. We all knew they were runnin' our slaves north, and he decided ta' do somethin' about it.

"And that's why we joined him on that raid. We wanted ta' get some of our own back. In hindsight now though, I wish I hadn't gone, 'cause I'm never gonna be able ta' unsee what I saw.

"The men got off easy. Yes, they did. We simply killed 'em right off. But the women," Mr. Collier shook his head, honestly ashamed. "Damn. I never thought it be possible ta' do that to a human being with them still be breathin'. Wissen and his boys, well, they weren't men anymore. They were mad with blood lust and killin' up close. They became animals. Worse than animals, 'cause I don't know of any beast in the woods that would treat its own kind that way.

"Even the little girl. She couldn'a been more 'n six years old and them boys took turns rapin' her. I'll never forget her screams, beggin' with them ta' stop. But they didn't stop. It was Wissen himself who raped that little girl so hard, he killed her. Then he chopped up her body like she was just a piece 'a meat."

"NO!" Julia Stanton screamed. "You're lying! You awful little man. How can you say my father committed such atrocities? He said he was never there, that it was you who led those raids. How dare you!"

Mr. Stanton grabbed his wife and forced her back into her seat.

"Shut up," he whispered through bared teeth. "You're making yourself look bad. Show some decorum, woman. We know he's lying and besides, he can't prove a word of it."

"Because it never happened!" his wife screeched back at him.

He cringed; his ears ringing.

Judge Lacey had had enough.

"Mrs. Stanton, you will leave this courtroom. Now! The bailiff will escort you to the antechamber where you will wait until you are recalled to the witness box."

Julia Stanton cried into her hanky, but there was little sympathy from those around her.

The bailiff approached to assist her from the courtroom.

"Ma'am, you will accompany me now. Mr. Stanton, you may join her in the antechamber if you wish."

"Yes, I—"

"No!" Mrs. Stanton turned on her husband. "You will stay right here and listen to what that bastard says. I want to know every word, you hear me?"

"But—"

"Every word!"

Then with a huff, she turned and strutted out of the courtroom with the bailiff close behind her.

Mr. Stanton sent a sheepish look toward the judge, but settled back in his chair to do his wife's bidding.

"Oh, thank goodness," Judge Lacey muttered, then nodded. "You may continue, Mr. Granger."

"Yes, Your Honor." Mr. Granger took a deep breath to calm his own nerves. He glanced at his client, but Jack sat, pale and quiet, looking at his hands. "All right, Mr. Collier. Is there anything more you wish to add?"

"Wull, I gotta admit, I'm surprised they didn't bugger them little boys too. Although, the one boy, we never saw him. I guess his ma hid 'im away somewhere. But the other one, the brother of that little girl, I don't know why they didn't do him too. They just left 'im. Probably figured he'd die in the fire."

"And now that little boy sits here in this courtroom, accused 'a murdering Cal Wissen. Wull, that ain't right. No sur, not right at all. Like I said before, if any man needed killin' it was him."

"Thank you, Mr. Collier," Judge Lacey said, "but you are only here to testify, not to stand in judgment. That is for the court to decide."

"I don't care what this court decides. That lad was within his rights."

"Thank you, Mr. Collier. Do you have more questions for your witness, Mr. Granger?"

"No, Your Honor, not at this time."

"Fine. Mr. DeFord. Your witness."

***

Mr. DeFord approached the witness. "Mr. Collier, you claim to have taken part in many raids along the Kansas/Missouri border, is that correct?"

"Wull, yes. I admit, we retaliated."

"Mm hum. How can you be sure that the atrocities you have described here actually happened at the Kiefer homestead? You, yourself stated that Mr. Wissen was a cruel man. How can you be certain that you are correct in the time and place?'

"As I said, this attack was late in the skirmishes. We hadn't gone on any raids for some time. It tended ta stand out."

"But how can you be certain, Mr. Collier, that it was the Kiefer homestead you attacked?"

"Because we targeted them, sur. They were assistin' our nigras to escape."

"But still," DeFord smirked, "it could have been any homestead along the river. You have no proof."

"What proof do I need? I recall clearly what happened that day. How can I ever forget?"

"But did it happen at the Kiefer homestead? That is the question, Mr. Collier."

"Of course, that's where it happened." Collier huffed. "As I say; those two families were targeted."

"Even if that is true, Mrs. Stanton insists that it was not her father who committed these atrocities. That it was more likely you, yourself, who committed them. Even if this did take place at the Kiefer homestead, how can you be sure after all this time that it was indeed Mr. Wissen who committed them?"

Mr. Collier puffed himself for a retort, but Mr. Granger beat him to it.

"Objection! Mrs. Stanton was out of line. She was not in the witness box and was not under oath."

"Sustained," Judge Lacey said. "Mr. DeFord, you will refrain from this line of questioning. Mrs. Stanton's accusation is not on record."

Mr. DeFord sighed. "Yes, Your Honor. Mr. Collier, is there any way you can prove that it was indeed the Kiefer homestead that was ransacked on that day, and that it was Mr. Wissen who led the attack and committed those crimes that you are accusing him of?"

Mr. Collier hesitated. "Ain't my word good enough?"

"Memories fade, Mr. Collier. Situations become confused. I'm sure what you described here did indeed happen. The question is, when and where did it happen? In the eyes of the law, Mr. Kiefer did not have the right to track down and execute Mr. Wissen, no matter what his crime. But, in the eyes of justice, if it can be proven beyond a doubt that Mr. Wissen did indeed commit these atrocities against the Kiefer family, then some leniency may be considered. What we need from you, Mr. Collier, is that proof."

"Wull." Mr. Collier looked around the courtroom. He met Jack's eyes, and the pain and sadness he saw there brought pangs of regret. "I tell ya, we didn't just burn a place, we plundered too." He sighed, thinking back to that day. "There was a rifle. Not just any rifle. A real nice one, and old. Brought up from the Revolutionary War. Now, Wissen, he took a fancy ta that rifle, and he kept it. Not a smart thing ta do, but he liked his keepsakes. If you can find that rifle, that would be proof, wouldn't it?"

DeFord nodded. "Indeed, Mr. Collier. If there is anything on that rifle to indicate that it belonged to the Kiefers', that would go a long way to proving your accusations."

"There ya go," Mr. Collier puffed up with importance. "All ya gotta do is find that rifle."

"Indeed. No more questions, Your Honor."

"Fine, you may step down, Mr. Collier. Court will adjourn for lunch. Mr. Stanton, you are not permitted to see or speak to your wife until after her testimony."

"But, Your Honor—"

"Court is adjourned!" And the gavel came down upon Mr. Stanton's protest. "Mr. DeFord and Mr. Granger, join me in my chambers."

***

"This is an interesting development, gentlemen. It appears that the only thing standing between Mr. Kiefer and the hangman's noose is this rifle." He cocked a brow at Mr. Granger. "Mr. DeFord, I expect you now agree that Mrs. Stanton has the right to address these new accusations."

"Of course. I will recall her."

"And then, Mr. Granger, you will have your opportunity to cross-examine."

"Yes, Your Honor. I'm not sure if she is deliberately lying or simply doesn't know."

"Indeed, Mr. Granger? With instincts like that, you might make a decent lawyer after all."

Steven Granger heard Mr. DeFord's quiet snort, but he refused to rise to the taunt. "Yes, Your Honor."

***

Jack paced the cell. With every new witness coming to the stand, more information was thrown out to haunt him. It was bad enough, coming to terms with his mother's rape, but to discover that his baby sister had suffered the same torture was causing his anger to rise again.

"Dammit." Jack ground his teeth. "I felt regret over killin' Wissen in front of his daughter and all, but not no more. I swear, if'n he was standin' in front a me right now, I'd rip his heart out and choke 'im with it. How can a man do that—?" The words strangled in his throat and, with teeth bared he circled the cell again.

"I know." Mr. Granger was apologetic. "Mr. Collier gave me details of the raid, but not that particular incident. If I had realized he would be so graphic, I would have warned you. That's not something you should have learned about during your trial."

"I shouldn't a learned about it period." Jack huffed. "I was ready ta accept any sentence the court deemed fit, cause 'a my own guilt. But now, I ain't ready at all. That bastard deserved dyin'—"

"I know. We find ourselves caught between what's legal and what is just. In the legal sense, Mr. Kiefer, you still had no right to be trial, jury and executioner. If you had a grievance against Mr. Wissen, you should have taken the proper legal steps—"

"Oh, come on!" Jack snorted. "I was sixteen! It was the law that put me inta that damned orphanage. It was the law that kept me starvin' on the streets. The law ain't never done me no favors, and they wouldn't a then, either. And you know it." He paused and sighed. He shook his head as though involved in a silent debate with himself. "But you're right. Killlin' Cal Wissen was the worst thing I've ever done. Not cause he deserved better, but because his daughter did."

Mr. Granger sighed and declined to answer.

"Do you recall this rifle that Mr. Collier mentioned? Could it be valuable as evidence here?"

Jack stopped pacing. With hands on hips, he stared into his own thoughts and considered the possibility.

"I think I remember the rifle he's talkin' about," Jack conceded. "I wasn't allowed ta touch it. My pa, he kept it above the fireplace, outta reach. But, every once in a while, Pa would take it down ta clean, and I saw it up close. It didn't look like much. The barrel was real long and seemed clumsy ta me. But Pa treasured it. It had a plaque on the stock. I don't recall what was engraved in it. Dang, for all I know, any writing might a been worn off by then."

"Hmm, maybe. But if it has your family name on it, and it's found in the Stantons' possession, that would be pretty damning."

176

"Yeah, I suppose."

Mr. Granger looked down at the untouched lunch set on the floor.

"I suggest you eat something, Mr. Kiefer. I'm going to get a quick bite myself. This afternoon could prove challenging."

Jack glanced at the plate and his stomach knotted. "I guess."

***

"Mrs. Stanton, you are under oath. That means you are required to tell the truth. Do you understand?"

Julia Stanton cocked an indignant brow at the judge. "Of course, I understand. I'm not uneducated."

"Is that so? Your earlier behavior in my court caused me to wonder. Mr. DeFord, continue."

"Thank you, Your Honor." DeFord approached his witness. "Mrs. Stanton, I realize you were young when you father died, but do you recall anything that might suggest any truth in Mr. Collier's testimony."

Julia Stanton sat firm and arrow straight in her chair, her lips were tight in suppressed anger as she glared at Mr. Collier. Then she met her lawyer's gaze. "No," she insisted. "There was nothing in our home that could even be remotely considered plunder."

"Do you still live at the property?"

"No, I do not. After my father was so brutally murdered, I was removed from my home and sent to an orphanage."

Jack groaned and ran and hand over his brow.

"And your possessions?" DeFord continued. "What happened to them?"

"As far as I know the property and all articles were sold at auction. The matron said it was to pay for my keep." She shook her head. "I never saw any benefit from the sale of my property. As far as I'm concerned, it's another example of the Union government stealing from us Southerners."

"So, you're saying that even if this rifle did exist and was in your father's possession, it was sold off to . . . someone?"

"It never did exist," Mrs. Stanton huffed. "But yes, all articles in the house were sold."

"Thank you, Mrs. Stanton. No more questions, Your Honor."

Mrs. Stanton stood up to leave, but Judge Lacey stopped her short.

"You have not been released from the witness box, Mrs. Stanton.

Remain seated."

"But what else is there to say? There's nothing to prove that—"

The loud bang from the gavel overruled her words.

"You will refrain from speaking out of line, Mrs. Stanton. Answer the questions presented to you and leave the court to decide what is proof and what isn't."

Mrs. Stanton hung her head, but her eyes were sharp points of resentment.

Judge Lacey motioned to the defense attorney. "Your witness, Mr. Granger."

"Mrs. Stanton," Mr. Granger acknowledged the witness. "How old were you when your father died?"

Mrs. Stanton scowled, frustrated at what she considered to be repetitive questions. "I was five years old when my father was murdered."

"And was it just you and your father living alone?"

"Yes."

"No servants?"

"Oh, well yes, of course we had servants. But they don't count."

"Of course not. Do you know what happened to them?"

"No." She shrugged at this being nonconsequential. "I expect they found other work. Perhaps they were auctioned off with the house and property."

"Auctioned off? But these people were paid employees, not slaves."

Mrs. Stanton rolled her eyes. "Of course, they were slaves, or at least the next best thing."

Mr. Granger hesitated. This was not a direction he had intended on going, but if he could invalidate Mrs. Stanton's testimony, this could be as good an avenue as any.

"But the war was over and the slaves freed. Why would you still consider them your property?"

"Because they were our property!" Mrs. Stanton rolled her eyes. "You Unionists. You think that because you won the war, you freed the slaves? Many of them had nowhere to go, Mr. Granger. You gave them their freedom, and that ended the matter as far as you were concerned. They had no money, no way to support themselves because no one would hire them.

"Many went north looking for opportunity. Some found it, but not all. Their lives were a misery. Before, if they had a good master, and our family was always good to our slaves, they had a place. A home, with shelter and food, and medicine when they needed it.

"But the war ended all that for them, and they were set adrift. Most of the plantations and ranches were in ruin. We could barely keep ourselves alive, let alone hire our own slaves back for paid wages. Those that were willing to stay under the proper circumstances were permitted to do so. And believe me, many of them did.

"With the help of those slaves, we finally got our plantation up and running again, but it was never the place it had been. Of course, I don't remember that, but my papa told me stories of its former grandeur. But that was all gone by the time I came along. Then my mother left and it was just me and Papa. And yes, the slaves who chose to stay loyal to us.

"Were these people present when your father was killed?"

"Well, not at the exact place. The house servants were in the house and the field hands were in the field."

"So, no one saw the incident?"

"I saw it, Mr. Granger."

"But you were only five years old."

"Objection!" Mr. DeFord interrupted. "We have already gone over this line of questioning."

"Sustained." Judge Lacey peered at Mr. Granger under dark brows. "This has already been determined."

"If I may," Mr. Granger said, "it has been suggested by the prosecution that Mr. Collier's testimony is unreliable based on the fact that these events happened years ago and therefore, his memory could be deluding him. If this conclusion is accepted, then I put to the court that Mrs. Stanton's testimony is also subject to error based on the years since it happened and her youthfulness at the time."

"I will never forget his face!" Mrs. Stanton insisted as she pointed an accusing finger in Jack's direction. "He did it! And he had no good reason to."

Again, the gavel rapped out a staccato. "Silence!"

The courtroom hushed.

Cameron sat with lips pressed tight. Though Caroline's hand held his, there was no conversation between them. Even David was tense and silent.

"This line of questioning is all based on conjecture," Judge Lacey declared. "Until such time as evidence can be presented this matter needs to be set aside. I have issued warrants for both the Wissen and Stanton properties to be searched, even though the plantation is now in possession of another party. And I hope, Mr. Granger, for the sake of your client, that this rifle can be found.

"In the meantime, I suggest we move on. Mrs. Stanton, now you may step down. But you are not free to leave town. Do you understand? If this rifle is found, you may be called upon to give further testimony."

"Yes, Your Honor." Mrs. Stanton stepped down from the witness box. "But I assure, no rifle will be found, because there never was one."

Judge Lacey's growling sigh was quite audible throughout the courtroom. "Call your next witness, Mr. Granger."

"Yes, Your Honor. I now call Mr. Jack Kiefer to the stand."

***

Jack groaned, and the knot that had been tying up his stomach now tightened into a sickening vice. He stood, and after acknowledging an encouraging nod from Taggard, made his way to the front of the courtroom.

The bailiff approached him with the bible, and Jack placed his right hand on it and lifted his left. His right shoulder protested at the movement.

"Do you swear to tell the truth, the whole truth, and nothing but the truth, so help you God?"

"I do."

"State your full name."

"Jackson Benjamin Kiefer."

"Take the chair, Mr. Kiefer."

Jack settled into the witness box, and then, just as Leon had done before him, he found himself surveying the spectators for the first time since the trial had started. For him, there were no surprises with the familiar faces looking back at him. He found himself smiling a greeting to Penny and Caroline, and then to David. He couldn't see Josey, but he was sure she was out there.

Mr. Granger was then in front of him, and Jack took a deep breath to calm his nerves.

"When were you born, Mr. Kiefer?" Mr. Granger asked him, again, starting out with easy, non-threatening questions.

180

"Ah, March 6th, 1853."

"And you were born in Kansas?"

"Yeah, I was."

"So, your farm in Kansas was the only home you had before the orphanage?"

"Ah, yup."

"And how many siblings did you have, Mr. Kiefer?"

"Two," Jack answered. "A brother who was older than me, and a," he hesitated and looked down, his jaw tightening, ". . . a younger sister."

"It is my understanding that you and your partner are related, is that correct?"

"Yes."

"In what way?"

"He's my uncle. Leon's half-sister was my ma," Jack answered. "She was the oldest daughter, I think. Anyway, the Navarres settled first in Philadelphia, as they had connections there from back home. Apparently, the family was big inta bankin', and real estate, and such. They wanted ta expand their holdings in this new country."

"I object, Your Honor," Mr. DeFord stood. "We already know the history of the families. Must we go through it all again?"

"Overruled," Judge Lacey proclaimed. "The court needs to hear how this tragedy unfolded from Mr. Kiefer's recollection. What Mr. Nash said at his trial should have no bearing on it. This is Mr. Kiefer's trial. Continue, Mr. Granger."

"Thank you, Your Honor." He sent a quick, hard look to his colleague, then returned his attention to the defendant. "Please continued, Mr. Kiefer. How did your two families connect?"

Jack sighed, frustrated with the interruption, then picked it up again. "Well, the family businesses were doin' okay, but then Louisa, my grandpa's first wife, caught the fever and died. He weren't happy in Philadelphia after that. He came west on his own, leavin' his family at home, there in the city.

"You can bet the folks in Europe were none too happy about it, when they found out. But by the time word had reached 'em, Frederick, my grandpa, had already decided that he liked it better out this way.

"I ain't sure how it happened, but he got in good with the Shoshones up around the Yellowstone area, and he up and married one of 'em. That did it for the folks in Europe, and they disowned him. I don't think he cared though. It was around then that he changed his name to Nash, which was his ma's family name. He got himself some land there in Kansas, along the border, and moved his family west.

"My pa was already staked out there, with a decent enough farm, and when he met my grandpa's daughter, well, it seems they hit it off well enough ta up and get married."

"Really?" Mr. Granger commented. "That's quite a colorful family tree. It is my understanding that the Navarres were a powerful family in Europe. Did you ever feel any resentment toward them for basically abandoning your folks to such a harsh life?"

"I never thought about it," Jack shrugged. "I never thought a myself as bein' a Navarre, or a Nash. I loved my grandpa, but he was grandpa, not pa. My pa was a Kiefer. Besides, I never heard anybody complainin' about our lives. Maybe bein' happy in a poor family is better than bein' smothered by a rich one."

"So, you don't harbor any resentment toward your mother's family?" Mr. Granger asked.

"No," Jack told him. "We were happy."

"Was it a difficult life?" Mr. Granger asked. "Homesteading, like that?"

"I suppose it was for our folks," Jack admitted, "but not for us young'uns. I mean, as soon as we were old enough, we all had our chores ta do, but life was good. We didn't know any different. The way I recall it, me and Leon had a lot a fun." He smiled in recollection. "Ran pretty wild too, I'd say. Occasionally, Leon's ma would take him up to the Yellowstone, to spend time with her people. It was kinda lonely for me then, but when he came back, he'd show me all the things his kin taught 'im, so that was worth it. We were always out somewhere, fishin' and ridin'. It was good livin' for us. Had to be home before dusk though. That was the rule. Yup. Trouble along the border; have to be home before dusk."

"Do you remember that? There being trouble along the border?"

"I remember bein' told there was. I don't remember ever seein' any. Not until . . . well . . . that day."

Mr. Granger nodded. "And you were at home the day your farm was attacked?"

Jack nodded. He mouthed his answer, but nothing came out. He coughed. "Yes."

"How old were you, when the attack happened?"

"I was eight."

A sympathetic murmuring rose amongst the listeners, and then settled again.

"And your siblings, how old were they?"

Jack shifted, feeling anxious as the questions pushed deeper. "Ah, well, my brother was twelve and my sister was five years old."

"What was the first indication of trouble? Do you remember?"

"The dog began barkin'," Jack answered. "Then I heard my pa yellin' at my brother to grab our sister and get to the house. I was still in the house, helpin' my ma get breakfast going. I liked helpin' her. And she looked so pretty that mornin'. She was wearin' the blue dress that was my favorite, 'cause the color of the fabric matched her eyes so perfectly. When she'd let her blond curls fall loose, they'd frame her face, real nice, and she'd look so pretty . . .."

Jack's voice trailed away as memories of his mother took over his thoughts.

Silence enveloped the courtroom as all ears strained to catch each word.

Jack took a deep breath, and, looking up, saw every face in the place focused on him. He felt embarrassed, talking about his ma like that, especially in front of so many strangers.

Nobody else thought it was silly.

"Take your time, Mr. Kiefer," Mr. Granger assured him. "Whenever you're ready."

Jack looked back to him and nodded. "I remember hearin' gunshots, and horses gallopin'. Everybody was screamin'. The horses were screamin', my sister and my ma were screamin'. I was screamin'. Even the dog was screamin'. I didn't know dogs could scream. I didn't know what was happenin' outside, I just could hear bangin', and men yellin'. My ma was at the window, shootin' the rifle she'd grabbed from above the fireplace. Then, I could smell stuff burnin'; wood and hay— and meat."

Jack stopped talking again and collected his thoughts. He sat quietly, looking at the floorboards. When he continued talking, he did not look up; it was as if he was all alone, and he was talking to himself.

"The screamin' had stopped outside, but my ma was still shootin'. Then, I guess she ran out of bullets or somethin', 'cause she turned from the window and ran over to me. She got me behind her, then turned and faced the front door. I remember, she was shakin' and mumblin' something. I think she was prayin'.

"Then the door burst open, and ma screamed and started backin' up, pushin' me back with her. I couldn't see what was happenin'. Then, ah . . ." Jack stopped. Jaw clenched tight, he fought for control. He swallowed, took a deep breath and ran a hand through his hair. But he didn't say anything; it was like he had come to a dead end.

"Oh no," Cameron mumbled, then thought, are we going to go through this again?

"Come on, Jack," David whispered, "don't lock up."

Jack took another deep breath and looked to his friends at the back of the courtroom. It was as though he had heard their quiet encouragements. He looked at the two girls and smiled at them, as though apologizing for what he was going to have to say next. To his surprise, they both smiled back.

"They grabbed her," he continued. "I got shoved down by the stove, and she was beggin' with 'em ta not hurt me." He gave an ironic laugh. "They were hittin' her, and she was beggin' 'em not ta hurt me.

"There were three of 'em," he stated, bluntly. "One of 'em pulled the tablecloth off the table and sent all the dishes flyin'. They crashed to the floor. I remember seein' my favorite plate landin' by the pantry and shatterin' to splinters, all in slow motion. I don't know how that happened.

"Then, one of the men grabbed her golden hair. He pulled her head back and kissed her. But it weren't a gentle kiss, not like when Pa kissed her. It was hard and cruel. Then, he ripped that pretty, blue dress. Ripped it right off a her. He pushed her onto the table and got on top of her, and I didn't understand what he was doin', but she was screamin', and they were laughin', and I knew they were hurtin' her.

"I ran forward and grabbed the six-shooter outta one of their holsters. I tried to aim it at the man, but the gun was too heavy for me." Jack's hands pantomimed the act of trying to hold up a gun that was too heavy for small, eight-year-old hands to manage. He shook his head, feeling the frustration all over again. "It was too heavy. I couldn't aim it and pull the hammer back, and I couldn't reach the trigger. It was too heavy.

"The men laughed at me—called me a dirty little jayhawker. They took the gun away and pushed me into the corner. I could hear screamin' and kind a realized that it was me doin' it. I was wonderin' where my pa was, and why wasn't he comin' ta help?

184

"I don't know how long they were there, takin' turns on the table. Time had no meanin'. I only knew that Ma eventually stopped screamin'. Finally, they were done and one of 'em took his revolver and . . . and he shot her.

"I was sobbin', I couldn't stop. I tried ta go to her, but they pushed me back, laughin' at me. Then I heard one of 'em ask, "What should we do with the kid? Shoot 'im?", and the other answered, "Naw, leave 'im ta burn."

"Then they left, and I started crawlin' to my ma. They came back, and I jumped into the corner, but they didn't care about me. They had brands with 'em from the fires outside, and they went around the kitchen, settin' fire ta anything that would catch easy. Then, they backed out the door, and were gone.

"I didn't hear 'em leave, I ran to my ma and started shakin' her, tryin' ta wake her up. I didn't realize she was already dead."

Jack stopped talking as the sorrow of that moment hit him. He looked to the back of the courtroom and gazed upon his two young friends sitting beside their father. Penny dabbed her eyes with a handkerchief, but she still attempted a smile when she saw Jack's focus on her.

"Mr. Kiefer."

Jack returned his attention to the lawyer.

"Are you able to continue?"

Jack nodded. "Yeah." He took a deep breath and forced his thoughts back to that awful day. "All I could hear was the fire cracklin' and burnin', and the room fillin' up with smoke, and the flames were startin' ta spread.

"But I had to wake my ma up. I was shakin' her and screamin' at her ta 'please wake up'! I started coughin', and my eyes started ta burn. It was gettin' hard ta see. I grabbed Ma's hand and tried ta pull her off the table, but she was too heavy. I couldn't move her. I was callin' for Pa to come help—but nobody came."

Jack hesitated, biting his lip as painful memories flood this mind. He felt something tickle his cheek and he wiped it away. He felt moisture and frowned at the patch of wet on the back of his hand. He wiped away more moisture from his eyes, then sighed.

"Are you sure you're able to get carry on, Mr. Kiefer?" Granger asked again. "Perhaps a class of water?"

"No, no." Jack waved him away. "Just let me get through this."

Granger glanced at Judge Lacey and that gentleman nodded.

Granger returned his attention to his client. "All right, Mr. Kiefer. Continue if you can."

Jack nodded. "The fire was takin' over, and part of the roof caught, and burnin' wood fell on both of us. I had ta let go of her arm. The fire was gettin' too close. I grabbed her foot and tried to pull her, but I still couldn't move her.

"The heat was intense, and the smoke got so bad I couldn't breathe. I knew I had ta leave her. I had to. I couldn't get her out—I weren't strong enough."

His voice became pleading, asking forgiveness. Asking for understanding as to why he left his mother behind.

He sighed and continued, back to speaking as though reading a story from a book. "I turned toward the door, and my feet got tangled in her dress. Her pretty, blue dress. I grabbed it and ran outside, so I could breathe. I couldn't run very far though, only as far as the well. My feet hurt bad, I didn't know why, but it was agony. I couldn't stand on 'em. I sat in a heap, while the house burned to the ground. Just sat there, sobbin' and clutchin' Ma's blue dress. Until Leon came."

An eeriness fell over the courtroom. The men remained silent, but many of the ladies present fought back emotion and dabbed at leaking eyes.

Jack sat still, staring at the floorboards, his mind temporarily trapped back in that day.

Mr. Granger got into Jack's sight and got him to focus again. "Do you remember what happened after your uncle arrived?"

Jack shook his head. "Not very much, no. I remember thinkin'; Thank goodness Leon's here. Leon would make things right. But there weren't nothin' he could do. I remember goin' inta town. I don't remember how we got there. Then, bein' hungry and alone. I didn't know where Leon was. I was in a strange place. Someone had taken my ma's dress away from me, and I didn't like that. I was hungry and scared, and I didn't know where I was.

"Then, I remember bein' at the orphanage. I didn't realize it was an orphanage at first, just some strange place, surrounded by people I didn't know. But Leon was there, and we stuck together.

Until, one day, he wasn't there. I didn't know where he'd gone, and nobody would tell me. All I knew was that he would never leave me if it were up ta him. He'd been forced ta go, and they hadn't even

186

let us say goodbye."

"Yes. That must have been difficult, to suddenly find yourself alone and with no allies."

Jack nodded, the similarities of what happened back then, and what was happening to them now, was not lost on him.

"Do you have any other strong memories of the orphanage, Mr. Kiefer?" Mr. Granger asked him. "Anything that epitomizes your life there?"

Jack looked at Granger, confused, his mind still thinking about the irony.

"What do ya mean?" he asked.

"Sums it up."

"Oh. Ah—hungry, all the time," Jack recalled, "and scared."

"Scared of what?"

"Scared 'a the other boys. Scared of the matron. Scared that Leon was gonna really get hurt. He was always gettin' inta trouble for stealin' food and for protectin' me. I often wouldn't tell him, if the other boys stole food from me, or beat me up, 'cause I knew it would make him mad, and I didn't want 'im bein' punished cause 'a me."

"Yes, I can understand that," Mr. Granger assured him. "As pursuant Mr. Charles' testimony, you didn't need your uncle to stand up for you anymore. You were learning how to do that yourself. That indeed, again as per Mr. Charles, you became 'dangerous'. Do you recall what brought about such a drastic change in your behavior?"

He sent another regretful look back to the two young ladies, sitting with their father. "Well, it was around that time I figured out what them men had done ta my mother." He hesitated again and felt ashamed. "I was filled with such anger. I remember wantin' ta kill 'em. But I couldn't, I was just a child. So, I took my rage and frustration out on anyone who gave me half an excuse."

"Did it help?"

"No."

"Mr. Charles also stated that the only one who could control you, during one of these rages, was your uncle, Mr. Nash. Would you agree?"

"At the time, yeah," Jack admitted. "Leon could bring me out of it, calm me down. After Leon was gone, the Sisters would simply dump a bucket of water on me and throw me into a room and keep me locked in there for a day or two. I have since learned how ta control my temper."

"I see," Granger stated. "So, is it safe to assume that when Mr. Nash returned for you, two years later, you were happy to see him?"

Jack's expression brightened. "Yeah! I knew he wouldn'ta left me on purpose. We were close, we watched each other's back." His eyes saddened as he went back to that time. "He told me some of what happened to 'im at that Residential School. It made Blessed Heart sound like a Sunday picnic."

Mr. Granger nodded. "And yet, when he suggested you leave with him, you were agreeable? To break out of that sanctuary and go it on your own?"

"Yeah," Jack repeated. "I was so happy to have Leon back; I weren't about ta lose sight of 'im again."

"You and your uncle do seem to have a symbiotic relationship," Mr. Granger observed.

Jack sighed in frustration and sent a long-suffering look to his attorney. "What does that mean?"

"I'm sorry, Mr. Kiefer," Granger apologized. "I simply meant that you appear to be very dependent upon one another. Even after a two-year separation, there was still a strong bond between you."

"Well, yeah. We grew up together; we've been through hard times together. Watched each other's backs. That means a lot."

"Indeed, it does," Mr. Granger agreed, "and yet, a few years after you and your uncle left the orphanage, you parted company. Why was that, Mr. Kiefer? What brought that about?"

"Well, we were with Fred Redikopp at that time, learnin' the con. I didn't fit in there. Not really. Leon was a natural, and Red was groomin' him ta—"

"Excuse me, Mr. Kiefer," Mr. Granger interrupted, "who is Red?"

"Oh, yeah. Sorry. That was Freddy Redikopp. It was just a nickname."

"Of course," Mr. Granger said. "Try to be clear, Mr. Kiefer, and stick with legal names during these proceedings."

Jack simply nodded. This was hard enough without having to remember these little legalities.

"Please, continue," Mr. Granger encouraged him.

"Ahh . . . yeah, Mr. Redikopp was groomin' Leon ta play the larger rackets. I still didn't have a handle on my temper, and Red—I mean, Mr. Redikopp knew it. He said, if'n I couldn't control my temper then

I wouldn't be able ta control the game, so I decided ta leave and go off on my own."

"Really?" Mr. Granger asked. "I find it odd that Mr. Nash would agree to this. He had gone through great pains to get back to you, had actually put himself at great risk to not only get placed back into the orphanage, but to also get the two of you out. He also knew you had a problem with you temper, and that he was the only person who could help you to manage it. Why would he let you strike off on your own, at that time? You must have still been quite young."

"Yeah, I guess." Jack shrugged. "We argued about it. He didn't want me goin' off alone. But he didn't wanna come with me, either. He figured we had thing pretty good there. But the rage I had inside 'a me, felt like it was burnin' a hole in my soul, and I couldn't settle there, or anywhere, 'til I found a way ta calm the anger. I knew Leon wouldn't let me go off, alone. If I insisted on leavin', he would 'a come with me, but he would 'a resented it. So, I waited 'til he was off, doin' a job, and I left. He was gonna be away for a few days, so I knew by the time he returned, I'd be long gone. There would be no way for him ta follow."

"How old were you then?"

"I was about sixteen."

"Sixteen, and on your own. How did you survive?"

Jack smiled. "Leon and I had learned how ta survive, Mr. Granger. It's not hard once ya get that sorted. When I could find jobs, I took 'em. When I couldn't, I stole. It weren't any different than bein' at Blessed Heart. I also became good with a six-shooter. I decided I was never again gonna be in a position where I could not protect the ones I loved. I learned how ta use a gun and ultimately, to my shame, I learned how ta kill."

A murmuring of voices came up from the spectators, and Jack saw Taggard's shoulders slump as he passed a hand over his eyes.

Jack felt guilt and regret over the things he had done during those years on his own. And now, he knew he was disappointing his friends. And not only his friends, here, in the courtroom, but Leon as well. Leon knew none of what was about to come, and he might feel their friendship betrayed because of it.

"I tracked Cal Wissen down. I had no doubt who he was," Jack continued. "I tracked 'im down, and I killed 'im."

Trying to ignore groans coming from the courtroom, Jack looked up and faced the spectators. The anguish and regret in his eyes were apparent to everyone.

"Mrs. Stanton," he began, fighting not to choke, "I know you're out there, listenin' ta me, and I know the hurt and anger you must feel toward me. I know you don't want to believe that your pa could have done such a thing, but he did. It was a time of war, and the whole country had gone mad. People did things they would regret later. I know it probably don't mean anything to ya, but from the bottom of my soul, I apologize. I am so sorry for what I took from you. I have come to realize that I had no right. I only hope, one day, you will find it in your heart to forgive me."

Heads in the spectators turned to gazed upon Mrs. Stanton.

She sat rigid, her mouth a straight hard line. Her eyes glistened with unshed tears, but those sitting near her could not see any forgiveness in them.

David had leaned forward during Jack's confession, his brow creased in concern. Jack was normally guarded in what he told strangers, and yet, here he was in the open courtroom, throwing all caution to the wind.

David nipped his lower lip. Jack didn't know it, but he was sending out clear warning signals, and David knew then what he needed to do.

Mr. Granger roused himself and brought the defendant's attention back to him.

"What did you do after that, Mr. Kiefer?" he asked. "Where did you go?"

"I don't know," Jack admitted. "I ran until the horse dropped out from under me. Then I don't know how long I lay in the dirt. I was tormented more than ever. The killin' hadn't eased my rage; it just added pain to it. Pain, in the realization that I had done a terrible thing. I had deprived a child of her father, just as I had been deprived of my family. It was the worst feelin' in the world.

"I knew then that killin' weren't the answer to anything; it only made things worse. I know I ain't lived a stellar life, and I have made a lot of mistakes along the way. Mistakes that can't never be taken back.

"But in all the things I have done since that day, I've tried ta respect and value the lives of others, and ta offer protection ta them who are weaker, or in need.

"It sounds like a contradiction, I know, but even though I've lived the life of a thief and a gunman, I've tried my best ta be an honorable man."

"Yes, I can see that," Mr. Granger commented, then continued with his questioning. "When did you return to your uncle?"

"It was shortly after that," Jack answered. "I felt lonely and lost. You are right, Mr. Granger; Leon and I were very dependent on each other. I had made the worst mistakes 'a my life when I was on my own, and I needed ta get back to the only family I had left. I tracked 'im down and was surprised that he'd left Mr. Redikopp's protection shortly after I did, and he had gone back to his mother's kin for a spell. I guess that didn't work out for 'im though, 'cause when I went ta Elk Mountain for the winter, he was already there.

"I was worried he wouldn't want me around after I'd run out on 'im. But it couldn't have been further from the truth. He even told the gang's leader, Joaquin Cortez, that he would leave with me, if'n I weren't permitted ta stay. So, we were partners then, and we've stayed together ever since—until now."

"All right, Mr. Kiefer, thank you. I have no more questions for you, at this time," Mr. Granger turned to the judge. "Your Honor, I request that we adjourn for the day. I'm feeling the need to regroup, and I'm sure my client must be feeling much the same way."

"Agreed, Mr. Granger," Judge Lacey answered. "I believe we could all use some time out. Court will adjourn until tomorrow morning at 9:00 a.m."

CHAPTER ELEVEN
THE GUNFIGHT

In the cellblock, Jack and Granger held a conference through the bars. They ignored the voices coming to them from the front office, where Jack's friends clamored for the right to come back to see him. Jack did not feel sociable and wished everybody would go away and leave him alone.

"Tell me, Mr. Kiefer," Granger asked him, "are you intentionally trying to put your head in the noose?"

"Why would I do that?"

"I don't know," Granger shrugged. "Guilty conscience perhaps? Maybe you decided you deserve to be punished.

Jack didn't answer at first. He stood, staring into space, his arms and chin resting on the bars.

"I suppose I felt Mrs. Stanton needed something more sincere than that. I know where her anger is coming from. I can never return her father to her, but at least I can willingly own up to it, and tell her why it happened."

"Was it worth your life?" Granger asked him. "You are aware of what this judge is capable of. He doesn't hold much with the sympathy plea."

"Then why put me through all this in the first place?" Jack demanded, as he straightened from the bars. "What was the point?"

"The jury, Mr. Kiefer. If the jury can be swayed by the trauma you suffered as a child, then the judge has no choice but to go along with their decision."

"Well that's just great," Jack complained. "They didn't seem ta have much sympathy for Leon, did they?"

"No, they didn't." Granger admitted. "But even these new jurors have had a taste of public opinion concerning that verdict, so they may hesitate to bring the same one down on you. On the other hand, premeditated murder is about as serious a confession as anyone can make. But again—on the other hand—there are strong, extenuating circumstances." He sighed and shook his head. "It could go either way."

"Great," Jack grumbled, "I kinda wish you hadn't stopped the trial, Mr. Granger. I wanna get this over with, one way or another."

"I know. But you can bet Mr. DeFord is going to go for the throat. I wanted you to have a chance to rest after today's testimony. I know it wasn't easy for you. Have something to eat and get some sleep. You're going to need your wits about you tomorrow."

"Yeah," Jack nodded and returned to the bunk.

"Would you like to see any of your friends?" Granger asked.

"I dunno," Jack mumbled as he sat on the bunk and drew his knees up. "I don't feel up to discussin' this tonight."

"All right. I'll tell them. I'll see you in the morning."

When Steven Granger returned to the front office, many sets of eyes turned to confront him. He held up his hands to quiet the barrage of questions thrown his way.

"He's tired," Granger stated, "he doesn't want to see anyone."

"He couldn't possibly mean me," Josephine insisted.

"Miss Jansen, he means everyone."

"I can understand the lad being tired," Coburn growled. "I suppose tomorrow will do. We can celebrate his acquittal from all this nonsense."

"Thank you, Mr. Coburn," Granger said. "Now, why don't we all retire to the café for supper? We can plan our next attack on the governor's office."

This suggestion was met with a chorus of approval, and the group headed out the door to the street.

There was one exception from this exodus that went unnoticed by the others. David had something to discuss with Jack, and the prisoner's decree that he didn't want to see anyone did not include his doctor.

Just in case the lawyer didn't agree with David's assumption, the doctor waited until the group left the office, then he caught Rick's eye and indicated the desire to enter the cell block.

Rick nodded. He got the keys and accompanied the doctor to the one and only occupied cell. He opened the door for David to enter, but the doctor lowered his head and whispered to the deputy, "Come in with me."

Rick was surprised at the request but entered the cell along with David and put himself on alert.

Jack, who was still sitting on his bunk, sent the doctor a long-suffering look, followed by just a flicker of a glance toward his pillow.

David picked up on it and knew then what he had to do. He made a beeline toward that pillow with only one objective in mind.

Jack's expression changed to one of alarm, and he was instantly on the move to get there before David did.

If Jack had been at the top of his game, he'd have beat the Doc, hands down. But as it was, the sudden movement caused sharp pain to shoot from his shoulder, right down through his elbow and into his hand.

David snatched that pouch of morphine out from under the pillow just a hair's breadth ahead of his patient.

But Jack didn't stop there; he continued to come and would have had David up against the bars, except that Rick was already between them.

The deputy grabbed hold of Jack's shirt and pushed him backward, across the cell. With an arm across the prisoner's chest, the deputy pinned him against the bars like a beetle on a display board.

Jack fought against him, then realizing the futility of the attempt, sighed and raised his hands in surrender.

Rick didn't release him; he kept him pinned against the bars, while he sent an enquiring glance to the doctor.

"That's all right, Deputy Layton. Thank you," David told him. "You can let him go. I expect he'll be fine now."

"Okay, Doc," Rick released his hold, "but I'll be in the office, so you give a shout if he tries anything. I'll hear you."

"Yes, I will. Here, better take this out with you," David handed the pouch to Rick.

The deputy took it, and with a warning look to Jack, left the cell.

David and Jack sent accusing glares to one another.

"Do you really think I'm a fool, Jack?" David asked him. "Did you really think I wouldn't check with Dr. Taff, to see what medications he's had you on?"

"What difference does it make?" Jack snarled as he cradled his throbbing shoulder. "According to popular opinion, I'm a dead man, anyway."

David sighed and looked down at his hands. "Tell you what, if the judge sentences you to hang, then I'll give you all the morphine you want. How's that?"

"Yeah, thanks a lot, David. You're a real friend!"

"Yes, I am," David answered, looking Jack in the eye. "You'd realize this if your dependency on that drug didn't have you running scared."

"I'm not dependent on it."

David's lip twitched. "You lied to me."

"I didn't—"

"You did!" David insisted. "You deliberately avoided telling me you were still taking it, when you knew I wanted you off it. In my book, that's lying."

Jack started to lose his bluster. He pushed off the bars and returned to the bunk. "I don't see the harm in it."

"No, you wouldn't," David softened his tone. "The drug itself is making you complacent and causing you to lower your defenses. You don't need it anymore, Jack, but your body is demanding it anyway, and your brain is telling you that it's all right. But I'm telling you it's not, and I'm asking you to trust me."

"I need it ta sleep," Jack insisted. "How else am I supposed ta get through this night?"

"I'll give you some laudanum."

"Laudanum doesn't help."

"Give it a chance!"

Silence ensued while the friends got over being mad at each other.

"Well," David began, "I'm hungry, and since I don't intend to eat alone, how about I ask Rick to bring a couple of meals over here from the café?"

"If you don't wanna eat alone, why don't you track down Cameron and the girls? I'm sure they would appreciate your company."

David understood where his friend's moodiness came from and tried to be sympathetic.

"Don't you want company during this time, Jack?"

"Yeah," Jack snapped back at him, "but he's not here, is he?"

David hung his head. "I know I'm a sorry substitute for your uncle, but I'm not leaving you alone tonight."

***

It ended up being a tough night for everyone in the jailhouse.

There were the two deputies, Larry and Chuck, putting in the night shift, but Rick opted to stay as well and tried sleeping on the cot in the back office. He woke up every hour or so and made a trip to the cell block to make sure the doctor was still alive.

Jack spent the evening pacing the cell and cursing, unable to relax, or even think about sleeping.

David sat on the floor, leaning against the bars, and propped up with some pillows. He sat there quietly and, with a grain of salt, accepted every form of verbal abuse his patient chose to throw at him.

"You're a mean-spirited man, David."

"So my wife tells me."

"You have no compassion for what other people go through, that's for sure."

"Yup. Totally oblivious."

"That's why you became a doctor, ain't it? So you could keep people under your thumb. Be in control. You like inflicting pain, don't ya? God knows, you keep hurtin' me."

"You certainly have me figured out."

By midnight, the verbal abuse eased off, and the pacing quieted down. By 1:00 a.m., Jack had settled on his bunk, and the two men sat in companionable silence. By 2:00 a.m., Rick came to the cell for the umpteenth time, looking bleary-eyed and disheveled.

"Finally," he mumbled. "Is he actually asleep?"

"Yes, I think so," David whispered. "I was beginning to think he would never shut up."

"You goin' back to the hotel?" Rick asked him.

"No," David answered with a sigh, "if you could open this other cell, I'll sleep on the cot in there. I don't want to leave him alone."

"Okay Doc, whatever works."

And that's how Taggard found them at 7:00 a.m., when he brought in the morning coffee; two friends, sound asleep, in adjacent cell.

***

"All rise. The Honorable Judge John Lacey presiding."

"All right, Mr. Kiefer. I trust you slept well. I also remind you; you are still under oath."

"Yes, Your Honor."

"Mr. Granger, do you have any further questions for this witness?"

"Yes, I do, Your Honor," Mr. Granger said, and he approached the stand. "Mr. Kiefer, we arrived at the point where you and your uncle joined up again. Did you ever tell him what transpired while you were separated?"

"No."

"Why not? Since those men were likely the same ones who attacked his home, I should think he would be pleased."

"I didn't tell him, 'cause I didn't want ta put that guilt and responsibility onta his shoulders. I'm the one who did it; no reason he should have ta carry the blame, too. I was also ashamed of it. I knew he wouldn't approve, and I, well, I couldn't bring myself ta tell 'im."

"I take it, Mr. Nash is against violence?"

"Well yeah. I thought that was obvious, considerin' our history."

"Of course, Mr. Kiefer," Mr. Granger explained. "I'm only trying to establish that the non-violent tendencies of your criminal careers were intentional, not accidental."

"Oh," Jack nodded. "Yeah. Leon was adamant with the members of the gang, there was ta be no killin'. Even if they were threatened—never shoot ta kill."

"That is certainly to his credit," Mr. Granger commented. "So, obviously Mr. Nash eventually took over leadership of the Elk Mountain Gang. Were there any grumblings about that from the other members, considering that Mr. Nash was still quite young, and relatively new to the organization? Obviously, he had jumped the queue—so to speak."

"Yeah, there was some. Gus Shaffer had been second-in-command until Leon came in and took over that position. When the leader, Cortez, disappeared, Leon kinda naturally stepped into the leadership role. Gus weren't too happy about that."

"Yes, I can imagine," Mr. Granger admitted. "Was there much threat of an up-rising from the other members?"

"Mr. Granger," Judge Lacey intervened, "As has been repeatedly pointed out; Mr. Nash has already stood trial. How does his position in the gang pertain to these proceedings?"

"I'm attempting to establish the timeline, Your Honor. How relationships within the group may have affected Mr. Kiefer's decisions."

The judge sighed. "Fine, Mr. Granger. But please get to the point."

"Yes sir." Granger returned his attention to his client. "Is this why you and your partner left the gang?"

"No. Gus didn't have much back up. The other gang members recognized Leon's intelligence and leadership qualities, and the gang prospered with 'im in charge. If Gus did start ta grumble too much, well, I had a reputation by then, and it didn't take much ta get 'im ta back off."

"Things were going well, I take it?"

"Yeah, they were."

"Then what did cause you to get out of the business?"

"Well, even though we were doin' good, we kinda figured our time was runnin' out. It weren't exactly a healthy lifestyle. Then Taggard switched sides, and though Leon felt betrayed by that at first, he come around ta thinkin' maybe Taggard had the right of it. Still, it took a particularly bad day before we seriously considered it."

"And this 'bad day' was after Sheriff Murphy had approached you with the governor's offer?"

"Yeah."

"But now, five years later, you have yet to be granted those pardons. Your partner is in prison, and you stand accused before this court. Why do you think that is, Mr. Kiefer?"

Jack sent a glance to Taggard, not sure how much to reveal about a deal that was supposed to be a secret.

Taggard smiled and nodded for him to go ahead. The governor's office wasn't holding up their end of the bargain, so why should they?

"I dunno," Jack admitted. "The deal was, we help the governor out for a year, then we'd get our pardons."

"A year?"

"Yeah."

"But it's been five, and three more governors."

"Yeah, I know."

"And yet, you kept trying for it?"

"It was important to us."

"That is apparent," Mr. Granger conceded. "So, what was it then, that led you to the killing of Quincy Bartlett? It must have been a serious offense on his part, considering your desire for those pardons, and your regret over the previous incident."

"Yeah, it was," Jack's jaw tightened at the memory of what had transpired. "After Taggard left the gang, Cortez brought in a couple a new members. One of 'em was Quincy Bartlett. He was an amiable fella, and everybody liked 'im. Everyone but me and Leon, we had our reservations."

"Why is that?"

"People accuse me a bein' a dangerous gunman," Jack sighed, shaking his head at the memory, "but Bartlett outshone me in that role. He was fast—real fast, and he was a killer in the truest sense of the word."

"Why would your boss allow him into the gang, if he was so dangerous?" Mr. Granger asked.

"Cause he was good at what he did," Jack said. "He had that look about 'im, and he could cow people into submittin' with just a glance. He got the job done."

"But Mr. Cortez had you for that. Why would he need a second gunman?"

"I was young, Mr. Granger; no more'n a lad. Cortez felt that an older man would have more of an effect."

"Of course," Mr. Granger agreed. "So, what went wrong?"

"One of our jobs went bad." Another sigh from Jack as he went back to that time. "It was a big one, too; thirty thousand dollars. Cortez and Bartlett took the money and headed off in one direction. The rest of us baited the posse ta lead 'em in the other direction. It kinda worked. Unfortunately, the posse also split up.

"All of us eventually got clear and met back up again at the hideout, but things had gotten hot for Cortez and Bartlett, and they hid the money, thinkin' they were gonna get caught.

"We couldn't go back and get it right away, as we needed ta give the law time ta get tired of watchin' us. That money stayed hid for about a month.

"Then, Cortez disappeared. We all got kinda suspicious, and Leon and Bartlett went to retrieve the money, hopin' that it would still be there. It weren't. We all came to the obvious conclusion that Cortez had betrayed us. That he'd gone back to the hidin' place, taken the money and disappeared.

"Leon took over as leader, and Bartlett was fine with that. He didn't have any interest in bein' the boss.

"The weather started turnin' cold, and some of the fellas, Bartlett included, decided to go winter down in Arizona, or New Mexico. That weren't unusual; it's a good place ta winter, if'n ya got no place else, but lots of the fellas had connections down south, so the population in Elk Mountain tended ta thin out when the snows were due. It was a good thing, 'cause that $30,000 was supposed ta be what we would live on through the dark months, so the fewer mouths there was ta feed, the better. Even at that, Leon had ta win a few hands at poker, and pull a couple a cons in order ta make sure we had enough ta eat. There was a lot of resentment toward Cortez that winter."

"Understandably," Mr. Granger agreed. "Mr. Cortez and the money were never found?"

"Yeah, they got found," Jack told him. "Come spring, a couple 'a the boys were clearin' away some winter fall that was cloggin' up the creek, and they come across Cortez's body. It weren't him that took the money after all. It was Bartlett.

"We figured he killed Cortez, then moved the money to a new hidin' place. Nobody knew he'd left the hideout, but he musta done. He followed Cortez and killed 'im, then snuck back into the bunkhouse, with none the wiser.

"He waited 'till the time was right, when it wouldn't appear unusual for him ta be leavin'. He retrieved the money and disappeared. None of us had any idea it was him 'til we found Cortez's body, then it all come together."

"I see. So, you and your partner decided to track him down?"

Jack shook his head. "No. The trail was cold by then. We had no idea where ta start lookin' for 'im. We had ta let it go. That is until Leon and me come upon 'im in Brown Creek, livin' high off the hog, with the gang's $30,000."

Jack frowned, his renewed anger causing his brow to crease, and his lips tighten.

"I was ready ta call 'im out for what he'd done to Cortez, but Leon talked me out of it. He gave all the right reasons about how we was tryin' so hard for the pardons, and it weren't worth riskin' our chance for a good life. It was past and done, so we oughta just let it go. Besides, Bartlett was fast, real fast. I think Leon was afraid I wouldn't be able ta beat 'im. And there'd be no walkin' away from it; Bartlett would go for the kill. So, I let Leon talk me outta it.

"But Bartlett had different ideas. We was outside, gettin' the horses ready ta leave, when Bartlett showed up, lookin' for a fight. He called me out, and he wasn't gonna let it go. He made his move first, but it turns out, I was faster."

"Come spring, a couple 'a the boys were clearin' away some winter fall that was cloggin' up the creek, and they come across Cortez's body. It weren't him that took the money after all. It was Bartlett.

"You killed him," Mr. Granger stated.

"Yeah. The sheriff witnessed it. He already knew what sort a man, Bartlett was, and he saw that Bartlett had started it. He pulled his gun first, so as far as the sheriff was concerned, it weren't murder. We never got any of the money back, and I had one more killin' ta deal with."

"All right, Mr. Kiefer. Thank you. I have no more questions."

Jack sighed. Here it was, barely midmorning, and he was already exhausted. His shoulder ached, and he shifted, trying to stretch the muscle and ease the pain. It didn't help, and he wished this whole thing could be over and done with one way or another. Then he found himself face to face with Mr. DeFord, and he knew that the worst was yet to come.

"Mr. Kiefer," Mr. DeFord addressed the defendant, "that's quite an interesting story. Just out of curiosity, has anyone ever beaten you to the draw? Anyone?"

"Yeah, one fella did," Jack admitted. "A Wells Fargo detective outdrew me once, about five years ago."

"Really?" DeFord exclaimed. "A Wells Fargo detective?"

"Yeah."

"One up for our side, then," DeFord commented. "Tell me, Mr. Kiefer, if a Wells Fargo detective outdrew you and had you in his sights, why didn't he arrest you? Or better yet, shoot you down where you stood?"

"Objection!" Mr. Granger came to his feet. "Mr. DeFord is deliberately baiting the defendant."

"Mr. DeFord," Judge Lacey agreed, "A little less drama, if you please."

"Apologies, Your Honor. I will rephrase the question. Why did this detective not arrest you, Mr. Kiefer?"

"He didn't know who I was," Jack explained. "It was a minor dispute, and we settled it."

"Hmm." Mr. DeFord cocked a brow. "How unfortunate, especially for Mr. Bartlett, that the only person to succeed in outdrawing you was so ill-informed, he didn't realize who it was he had in his sights. It might have saved us all a lot of bother."

Judge Lacey sighed loud enough for those near the bench to hear him. "Mr. DeFord, you are stepping over the line. Again. Please stay on track."

"Yes, Your Honor. My apologies. Mr. Kiefer, you stated that you and your partner took over leadership of the gang. Obviously, Mr. Nash was the brains. What was your role in that partnership?"

"Security," Jack said. "I decided who we let into the gang, and it was up ta me ta keep 'em in line."

"With your gun."

"Well—yeah. My gun, and then my reputation, were tools of my job. I used them whenever I needed ta keep order. I rarely had ta actually shoot anyone."

"How admirable of you," Mr. DeFord commented. "Still though, how many times have you pulled and aimed your weapon at another man?"

"Objection," Mr. Granger spoke up though he didn't bother to stand this time. "This question is ridiculous. How could Mr. Kiefer possibly know how many times he has pulled his gun over the last fifteen years? This question only serves to muddy the facts."

"Sustained," Judge Lacey stated. "Get to the point, Mr. DeFord."

"Let me rephrase the question. You state that you rarely had to shoot anyone. All I ask is that you be more specific. How many times, in the course of 'doing your job', did you shoot another person?"

Jack shook his head. "I'm sorry, Mr. DeFord, I can't really say. Usually, I'd outdraw my opponent so easy they wouldn't have cleared their holster. Seein' my gun pointed at 'em would end the dispute, then and there."

"So, if I may confirm, you have only killed twice in your life. One in self-defense, the other still not determined. Is this correct?"

Mr. Granger groaned, coming to his feet. "Objection!"

"No, it ain't." The admission was out of Jack's mouth before the defense attorney could stop him.

Taggard closed his eyes, shaking his head. This was not going well.

Mr. Granger pounded the table in front of him. "Objection!" he called out over the loud mumbling that rumbled throughout the spectators. "Your Honor, I request a recess."

"Sustained." Judge Lacey's tone was long-suffering. "Mr. Granger, you have an hour to advise your client, then I want both you and Mr. DeFord in my chambers. Again! Court will reconvene at 1:00 p.m."

***

"I can't believe this." Mr. Granger paced the aisle while Jack leaned against the bars of his cell. "You do have a death wish, don't you?"

"Better than goin' ta prison."

Granger stopped; his whole demeanor ready to explode.

"Again, I strongly recommend that we request a new trial. Give me some time, for Christ's sake. I'm trying to keep you alive. Don't you understand that?"

"Yeah, I understand it," Jack snapped back, "but there ain't no point. Mrs. Stanton's father was murder. There ain't no escapin' it. I don't wanna meet my maker carryin' the others." His voice rose with his own frustration. "And like you already pointed out, there ain't nobody here layin' those charges against me. I ain't on trial for 'em. If I chose to own up to 'em, then that's on me. I just want this over with! Can't you understand that?"

"I understand that you have openly admitted to two more homicides. Have you decided that Mr. Wissen and Mr. Bartlett aren't bad enough so you're throwing in the other two just to make sure? I thought we had agreed to focus only on the two you have actually been accused of."

"But DeFord asked me, point blank. I weren't gonna lie."

"I put in an abjection to stop that line of questioning. Why did you push through me?" Granger started pacing again, his hands attacking the hair on his head. "My objection was sustained; you would not have had to answer that question."

"But it was already out there," Jack reasoned. "People, includin' my friends, woulda been left wonderin' why I didn't answer. I'm sick and tired of hidin'. I ain't on trial for them other two. If I'm gonna be hanged, it'll be for Wissen, not them."

"But Mr. DeFord can still use that information against you. Your open admission is all he needs to discredit you."

"The way I see it, I've already done that to myself."

Granger slumped. "How can I help someone so determined to stick his own head in a noose?"

His only answer was silence.

***

Judge Lacey confronted his two lawyers. "Well, here we are again, gentlemen." He focused on Mr. Granger. "Is your client determined to sabotage his own defense?"

"My client only wishes to clear his conscience, Your Honor."

"And he is certainly doing a fine job of it." The judge turned to Mr. DeFord. "If the defendant wishes for an accounting of past deeds before this court and Almighty God, then I won't stand in his way. But keep in mind, Mr. DeFord, no one has brought forth these charges, and he is not on trial for them. View it as privileged information."

"Of course, Your Honor."

Judge Lacey narrowed his eyes as the prosecutor, sensing the duplicity in his assurance. "Mr. DeFord, excuse us."

DeFord glanced at Mr. Granger, then back at the judge.

He nodded acquiescence. "Of course, Your Honor."

Once the door closed on Mr. DeFord, Judge Lacey turned to Mr. Granger.

"I realize you are new to the bar, Mr. Granger, and this has been a most challenging trial. Are you sure this is the route you wish to take?"

"No, Your Honor, I am not. But my client is. He can be a most obstinate man and he will not budge."

Judge Lacey sighed. "Fine, we will continue. But stay on your toes, Mr. Granger. Mr. DeFord is going for blood, as he should. And I must admit, he has a strong case. Keep your wits about you."

"Yes sir."

***

Mr. DeFord approached the defendant. "That was quite an announcement you made right before recess, Mr. Kiefer. Would you like to elaborate?"

Jack swallowed, feeling the bile wanting to rise. "Yeah. There were two others besides Wissen and Bartlett."

An undertone of murmurs invaded the courtroom, but Mrs. Stanton's remark soared above them.

"I knew it! He's a murderer. He's admitting it!"

The gavel struck. "Mrs. Stanton! My insistence that you remain in town does not necessarily include this courtroom. You have been removed once for speaking out of line. Do it again, and you'll be out for the duration. Mr. DeFord, continue."

Mr. DeFord turned his attention back to the defendant. "Four?" The lawyer feigned surprise. "You've killed four men?"

"Yeah." Jack looked to the back of the courtroom and the heartbreak in the girls' eyes made him feel sick.

206

"We already know about two," Mr. DeFord pointed out. "Please, Mr. Kiefer, bring us up to date on the others."

"Objection," Mr. Granger was prepared for this eventuality. "My client does not stand accused of any murders other than Mr. Wissen and, possibly, Mr. Bartlett. I insist the prosecutor focus on these two charges only."

"Overruled. The defendant himself brought this information to the court's knowledge. Though he has not been charged, this information cannot be ignored. But having stated this, Mr. DeFord, what is your intention here?"

"I am merely attempting to establish a pattern, Your Honor. Mr. Kiefer is accused of having a violent temper and is obviously capable of murder—"

"Objection!"

"Sustained." Judge Lacey pointed his gavel at the prosecuting attorney. "The defendant has not been found guilty of any charges at this point, Mr. DeFord. If the defendant is willing to discuss these matters, then so be it, but he will not be badgered. Do you understand?"

"Yes, Your Honor." Mr. DeFord turned away from the judge and sent Jack Kiefer a look of hostile determination. He knew the defendant was guilty of all charges against him, and he was determined to bring the defense to its knees.

But when he spoke again, all hostility was gone to be replaced by subtle distain.

"Well then, since we are still waiting for non-existent evidence in the Wissen case, we shall leave that until later." Mr. DeFord smiled, but not one intended to put the defendant at his ease. "We also have your admission of two other incidences where a life was ended. With the court's permission," and he nodded to the judge, "may we have some enlightenment on how those came about?"

Judge Lacey cocked a brow at Mr. Granger.

The defense attorney sighed, but conceded.

Jack sighed, collecting his thoughts on these issues for the second time.

"The first was an accident," Jack explained. "I was young, no more n sixteen. I was fast, but I weren't accurate. This fella couldn't a been much older n me. He saw that I wore my gun tied down, so he figured he'd make a show in front a his friends. He started pushin' for a fight. He weren't very fast. I beat 'im easy and was tryin' ta scare 'im off, but

I missed and got him in the gut. He died a few hours later."

"What happened after that?"

"I threw up."

Mr. DeFord sniffed. "Yes. Then what happened?"

"I left town. The sheriff, he knew them boys, and knew they were troublemakers. He didn't blame me for it. Said that kid probably had it comin'. But his friends were out ta get me, so I high-tailed it outta there."

"How convenient that the local law always seemed to be around to witness these killings. And it's never your fault." Mr. DeFord shook his head. "What a shame we don't have any of these gentlemen here in court today."

Mr. Granger silently agreed with this statement.

Jack made no response; he was learning how to recognize rhetoric when he heard it.

"So, that was the first," Mr. DeFord continued. "What about the second one?"

"The fella I run down, was a two-bit outlaw named Clyde Ross. He was runnin' with a band a thieves down Arizona way. Once he figured out who I was, he came at me with a two by four, yellin' that he shoulda cut my throat, just like he did my brother's. That was the last thing he said.

"A couple of 'em were already dead. Apparently, one was killed the day of the raids. I assume it was at the Nashs' place. I heard the other was killed in the war."

Jack swallowed the rising bile in his throat. Digging up these memories was proving to be far more difficult without the dose of morphine to calm his nerves. "The third man I killed was Cal Wissen, who was Mrs. Stanton's father. And I'm sorry, Mr. DeFord, but the sheriff weren't around ta witness those ones. Only Wissen's daughter witnessed the last, and I don't think she has any doubt as ta who's ta blame."

Mr. Granger groaned again. His client was trying to get himself hanged. The lawyer was about to call for a recess, to get Mr. Kiefer calmed down, but then the defendant managed to do that himself.

Jack continued, "The fourth was Quincy Bartlett."

"Yes. Here we are back to Mr. Bartlett again," Mr. DeFord observed. "I'm curious, Mr. Kiefer. You claim to have lost your taste for killing after your revenge rampage, choosing instead to slightly wound or intimidate your adversaries into submitting. Yet, you killed Mr. Bartlett. Why didn't you simply wound him and leave it at that?"

"Because Bartlett was a killer," Jack shot back, getting mad again. "I thought that was already clear. Mr. Jaxton told ya about the cowboy Bartlett shot the day before. Leon and me witnessed that shootin', and there was no reason for it. That kid was no gunman, certainly no match for Bartlett's speed, and Bartlett knew that. But he killed 'im anyway. I knew if Bartlett and I squared off, it would be to the death.

"I also knew, if I beat 'im and left 'im wounded, he would come after me. And knowin' then, that I was faster than him, it wouldn't be a straight up gunfight. He'd come at me from behind. He would not let it rest until one of us was dead."

"Did Mr. Bartlett know how fast you were?" Mr. DeFord asked. "Did he realize he was challenging The Great Kansas Kid?"

"Objection. Mr. DeFord is badgering the witness."

"Sustained. I understand where you are going with this, Mr. DeFord, but be careful how you present your case."

"Of course, Your Honor. My apologies." He smiled at Jack. "Was Mr. Bartlett aware of your reputation?"

"A course he knew who I was. We were in the same gang together."

"But, by your own admission, you were a greenhorn at that time. Even the gang leader didn't think you were good enough to be threatening. Did he realize the level of your expertise at the time he challenged you?"

"He suspected I was fast, but he didn't know for sure," Jack admitted. "He knew I had a reputation, but that don't always mean anything."

"Well, even suspecting," Mr. DeFord continued, "that should have been enough to convince him not to challenge you."

"Not necessarily, Mr. DeFord. Nine times outta ten, a reputation will cause a person ta back off. But there's always that one who thinks he's faster and wants the reputation for himself. Mr. Bartlett wanted that reputation."

"Of course. That would be quite a feather in his hat. But you don't know for sure if he respected your reputation, or if he still thought of you as the wet-behind-the-ears youngster who only had a place in the gang because of his uncle's influence. Quincy Bartlett was not aware of whom or what you had become after he left the gang, and then you killed him, well, that could be tantamount to murder, don't you think?"

Jack gritted his teeth, feeling the edge that only morphine could ease.

"It wasn't murder!" he yelled, his fist hitting the arm of the chair. "It was self-defense!"

"Temper, temper, Mr. Kiefer." Mr. DeFord's smile sent a shiver down Jack's back.

Jack took that chill and channeled it through his blue eyes, sending the lawyer a cold stare, but he still had enough wits about him not to send him his deadly one. He knew he had to calm down, or Mr. DeFord was going to back him into a corner he would not be able to get out of. Just like he had done to Leon.

"It seems convenient to me," Mr. DeFord continued, "that the only shooting you will admit was in cold blood is the one where you really cannot deny it. The other three killings were accidental or in self-defense—according to you."

"Objection!" Mr. Granger was on his feet. "The defendant has only been charged with two killings, not four."

"Sustained. Mr. DeFord, keep your questioning relevant to the charges. Since the defendant willingly divulged the nature of the previous two incidents and no charges have yet been laid, he is not required to offer defense for them."

Mr. DeFord again apologized, but it stuck in his craw. He turned back to the defendant; his eyes dark with suppressed frustration. "The second killing, you insist was in self-defense, but since we have no witnesses to verify that, we only have your word this is how it transpired.

"You claim the lawman in Brown Creek supported you in stating it was self-defense, yet, I don't see him here in the courtroom willing to testify. All we have, Mr. Kiefer, is your word."

"That's how it happened," Jack insisted. "Considerin' I have already agreed that the killin' of Cal Wissen was in cold blood, why would I need ta lie about Bartlett?"

"Well, one murder—considering the circumstances surrounding it, might simply warrant you a prison term," DeFord explained. "But two, possibly four? I think you know that four cold-blooded murders cannot so easily be explained away. Four would suggest that you are exactly what certain witnesses here today have accused you of being; a cold-blooded and dangerous killer."

"Objection." Mr. Granger was feeling frazzled. "Again, my client stands accused of two homicides, not four."

"Overruled," Judge Lacey said. "Your client has already admitted to these other incidences. Though not on trial for them, this knowledge cannot be denied. Carry on, Mr. Kiefer."

"Yes, Your Honor." Jack shot over a glace that encompassed both his attorney and Taggard. Then he returned his attention to Mr. DeFord. "You heard Mr. Jaxton's testimony. He described the gunfight between me and Quincy Bartlett. He told you Bartlett drew first. This backs up what I already described as how it happened."

"Yes, it does," Mr. DeFord agreed. "But, as pursuant your own admission, you were aware that, according to the sheriff of that town, whoever drew first was automatically the one at fault. You knew you could not draw first, because then, even if you won, you would be arrested for murder.

"Mr. Jaxton also stated he saw you and Mr. Bartlett in conversation, though he could not hear what you were saying. You, apparently, turned to leave, and it was this action that prompted Mr. Bartlett to draw his weapon.

"Now, this is the question that comes to my mind, Mr. Kiefer: Was it your intention to walk away, or was it a deliberate feint to push Mr. Bartlett into making the first move, thereby absolving you of any guilt?"

Jack hesitated, tying to think of the best way to answer.

"It might not seem like it to a casual observer," Jack explained, "but being the one who walks away after a gunfight, involves subtle strategy and the ability to read your opponent. Bartlett was determined to push that situation to a fight; I simply offered him the opportunity to do so. It was his decision to take it."

"Indeed," Mr. DeFord conceded. "And a fatal decision, at that. I also find your explanation concerning the subtleties in a gunfight, chilling to the bone. In fact, I feel it only serves to support the opinion that you are a calculating and cold-blooded killer, and it is past due for judgment to be brought down upon you."

"Do you think I don't carry the guilt of those deaths with me every day?" Jack demanded. "Even Quincy Bartlett continues to haunt me and will for the rest of my life."

"Well, you can take some comfort in the probability that they won't be haunting you for much longer," Mr. DeFord sighed and looked to the judge. "I have no more questions for Mr. Kiefer, Your Honor."

"Thank you, Mr. DeFord. Mr. Kiefer, you may step down."

Oh finally! was all Jack thought as he pushed himself to his feet and returned to his seat. He could feel the tension in the air, and the look he exchanged with Taggard was not encouraging.

"Gentlemen," the judge continued, "it is late in the day. Court will recess and reconvene at 9:00 a.m. tomorrow. Please have your closing statements prepared.

CHAPTER TWELVE
THE VERDICT

Taggard, will you please talk to me? You've hardly sent two sentences my way in just as many days."

Taggard had secured Jack in his cell and was turning to leave, when Jack's heartfelt request stopped him in his tracks. Taggard sighed, and tried, unsuccessfully, to relax his tense stance.

"I ain't mad at ya," Taggard finally responded. "I'm just havin' a hard time adjustin' ta all this." He hesitated, furrowing his brow, then continued with some irritation. "No. Actually, I am mad at ya. You keep quiet about all this for fifteen years and then decide to confess in the middle of a courtroom? What the hell were you thinkin'?"

Jack shot up his hands in frustration. "I know. I'm sorry. But they already had me for Bartlett and Wissen. I figured if I was gonna hang for them, I may as well put the other two ta rest."

"Jack, you don't know it's gonna go that way," Taggard softened his tone. "You just made it appear a whole lot worse by admittin' to the other two, that's all. And I wish you'd a told me about it."

"I didn't even tell Leon," Jack pointed out. "I was just . . . I'll never forget that little girl lookin' at me like that. Knowin' what I had just done to her, what I had just taken from her. I guess, I thought if I didn't talk about it, it would go away, that guilt. But it never did. I shouldn 'a done it, Taggard. For her sake, not his. He weren't even armed, and I shot him down in cold blood right in front of her. If the law decides I should be hanged for it, well, then maybe that's right."

"No, Jack. It ain't right," Taggard said. "There were extenuatin' circumstances with all of 'em, even Wissen. You were young and had witnessed a terrible thing. I can't even begin to imagine what that musta been like. But I know it ate at ya and drove ya ta do things ya never would have dreamt of doin', otherwise. You're not a cold-blooded killer, Jack. I know that, and so does Leon."

The block door opened, and Steven Granger came in.

Taggard and Jack straightened up from the bars and addressed the lawyer.

"You need ta talk to your client?" Taggard asked, surprised. "I thought you were workin' on your closing statement."

"No time," Granger announced. "Myself and Mr. DeFord have just come from Judge Lacey's chambers. There has been another surprise development, Mr. Kiefer, and court will reconvene in fifteen minutes."

Taggard and Jack exchanged a snap glance, then Taggard looked at the lawyer. "The rifle couldn't have shown up already. Or was it found right away and the law down there simply sent word?"

Mr. Granger cocked a brow. "No. The rifle has not been found and now, it wouldn't likely do us any good, anyway."

***

In the courtroom, everyone sat in strained anticipation of what the verdict was going to be. The short recess had taken everyone by surprise and some actually packed their half-eaten sandwiches back into the courtroom with them. No one wanted to miss this.

The court was called to order, and everyone waited.

"I apologize to the jury for calling you back into session so quickly," Judge Lacey stated, "and I apologize to this court for apparently wasting your time." He sent a disapproving look to the defendant. "Jackson Benjamin Kiefer, please stand."

Aww no, what's going on? Jack was visibly shaking. He knew all eyes were upon him as he pushed himself to his feet. He kept a hand touching the table in front of him, just for added security. His knees felt as though they were going to give out beneath him.

"It would seem, Mr. Kiefer, that Governor Warren has allowed public opinion to addle his brains," Judge Lacey announced. "Apparently, the law-abiding citizens of this territory are going to have to be satisfied with Mr. Nash paying the debt you both owe. Be thankful, Mr. Kiefer, for the 'lucky' twist of fate that brought your partner, and not you, to trial first, because without the rifle to show just cause, you were looking at murder. As it stands, Governor Warren has seen fit to grant you your pardon."

The courtroom erupted into turmoil The noise was deafening, from whoops and clapping of approval and relief, to boos and hisses, and yells of anger, accompanied by the pounding of fists on wood, demanding justice.

Jack Kiefer just about fell over. He couldn't believe he had heard right. After all this time, it was just to be handed over to him in such a volatile and conflicted atmosphere as this? It was not how he had imagined it.

The judge's gavel worked overtime to bring the courtroom to order.

"Court is not adjourned, ladies and gentlemen! Quiet down and please return to your seats."

It took a few moments for the gathering to heed the judge's order, but gradually everyone complied, and the courtroom quieted.

"The governor's office is still in the process of getting the paperwork in order," the judge continued. "Mr. Granger, as soon as I hear word that they are ready, I will inform you, then you and your client will meet with the governor at that time to get them signed. You will also need a witness, Mr. Kiefer, make sure that person accompanies you.

"I also say to you, Mr. Kiefer, in my opinion the outcome of this trial is a disgrace. I can only hope you will realize the opportunity that has been handed to you, and that you will not throw it away. But I warn you; if you ever stand before me in this court of law again, even for so much as expectorating in public, I will make sure the full force of the law, and the punishment you deserve will be forthcoming—do you understand?"

"Yes, Your Honor," Jack answered quietly, wondering how it was he was still on his feet.

"This court stands adjourned!"

BANG!

Again, there was an eruption of voices, and everyone was on the move at once.

Jack found himself amidst wild activity as people he knew, and didn't know, bombarded him with handshakes and slaps on the back.

He heard Josephine coming, "Jack! Oh, Jack." Then, there she was, with her arms wrapped around his neck and yet another very affectionate kiss planted upon his lips.

This time, he didn't even try to push her off, and he wrapped his arms around her slim waist and returned the kiss, wholeheartedly. This was accompanied by more back slaps and loud "whoops" from the numerous males in attendance.

If Jack had thought to look up, he would have been met by one, very horrified look coming from another young lady. Penelope Marsham had rushed forward to congratulate her friend when she was brought up short by someone else beating her to it.

Who is that woman kissing my Mathew with such . . . well . . . such . . . affection? And why is Mathew returning it with such . . . well . . . returning it?

Poor Penny stood with her mouth open, not sure what to do or even where to look. Fortunately, her sister was not deterred by the usurper, and she did not hesitate to cut in and present Jack with her own congratulatory hug.

Following Caroline's example, Penny came forward, and the two young ladies ended up, one under each arm.

Josey backed off, not at all offended.

Then, Jack felt someone touch him on the shoulder. He turned to find himself face to face with Rick.

"Deputy," Jack greeted him.

"No," Rick corrected him, "just Richard Layton. It's time I got back to my ranch. If you ever need a job—"

"As a ranch hand?" Jack cocked a brow.

Rick smiled. "Yeah, I know."

Rick held out his right hand and Jack, unwrapping his arm from around Caroline's shoulder, grasped it.

"Goodbye, Mr. Jackson Kiefer. And good luck to you."

Jack smiled. "Thanks. Goodbye, Mister Layton."

Rick turned and walked down the aisle toward the exit, removing what appeared to be his deputy's badge as he went.

Steven Granger took the opportunity to nip in and have a quick word with his client.

"That certainly ended a lot better than I thought it would," the lawyer understated. "I know you and your friends will want to celebrate, but I suggest you don't go far or drink too much. You will need to be sober to sign those pardon papers. It shouldn't be too long before the governor has them ready for us."

"Yeah, a course," Jack agreed. "I don't think we'll be goin' far. And Mr. Granger, thank you. For everything."

"You're welcome, Mr. Kiefer," he responded with a smile. "I'll

216

come and join you soon."

He turned to leave, and Caroline quietly slipped away from Jack and, following Steven to the exit, caught up with him and slipped her hand in his. He smiled at her, and they left the courthouse together.

Jack smirked and did a quick scan of the room, looking for Cameron. There he was, talking to Taggard and David. Cameron hadn't noticed his eldest daughter slipping away. There were going to be fireworks later.

Jack looked down at the young lady who was still under his left shoulder. Her arms were wrapped, contentedly, around his waist. He was met with such a warm and congratulatory smile from his young friend that he couldn't help but smile back at her.

Then he almost ended up going headlong into the floorboards. Max, who had taken a little longer than everyone else to arrive at the front, gave Jack such a wallop on the back it set his teeth to chattering.

"What did I tell ya?" Max growled. "The law wouldn't dare hang ya, not with me in town. I shoulda been here for Peter. But that's not over yet, dammit."

"Hey, Max," Jack greeted him, once he got his wind back. "Good to see ya. And, thanks, for comin'.'"

"Anything for our little family," Max insisted. "And don't you worry about Peter. We'll handle that business, no matter how long it takes."

"Oh, Mr. Coburn, you are such a bear," Josephine stated in a teasing manner.

Max's face cracked into a smile. "Well, thank you Miss Jansen," he tipped his hat. "Would you care to join me for some refreshment?"

"Why, Mr. Coburn, how kind of you to offer," Josey accepted with a smile, and a twinkle to Jack.

"Now, Max, you be careful," Jack called after them. "Remember, you're a married man."

"Penny," Cameron's voice sounded close behind them. "Where's your sister?"

"I don't know, Papa."

Cameron looked around with furrowed brow. The courtroom had emptied out now, but no Caroline in sight. Where in tarnation had that girl gotten to now? Keeping track of his two young ladies was like trying to keep two squirrels on a leash, and it was starting to wear on his nerves.

"Come, and help me look for her," Cameron instructed his younger daughter.

Penelope slumped in disappointment. She was content to stay where she was.

"You go on, Penny," Jack told her. "I'm sure I'll be seein' ya at supper. And I need ta talk ta Sheriff Murphy for a bit."

She smiled up at him. "Okay, Mathew. I'm so glad everything worked out."

"Yeah, me too."

Jack approached his two friends, feeling apprehensive. He knew all this had been hard on them both, and he hadn't been so far gone last night that he didn't remember some of the things he had said to David. But as he joined them, both men turned to him with smiles and congratulatory handshakes.

"Well Jack, has it sunk in yet?" Taggard asked him.

Jack sighed and shook his head. "No, not really. For one thing, this ain't the way it was supposed ta be. Leon should be part a this. I never would a made it this far without 'im."

"I know," Taggard said. "We were just discussin' that very thing with Mr. Marsham. We're not gonna stop in our efforts ta get Leon pardoned. In the words of your friend, Max Coburn; this ain't over yet."

"Yeah," Jack agreed. "Well, what now? I sure ain't goin' back ta that jail cell."

Taggard and David both smiled.

"No," Taggard agreed. "We'll get you a room at the hotel. Then you can have a bath and a shave, and some clean clothes." The three men headed for the exit. "You'd probably appreciate a beer too, huh? And I must admit, the ladies at the saloon are all very pretty."

"Uh huh," Jack commented. Then, "David?"

"Yes?"

"What's expectorate mean?"

***

Jack couldn't believe how nervous he was during the ride to the governor's office. After the events of the two previous days, he was certain nothing would ever faze him again. He was wrong.

Man, you'd think they were takin' me on my last ride to the gallows instead a my first ride ta freedom!

218

Taggard maneuvered the horse and buggy to the hitching post at the main building. A liveryman came out of nowhere to hold the animal's head, while Taggard, Steven and Jack stepped out. Leaving the horse and buggy in the capable hands of the employee, the group went up the steps and entered through the impressive front doors.

The receiving hall was luxurious, with high ceilings and beautiful hardwood floors adorned with plush carpeting.

Jack gazed at the row of large portrait paintings hanging on the walls, each one showing the stern, almost accusing gaze of previous governors during their tenure and residence. The larger portrait at the end of the room showed an equally impressive President Cleveland scrutinizing all who entered.

Jack felt unnerved, like all these haughty men were judging him and finding him wanting. Then his eye caught the glitter of gold pen holders and other items of such value as to make any thief tremble with temptation. Jack was no exception. He found himself pondering the value of the items that were within easy reach, and calculating the distance from the front door to the nearest alternate escape route. He brought himself back to the present with the reminder that they weren't doing that anymore.

The visitors were met by another lackey who showed them the way into a spacious waiting room that was even more posh than the receiving hall. One noticeable difference was this room included numerous cushy chairs that silently enticed the visitors to sit and relax, and not worry about how much time they were being forced to wait for their appointment with the governor.

As it turned out, the three men did not have to wait. They didn't have a chance to indulge in the fine upholstery before the secretary, Mr. Higgins, entered from another doorway and summoned them to the main office.

Jack felt uncomfortable, as he often did when he found himself in an atmosphere of obvious wealth and power. Leon could always fit into this type of environment as though he had been born to it. But not Jack; it made him feel vulnerable and off-balance. The governor's office was no exception.

The smell of fine wood and the feel of carpeting, like velvet spring grass under his feet, as well as impressive bookcases and more paintings, added to Jack's feeling of uneasiness. The large oak desk and the previously elusive Governor Warren stepping forward to shake their hands, combined to make Jack feel insignificant.

"Sheriff Murphy, how very good to see you again," Governor Warren lied through his teeth. He shook hands with Taggard, then turned to the other men. "You must be Mr. Granger, Mr. Kiefer's attorney."

"Yes sir," Granger answered, shaking his hand. "Pleasure to meet you, Governor."

"And now, the very elusive Kansas Kid, himself," Governor Warren said, as he offered his hand to the ex-outlaw. "What a pleasure to finally meet you."

"Ah, thank you, Your Honor," Jack answered, feeling like he'd already said the wrong thing. He thought it odd the governor described him in the same way, Jack had been thinking about the governor. Elusive.

"Please gentlemen, be seated," the governor offered. The four men took chairs around the desk and prepared to get down to the business at hand. "Higgins! Brandy, all around."

"Yes sir."

"Well, gentlemen," Governor Warren began, while Higgins turned to the small bar to prepare the drinks. "I have the papers right here and ready to sign. If you wish to look them over, Mr. Granger, I can give you a few moments to do this."

Higgins placed the brandy snifters on a tray and discreetly made the rounds, offering them to the visitors before placing the fourth on the desk in front of his boss. Setting the tray aside, he picked up the documents and handed them to Mr. Granger.

The lawyer accepted them. He placed his brandy on the small side table and began to scrutinize the fine print.

"Ah, Your Honor," Jack began, pushing his way past his nervousness, "what about my partner, Napoleon Nash?"

Mr. Granger paused in his reading, not sure if now was the right time to bring this up. But his client was not waiting for approval from him.

"What about him?" Governor Warren inquired.

"The pardons were supposed ta include him as well," Jack reminded the honorable gentleman.

"Mr. Nash had his trial and was convicted. You were the only one to receive a pardon. That's the end of it."

"No, it ain't."

"Mr. Kiefer . . ." Granger warned him.

Taggard sent his friend a cautious look, but Jack ignored them both.

"How can that be the end of it? Leon deserves this more n I do."

Mr. Granger was preparing to say more to his client, but the governor raised his hand to stop him. He turned to his secretary.

"Mr. Higgins."

"Yes sir."

"Please bring in the rest of the paperwork associated with this matter."

"I'll need help with that, sir."

"Use as much help as you need."

"Yes sir."

The four men waited while Mr. Higgins left to complete his errand.

Mr. Granger returned to studying the pardon document, but with the rising stress level in the office, it was hard to concentrate.

Fortunately, Higgins was not gone long. He, with two assistants, entered the office and waddled to the desk, lugging large, bulging, mail sacks, filled to the brim with correspondence. The three men plopped the large bags on the carpet and opened them, just enough to reveal a variety of shapes, sizes and colors of envelopes, telegrams, and parcels, which began to spill onto the floor.

"This, gentlemen," Governor Warren announced in irritation, "is just a sampling of the mail that has been inundating my office for the past month. These are the ones we haven't had time to open and read yet! We don't have to open them to know what they say; they're all the same. People insisting this Office honor the supposed deal which was made with Napoleon Nash and Jack Kiefer. I even had some boisterous rancher from Texas—Texas, of all places—barge in here like he owned the place, demanding I stop your trial and pardon Napoleon Nash, right this instant, while expostulating about "what good boys they are—good boys—both of 'em!" The man was relentless."

Taggard and Granger covered their mouths to hide their amusement.

Jack sent the governor an exasperated look that this demand had not been met.

Governor Warren answered his silent inquiry.

"The problem, Mr. Kiefer, is there are almost as many letters and telegrams demanding I allow justice to take place. The Kansas Kid must face whatever judgment is coming to him, and Napoleon Nash better stay right where he is. Not to mention, I had representatives from the Railroad Commission, the Banker's Association, and the Cattlemen's Association, all in here, practically threatening my life if I dared to give the Kansas Kid and Napoleon Nash pardons.

"Finally, in order to appease everybody, it was agreed, since Napoleon Nash had already gone to trial, been convicted and was incarcerated in the Laramie Penitentiary, then he could bloody well stay there.

"That took care of the Associations and their followers. To quiet down the opposition," he sent a disparaging look to the sacks of mail, "it was agreed to give the other partner the pardon. Someone had to be thrown to the wolves, Mr. Kiefer. Perhaps you should be thankful it wasn't you!"

Jack sat, tight-lipped with anger, the color drained from his face, as he barely held onto his self-control.

Seeing the real threat of the explosive temper Mr. DeFord had tried to ignite, Taggard stepped in to defuse the situation.

"I think Mr. Granger and I need to take a few moments to discuss this with Mr. Kiefer. If you don't mind, Governor."

"Yes, yes, of course," Governor Warren agreed. "But don't take too long, gentlemen. I have a busy schedule, and it's the only deal you're going to get."

The governor nodded to Mr. Higgins and those two gentlemen exited the office.

"Jack, what do you think you're doing?" Taggard seethed. "Now is not the time to get stubborn."

"It ain't right, Taggard. How can I sign this agreement, knowin' that Leon is the one payin for it?"

"Sometimes, discretion is the better part of valor, Mr. Kiefer," Mr. Granger pointed out. "You sign the agreement now, you'll be a free man and you can continue the fight along with the rest of us, to get Mr. Nash pardoned. You dig in your heels and refuse it, you can bet, Governor Warren will throw you back to Judge Lacey, and then what help will you be to your partner?"

"You best listen to him, Jack," Taggard strongly recommended. "Ya gotta look at the big picture here."

Jack sat back with a frustrated sigh, but his anger was dissipating. He struggled with this situation. It went against his grain, but he knew that Taggard and Granger were right. He nodded his consent.

***

That evening, Maxwell Coburn reserved a private dining room in the finest restaurant in Cheyenne. Everyone anticipated a more enjoyable experience than what this city had so far offered them.

Caroline and Penelope were elated at the prospect of being included in such a grand affair. They giggled and laughed, spluttering with their first taste of champagne.

Cameron sat between his two girls, in hopes of keeping an eye on them, but they still managed to have their own way in the seating arrangements. Caroline, to his left, had maneuvered a co-operative Steven Granger into the seat next to her. Penelope, to Cameron's right, accomplished the same feat with Jack. Both young ladies were having the time of their lives. David sat on the other side of Jack, then Taggard and, finally, Josey with Max beside her.

Jack couldn't help but smile, watching Josey rejoice in her element.

Josephine loved men. She had never married, because she had yet to meet a fella who would make it worth her while to forgo all others. Even with Leon and Jack, she was never able to say goodbye to one, in order to commit to the other, so she remained free and enjoyed them all. Big men, little men. Rich men, poor men; she didn't care. She loved them all and flirted, shamelessly, with whoever gave her free rein.

She happily gave equal attention to both Taggard and Max, and those gentlemen greatly enjoyed her company. Though never divulging any secrets, Josey carried on an endless chatter about everything and anything from boyfriends and girlfriends, to her life in Denver. When her escapades with Leon and Jack became the topic of the evening, everyone joined in to relate some of their own adventures with the incorrigible duo.

Great food, fine champagne and stimulating conversation, flowed freely and a good time was had by all—except one.

Jack Kiefer tried hard to join in on the festivities. He ate the food, drank the champagne, and joined in on the toasting, congratulating, and all the spirited conversation. But his heart wasn't in it. The one person who should be with them was locked away, shivering in a prison cell. How could he enjoy this fine dinner, knowing that? How could he be happy and content with his good fortune, knowing that?

Occasionally, he caught Josey's eye, and through her happy conversation and giggling flirtations, she would send him a soft compassionate hug across the table, all encompassed in a warm look. She knew what he was going through. Indeed, all his friends knew it, and they each sought to bolster his spirits the only way they knew how—with the offer of good companionship.

Gradually, the evening wound down. Despite moans and groans of belts being too tight, desserts found their way around the table. After that, everyone still managed to find room to finish off with brandy or coffee, accompanied by more sedate conversation.

The topic of what Jack's plans might be came up, and he had to admit to being completely at a loss.

"Please come home for Christmas," Penny got in there before any other suggestions could be brought forth.

"Ahh . . ." Jack hesitated.

"Yes, Mathew," Caroline seconded, "it would be wonderful to have you come for Christmas, and why not Thanksgiving too? Mama would love to have you come and stay."

Jack didn't buy it. "Oh, your mother would love it, would she?" he questioned, with a smile in his voice.

The girls looked sheepish. They knew he knew they were using that reasoning as added pressure.

Cameron smiled at his daughters' strategies.

"Still, they are right, Jack. You're more than welcome to stay at the ranch through the winter. Maybe give you some time to find your footing and decide what you want to do. I seem to recall saying once before; if you get bored, I can always put you to work."

"Uh huh," Jack commented. "I dunno."

"It might be a good idea, Jack," Taggard mentioned. "Maybe you should get out of Wyoming and lay low for a while."

"Why?"

"It seems ta me there were quite a few people in that courtroom who were not happy with the way things ended," Taggard explained. "Seein' you out and walkin' about, might encourage some of 'em inta takin justice into their own hands. You don't need that kind of trouble, right now."

Jack sighed. "Yeah. I never thought about that. And my shootin' arm sure ain't what it should be."

"If you come back to Arvada for the winter, we can do some work with that," David offered. "Goodness knows, if you want to be there for Christmas, you're going to be snowbound then, anyway."

The girls' hopes increased that their suggestion was going to be taken up. But still, Jack hesitated.

"Yeah, but . . ."

"You can't get in to see Leon, anyway, Jack," Taggard reminded him, suspecting this was the reason for him not wanting to leave the territory. "The three-month ban on visitors won't be up until after the holidays. And then, the weather could make it difficult to get there, even from Medicine Bow. It'll likely be spring before you get up to the prison to see him, the way things are going."

"Yeah. If he even wants ta see me," Jack mumbled.

Taggard frowned. "Of course, he'll want to see you. Why wouldn't he?"

Jack shrugged. "I dunno."

Taggard thought it was an odd thing for Jack to say, but he dismissed it.

David also thought it was odd, but he did not dismiss it.

Before anything more could be commented upon, the two youngest members of the dinner party yawned in unison. They apologized profusely, blaming the taste of champagne for their drowsiness.

Cameron laughed. "Yes. Or it could also be the late hour. I think it's time for some of us to be retiring."

"Oh, Papa!"

"We don't want to leave yet."

But Cameron had made up his mind. The hour—believe it or not—was close to midnight. It was past time his girls were in bed. He got to his feet. His daughters, accepting that the decision had been made, pushed themselves from the table as well.

The gentlemen present, all stood to say goodnight to the ladies.

"Well, if Mr. Marsham is escorting his daughters to the hotel, I believe I will join them," Josey announced. "It's getting late for me, too. I'll leave you gentlemen to your brandy."

"Oh, Miss Jansen, must you take your leave?" Max complained.

"Oh yes. A lady must get her beauty sleep."

"Oh well, you have nothing to worry about there, ma'am," Max assured her.

"Why, Mr. Coburn," Josey flirted, "you are such a gentleman."

Jack rolled his eyes. Both were having fun, playing their little game.

He felt Penny's warm hand slip into his and give it a tight squeeze. Jack, surprising himself, felt a tingling of pleasure at her touch, and he smiled at her.

"Goodnight, Penny."

"Goodnight, Mathew."

Finding himself surprised again, she reached up and gave him a brush of a kiss on his cheek. Her brown eyes smiled at him and then she slipped away to the door.

Cameron walked by, sending Jack 'the look' that all fathers send to prospective suitors, making sure they remembered their place.

Cameron heard Caroline give Mr. Granger a sweet goodnight, and that gentleman's equally pleasant response. The paternal figure recognized that there was another young man he needed to have a word with.

As Cameron and the ladies left the room, David stood up and stretched.

"Gentlemen, I believe I will retire, as well. Mr. Coburn, thank you for a wonderful dinner. Perhaps I'll see you all in the morning, over breakfast."

"Certainly, young man," Coburn boomed. "You keep up the good doctorin' you're doin' with Mathew there. I might be needin' him for a job or two in the future. I'd like to think he can still look after himself."

David smiled acknowledgment as Jack rolled his eyes. What did that mean?

As David sauntered over to the doors, he motioned Jack to come with him, out of earshot of the other gentlemen.

Jack felt a twinge of irritation at this beckoning but followed him anyway.

"What, David?" Jack asked, not being able to hide the edge in his voice.

"How are you feeling?" David asked. "Coming off morphine can have some nasty affects. I'll stay with you tonight, if you want."

Jack sighed; his lips pursed tight. "I'm fine. Will ya stop hoverin' over me like a mother hen?"

"All right," David agreed, not taking offense. "You have some laudanum, but if you find yourself feeling restless and still can't sleep,

226

don't hesitate to knock on my door. Okay."

"David, you hardly got any sleep last night. I'm not gonna bother ya."

"It's no bother. I'd rather you wake me, than go out and do something—rash. So, if you can't sleep and start feeling irritated, you let me know."

"Okay, David," Jack threw back at him. "I'm feeling irritated. Leave me alone."

David smiled. "Okay. I'll see you in the morning." He glanced at the group, still sitting and enjoying the last of their drinks. "Gentlemen, goodnight."

***

Cameron and David passed each other on the boardwalk leading to the hotel, and they said their goodnights.

Cameron sighed in disappointment, watching David continue on his way. Cameron would like nothing better than to do the same thing. It was late, and he was tired too. But he was a man on a mission, and one more thing had to be taken care of before they went their separate ways.

As soon as he returned to the dining room and poured himself a final brandy, he pulled Steven Granger aside and prepared for the father/suitor talk.

"Mr. Granger, I know I am paying your fees for these two cases, which I am quite happy to do. What I didn't realize, was that those fees would include my first born."

"Oh . . . ahh," Steven found himself without words. "Yes, of course. My apologies, Mr. Marsham . . . I didn't realize. Oh, dear."

Cameron smiled. Sometimes it could be fun, putting these young bucks in their place. "I believe I have the right to know your intentions," the father continued. "After all, Caroline is not yet twenty, and hardly in a position to arrange things for herself."

"No, no, of course not," Steven stammered. "You are quite correct. I should have spoken to you sooner, but it all came up rather quickly."

"Uh huh." Cameron waited. Nothing more came forth. "Mr. Granger, what are your intentions?"

"Oh! Ahhmm. Well, over this past month, Caroline and I have become very involved." Cameron raised his eyebrows. "Oh. No. Not that way." For an articulate lawyer, poor Steven was having a hard time. "I mean, with getting our strategy worked out, and our assault on the governor's office put into motion." He smiled at the memory of his visit to see the governor earlier that afternoon. "We seem to have been quite successful, too. Still, we have a long way to go. I have been needing an assistant, and at first, I thought Caroline would fit well into that position . . ." Cameron's brow went up even more. "No, but then, I realized that wasn't going to wash. A young woman, like herself, coming to live here on her own, would certainly not be acceptable."

"You're quite right there, Mr. Granger, it would not." Cameron enjoyed watching the young man squirm.

"Then I thought, perhaps if I moved my practice to Denver."

Cameron found himself genuinely surprised at this offer. "You would be willing to pack up and move to another territory, to continue seeing Caroline?"

"Yes," Steven thought this should be obvious. Then he realized he wasn't following proper protocol and, taking a deep breath, he stood up straight and looked Mr. Marsham in the eye. "Sir, I ask your permission to formally begin courting your daughter."

"Really?"

"Well, yes."

"And how does Caroline feel about this?"

"Oh. I haven't actually asked her," Steven admitted. "I assumed she would want to."

Cameron smiled and laid a hand on Steven's shoulder.

"A word of advice, Mr. Granger. When it comes to young ladies, don't ever assume anything."

"Oh. Ahh, well, I suppose I should . . ." Steven was losing ground again.

Cameron took pity on the young man and decided it was time to put him out of his misery.

"Tell you what; I can't really give permission for anyone to court one of my daughters without their mother having a say in it. Since she has yet to meet you, I'm afraid it's not possible at this point."

"Oh. Yes, of course."

"But," Cameron continued, "if you would like to join us for Thanksgiving next month, you can be formally introduced to my wife, and we can discuss this matter further."

"Oh! Yes, of course." Steven brightened up. "Yes. I'd like to come out to your ranch and meet your wife. Thanksgiving. Yes, I'm sure I can manage that."

"Good, Mr. Granger. Fine." The two men shook hands, then Cameron addressed the group. "Gentlemen, I'm exhausted. It has been a very busy and unusual day. I must say goodnight. Thank you, Mr. Coburn, for a fine supper, and I hope to see you all in the morning— or, I should say, later in the morning, since it is well past midnight."

Goodnights were said all around, and everyone headed off to their various beds for what remained of the nighttime hours.

CHAPTER THIRTEEN
SURVIVOR'S GUILT

Jack paced and fidgeted, grumbled his discontent and paced some more.

First time in how long, he had a real bed to sleep in, and he couldn't settle enough to enjoy it. "Damn that Warren. Who the hell did he think he was—playing with people's lives like that? "Somebody had to be thrown to the wolves, Mr. Kiefer. Perhaps you should be thankful it wasn't you." Damn him to hell. It ain't right—it ain't fair. If one of us had ta go to prison, it should'a been me. I know that. I'm the one who actually killed people, I'm the one who doesn't deserve to be the free man. Leon never hurt a fly, at least, not intentionally. And now, there he is, stuck in that bloody prison. It weren't right. I would have stood a better chance of surviving in prison, but not Leon. Leon can't stand being cooped up. It'll drive him mad. Slowly, but surely, it will kill 'im."

Jack was ready to explode. What a time for David to take away the morphine. Dammit. A few more days on it, just to get me through this time. But no, dammit to hell. He's a control freak is what he is. Well, if I can't have morphine, then I'll find something else. Maybe the opium den. No, opium won't do it. I need somethin' stronger. Dammit.

He snatched the bible off the nightstand and threw it against the far wall, cursing a blue streak as it hit then clattered to the floor.

There's no way I'm gonna sleep tonight. I have ta get outta here.

Mr. Granger had stopped by the jailhouse earlier that day and retrieved Jack's meager belongings. Jack grabbed them now. His gun and holster, he strapped on, though he'd probably shoot off his own foot if he tried a fast draw. It was just a habit to strap it on; it made him feel complete. He threw on his coat and his hat, made sure he had money on him, and headed out, toward the nightlife side of town.

Aftershock

It was a beautiful night; clear and crisp, with the stars like diamonds in a black velvet sky. But Jack didn't notice, as he approached the bright lights and loud tinny music coming from one of the local saloons. All he cared to notice about the night was that it was cold; he could see his breath in the air. He blew into his hands to warm them. He could smell snow.

Winter was coming.

The opium den beckoned him, but he ignored the call; he knew what he wanted, and it wasn't a drug to nullify, no. He could have taken laudanum for that. No, he needed something to vent his anger and frustration. He needed a release.

He opened the doors of the saloon, closed against the Wyoming night chill, and entered the warm inviting establishment, welcoming all those who would rather drink and gamble than sleep through the night. A few heads turned at the opening of the door, but quickly went back to their original entertainments as soon as the newcomer was recognized.

The Kansas Kid was feeling mean, and it showed. His blue eyes that turned to icy daggers when angry, now brought a feel to his countenance that was as rare as it was contrary to the norm. Death Valley heat, like the summer sun smoldering on a mirage sizzled anyone who dared to meet his gaze.

Nobody wanted to tangle with him.

With barely a glance at the other patrons, Jack headed for the bar where a couple of local customers shuffled down to make room for him. He snarled at them in his irritation. The barkeep approached, feeling safe in the knowledge that he was expected to do so.

"What'll ya have, Mr. Kiefer?"

"Whiskey. Bring the bottle."

"Yes sir."

The barkeep departed but returned quickly with a bottle and a shot glass. With a steady hand he had to work to achieve, he poured the customer his first drink.

Jack tossed payment onto the counter. He downed the first shot in one go, poured himself another and turned to survey the room before him.

He looked over at the group that made up the evening crowd and, very quickly, his gaze picked out the one person he was looking for

He didn't have enough money to visit the higher-class

establishments in town, but he knew that most saloons had their share of the less expensive 'upstairs girls'. Often these young ladies had an older, more experienced matron watching out for them, and this was whom Jack's gaze settled upon. The middle-aged woman, dressed like she owned the place, purposely stood out from the crowd, and a subtle nod from Jack was all it took to get her coming his way.

"Good evenin', Mr. Kiefer," she greeted as she sidled up to the bar beside him. "I hear you've had quite a day. Are you looking for quite a night, as well?"

"Yes ma'am, I surely am."

"Oh, don't go ma'amin' me," she told him. "Name's Lucy, honey. Now, you tell me what it is you're lookin' for, and I'll see what I can do for ya."

"Well, first off, can I interest you in a drink?"

"You most certainly can."

Jack nodded to the barkeep to bring over another glass, and he poured the lady a shot.

"You know what I'm lookin' for, Lucy," Jack said, as he downed his third shot. "Who do you suggest?"

Lucy, being the experienced and professional Madam that she was, noticed Jack the instant he'd walked into the establishment. It was part of her responsibility to look after her girls, so being able to judge a man's mood and temperament before sending him upstairs, could make the difference between a mean drunk and a happy customer.

She read Jack's mood correctly. He was antsy, seething almost, and there was a wild look to his eye; like a young stallion that'd been cooped up in a stall for too long.

Lucy did a quick once-over of the room and lighted on one of her girls. The matron beckoned her over.

The lady in question smiled and made her way to them. She was young, but not too young, with long blond hair and smoky brown eyes.

That's appropriate, Jack thought, and his eyes traveled over her tightly-corseted figure as she approached them.

"Mr. Kiefer, this here is Becky," Lucy introduced them, "and I think you will find her quite to your liking." She leaned close and added in a conspiratorial tone, "Becky don't mind at all, if you get a little— rough."

Jack smiled. Obviously, Lucy did know what he needed.

"Howdy, Becky," he greeted her, looking everywhere but in her eyes. "How'd you like a drink before I take you . . ." his smile broadened, ". . . upstairs."

Becky and Lucy exchanged a look. This one might be trouble. Lucy left it up to Becky to decide.

Becky smiled back at her customer, the lure of spending time with the infamous ex-outlaw overruling her common sense.

"Why, I'd like that fine, Mr. Kiefer."

"Aww, Sweetness," he said, as he watched the bartender pour her a drink from the 'ladies' bottle, "you best call me Jack. I intend to get real intimate before this night is done."

Becky sidled in closer. She took her drink and downed it in one swig.

Lucy discreetly departed, leaving the two to get on with business.

After a few more drinks and a little more small talk, Jack tossed additional coins on the bar in payment of the upcoming services. Having had enough of the preliminaries, he took Becky around the waist and steered her to the staircase.

Lucy watched them with a concerned look on her face. As soon as the couple disappeared into one of their rooms, she called to another of her girls. "Suzy, sweetheart, do me a favor, will ya?"

"Sure, Miss Lucy. What is it?"

"You go up and settle yourself into the room next to Becky's, all right? The customer she's with is in a mean spirit, tonight. If she gives you the signal that it's gettin' too much for her, you let me know, right away."

Suzy looked confused. "But, what's the problem? Becky likes it rough."

"Yeah, honey, but there's rough and then there's brutal. You just listen over her. If she gives the signal, you let me know, ya hear?"

"Yes, Miss Lucy." Suzy trotted up the stairs to begin her guard duty.

***

Leon and Jack were on the run—again.

Both their horses ran flat out, but they couldn't seem to lose the posse that had picked up their trail an hour and thirty miles ago. This was worrisome. They rode over flat, open terrain, so trying to hide anywhere was pointless, and all their tricks of the trade to confuse pursuers, weren't working.

The horses were tired, but Jack pushed Midnight as hard as he could. He knew his stalwart gelding was getting long in the tooth, and these kinds of frantic races were too much for him now.

Midnight gave his best effort, solid fellow that he was, but he couldn't match Karma's speed.

Leon was holding her back, Jack could tell. Holding her back, so he wouldn't leave Jack behind; so they wouldn't get separated.

"Let her go, Leon," Jack yelled at him over the sound of rushing wind and pounding hooves. "Let her run. Get outta here!"

"No!" Leon called back over his shoulder. "C'mon. We'll lose them in the ravines."

Jack kept on, pushing Midnight as hard as he could, while at the same time, afraid he was going to push his honest horse right into the ground. He kept his eyes on Leon's back, following him at that breakneck gallop toward the ravines up ahead. He prayed Leon was right; that they would lose this determined posse within those twisting, winding trails.

The posse narrowed the distance between them; Jack could hear the pounding of their hooves as they closed the gap between themselves and the outlaws. He heard rifle fire and prayed none would find a mark. They kept going, Leon holding Karma back, Jack pushing Midnight as much as he dared.

Then a different sound boomed out behind them. A Sharps rifle let fly, and Jack screamed as he saw Leon's back violently arch over in an unnatural manner. Leon plunged forward into Karma's neck and tumbled to the ground.

Karma, panic stricken, kept running. Midnight charged past the crumpled figure, but Jack hauled ruthlessly on his mouth, sending him around and back to his partner.

Jack didn't attempt to slow Midnight, and he bails off at the gallop to plow into the ground, close to Leon. He scrambles to his uncle and puts a trembling hand upon the motionless shoulder. Jack can't see his face; Leon lay on his stomach, but his back is a solid mess of blood and broken bone.

Jack screams again.

The posse's horses surround them, galloping in a circle, encompassing them both.

Jack launches to his feet and pulls his gun; he's in a fury and starts shooting. A horse goes down, and a man plunges to the ground. Another man screams and falls. Jack keeps shooting, fanning the hammer and screaming his rage, until the gun clicks on empty.

A horse plows into him from behind and he is sent sprawling to the ground, his gun flying across the dirt, to land well out of reach.

The men are off their horses and diving toward the outlaw. Rough hands grab Jack and haul him to his feet, pinning his arms behind him. Another arm circles his throat and squeezes, until Jack can barely breathe.

One of the lawmen approaches Leon and, with a toe under the outlaw's shoulder, rolls him over onto his back.

Jack groans. His throat and eyes burn as tears roll down his cheeks.

Those dark brown eyes that were so often glinting with mischief and good humor, now stared, dull and sightless, up to the heavens.

"He's dead, that's for sure," smirks the man who had rolled Leon over.

"Good," the apparent leader responds, "one less to worry about."

Jack groans again, his yell of rage and torment strangled by the squeezing hold on his throat. He struggles, fighting back, but the men hold him firm and their only response is to laugh at him. His sobs fight to come forth, but all he can do is choke on them.

"That's $10,000 lying there, in the dirt, boys," the leader proclaimed. "Talk about a good day's work."

The jovial countenance dropped from his demeanor, and he glared at Jack. As he approached the outlaw, he pulled his gun and brought the weapon down, hard, against the side of Jack's head.

Jack gasped and would have fallen to his knees, if not for the men holding him up.

"On the other hand," the leader snarled, "you killed four of my men, Kiefer. And you're gonna pay for that. Hold out his right hand, boys. Hold it out there—let's see it."

The men holding Jack started to snicker. One of them grasped Jack's right wrist and pulled his arm away from his body, holding his hand in the clear.

Jack struggled, frantic to get away. He knew what was coming.

But even through his terror and his anguish, he knew there was nothing he could do to stop it. He screamed silently, fighting against the unyielding hold, but he couldn't break away. He was held firmly in place while the leader pressed the muzzle of his six-shooter into the palm of Jack's trembling hand and pulled the trigger.

Jack's scream was loud and fraught with anguish, as the men holding him let him drop to the ground. He clutched his right hand and writhed in agony. He could hear their laughter; the voices in the distance, mocking him.

"C'mon, Jack. What's the matter?"

"Hey Jack. Settle down. There's nothing to get upset about."

The ground shook him. He awoke with a violent start and went for his gun, but it wasn't there. David's face came into focus. The doctor stood over him with concern in his eyes.

"Wake up, Jack," David said. "It's all right; you're just having a bad dream."

Jack lay, propped up on his elbows. He shook and gasped for air, confusion in his eyes, as he stared at David and tried to let go of the nightmare.

"It's all right, Jack," David repeated. "You're safe; it was just a dream."

Jack let go a sigh as his ragged breathing began to slow and the tingling gradually retreated from his limbs. He was on a train; he could tell that by the rocking motion and the clackety-clack of the wheels rumbling along the tracks. He was on his back, across two seats, with his coat draped over him. There was a makeshift pillow stuffed against an armrest, to cushion his head while he slept.

He lay back down, feeling weak. It was daylight, but he couldn't remember getting on the train. He couldn't remember anything after leaving the supper party—the previous night?

David gave Jack a pat on the knee, then returned to his seat, facing him.

Jack looked at him and noticed Cameron sitting beside the doctor, by the window. There was an odd expression on his face. Jack couldn't decide if it was concern or anger.

He then heard Josey's laughing voice coming from further down the car. Apparently, they had the whole area to themselves. Penny and Caroline sat with her, delighting in hearing all her wild stories of her adventures with Leon and Jack, properly embellished with damsels in distress and outlaw heroics.

Once Penny realized that Josey was no threat to her designs on Jack, all three ladies became fast friends, and the animated stories were doing a lot to help pass the travel time.

Cameron frowned, not sure if he approved of the stories the free-spirited woman was entertaining his daughters with. But then he cast a side-long glance at Jack and a deeper concern took over.

Josey had paused in her narrative, and all three ladies looked, with concern, to where the three men were situated. The sounds of Jack's frightened cries had instantly drawn their attention. But they soon realized that it was just a dream and that Cameron wasn't taking the man apart, limb by limb.

"You all right now, Jack?" David asked.

"Yeah."

"Must have been some dream you were having."

"Yeah."

"Do you want anything?"

"No."

Jack pulled his coat over himself and lay back on the seats to continue sleeping.

Cameron and David sat quietly, lost in their own thoughts. Cameron watched the scenery slide by the windows, and David watched the prone man across from him. Both of their expressions were strained.

When enough time had elapsed for Jack to fall back to sleep, Cameron picked up the conversation where it had been interrupted by the violent dream.

"I dunno, David. I don't know how I could have thought I knew these two men, simply based on a few months' acquaintance four years ago." Cameron frowned and looked at the sleeping man. "One thing is for sure; he'll be sleeping in the bunkhouse with Sam until he proves himself worthy of sharing our home again. What the hell is the matter with him? I swear, if he even thinks of treating Penny the way he treated that girl last night, I'll kill him. I dread to think how much worse it would have been if that madam hadn't gone in there and broke it up."

"I know," David responded. "I can understand your concerns, but try not to be too hard on him, Cameron. Don't give up on him yet."

"Yeah, right," Cameron grumbled. "With all the stuff that came out at his trial, and him insisting he was sorry, and he knows better now. Insisting he has his temper under control, then he goes and does that. I'm beginning to think, rather than being under control, his tempter has been lying dormant, waiting for an opportunity to explode. I don't want Penny anywhere around him when it does."

"Last night was completely out of character. You know that just as well as I do," David insisted. "And what happened was just as much my fault, as it was his."

"Oh, David. How could it have been your fault?"

"Before I left the dinner party, I knew he was depressed. I knew he was edgy. I could see it. I tried to get him to talk with me, but he got angry and pushed me away. I shouldn't have accepted that; I should have stayed by him."

"You were exhausted," Cameron reminded him, "you were up with him most of the previous night, then we were all up late, last night. Even now, you look like you could use a few hours."

"Doesn't matter," David shook his head and sighed. "I should have done something. Even parking myself outside his room might have helped. I might have been able to stop him."

"Yeah, or he might have flattened you and gone anyway," Cameron sent a frown to the sleeping man. "What's gotten into him?"

"The last four months have been hard," David mused. "He's depressed over what happened to Napoleon. I also believe, he is still going through a mild withdrawal from the morphine."

"Mild withdrawal?" Cameron glanced at David in disbelief. "You call that mild?"

"Yes." David was emphatic. "He wasn't taking enough of the drug to really become addicted. He was only becoming a little dependent on it, when I cut him off. I'm still irritated at Dr. Huff for continuing to give Jack that drug, after I told him not to—and why. But he's an old-time doctor and doesn't understand the dangers of opioids. He probably thought I was being an old fuddy-duddy."

David stopped, regretfully gazing at his sleeping friend. "Morphine is a wonder drug when it comes to sedation and pain relief, but it's insidious. With the long-term use, a person will become addicted to it without realizing what's happening. Until they can no longer get it, then their whole world falls apart. They become stressed, agitated, abusive, and often violent in their need for the drug. Even experiencing black outs and memory loss. In extreme withdrawal, the addicted person suffers crippling headaches, seizures, convulsions, vomiting, extreme constipation—everything nasty under the sun. Some so bad, they can die from it. So, yes; what Jack is going through now, I'd call 'mild'."

Cameron looked at David, almost speechless with shock. "Oh my

God."

"Yes," David agreed. "So, try not to be too hard on him. He'll come around. I'm sure by the time we get home, you will have noticed a marked improvement. The holidays will be the hardest time for him. If we can get through Christmas without a crisis, then he'll be well on his way to a full recovery."

"Yeah, well, all right, David. I'll give him some time. But he's still sleeping in the bunkhouse. He's got a long way to go to redeem himself if he has any notions of courting my daughter."

CHAPTER FOURTEEN
SEVERED LINK

Laramie, Wyoming
Autumn 1885

Leon did his best to work through each day without getting into trouble. This was not an easy feat, since Carson or Bowman were often on the prowl looking for a fight. Being in the warehouse was a challenge, and Leon constantly had to watch his back.

He smirked at how he thought riding the outlaw trail was dangerous; too many people out to get them. But that existence was easy compared to what he had to deal with in the prison. At least on the outside, they had some measure of control over their lives. But in here, he wasn't even allowed to fight back. If a guard came at him with a billy club, he had to take it, or end up in the dark cell, and that was worse than any beating he'd ever had.

So, when the guard, Pearson, approached him with the usual "Convict, follow me", Leon's initial trepidation over where he was being taken turned to guarded curiosity when he found himself in the laundry room. Curiosity was followed by relief when he was informed that he would now spend one day a week on laundry duty.

Leon never thought he would ever look forward to washing sheets and scrubbing prison tunics, but that one workday a week, when he could spend time alone in the laundry room, became a blessing that helped him to hang on. He didn't have to be as diligent when watching his back in there, so he could be alone with his thoughts.

When he first started this duty, his thoughts were on his partner and how the trial was going. Carson's attempt at emotional torture had been successful for the first day or two, but when nothing official came down the pike, Leon started to relax and to take some comfort in the idiom that no news was good news.

Then, one evening, Leon returned to his cell with a cup of coffee, intending to read the next chapter in 'Drug Addiction and its Consequences', when he noticed a newspaper lying on his cot. He set his coffee cup on the small table, and, picking up the paper, sat down to browse through it. His heart was instantly in his throat.

THE CHEYENNE GAZETTE"
NOTORIOUS KILLER GRANTED PARDON

Leon frowned. *Notorious killer? What was that all about?* He began to read.

He read it through quickly the first time to find out all he could as fast as possible, but by the time he got to the end of the article, he was more confused than ever.

He read it a second time, more slowly, trying to take it all in. He still had a hard time digesting it.

Jack had killed? Not once; not just Bartlett, but three others as well? Why had he never said so? Why hadn't Jack told me this?

He settled in to read it a third time, his coffee cold and forgotten.

When he was done, Leon lay back on his cot, staring at the ceiling, one arm curled behind his head. He was hurt that Jack had chosen to not confide in him; to tell him what had happened. What a weight for his nephew to have carried alone, all those years. Leon surmised that Jack didn't think his uncle would understand.

He probably thought I would be angry, that I would have turned away from him. But I would never have done that. It's a hard thing, but I would have understood. I do understand.

Leon's thoughts went deeper, and he chewed his lower lip with the memories that came back to him.

He had to admit, now that he had the missing pieces, it all kind of made sense. After the showdown with Bartlett, Jack had been upset at the killing, but not devastated as one would normally be. Leon had often wondered about this. Surely, if that had been the first time Jack had killed someone, it would have been far more traumatic for him. But it hadn't been. Jack had seemed more disappointed than traumatized by it, and this had always struck Leon as odd. But Jack didn't say, and Leon didn't ask.

But now it was all coming together and, finally, it made sense.

242

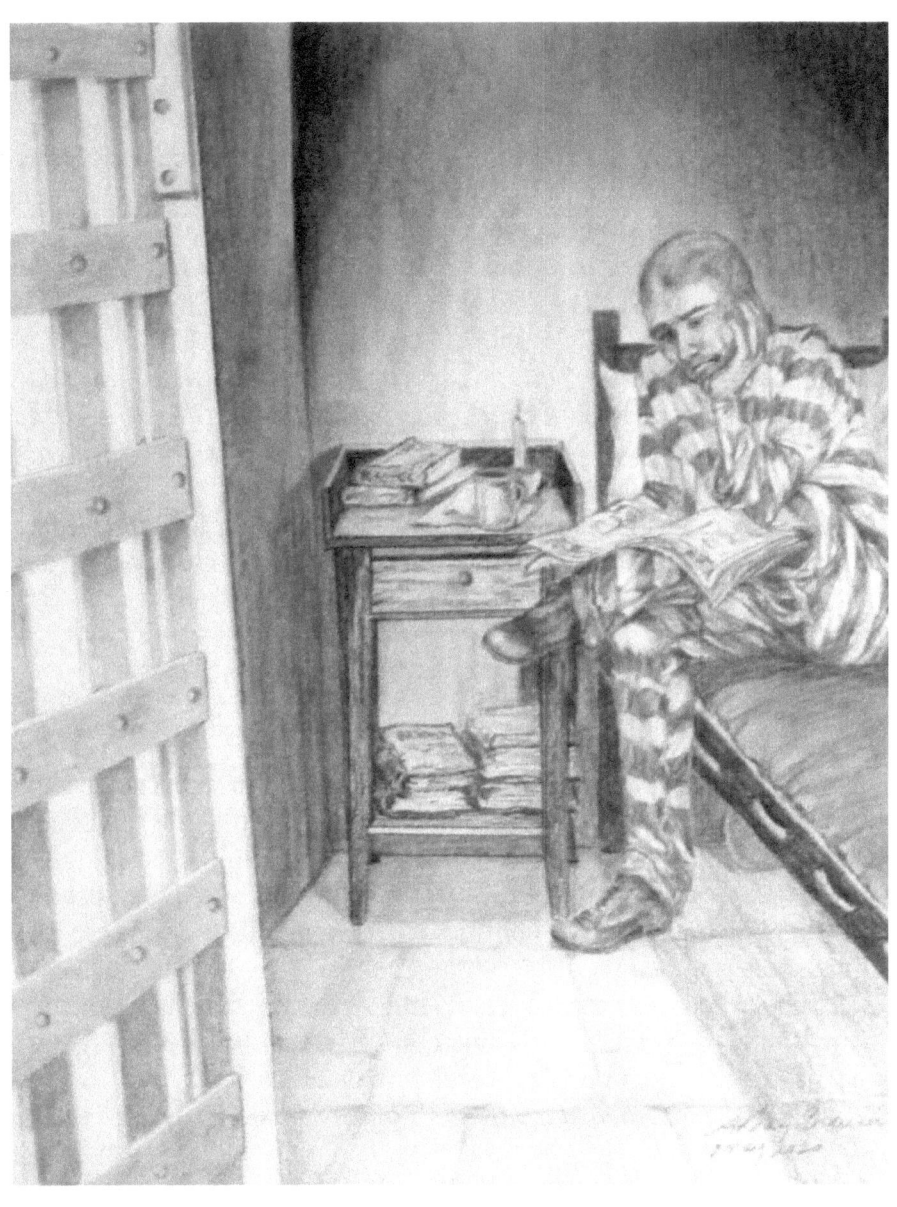

He read it a second time, more slowly, trying to take it all in. He still had a hard time digesting it

Even at Blessed Heart, Leon knew there was something insidious eating away at his nephew. Those temper tantrums and ultimately, the blind rages that came on him, those weren't coming from nowhere.

What happened to their folks had been hard on them, but the way they each dealt with it had been an example of extreme opposites.

Young Napoleon had simply forgotten the worst memories. Buried them away in his subconscious mind, not to be heard from again until they had been forced out of him at the trial.

Jack, not being able to forget, had acted out instead. Releasing his anger the only way he knew how, by lashing out and then, ultimately, by killing.

Leon sighed. *Poor Jack. I don't know what would have been worse; remembering or not remembering. Oh, but at least he got the pardon. Finally. Thank goodness for that. At least one of us was able to avoid this hellhole.*

Leon was curious how Jack had been given a pardon while he was thrown in prison. He was happy for Jack, and it gave him hope, because now, Jack would do everything he could to get Leon out.

Yes, this is a good thing.

***

Leon tried to be patient as he waited for word from his nephew. He knew the first Saturday after reading the paper would be too soon to expect a letter. Besides, the snow was beginning to fall now, so even letters and parcels would be delayed in getting to him. He'd just have to wait and continue to be confident that he would receive word from Jack, sooner or later.

But as the weeks went by, and letters from the Marshams and even from Taggard arrived, there were none from Jack. Nobody even mentioned Jack. Leon began to feel hurt again.

Why haven't I heard anything? What's going on? Is Jack mad at me—but for what?

Leon could not understand. Why had his nephew not written to him?

Eventually, Leon got tired of waiting and he sent a letter to Taggard, asking that very question. The response, a couple of weeks later, did not help to clear things up. All Taggard said was that Jack was staying with the Marsham's through the winter, so Leon should get in touch with him there. He also mentioned, somewhat obscurely, that Jack was going through a 'hard time'.

This got Leon's dander up.

Jack was going through a hard time? What about me? Talk about hard time. At least Jack is free. I mean, come on; staying at the Marshams' ranch through the winter? How could that be considered hard time?

Leon couldn't figure what the hell was going on. Didn't Jack know how much Leon needed to hear from him? All the questions about Jack's trial and what had gone on during their separation were burning holes in Leon's shoes.

Ah, but maybe that's it, Leon mused. *Maybe he's ashamed of what happened and doesn't want to face me. Maybe. But come on.*

Leon felt abandoned; like his best friend had hung him out to dry.

He next wrote to Cameron, hoping to get some explanation from the rancher. But again, when a response did arrive, it didn't offer much comfort.

Leon sat on his bunk with letter in hand and a frown upon his forehead.

> *"Napoleon,*
>
> *God only knows what's going on with Jack. David says it's coming off the morphine that's causing him to behave so erratically. I've about had it with him. I'm disappointed but not surprised he hasn't written to you. He's not much good to anyone these days."*

After reading the letter from Cameron, Leon became depressed and sullen to the point where even reading the medical journals wasn't helping to raise his spirits. It was becoming too cold for the inmates to have much time outside, and the wind and snows were blowing, so he had also lost that relief from the mundane. The weekly sermons in the chapel did nothing to bring light or hope into his heart, and his appetite diminished, so his weight dropped dangerously low.

He had thoughts of suicide. Him, of all people! But what was the point of hanging on? His best friend had abandoned him and now he was never going to get out of here. Then he berated himself for allowing pity to cloud his mind and rob him of his courage, and he'd pick himself up and carry on.

Christmas was coming; it was just around the corner. Would that help to brighten his mood, or make it worse? They would not have to work on that day, and there would be a special Christmas sermon for those who wished to attend. Leon doubted he would. Why bother?

Word was the Sisters of Charity, from the nearby orphanage, would be coming to the prison on Christmas Day to distribute gifts to the inmates. Usually they were sweaters, socks, and mitts, that had been knitted by caring citizens who felt a need to send help and hope to those less fortunate made up the Christmas packages.

That might make it worthwhile, Leon supposed. *Oh well, whatever.*

***

The days dragged by. He continued to receive letters from Caroline and Penny, and they delighted in telling him all about the goings on at the ranch. Caroline mentioned something about Mr. Granger coming for Thanksgiving.

Mr. Granger? The lawyer? What was that all about?

There was some talk of Jack being there. He was helping at the ranch, doing odd jobs, but he often disappeared into town and would not come back for days. Then, they would make some comment about how Leon must already be aware of that stuff, since, surely, Jack was writing to him and keeping him up to date.

Then Leon sank deeper into a depression. He retreated into his cave and shut out everything and everyone.

December came in white and cold. Christmas was a bad time for people who are already lost, and Leon dreaded the coming of that day.

Even at Blessed Heart, Jack had been with him. But not this year. This year, he was isolated, in his heart, his mind, and his soul.

He lay on his cot in his cell, staring at the ceiling he couldn't see.

So many images had been fixed upon that surface—that surface he couldn't see—that if it had been the pages of a book, the stories it could tell of its current resident would be an epic tale of loneliness and despair.

Though there were no timepieces in the tiny cell, Leon had developed a keen sense of the passage of that line into the future. So many nights he spent laying on his back, staring up into the darkness that he seemed to know when he was at any given point during the night. Now, for instance, it was coming up on midnight of Christmas Eve.

A heavy sigh passed through his lips. He missed his nephew more than he thought was possible. But Jack wasn't with him anymore, just as surely as his own folks weren't with him, and his sister wasn't with him. At least with his folks, he knew it wasn't their choice to be away from him. Death is a one-way street, after all.

But Jack?

Why has he shut me out?

Try as he might, he couldn't understand it. The one letter Leon sent to him remained unanswered. Jack, withdrawing his support, was the worst thing that had happened to Leon throughout this whole miserable chapter of his life.

His nephew, his closest friend, was lost to him, and the thought of that loss, and of the precious link that had been severed, threatened to break his heart all over again.

He felt his throat tightening, and the tears behind his eyes fighting to spill out upon his cheeks. He quickly wiped a shirt sleeve across his face and swallowed the tightness. He knew he could not afford to allow that to happen.

Even here, in the darkness and solitude of his cell, he couldn't allow himself to cry because he knew once the tears started, they would be endless. If he allowed himself the luxury of tears here, then he might not be able to stop them the next time they threatened, and the next time could be in the workshop.

He dreaded to think what would happen if Carson caught him crying. He'd seen it before with one of the younger inmates who didn't have the fortitude to stand up to the bullying. He had broken down and allowed the tears to come. He had begged to be set free, so he could go home.

Carson's expression had turned to malicious glee, and he set upon the young man with brutal words and hard kicks, until he curled into a ball and begged for his mother.

Leon shivered; that was never going to be him, he would never allow the tears to come.

His mood changed from self-pity to anger as he thought of Carson and the things that guard took pleasure in doing.

He's another Morrison—no, actually he's worse than Morrison. The marshal, at least, was honest. It wasn't that he took pleasure in the things he did; it was simply the only way he knew of to get the job done. And he did get it done, no doubt about that.

Leon looked back at the time he had spent in the company of the marshal, and he had to admit to himself, even if he had been trying to break custody, he would not have succeeded. Morrison had been a step ahead of him all the way, blocking every conceivable move the outlaw could have made. The only time Leon might have succeeded in escaping, was when he was in the Cheyenne jail, and no longer in Morrison's custody.

The fact that Leon had decided not to leave then was a decision he now regretted more than any other he'd ever made. Promises be damned.

I'm heading into self-pity again. He shifted on his bunk. I have to get away from that line of thought. I've been going there too often, these days.

He rolled onto his side and hugged his knees.

This was one of the positions he preferred lately. He didn't look too deeply into why he did it; he never used to sleep like that. But lately, well, he told himself, it was to keep warm. There were fireplaces at both ends of all three levels of the cell blocks, but often they were left empty, and the draft coming down the chimney made it worse.

Snow flew across Wyoming and the temperatures dipped below freezing.

Leon's three months of "settling in time" would be over soon, but he came to realize, no one would be coming to visit during the winter months. Travel was almost impossible, and downright dangerous. It was going to be a long, lonely winter—and cold too, with only the hope of a letter or a parcel making it through to him.

He thought of the Marshams, since they, and sometimes Taggard, were the only ones to send him letters or parcels. The last one, from Jean, had been a nice, warm sweater—thank goodness. Kenny made sure he got it, too. He wore it now and, feeling the warmth it provided, he sent out a wish to them that they would enjoy a Happy Christmas, and not have it marred by worries of him.

Then he felt the pain hit him again, as memories of one of the last conversations he'd had with Jack came back to him, unbidden:

'Then there's Thanksgivin'.

Yup.

Then Christmas. Sure would be nice to spend Christmas with a

248

family again.

Sure would.'

Jack was obviously going to be getting his wish; Christmas with a family.

Leon thought back to the last Christmas he had spent with family, so many years ago. It had been wonderful. Little Jenny had been there, still sparkling brand new. Leon remembered being so proud that he was now a "big brother".

It had been the Nashs' turn to host the Christmas dinner that year, and the Kiefers had come over in their sleigh in the early afternoon. Everyone had been in a festive spirit.

Leon and Jack spent the afternoon outside building a fort and engaging in snowball fights. Then, as the light waned, they went inside to sit by the fire and drink hot apple cider until supper was ready. And what a supper it was. This was something that Leon always remembered the most: the heavenly aroma of roasting meat and baked apple pies, even if they were of the vinegar variety. Warmed up and cover with their fresh ice cream, it was heaven.

Afterward, with tummies full and spirits glowing, they'd all stayed up past midnight, telling stories and singing carols until exhaustion sent them all to bed.

The following morning produced another great and memorable meal. Everyone sat around the breakfast table drinking coffee and warm milk sweetened with honey until it was time for the Kiefers to head for home. It had been a great Christmas.

Then, Leon's thoughts turned to his sister.

What would life be for her now, if she had lived? Would she be married, with children of her own? Would she be celebrating Christmas with her family? Would I have even taken to the outlaw trail, if I'd had a sister to look after? Oh, damn, what am I thinking? It would never have been like that. Look at Josephine; what choices had she faced?

Leon pursed his lips with resentment.

Most of the girls went into arranged marriages right out of the orphanage, and usually to a man who was much older than they were, who was only looking for a vassal and a nanny. Those who weren't fortunate enough to warrant an arranged marriage were left with two extreme options: the nunnery or the brothel. After the way they'd been treated at Blessed Heart, it's not surprising Josephine hadn't taken the pious route. She had taken the only option open to her, and she wouldn't have had it any other way, but she would be looked down on for the rest of her life because of it.

Jenny wouldn't have had it any different.

Leon had often enjoyed the services of prostitutes, but he didn't look down on them; on the contrary, he honored and respected them. Maybe he viewed them as being from the same mold as himself; two lost and lonely souls taking comfort in each other's arms.

Of course, Josey may have had a hand in instilling that respect into him. He never thought of Josey as a prostitute. He thought of her only as a friend. He knew her profession, of course, but he had never availed himself of her services, and, presumably, neither had Jack. They simply did not see her that way.

Then another young woman came to mind.

What was her name? Lorna? . . . Louise? . . . Linda? . . . No, Lindy. That was it.

Leon hadn't thought of her in years. Oh, in his mind's eye, she was so pretty, so exciting. He had been sixteen when she had taken him into her bed. She was so much older than him, well, he figured, twenty. But when you're sixteen and inexperienced, twenty seems so much older, and wow, was she ever experienced.

She knew, of course she could tell right away, that Leon was new to this. But she treated him like a man and gently showed him the way. She took his virginity, wrapped it up in sweet kisses and returned it to him in a warm and sensuous package.

Leon smiled at the memory of her: the scent and the feel of her, and ohh, the warmth of her.

Then he groaned at the uncomfortable urgings growing inside him.

Oh no, I really shouldn't think about stuff like this. All it does is add to the frustration. Ohh, damn.

The aching inside him demanded attention.

He shifted position, so he could tend to his need. It wasn't an easy thing to do, considering how he was bundled up in clothes and blankets in a futile effort to stay warm. But there's nothing like incentive to get a job done.

In the utter darkness of his cold cell, he managed to give himself some comfort and release from the stresses that had been building up day, after day, after day.

With the job done, he relaxed and sighed deeply. He closed his eyes and lay back, hearing his heart beating in his ears, and his breath coming heavily. But for now, at least the tension was gone from his body.

Then he noticed his blanket was wet.

Dammit. Nothing good comes without a price.

He shifted position again, hoping to get comfortable. He snuggled in, hands pressed between his drawn-up knees to stay warm. He stared into the darkness, feeling his respiration softening and his heartbeat slowly returning to a normal rhythm. He hoped that, maybe now, he could get some sleep.

***

Christmas dawned cold and clear, which boded well for the Sisters from the local charity association to make it to the prison for the afternoon.

The inmates were allowed an extra hour of sleep for Christmas morning, but it was still a dreary and chilly operation. Leon kept his blanket wrapped around him as he climbed out of bed and stood at the cell door for rollcall. Everyone hugged themselves and shivered.

Certain he could see his breath, Leon glanced to the end of the aisle to see if the fireplace was lit. He hoped on this morning, of all mornings, the warden would see fit to light all the fireplaces and bring heat into the prison. If not for the inmates, then at least for the comfort of the visiting Sisters. He almost smiled with relief when he spied one of the guards stoking their fireplace into active duty.

Next was a breakfast of oatmeal and coffee. At least it was warm.

The breakfast dishes were cleared away, and the common room transformed into a makeshift chapel.

Leon made sure he sat as far away from the "pulpit" as possible. If he had to be here, at least he could choose not to engage. So, he sat, along with the other inmates who grumbled about the necessity of being here and waited for the sermon to begin.

As the minutes ticked by, he considered the men whose company he shared, and he noticed something disturbing. The three other inmates wore surly, angry grimaces. When the Sisters entered the hall to begin the service, these men showed their disdain with silent snorts and lewd glances.

Leon frowned. Is this what I look like? Are my thoughts so obvious to the casual observer?

He looked forward again and decided that if this was the warden's idea of Christmas, he would ignore those seated around him and make the most of it.

Once his mood and intention changed, the service turned out to be uplifting enough to help him feel a bit better about himself.

But then after the sermon, Warden Mitchell stepped to the pulpit to make his grand announcement, and Leon's mood turned dark again.

"Good morning, and Merry Christmas," Mitchell declared to an unappreciative crowd. "I'm pleased to inform you all, that the Sisters of Charity have arrived at the prison and will soon be entering the hall with gifts for everyone. You are to stand quietly and wait for a Sister to come to you. Each inmate will accept the gift offered to them, then you will return to your chairs and wait until the distribution is completed. There will be no talking other than a brief acknowledgement of your gift. Otherwise, do not speak to the Sisters unless spoken to directly. Under no circumstances are you permitted to touch any of the Sisters. Any infringement of these rules, and the perpetrator will spend the rest of the day in the dark cell. But first, Dr. Soames has kindly offered to lead you all in a Christmas sermon."

Leon groaned. *Dr. Soames. Well, at least it's someone new.*

"Thank you," Mitchell continued, "and I wish you the best of the season. Good day!"

The warden gave a curt nod to the assembly, straightened his suit jacket and made a hasty exit. He had a few minor details to attend to in his office, then he would walk the short distance to his home to spend Christmas Day with his own company.

Leon frowned as he watched the man stride across the room and disappear.

That was rather cold and impersonal for a Christmas message. Oh well. I suppose I shouldn't have expected anything more. Everything is cold and impersonal in this dismal place; may as well make Christmas that way too.

It was then he noticed a change in the mood of the spectators. Men shifted in their chairs, others spit in their hands and slicked back non-existent hair. There was a feeling of anticipation.

Leon frowned. Did they know something he didn't? He cast quick eyes over his fellows. Some grinned like fools, while others licked their lips as though in anticipation of a good meal. Something was up.

Much to his surprise, the attending preacher turned out to be a woman. He again glanced around at the other attendees and noted that every one of them was at full attention.

That's odd. Well, perhaps the prison couldn't find a real minister to come here. Took what they could get, I suppose.

Then she smiled at the spectators before her, and Leon's heart jumped.

He knew her.

Her eyes scanned the many faces before her as she opened the bible.

"Good morning, gentlemen."

A rumbling of voices responded. "Good morning, Dr. Soames."

Leon frowned. *This is extremely odd. And she's a doctor? I knew she was well educated, but . . . and a preacher? Damn. And I liked her, too.*

"Gentlemen, today, being Christmas and a time of rejoice and charity, I'm going to talk about how big results can come from small efforts . . ."

Oh, here we go. Leon sighed, then he ducked as her eyes scanned his section. A sense of shame washed over him and now, more than ever, he did not want to be noticed.

Their original encounter had happened by chance. It was during the time when he and Jack were still working for their pardons, when they came across a middle-aged woman stranded in the middle of nowhere. Her buggy had broken down and the horse run off, so she truly was in a fix.

Of course, they had helped her; no decent man would leave a woman stranded like that. They became friends in the three days it took them to get to the nearest town, both men enjoying her wit and ready intelligence.

She dressed as most women dressed, so there was nothing to give away that she was a well-educated woman. She spoke briefly of her spiritual leanings, but it never occurred to the two outlaws that she was actually in a position to lead a sermon. As far as they were concerned, she was heading to Kaycee, Wyoming, to take up the position of schoolteacher.

Mariam Soames didn't know who he and Jack were, having been introduced to them as Peter and Mathew, and now, he did as Kenny suggested, and hid in the shadows.

But as the session went on, he relaxed some and was surprised to note that instead of blocking her out with his own musings, he was listening to her.

Her sermons differed from those of her male counterparts. The men who preached at the prison came at the congregation with shaking fists, and fire and brimstone spewing out to intimidate. But Mariam never went in that direction. All her sermons were of happiness and hope, and love for your fellows. They were like a ray of sunshine in that bleak and bitter existence that was the lot of a convict.

Everyone sat, with only the occasional cough breaking the silence, but otherwise, nothing moved. Even the guards who were unlucky enough to pull Christmas duty, stood placidly waiting for the event of the day.

Leon glanced up at one of the two guard "cages" that were barred-in lookouts where armed guards stood overhead and watched the common area. These lookouts were positioned in strategic locations throughout the prison, and for this occasion, both the cages in this area were occupied.

Again, so cold and impersonal. Leon longed for those cold Christmases, holed up in some miserable shack with just his nephew and a hasty fire for company. If they were lucky, they had fresh game for dinner, but usually it was beans and biscuits, with coffee. If times were tight, maybe dinner would be jerky and whatever they could scrounge out of their saddlebags.

At the time, those Christmases seemed bleak and they had reminisced about the holidays spent in the cabin at the Elk Mountain hideout. Yet, when they were at Elk Mountain, they would lament the happy times and wonderful meals their families had shared when they were children.

That one Christmas they spent with the Marsham family had been enchantment itself. Leon and Jack had gotten lost in a blizzard, trying to elude an extremely determined posse, when they had been fortunate enough to stumble across the Marshams' dilapidated ranch. They were both near frozen, with Jack being the worse off as he had fallen into the river. He had been barely conscious when Leon practically crawled onto the front porch to beg for help.

He hadn't even had the strength left to knock on the door, and only the barking of the ranch dog alerted the rancher that two sorry strangers were frozen to the front yard.

Cameron took them into his hearth and home without a second thought. The family had gathered around, tended to their frozen condition with dry clothing and long johns, heavy socks and warm blankets. Jean had settled them by the fire and given them hot stew and warm, spiked coffee, and the two girls lit up with excitement due to the company they would have for the special day.

Dinner of roasted quail with potatoes and root vegetables had been a banquet to the two lost men. The warmth of the heated alcohol equaled the warmth extended to them from this family. They had been so fortunate to stumble across the ranch, out there, in the middle of a white, frozen expanse that surely would have killed them, otherwise. The only good thing about the weather that Christmas, was it forced the posse to give up on them and go home, until spring.

Christmas that year had been special and neither Leon nor Jack ever forgot it. Every year since, Leon hoped that the next Christmas would be just like that one, yet it seemed they only got worse. Now, here he was, the dreariness of his situation made more acute by the absence of his closest friend, and the knowledge that this friend was again spending Christmas with the family who had once made it so special for them both.

He felt his heart break again. Why had Jack abandoned him?

Activity by the entrance caught his attention. Boxes containing brown paper-wrapped parcels were dragged into the hall, and the two Sisters, hindered by their bulky habits and extensive head coverings, hovered around them, waiting for their cue.

Carson stepped forward to address the inmates.

"All of you will stand," he ordered. "Remain by your chairs until the Sisters have completed their rounds. Do not leave the room until you are ordered to do so."

The sound of scraping chairs took over the silence, as the inmates came to their feet.

Carson turned to the Sisters and nodded. They reciprocated, and with each Sister accompanied by a guard, the gift-giving began.

Leon sighed. He felt uncomfortable with this and regretted his decision to stay for this traditional act of passing out gifts to the inmates. He'd rather work for what he got, even if that work consisted of planning a bank heist or blowing up a train trestle. He didn't like accepting charity, it made him feel—inadequate.

His anxiety worsened when he noticed Dr. Soames join the Sisters and, taking some of the wrapped parcels from one of the nuns, she helped to distribute the items. This itself was not a bad thing, but she slowly made her way toward Leon, and this was something he did not want to happen.

Shame filled him and he glanced around for an escape route, even though he knew there wasn't one. He was stuck.

Dammit. Of all the prisons dotted throughout the West, why in the world did she have to wind up here?

The instinct of the hunted took over, and he scanned the area, still hoping to find an escape route. None presented itself. Then it was too late; she was almost level with him.

She won't recognize me, Leon told himself. *I'm not the same man I was then. I've lost weight and my head is shaven. That changes a person's appearance; she won't know me.*

He kept telling himself this, but in his heart, he knew his dark eyes and those persistent dimples were very distinguishing. Even with the law not having pictures of him, it was amazing he had stayed free for so long, because once having seen him, people tended not to forget him.

He kept his mouth neutral and turned his eyes away from her. He looked down at the floor and refused to make eye contact. This was a typical stance for an inmate; it would be expected. It would be all right.

Then Mariam touched his arm.

Though approaching the furthest end of middle age, Mariam Soames was still a comely woman who, to this day, carried a spark in her eye and a ready smile upon her lips. She was a kind and loving soul who moved with grace and elegance. Any man would have been proud to have her on his arm.

But Leon turned away.

She took no offence at the inmate not raising his eyes to meet hers; she knew what it was like for them here. She smiled and handed him a soft parcel, probably a blanket or a sweater.

"Merry Christmas, young man," she greeted him. "Please accept this. I hope it will give you some comfort through the winter for you."

Leon did not lift his eyes, but he couldn't help the hint of a smile that triggered his dimple as he accepted the package.

"Thank you."

Mariam nodded acknowledgement and turned away.

Leon breathed a sigh of relief, but it was short-lived.

She stopped and took a closer look at him. Again, she gently touched his arm.

"Peter?" she asked. "Peter Black?"

Leon silently groaned.

The guard, Pearson, spoke up. "No, ma'am, you're mistaken. Black was his alias. His real name is Nash."

"No. That can't be. Peter—please, look at me."

Leon's jaw tightened. Could his degradation plunge any further? Must he be humiliated like this?

Then he felt Pearson's billy club smack him on the butt.

"You heard the Preacher-lady, Nash. Let her get a look at your ugly mug."

With a resigned sigh, Leon lifted his chin and looked the doctor in the eye. Now that his cover was blown, he smiled a greeting as he saw recognition wash over her features.

She openly smiled back at him.

"It is you. I thought so. But . . . Mr. Nash?"

"Yes, Doctor," Leon admitted.

"Oh. I see." Her expression changed to one of concern. "Of course, we had heard of the capture of Napoleon Nash and Jackson Kiefer, but we don't get newspapers at the orphanage. We never saw any pictures. It never occurred to us that . . . does this mean that Mathew is really . . .?"

"Yes, ma'am," Leon answered. "Mathew White is Jack Kiefer."

"Oh dear. This is surprising news, indeed." She glanced around and realized she was holding things up. She squeezed Leon's arm and smiled at him again. "I must carry on, but I will speak with you later."

Dr. Mariam and Officer Pearson moved on.

Leon watched them out of the corner of his eye, as the Sisters finished with their errand.

What did that mean? his suspicious mind asked. *I'm not permitted visitors yet. Did Mariam have special privileges here? Well, I suppose that would make sense. But what do we have to talk about? Am I in for a reprimand? Is she going to turn the wrath of God upon me?* He sighed. *That's the way it always happens. They're nice to you, ingratiating themselves with you, and then, when your guard is down, they attack you with righteous damnation. They're all the same. But I thought she was different . . ..*

He was jolted out of his musings by Carson's loud voice giving orders.

"Listen up! Through the Christian generosity of Warden Mitchell, you have all been given the day off. Use it wisely."

The shuffling of feet and scraping of chairs followed this announcement, as some inmates chose to leave the common hall, while others pulled out books, or writing paper and sat down to pass the day in silent commune.

Leon returned to his cell.

***

Leon shivered. Even with the fireplaces lit, the prison maintained its chill. But he held onto his holiday spirt as he leaned back on his cot, with his pillow against the wall, and opened his Christmas present.

Yes, it was a blanket, and a pair of socks.

He smiled with unexpected pleasure as he removed his shoes and pulled the socks onto his cold feet. Instantly, he felt the warmth invade his toes. He closed his eyes and sighed with the ecstasy of it. He couldn't remember ever receiving such a welcome gift. He wrapped the blanket around his shoulders, and settled back into the comfort of his pillow again.

What a pleasure it was to feel warm.

After a few minutes of pure indulgence, he turned to his table to retrieve the latest medical journal, only to find himself staring at another parcel sitting there. It was obvious the paper wrapping had been removed, and the contents inspected. But the guard who had done it took care to rewrap the gift before placing it in Leon's cell. Half the fun of receiving a gift was the unwrapping of it.

Hmm, who could this be from? He'd already received a sweater from the Marshams and couldn't think who else would be sending him a gift. Taggard, maybe? His breath caught, could it be Jack, sending a peace offering?

He picked it up and looked at the writing, and his heart sank.

No, it's not from Jack. Still, it's from Josey; at least she hasn't forgotten about me.

He felt a boyish excitement at receiving another gift and tore off the paper wrapping to find himself staring at a book, *Around the World in 80 Days.* He chuckled at that. Trust Josey to give him a book about traveling when he was stuck in a prison cell.

Oh well, I hear it's a good read. It just might help me forget about this place for a while.

He opened the cover and a letter fell out. Oh! Finally—maybe some news.

He began to open the envelope when he heard a rapping on his cell door. He looked up to see Officer Pearson standing there.

Leon slumped in disappointment. Now what?

"Convict—follow me."

Leon tucked his letter back inside the book and placed both on the table. He swung his legs off the cot and put his shoes back on, before standing up and following Pearson to wherever they were going.

They headed downstairs to the ground level, then to a small room tucked in beside the washroom. Pearson unlocked a door and ushered Leon inside where there was a bench and numerous sets of shackles and leg irons hanging on the wall. The other guard, Murray, followed them in and stood to the side, holding a rifle and watching every move Leon made.

Leon was apprehensive. What was going on?

"Up against the wall, Convict," Pearson instructed him, "hands above your head."

Leon complied. He felt Pearson put pressure between his shoulder blades and push him harder against the wall. He felt his legs being whacked apart with the billy club followed by Pearson giving him a thorough search.

Leon hadn't been given a patting-down like this since Morrison.

What are they looking for? he wondered, as he subconsciously chewed his lip. *Do they think I've stolen something?*

Pearson finished the search, but he didn't give Leon permission to move, so the inmate stayed where he was. Then Pearson wrapped that damned belt around his waist and snuggly cinched it up.

Am I going somewhere? In this weather? Oh crap.

"Turn around."

Leon did so, and his hands were snapped into the cuffs attached to the belt.

Pearson squatted and clamped the leg irons around Leon's ankles. He brought the chain up with him as he stood and attached the end of this to the belt. Finished with the security precautions, he grabbed the inmate's arm, turned him toward the exit and shuffled him into the main aisle again.

Pearson led the way past the cells and stopped in front of the door that led out to the offices. He unlocked it, and the three men continued past the door of the warden's office, past the entrance to the main hallway, and then stopped at the door to the processing room.

Leon had been here before, on the day of his incarceration, and he felt anxious about being here again. If he were leaving the prison, wouldn't they have simply gone through the door to the hallway that led to the front entrance? Did he have to be processed out, and if he was going out, where was he going?

Pearson opened the door and motioned Leon into the processing room. It looked much the same as the last time he'd been in here, though the camera wasn't set up. No new prisoners coming in today.

Pearson took him to the table and pushed him onto the chair. Another chair faced him on the opposite side of the table, and he stared at it as though it had the answers to all his questions. It didn't.

He noticed that it was warm. He considered pulling off the sweater he wore over his prison garb but he was too securely restrained.

Pearson then took his position by the door to await whomever was coming.

Leon turned eyes forward and stared at the empty chair on the other side of the table. Was this to be another interview with the warden? If so, hopefully he wouldn't have to wait too long. He had an important letter to get back to.

The door leading to the office hallway opened, and Doctor Mariam walked in.

Leon hadn't realized how tense he had been until he saw her, and relief washed over him.

Mariam met his eyes and sent him an open smile.

Leon smiled back, no longer feeling embarrassed by his predicament, or worried about her motives. The kindness in her eyes alleviated his suspicions, and he now looked forward to having an honest-to-goodness conversation with a real person.

Mariam closed the door behind her. She nodded a greeting to Pearson, then sat down in the second chair. She had a book with her.

"Peter," she greeted him, then hesitated. "Or, I suppose, I should call you Napoleon."

"It doesn't matter," he told her. "Whichever one you're comfortable with."

"Well," she smiled, "To me you are Peter, so I'll stay with that for now. Perhaps, as I come to know Napoleon Nash, it will change."

Leon smiled with an openness that was rare even on a good day. It was so nice to see her like this, face to face, rather than from the distance of the pulpit to the far corner of the common room. Somehow, her presence here was proof that life still did exist "out there".

"I have brought you a gift," she informed him.

"Another one?"

"The previous one was from the Women's Auxiliary and Charitable Deeds Association," Mariam explained, "this is from me to you. I seem to recall you enjoy reading. I thought you might like this. It's not a new copy, but it is intact."

She presented him with the book and waited for him to accept it. The table blocked his lap, so she could not see that he was shackled.

He smiled self-consciously and shook his hands, causing the chains to rattle.

"I'm afraid I'm a little confined here, Doctor," he explained. "If you could put it on the table, I'll be sure to pick it up when I leave."

"Oh, of course," she said. "I'm sorry, I should have realized."

Leon shrugged, dismissing her apology.

She placed the book on the table, and he leaned forward to read the title.

He smiled with pleasure. "Oh. Gulliver's Travels. Thank you."

"I wasn't sure if you had already read it, but if you have, I always felt a good book is worth visiting again."

"Yes, I have read it before," Leon admitted, "but I agree; it is worth another visit. Like going to see an old friend."

"Speaking of friends," Mariam inquired, "how is Mathew?"

The smile dropped from Leon's face.

Mariam frowned, seeing pain flicker through his eyes. "What is it?"

"I don't know how he is," Leon admitted. "I haven't heard from him."

"Really?" Her frown deepened. "I was under the impression that the two of you were close."

"Yes. So was I." He looked at his hands, avoiding her eyes. He felt the tightness return to his throat and he tried to swallow it down.

Mariam's frown lifted into a sad smile. His torment was obvious. She wanted to go to him, to take him in her arms and hug his loneliness away. But she knew the rules, and in these circumstances, she was not permitted to approach the inmate.

Yet, when she came to assist the prison doctor, she tended to the patients' needs on a regular basis, so, perhaps . . .. She reached a hand toward him, to offer him some solace.

Instantly, there was a discreet cough from the guard still standing behind Leon. Mariam glanced at him and he shook his head. In here, even with the doctor, physical contact was not permitted.

The warning from Pearson brought Leon out of his musings, and he smiled to lighten the mood.

"It's all right," he assured her. "Jack has a chance at a good life, now. I can't blame him for going after it."

"Well, hopefully you'll hear from him soon. In the meantime, I know you are permitted to write one letter a week; why don't you write to him?"

"I have. He has not responded."

"I see. Please keep trying. There may be things going on in his life that you know nothing about. Don't give up on him yet."

"All right. I won't."

"In the meantime, with the help of three Sisters, I run a small orphanage on the other side of Laramie," she informed him. "I also help Dr. Palin in the infirmary when things get too busy for him. So, you see, now that I know you are here, you are not going to be getting rid of me. I will keep in touch."

Leon's smile was genuine. "Yes, ma'am. I admit, I didn't realize you were Catholic."

"I'm not."

Leon frowned. "Now I really am confused. I didn't think the Catholic church permitted women to be ordained, but . . ."

"No, they don't." Mariam smiled at his ordeal. "I was raised a Unitarian, and my father often lectured at the weekly meetings. I learned a lot from him about how to keep an audience interested. He encouraged my education and I was fortunate to attend university. I have degrees in theology and the sciences. I am also a Doctor of Philosophy. I offer my services as an instructor and a lecturer, not as a minister, but, when the need arises, I can do both."

A spark of interest lit Leon's eyes. "Science and philosophy? And a doctorate degree at that. I'm impressed."

"Perhaps we can get together sometime and share our views."

"Hmm." Leon's interested dipped as he glanced around at the guard. "Yeah, maybe." He sighed and returned his attention to his friend. "I must admit, I've never heard of the Unitarian Church. Is it a form of Christianity?"

"In a way. Perhaps, when we have more time, we can discuss this topic further."

The cloud that was again settling over Leon, darkened.

Oh, here we go. I knew it; another lecture.

Mariam read his thoughts and sought to put him at ease. "When you're ready, or even just interested. I'm not trying to convert you, Peter. That's not what we do. You must find your own path."

"Really?" Leon's relief washed away the cloud. "Fine. I don't choose any path."

Mariam chuckled. "But you are on a path, whether or not you're aware of it." She saw the block come down again. "Never mind. I'm not here to preach at you." She twinkled a smile. "I'll save that for Sunday services."

Oh, thank goodness. Leon relaxed and picked up the conversation where he was more comfortable. "So, if you're not Catholic, why are you living in a convent with a bunch of nuns?"

Mariam laughed. "Oh, Peter. It's not a convent. Witnessing the unfortunate plight of so many orphaned children, I felt I wanted to do something to help. When we first met, Mathew let slip about your years in an orphanage. Hearing his stories added fuel to my convictions."

Leon rolled his eyes. "Jack isn't usually that forthcoming. But he sure didn't have any trouble filling you in on that part of our lives."

"Oh dear. Yes, it's Jack, isn't it? I can see it's going to take me a while to get used to your names."

Leon nodded. "That's okay. Whatever you're comfortable with. But how did you end up working for the church?"

"I'm not working for the church. They're working for me."

Leon leaned back with a skeptical gaze. "How's that?"

"Well, I wanted to open a school and orphanage for unfortunate children, to give them a better start in life. I came into money and began looking for the right place. And I found it, right here in Laramie. It's an old hotel, but it's perfect. It has its own stable and kitchen, as well as dining area and lecture halls for classes. And there's no shortage of bedrooms. It's run down, and always seems to be in need of repair, but it works."

"So, you own it?"

"Yes."

"And the Sisters? How is it they work there with you when you're not Catholic?"

"I knew I couldn't run it on my own, but nor could I afford to hire staff. So, I asked the church in Cheyenne if they could spare three Sisters to come work with me. I offered to cover their room and board, and since it was for a worthy cause, it was agreed to."

"That's amazing." Leon gazed at her with heightened respect. "You have the church working for you? And all you're covering is their room and board?"

"That's all they get at the convent." She leaned forward with a sly smile. "Besides, I give them a small wage for pocket money, but if I told the church administrators that, they would confiscate it. So that's just between us."

Leon chuckled. "You, me, and Officer Pearson."

"I'm sure the officer will keep our little secret. Won't you, Officer Pearson?"

Pearson twitched a smile. "Yes, ma'am."

Mariam looked at Leon again. "You see? All is good. Now, I'd best be going. The Sisters are waiting for me."

"Yes, of course," Leon accepted that. "Thank you for coming, Doctor. And thank you again, for the gifts."

"I'll look forward to speaking with you again," she said, as she got to her feet. "And no need to be so formal. We are friends first, are we not? Goodbye, for now, Peter."

Leon started to get to his feet, as any gentleman would do, but was instantly reprimanded.

"Stay where you are, Nash," Pearson ordered him. "Don't move."

Leon sat back on the chair and sent an apologetic smile to the doctor.

She returned an understanding nod and then was gone.

Pearson opened the back door and ushered Leon through. "I've never heard of Unitarian either. It must be some new-fangled religion. It takes all kinds, I suppose."

Leon shrugged. "The inmates seem to like her."

The words slipped out before Leon could bite them off. Then he tensed, expecting a reprimand.

There was a slight heaviness to the air as they continued along the hallway, and Leon could feel the guard considered his options.

They entered the cell block and the moment for reprimand had passed.

Leon relaxed and returned to his cell. He knew he'd sidestepped the punishment. If he'd been with Officer Murry, he'd be nursing a bruised ribcage by now. He still had to learn to keep his mouth shut.

As time went on, he found himself looking forward to the sermons that Dr. Soames delivered, if for no other reason than to hear a woman's voice, speaking passionately about reformation, and forgiveness, and of God's love. He still wasn't buying it, but hearing Mariam speak took him back to happier times and filled him with a contentedness he thought he'd lost.

***

Leon wrapped his new blanket around himself and settled into his pillow to read Josey's letter.

He smiled as he read; she wrote just like she talked, high energy and all over the place. A lot of what she said concerned Jack's trial. Much of it, Leon had already heard from Taggard, but it was good to get it now from Josey's perspective.

Leon was surprised to learn that their Texas rancher friend, Maxwell Coburn had testified in person and had given quite a commanding statement, even putting the judge in his place.

Good for him. Leon smirked. *Nobody like good ole Max to barge in there and stir things up.*

Leon wondered if things would have gone differently if their negotiations had not worked out. Or worse, if the woman in question had turned out to be a shrew of a wife. Geesh. He and Jack would probably have ended up swinging from the gallows. As it was, it all worked out well for Jack, and Josey insisted that Max wasn't going to give up on Leon, either. He wasn't to lose hope; nobody was giving up on him.

Leon sighed. *Yeah, nobody but Jack.*

Moving on, he was amazed to hear that Josey and the Marsham girls—or, more appropriately, young ladies—had struck up a friendship.

> *"Caroline is apparently planning on starting a job in Denver this spring and will be staying at Miss Hardcastle's Boarding House for Young Ladies. I pity her*

having to deal with that dried up old prune. I think it ironic that her Christian name is Prudence, as none other could be more fitting. I'd suggest she stay with me, but somehow, I doubt her parents would approve given my current situation."

Leon laughed. No, that probably wouldn't work.

"Still," Josey's letter continued, *"I don't mind showing her the sights. I'm sure a young lady, away from home for the first time would appreciate a friend close at hand. Goodness knows Miss Prudence Hardcastle won't give her any leeway. That woman is like a vulture lying in wait for any sign of anyone under her roof actually having a good time.*

Well, now I suppose I should get down to the meat of the matter. Never, in all my born days, would I imagine Jack behaving the way he is these days. My goodness, he has always been such a gentleman, even when we, oh, no. Never mind about that, Napoleon.

Anyway, I should have thought he'd be happy to have won his pardon, or at least relieved. Then eager as the rest of us to get after Governor Warren to rectify your mistreatment. I've even had a word with dear Ben, who was recently appointed governorship of Colorado, to have a word with Mr. Warren concerning this situation. But it was all for naught.

He practically threw me out of his office! I couldn't believe it. I reminded him of all the favors I've—Oh, but I digress again. Long story short, he would have nothing to do with discussing this situation with Governor Warren. Good heavens! What's the point of making friends with these people if they refuse to return a favor? I mean, really!

But, back to Jack. As I said, we all thought he would be happy, but instead, he is sullen and miserable. He often disappears for days on end, getting drunk and causing trouble in town. Dr. Gibson is at a loss. Mr. Marsham is ready to wring his neck. I am sorry to say it, but your nephew has turned into a drunken bastard.

He's also spending way too much time at the brothel in Arvada. I hear from the gossip circles that Miss Penny is taking this behavior to heart. Apparently, she has designs on Jack, herself, and can't understand what he's getting from 'those girls' that he can't get from her.

Well! All I can say to that is if her parents haven't told her about the birds and the bees yet, then it's hardly my place to do so!

I hope that Miss Caroline isn't quite so naïve, or we won't have any fun at all! Oh, but good fun of course. Nothing sordid. You can rest assured; I shall be very selective on which sights I expose her to.

Well, there you have it. This is all I know about the matter, dear Napoleon. We are at our wit's end. I shall, of course, keep you posted, although, with the state of our postal service this time of year, it's likely all will be remedied before you hear anything more.

We can all hope so, anyway.

Goodbye for now. I hope Christmas hasn't been too bleak for you there."

Leon finished the letter and shook his head in dismay. What's going on with him? This doesn't sound right at all. In one way, the information worried Leon, as it was so uncharacteristic of Jack to behave in this manner. But, in another way, it made Leon feel better. Obviously, there was something wrong. This also meant that Jack's apparent abandonment of him had nothing to do with his nephew not caring. If anything, it suggested the opposite.

Leon fretted over his own inability to help his friend. He had to count on others to step in and take over, but none of them understood what was wrong, either. Leon sat on his cot, wrapped cozily in his new blanket, and stared into space. He thought, and he worried, even though he knew there wasn't a damn thing he could do about it.

Eventually, he scooped up his worn-down pencil and last sheet of paper. Using one of his new books for support, he focused on writing a letter. He wasn't sure how to start it, or what questions to ask. He just knew he had to contact someone who would be willing to give him some information, so he could feel he was a part of what was going on at home.

He sat for a moment, collecting his thoughts, pencil poised over the paper. He frowned, made a decision, and began to write:

Dear David . . .

CHAPTER FIFTEEN
THE LETTER

Arvada, Colorado
Winter 1886

It was evening, at the beginning of the second week, of the New Year, when David sat down at his desk to write a letter. He contemplated his words, quill in hand and not sure how to begin. He decided that at the beginning was probably best. He dipped the quill in the ink and began to write:

Napoleon,

I apologize for not writing to you sooner. You are correct, of course, in requesting information concerning your nephew. You are, indeed, his closest friend and only legitimate family, so you have the right to know. I should have written to you sooner, but things have been so tumultuous here since our return from Wyoming, I didn't think to do so. It is well passed time to rectify this omission.

I suppose, another reason for not writing to you, is that I don't understand what is going on with Jack. Part of his distress, at first, was due to withdrawal from the morphine he had been taking, but he's well past that now. Yet, he is still behaving erratically. He has simply replaced one drug with another—the other being alcohol.

I also suspect he is visiting the opium den which would also explain his erratic behavior and long absences. I have not been able to catch him at this however so it can remain only a suspicion.

I realize he is doing this because he is depressed, but it is the reason for the depth of his depression that I don't understand. He is naturally upset over your fate, as we all are. But though the rest of us are doing what we can to pressure the governor into granting your pardon, Jack seems to prefer simply getting drunk every night. We are all surprised

and confused by this behavior, not to mention disappointed. We assumed he would be the first to come to your rescue.

I have sent a letter back East, to a friend of mine who has done some study on addiction and acute depression. I am hopeful he can give me some insight into Jack's problem.

Meanwhile, I am available to Jack whenever he wants to talk, but if he won't even try to help himself, it's difficult for me to force it onto him. As far as I am aware, he is not even continuing with the stretching and exercises I gave him, to help his shoulder heal properly. Before his trial, he was consistent with keeping this up, but now, it's like he doesn't care anymore.

Fortunately, throughout most of the trip home from Cheyenne, Jack was asleep, only waking occasionally due to bad dreams or necessity. We all disembarked in Arvada, except for your friend, Miss Jansen, who continued on to Denver. I also parted company with the Marshams at this point and walked the rest of the way to my home. I believe Cameron hired a buggy to take the rest of them out to the ranch.

***

Arvada, Colorado
Autumn 1885

Jack sat in the front seat of the buggy. Cameron sat beside him, driving the pair of horses along the familiar road to the ranch. Penny and Caroline sat in the back, bundled up against the chill, but still talking and laughing about their adventure.

270

The two men up front were quiet. They each remained with their own thoughts until the horses jogged down the tree-lined lane leading to the Rocking M. It was then that Jack spied ole Midnight still out in that same field with Karma.

"Cameron. Stop for a minute, will ya?" Jack asked, "I'd like to say hello to my old friend out there."

"Sure," Cameron agreed, and pulled the pair to a halt.

The two pastured horses, both looking fat and shaggy with their winter coats on, snorted and trotted over to the fence in greeting. They appeared bright-eyed and healthy, and Midnight gave a nicker as he recognized his human.

Jack smiled and gave his big gelding an affectionate slap on the neck.

"Hey there, old friend. How ya doin'"

Midnight gave him a boisterous head butt, as though asking the same question.

Karma was standing by, and she stretched her nose out to Jack and gave him a checking over. She made sure he was whom she thought he was. Then she turned her attention to the lane, and with head up and ears pricked to their utmost, she scanned the distant horizon, waiting expectantly for her own human to appear.

She opened her mouth and set forth a whinny, then continued to watch and wait, hoping to see the familiar figure come walking over the ridge.

Jack felt his heart break in two. He gave her a pat on the neck and rubbed her mane.

"No, Karma. He ain't here. He ain't comin'."

Karma cocked an ear toward him and then, as though in understanding, she relaxed her stance and brought her head around to give Jack a friendly nuzzle.

He gave her a gentle rub, then she turned and, along with Midnight, trotted back into the field to continue with grazing.

Jack stepped up into the buggy.

"They're lookin' in good shape," he said to the ladies. "You've done an excellent job of takin' care of 'em."

"It was a pleasure to look after them for you, Mathew," Caroline assured him. "They're wonderful horses; both of them. We can see why you and Peter are so fond of them."

Jack simply nodded.

Cameron clucked to the pair and they continued on to the barn yard.

Rufus finally appeared, better late than never, to greet the home comers. He woofed excitedly, his tail wagging as he trotted stiffly over to meet the buggy. Peanut and Pebbles charged out of the barn after him, yapping excitedly in their own form of greetings.

Close behind them, came Sam.

Cameron turned the buggy toward the second barn, and Sam stepped forward to hold the bridle of the near-side horse, while everyone disembarked.

"Afternoon, Sam," Cameron greeted him. "Everything all right?"

"Yes sir, Mr. Marsham," Sam assured him. "Everything is fine. Hello Miss Penny, Miss Caroline."

"Hi Sam," Penny greeted him.

"Hi," Caroline answered, but barely gave him a smile or a look.

Sam sighed and looked to Jack.

"Mr. Kiefer." He felt apprehensive, as if he wasn't sure what kind of reception he would receive from this gentleman. "I'm glad to hear everything worked out for you."

"Hello, Sam," Jack answered and stepped forward to shake his hand. "It's good to see you again."

Sam smiled, relieved. It seemed Mr. Kiefer, at least, had forgiven him.

"Take the horses in and settle them for the night, Sam," Cameron instructed him. "You can return them to town tomorrow when you go in."

"Yes, sir."

"Mathew!"

Jack turned to the house to see Jean come down the steps and run toward the group.

"Oh, Mathew. Welcome home. It is so good to see you."

Jack grinned. "Hello, Jean."

She came up to him and gave him a big hug. He returned it with a kiss to her cheek.

"Come into the house," she said. "I've had a chicken stew simmering on the stove, just waiting for you to get home. You all must be chilled to the bone."

This statement was met with agreement from all quarters. Everyone headed for the house, looking forward to the opportunity to

272

warm up and settle in.

Jean turned to Sam as he was leading the team into the barn.

"You come in and join us, Sam. As soon as you get those horses put away."

'Yes, ma'am. I will. Thank you."

***

Inside the ranch house it was warm, and should have been inviting, but Jack felt uncomfortable. Everyone removed their heavy coats and scarves, then settled in around a new dining room table. They were soon tucking into hot soup and warm, fresh-baked bread.

Jack joined in, as was expected of him. He laughed and talked as everyone discussed the ranch and the current events of the town, but just like at the dinner party in Cheyenne, his heart wasn't in it. All he wanted to do was run away and cry somewhere. But there was nowhere else for him to go.

Jean noticed his distraction and tried to bring him back into the conversation.

"I've set up the same room for you, under the stairs," she informed him. "I hope that will be all right for you."

"Ahh," Jack glanced at Cameron, not sure where to go with this.

"Jack's going to sleep in the bunkhouse with Sam," Cameron informed his wife. "At least for now."

Jean frowned. "Whatever do you mean? Why can't he simply return to his old room?"

"We'll discuss it later." Then, to avoid an argument, he turned to Jack. "David suggested I put you to work right away, but if you want to take a day or two—."

"No!" Jack snapped out. "I need somethin' ta do. Whatever you want, Cameron."

Cameron and Jean exchanged a quick look and the girls were suddenly silent.

"Okay, fine," Cameron agreed. "Tomorrow morning, when Sam takes the buggy back into town, why don't you go with him. You can drive the buckboard, and the two of you can bring back the supplies for the week."

"Fine."

Sam came in the front door and, removing his heavy coat and work boots, came and joined them at the table.

Jean was quick to put a bowl of soup in front of him and offer him some bread. That done, she headed for the day nursery, as Elijah had started to stir and was making it clear he wanted to join the family.

"Jack's going into town with you, tomorrow, Sam," Cameron said, "give you a hand with the supplies."

"Oh sure," Sam smiled, glad of the help. "I hope we can get there and back before the first snows hit. You can practically smell it in the air."

Jean returned with Eli. It was obvious, even wrapped in a blanket, that he had grown plenty in the few months Jack had been away. Even at that, the scene around the table was a disturbing déjà vu. It was so much like the first lunch he and Leon had enjoyed in this room, that Jack felt like he was going to throw up.

"Mathew, why don't you take Eli for a bit?" Jean suggested. "Get reacquainted."

"No!" Jack practically shouted at her. He shoved his chair away from the table and was on his feet in a flash, backing away from her.

Jean jumped in surprise and took an involuntary step back.

"Jack . . ." Cameron's voice held a warning tone.

"I'm sorry," Jack mumbled, trying to calm down, knowing he was behaving in an unacceptable manner, but unable to stop himself. "I'm sorry. I'm tired. I'm just gonna go ta my room for a while." And with all eyes upon him, he turned and, through force of habit, disappeared into the room under the stairs.

Jean sent a questioning look to her husband. Cameron sighed and shook his head. He could tell there was going to be some more "pillow talk" come evening.

***

Jack closed the door behind him and was instantly pacing the room. He felt agitated, frustrated, angry and hurt. All these emotions hitting him at once, and he had no control over any of them. He felt like he needed to hit something or someone!

He unstrapped his gun belt and threw it on the chair. This action itself suggested his uncharacteristic moodiness, as he generally treated his colt 45, far better than he did himself. He turned his back on the holstered gun and ran his hands through his hair, clenching his fists around the curls as if his very life depended on it.

His sob came suddenly and uncontrollably. He clamped down to suppress it but failed completely. Fighting for control, he sat on the bed and stared out the window at the two horses grazing in the field. And the sobs attacked him. He grabbed the pillow and, flinging himself back across the bed, he hugged it to his face to suffocate the sounds, or suffocate himself, whichever came first.

He rolled onto his side and, pulling his knees up, he cried into the pillow like a baby. The sobs racked his body until he fought just to breathe; his chest ached, and his throat burned, yet he continued to sob.

Somewhere, in between the gasps and the anguish, he heard a strangled voice pleading, "Leon, I'm sorry. I'm sorry . . .", until the sobs took over completely and his words were drowned.

***

"What in the world was that all about?" Jean asked as she snuggled in her husband's arms. "He didn't even come out for supper."

"I don't know. David says he's depressed, and we need to give him some time. But I'm at a loss as to how to deal with it. I guess just putting him to work would be the best thing, right now."

"Yes," Jean agreed. "Keeping him busy can't hurt. And I'm sure the girls will help to bolster his spirits." Cameron shifted a little and Jean felt him tense. "What?"

Cameron sighed. "Well, I wasn't sure how to tell you this, but you do need to know. The morning after the trial, we all met at the café for breakfast, but Jack didn't show up. David decided to go back to the hotel to check on him, and he wasn't in his room. Nor had his bed been slept in. So, the two of us went in search of him. We found him, passed out in one of the seedier saloons in town.

"Apparently, he went there shortly after we had all retired for the night. He took one of those gals, and he treated her roughly. I swear, I felt like beating some sense into him myself—give him a taste of what he had been dishing out. But he was passed out cold from all the drinking and wouldn't have felt it anyway. Plus, David wouldn't let me, though he was sickened by the whole affair, as well.

"The Madam told us not to worry about it, that it was common for some of the customers to get a little rough, no big deal." Cameron sighed again, and Jean could feel him shake his head at the absurdity of the whole episode. "So, David and I hauled Jack back to his hotel room to sleep it off until the train was due. Then we loaded him onto the train and brought him home. I haven't had a chance to speak with him about it, because the girls have always been around, so maybe tomorrow. Still, I don't really feel comfortable with either of the girls being around him without one of us being there. At least for now. I just don't trust him."

"Oh no," Jean whispered. "Poor Mathew."

"What?" Cameron wasn't sure he'd heard correctly. "What do you mean, 'poor Mathew'? Didn't you hear what I said? That prostitute took a beating, but it would have been a lot worse if the Madam hadn't gone in there to break it up."

"No, I know," Jean insisted, as she gave her husband a light squeeze on his arm. "I'm not saying it was acceptable—of course it wasn't. It's just that Mathew is such a gentle soul."

Cameron barked a laugh.

"I know," Jean repeated, "but if you weren't so angry with him right now, you would realize how much pain he must be in, to cause him to behave that way.

"I hate to admit it, but I would be more inclined to believe Peter had done something like that, rather than Mathew. Peter can be masterful and intimidating sometimes. I have no trouble believing he was the leader of the Elk Mountain gang—he has a way about him, he naturally takes control. But not Mathew; he's too kind."

"I don't know, Jean. You didn't hear the testimony at the trial. More than one person commented on Jack's temper and that Leon was the only one who could control him when he got like that. And he has killed. More than once."

He felt Jean stiffen with this news, then release a sigh.

"Oh dear."

"Yes. I was asked if I had ever felt threatened by either of them or concerned for the safety of my family with them around. I answered truthfully at the time, that I never had. But now? I would not be able to give the same answer. I do fear for their safety around Jack now, and I don't want either of the girls to be alone with him, until he can prove to me he is worthy of our trust."

"All right," Jean agreed. "I don't believe he would ever hurt any of us, and if he has killed, then there must have been some good reason for it."

"Yes, his rationale was convincing. But the prosecuting attorney also made some valid points. Still, Jack was repentant, and even apologized to the daughter of one of the victims."

Jean nodded. "That sounds more like the man we know. But I'll accept your decree. At the same time, though, I am also going to do everything I can to help Mathew get through this. I know he's a good person, and now that he has his freedom, I'd hate to see him throw it away. We need to help him find his footing again. These last four or five months have been very hard on him."

Cameron chuckled and gave his wife a hug. "Oh brother. You and David. You're each just as stubborn as the other."

"Yes, we are," she agreed. Then her tone turned serious. "Now, what about this Mr. Granger, whom I am apparently going to be entertaining at Thanksgiving?"

"Oh no," Cameron groaned.

"What?" Jean asked. "Don't you like him?"

"No, no, I like him well enough. It's just that I was hoping to actually get some sleep tonight."

"Oh, a couple of more minutes won't hurt you," Jean insisted. "I'm just curious. You wouldn't have invited him all the way here for the holiday, if you didn't think he was worthy. You saw him in action in the courtroom—does he appear to be an honorable person?"

"Well, yes," Cameron admitted. "He worked hard on both cases and certainly spearheaded the campaign to persuade the Governor's Office into keeping the promise that was made. This course of action did help in Jack's case. And, he's willing to stay with it to get Leon pardoned. It's not going to be easy."

Jean nodded, then elaborated. "Still, often, some lawyers can bend the truth a bit to ensure a win; twist people's words to mean something that wasn't intended. Did you see any of that with Mr. Granger?"

"No. Indeed, that is a better description of the prosecuting attorney, Mr. DeFord. He had quite the talent for leading witnesses in the direction he wanted them to go. Indeed, he would have won both cases if the governor hadn't stepped in with Jack's. He was this close to getting that young man hanged. I may be angry with Jack right now, but I don't believe he deserves that."

"So, are you saying you think Mr. DeFord is a better lawyer than Mr. Granger?" Jean asked.

"No," Cameron defended himself. "Not a better lawyer as such, but a lot more vicious in his manner. Mr. Granger is still a young man and new to the bar, which is the only reason we could retain him for the defense; no other lawyer in town wanted the job. In that light, I think he did very well, and once he gets more experience under his belt, he should make a fine attorney. And from what I've seen, an honest one as well."

"He should be able to provide for Caroline and a family without too much hardship," the practical side of the mother observed.

"Certainly. I think he will be very successful."

"And Caroline is obviously fond of him," Jean stated. "That was clear as soon as she got home from Peter's trial."

Cameron sighed. "There you go again. How could you have possibly known that?"

"There was far too much correspondence between them for it to just be about their campaign," Jean explained. "Her letters to him were time consuming and well thought out. Whenever a letter arrived from him, she retired to her room to read it alone, before letting Penny in on what was said. If it was all just about their assault on the governor, she would have been sharing those letters with Penny right away."

"So, this isn't news to you," Cameron stated with some disappointment.

Jean smiled and again gave her husband a squeeze on his arm. "No. I wasn't at all surprised when you told me of his intentions."

"You're too much. How am I supposed to surprise you with anything when you're always two steps ahead of me?"

"Well, I'm not always, dear. Just when it comes to our girls and affairs of the heart."

"Okay, fine," Cameron conceded. "Still, personally, I think Mr. Granger is a good sort, but of course, I wanted you to meet him before giving permission for anything official. But I think you will like him."

"I'm sure I will," Jean agreed. "It will be a full house here for the holidays!"

"Yes, it probably will be," Cameron gave his wife a hug. "So, can I go to sleep now?"

Jean chuckled. "Yes, you may. Love you."

"Love you too. Now goodnight."

***

The next morning was a surprise for Jean and Cameron. Jack was up early and already had the fire stoked and the coffee going, when Jean came down to start breakfast. She smiled at him and, putting Eli on the floor to entertain himself, she gave Jack a morning hug.

"You're looking in better spirits today, Mathew. Did you sleep well?"

"Yeah, I did," he lied. "Thought I would get an early start on things since it is my first day on the job here."

"You must be hungry, since you didn't eat any supper last night," Jean said. "We'll get some oatmeal going first and then how about some flapjacks and bacon?"

"Fine."

"Sam ought to be in soon," she said. "He generally takes meals with us now, since the other hands are up at the line cabin to take care of the stock through the winter. It gets kind of lonely for him in that bunkhouse, all by himself."

"Sam is working out okay here, is he?" Jack asked.

"Yes, he is. He works hard and has done nothing to make us regret keeping him on after, well, you know."

Jack smiled. "Yup." He poured coffee for them both, while Jean set the pot on the stove for the oatmeal. "It don't appear that Caroline has quite forgiven him though."

Jean sighed as she hugged her cup of coffee. "No. I think Sam has burned his bridges there. But he does seem to be getting on well with Maribelle Willis. I don't think he's going to be too heartbroken that Caroline has set her sights on another."

"Ohhh, so Cameron has told you about that, has he?"

"Oh yes," she said, with a smile. "What do you think of him, Mathew? Is he worthy of our eldest daughter?"

"After what happened ta Leon, I was ready ta write him off as useless," Jack said. "But once I got a taste of how ruthless it is in a courtroom, I ended up admirin' 'im just for bein' able ta stay afloat." He nodded his confirmation. "Yeah, I think Mr. Granger would make a good match for Caroline. If my opinion counts for anything these days."

"Of course, it counts," Jean assured him. "And from what I am hearing of this young man, I think you are probably right. He seems to be willing to carry on pushing for Peter's pardon as well, so that certainly speaks well of him."

Jack's smile dropped and was replaced with an anxious, almost guarded, demeanor.

Jean frowned, noting the change in the atmosphere.

"Have you been in touch with Peter yet?" she asked.

"No. I doubt he would wanna hear from me."

"Why would you think that? Of course, he'll want—"

"No!" He looked at her with eyes on the edge of threatening, and he backed away.

"It's all right, Mathew." She put a quiet hand on his arm, instinctively seeking to calm him; to prevent him from bolting to his room again. "Don't worry about it. Come, help me slice up some bacon for breakfast."

Jack's demeanor softened, and he relaxed with a self-conscious smile. He stepped forward again and focused his attention on getting breakfast ready.

Jean sent up a silent prayer of thanks. Unlike her husband, she could see right away that Jack was deeply wounded. But just the same as everyone else, she couldn't understand why. But Jean, being Jean, would take him under her wing and do everything she could to help him heal, and hopefully understanding would come in time.

Then there was a stampede on the stairs as the rest of the Marsham clan came down for breakfast.

Eli started to cry.

***

Early afternoon found Cameron sitting at the large table, doing paperwork for the ranch, when he heard the buckboard returning from town. The inevitable chorus of dogs barking in joyous greeting confirmed the arrival. He put aside the figuring, shrugged on his coat and headed outdoors to help with the unloading. But as soon as he got to the porch, it was obvious that something was wrong, no Jack.

Cameron growled to himself.

He plunked down the steps and headed to the buckboard where Sam had parked it, in front of the storage barn. He took hold of the near horse's bridle as Sam climbed down from the driver's seat, already shaking his head.

Cameron's jaw tightened.

"Where is he?"

"I don't know, Mr. Marsham," Sam answered, feeling like he was to blame. "We got into town fine. He seemed to be in good spirits. I went straight to the mercantile, and Mr. Kiefer, he took the pair and buggy back to the livery stable.

"Anyway, short time after that, he met me at the store and helped to get everything loaded into the buckboard n' all that. We were gettin' on fine, talkin' about stuff, you know, but then when we was gettin' ready to come back here, suddenly he says he's gonna go to the saloon and play some cards n' stuff, and he'd make his own way back. Well, I didn't know what to say to change his mind n' all, and he didn't give me a chance to anyway—just walked away."

Sam shrugged, feeling responsible, but still hoping he wasn't going to get yelled at.

Cameron sighed, and his jaw tightened even more, as he tried to keep his frustration and anger in check.

"It's all right, Sam," he assured the young man. "It wasn't your fault."

"Yes sir."

"Where's he getting the money for all this?" Cameron commented, more to himself than anyone else.

"I dunno," Sam answered with another shrug, then began unloading the wagon.

Cameron stared off down the road toward town, a pensive expression on his face.

"He better not be visiting those opium dens. David will have his head, if he is. Then I'll take care of the rest of him."

***

When Jack finally returned, it was three days later, and he was riding a rented horse. He wasn't drunk, nor was he hung-over, and he didn't look like he'd been in any fights, but he was tired. Actually, exhausted would best describe his condition. He tended to the horse, more out of habit than through any sense of responsibility, then staggered into the house. Without a word to anyone, he disappeared into his room and collapsed on the bed. He didn't move for the rest of that day and all that night.

The next morning, he was again up early and getting coffee going before anyone else had begun to stir. He said not a word about where he'd gone, or what he'd done, or even any apology for causing days of needless worry for three ladies who cared deeply for him.

Cameron was ready to wring his neck.

Jean kept the peace.

That day, he helped Sam with the chores around the barns and then saddled up Midnight and joined Sam on a ride up to one of the northern pastures. It was time to check on the livestock, and make sure they were all getting enough to eat in preparation for the upcoming winter months.

It started to snow. It was just a dusting down on the lowlands, nothing to panic about but that didn't stop Caroline from worrying.

"What if Stev . . . err, Mr. Granger can't make it for the holiday? Nothing could be worse than that."

***

The next morning, Jack saddled Karma, since Midnight still seemed tired from the previous day's excursion, and, giving assurances that he would be back in a few hours, headed into town, leading the rental horse back to the livery. Everyone was on pins and needles, wondering if he would indeed return, and what would be the consequences if he did not.

All went well though. Two and a half hours later, he and Karma came trotting back into the yard, just as more snow began to accumulate. Jack tended to Leon's mare and got her, and Midnight, settled for lunch, then entered the house to get some lunch for himself.

For the rest of the afternoon, he busied himself with what chores his injured shoulder would allow and helped Sam get the barnyard livestock tended for the night. Everyone breathed a sigh of relief. Maybe Jack was finally starting to settle in, and everything would be fine.

***

Laramie, Wyoming

By the time Leon received David's letter, it was well into the final week of January 1886. There had been such a heavy snowfall over the Friday night that several inmates were volunteered to go outdoors on the Saturday and shovel the yard, so horses and wagons could get into the prison. Since Carson took great pleasure in antagonizing the "great outlaw leader", Leon, along with Boeman, was doomed to be part of that work detail.

Leon wasn't sure if Carson was trying to organize things so the two adversaries would end up in a scuffle, or if he simply liked asserting his dominance over the two alpha wolves in the pack, to remind them who was really in charge. Unfortunately, Boeman wasn't smart enough to realize the head guard was manipulating him, and he seemed to think Leon was being deliberately antagonistic. Leon did his best to avoid both gentlemen.

Being a man who didn't care much for physical exertion when it could be avoided, Leon found the job of shoveling snow exhausting work. He knew he was going to be sore the next day and that put him into a snarky mood, even before the muscles started to ache. To add to his irritation, Boeman took every opportunity to bump into his rival, knocking him off balance on the slippery footing. He also tended to misjudge where his shovel was going and gave Leon more than one sharp rap on the ankles.

Every time this happened, Leon sent a quick glance to Officer Carson, expecting him to give Boeman a reprimand, but none ever came. Carson simply smiled and watched, obviously anticipating an entertaining scuffle, once Leon got tired of the abuse and lost his temper.

It never happened.

What did happen, came at the end of the day, when Boeman showed up for supper, arriving in the common hall with a limp, a black eye and a split lip.

When Kenny asked him about it, he simply stated that he had fallen on the slippery steps outside and had no other comment to make. The odd thing was, nobody recalled seeing him slip. Kenny was suspicious, and Carson felt he had been cheated out of his fun.

Once supper was over with, a sore but self-satisfied Leon returned to his cell with a cup of coffee. He felt chilled from his time outside and it was his intention to curl up with his blanket and continue reading Around the World in 80 Days.

Instead, he found David's letter waiting for him. Finally, news from home. Some news that might actually make sense. Surely David, being an educated medical man, would know what was going on with Jack.

But once he settled in to read the narrative, his hopes fell. Just as Josey had stated in her letter, David was at a loss. Jack seemed to be getting over his moodiness early in November, and everyone had breathed a sigh of relief. The month had gone by quickly, and the Marshams were busy getting ready for the first of the big holidays, especially since company was coming. Jack had volunteered to stay in the bunkhouse with Sam (Leon bristled at the mention of that young man's name), so Mr. Granger could occupy the spare room during his visit.

All seemed well.

CHAPTER SIXTEEN
DIRE STRAITS

The Rocking M
Colorado

The afternoon before Thanksgiving, Jack drove the buckboard into Arvada to collect more supplies and pick up Steven Granger at the train depot. There was a layer of snow on the ground, but the day was clear and bright, and the roads were hard-packed and easy to traverse. Much to Caroline's relief, all her fretting had been for naught. The train even arrived on time, which was a most unusual occurrence and would hopefully bode well for the holiday.

"Mr. Granger," Jack greeted the attorney as he disembarked, "how was your trip?"

"Mr. Kiefer. Fine, fine." Steven hoisted his one satchel onto the buckboard. "I take it you're settling in all right?"

"Yeah, sure."

The drive to the ranch went by quickly as the conversation flowed easily between the two men.

"How is Caroline?" Steven asked as the buckboard headed out of town.

"Fine," Jack assured him. "She's lookin' forward ta seein' ya."

Steven grinned. "And I her. And Mr. and Mrs. Marsham? Are they well?"

"Yup."

"Have they said anything about me?" Steven continued to dig as he absently chewed his lip. "Do you think Mr. Marsham is in favor of me?"

"Dunno."

Steven sighed. "And Mrs. Marsham? Is she open to my visit? Do you think she'll like me or is she strict and hard to please? What does she think about me courting her daughter? Is she open to that? And what about Caroline coming to work for me in Denver? Have you heard anything at all concerning that issue?"

Jack smiled and patiently listened to this monologue of questions, until they eventually petered out.

Steven finally stopped talking and sat there, looking pensive.

"Well, I tell ya," Jack commented now that the barrage had ceased. "Jean Marsham is one of the kindest women I've ever met. She'll put ya at your ease. Just be yourself and try not ta try too hard."

"Yes, of course." Steven didn't sound convinced.

***

Later that day, Steven had to admit that Jack was right. Once he had been welcomed into the Marshams' home, Jean's natural warmth and kind spirit quickly put him at his ease. Then, when Caroline entered the room, well, the instant and obvious pleasure that beamed from his countenance upon seeing her again, made everyone smile.

***

As it turned out, Jack ended up having the bunkhouse to himself and the dogs. Sam had been invited to spend the holiday in town, with Maribelle and her folks, and Jack had volunteered to take over his duties so the hired hand could have a few days off and enjoy himself. Caroline couldn't have been happier with this development, since the last thing she wanted was that puppy hanging around when she had a real man showing her attention.

Cameron had begun to ease up on his decree concerning Jack. It had been over a month since the last incident of bad behavior, and Jack seemed to be in a much better frame of mind.

Penny was pleased to have her friend joining them at the table for Thanksgiving dinner, and she spent most of the evening chatting with him exclusively. She flirted with him, shamelessly, but so sweetly, no one was offended. On the contrary, Jack seemed to be enjoying the attention and was the perfect gentleman for the duration of the evening.

Throughout dinner, the discussion did turn to Steven moving his practice to Denver, in the hopes of furthering his acquaintance with

Miss Marsham. It was also suggested that Caroline go to work for Mr. Granger, as his assistant, as she obviously had an interest in the law and had an extremely bright mind to go along with it. There was some hesitation
about this, as it seemed to both parents that Caroline was a bit young to be moving to the big city on her own. It was at this point when Jack stepped in, much to Steven's undying gratitude.

"Ain't there a lady's boarding house in Denver?" Jack queried. "I hear tell the matron is real watchful over her ladies there, so Caroline would be safe enough. And Josey lives right there in town. She and the girls seemed to get along in Cheyenne, so I don't think she would mind keepin' an eye on her."

Steven and Caroline looked hopeful. Jean and Cameron looked skeptical.

"Is she responsible?" Cameron asked. "Considering her—" he sent a quick glance to his two young maidens. "I mean to say, she was quite a free spirit with the gentlemen in Cheyenne."

"Well, yeah, she can be," Jack admitted. "But she ain't a floozy, Cameron. I would never suggest her if'n she was. She has a solid character and would take the responsibility seriously. I know she would look out for Caroline's best interests. She'd certainly see the pitfalls long before Caroline walked into 'em."

"Papa, wouldn't that be all right?" Caroline asked, hopefully. "I mean, you have met her, and she is an older lady, and we do get along."

Jack smiled at the "older lady" reference. Josey probably wouldn't appreciate that description.

"Well," Cameron contemplated, "we'll see. If you're able to get lodging at the boarding house, we might consider it. Perhaps the proprietor would have a suggestion for a chaperone."

"Oh, Papa. I don't need a chaperone. Good heavens, I'm almost twenty."

"Twenty, and the first time away from home on your own. You will have a chaperone, young lady, or you don't go at all."

Caroline pouted. "Well then, Josephine. I'll accept her."

"We'll see."

"But Jack says she would be fine."

Cameron flashed a look to the man seated across from him, the thought occurring that he wasn't too sure about Jack's discretion let alone trust his assurance in this matter.

Steven chose this moment to step in. "Perhaps we should see if Miss Hardcastle has room first, then discuss the possible chaperones. You really do need to have a lady companion."

Caroline harrumphed but realized she was outnumbered. "Fine. A chaperone it is. As long as she's not some dried up old—"

"Watch your manners, young lady."

Sigh. "Yes, Papa."

Jack chuckled. "I'm sure it will all work out."

"I'll send Miss Hardcastle a telegram tomorrow and see what she says," Cameron concluded. "One step at a time."

Then, unfortunately, but not surprisingly, the topic turned to Leon and his pardon. Jean noticed right away that Jack's demeanor changed, and he became withdrawn. No one else took note and the conversation continued along that line.

"We really need to hit the governor hard now," Steven said, becoming animated with the topic. "He thinks the pressure is off, because he granted Jack his pardon, but we have to let him know it's not over yet."

"I've already sent letters to people who wrote in before," Caroline stated, "asking them to do so again. Plus, Mr. Coburn and Miss Jensen agreed to get right on it once more. No one is giving up, that's for sure."

"Yes. Sheriff Murphy is also sticking to it," Steven informed them. "Oh, and I received a telegram from a Mr. Carlyle, apparently from the Wells Fargo Detective Agency?"

Jack groaned. Oh no. "What did he have ta say," he asked, already feeling apprehensive.

"He apologized for not getting in touch sooner," Steven explained. "Apparently, he has been out of the country for the past six months, working on a case. He didn't even get the telegram Mr. Nash sent him, until after the trials had begun. Otherwise, he insisted he would have been right there, testifying on your behalf."

"Uh huh," commented Jack. "I don't like countin' on 'im though; he's so damned hard ta pin down."

"I haven't responded to that telegram yet, Mr. Kiefer," Steven informed him, sensing the reluctance. "Would you prefer I ignore it?"

Jack sighed. "No, I guess not. Frank can be resourceful. He just tends ta put people off. He ain't really the friendly sort."

"Fine," Steven agreed, though he wondered at the relationship his two clients had with the agent. Jack seemed cautious of him. "I'll get in touch when I get home. Let him know that any support he can give would be welcome."

***

Dinner wound down, and Eli demanded attention. Penny went off to tend to her brother, while Jean and Caroline cleared the table.

Cameron offered brandies to the two young men still seated at the table, but Jack declined the offer and got to his feet.

"I'm tired," he offered. "I'm gonna retire to the bunkhouse." He promptly made a discreet exit.

Cameron watched him leave, a concerned expression on his face. Jack Kiefer had always been open and friendly, far more so than his partner. But lately he was like a closed book, shutting down and backing off if anyone got too close, even to the point of becoming angry.

Cameron acknowledged that Jean was able to draw the man out more than he could. David seemed to be able to, as well. There was obviously a friendship there between Jack and David, but even that relationship was strained these days.

Cameron sighed and turned his attention to the young man still sitting at the table.

"So, Mr. Granger," he began, as he poured them a couple of drinks, "when exactly do you intend on moving to Denver?"

***

Steven stayed on for a few days but then was forced to depart. He did have a practice to run, not to mention a governor to harass. But he promised to keep in touch, both on the personal level and the professional one. He also gave Caroline many assurances that he would start making plans to move his practice to Denver in the springtime, and to officially begin courting her at that time.

Cameron and Jean both seemed agreeable to this arrangement, so long as Miss Hardcastle could accommodate her at that time.

Jack continued to work at the ranch and was reliable so far as his duties were concerned. But he still tended to disappear on Friday nights and not return until Sunday afternoon. Cameron was again becoming concerned about the man's state of mind.

David tried to keep an eye on their wayward friend, but all those years of eluding the law had taught Jack well how to hide his tracks. The doctor even made unannounced visits to the opium den, both hoping and dreading to find Jack there. But Jack was either too wily for him or was sticking to alcohol as his chosen pain killer, because he was never found within those hazy walls.

Penny was disappointed. After the Thanksgiving dinner, she thought Mathew enjoyed her company, but now he was back to barely acknowledging her. One evening after supper, when it was Caroline's turn to tend to their brother, Penny broached the subject while helping her mother with the dishes.

"What's the matter with him, Mama?" she asked, all concerned. "He never used to behave like this."

Jean sighed. She knew this conversation was going to happen sooner or later. "I know, sweetheart. I don't fully understand it either. I just know that what happened to Peter has hurt him deeply, and he's struggling with it."

"But I thought he would want to help Peter, just like the rest of us," Penny reasoned, "but he's not doing anything. He just keeps going into town to drink and spend time with those girls."

"Penelope!"

"Oh Mama. Do you really think I don't know what goes on there? I'm not a child, you know."

Jean sighed and relaxed her indignant stance.

"No, you're not, are you? I keep forgetting how quickly you girls are growing up. Now, there's your sister already on the verge of being courted by a noteworthy young man." Her smile was sad with acceptance as she brushed a strand of loose hair from her daughter's brow. "You're not little girls anymore."

"So, what do I do?" Penny asked. "How do I get Mathew to notice me?"

"He notices you, sweetheart. Believe me, he does. But he has his mind on other things right now. Until he comes to terms with that, he's not going to be ready for anything more."

"But he doesn't seem to mind spending time with the girls at the saloon," Penny pointed out. "Why does he prefer their company over mine?"

Jean had to stop and think about that one.

"The girls there are just a diversion," she finally explained. "He's not serious about them. They're just frivolous company; they help him to feel better for the short term, because he's not ready for anything long term yet. In a way, he's showing his respect for you by backing away and not taking advantage of your feelings for him."

"But I want him to take advantage of my feelings for him."

Jean laughed, knowing her daughter was still too naïve to understand what she was saying.

"No, you don't. You want him to respect you. You want him to court you the way Mr. Granger is going to be courting your sister. And believe me, courting is not what Jack is doing with those ladies in town."

"Yes, I suppose," Penny admitted. "But how do I get him to do that?"

"Give him time," Jean told her daughter, "Don't chase him. Be there for him when he wants your company, be supportive of him when he needs your support, but don't chase after him. Wait until he's ready to come to you."

Penny gave a long-suffering sigh. "That could take forever."

"Yes," Jean agreed. "Sometimes it can take a long time to convince a man that it's his idea to come courting."

***

Laramie, Wyoming

Leon ran out of candlelight before he could finish David's letter, but he decided, maybe this wasn't such a bad thing. David's news seemed to be all bad, and Leon had a hard time digesting it in one go. He didn't feel well, as he had a bit of a headache, and a slight cough was invading his chest. A day of working outside in the cold had not done him any good.

It was still early evening, but the cells had been locked down for the night. Leon blew out what was left of his candle and decided to settle in to get some rest. Maybe he would feel better in the morning. After all, it had been a strenuous day, and he was tired.

He fell asleep quickly and stayed asleep until the early morning hours. Then, he lay awake, bundled up in his clothing and blankets, waiting for the morning buzzer to sound. He thought that he had dodged a bullet, as he really didn't feel too bad after his rest. Could be, the sudden outdoor exercise had taken his system by surprise and all he needed was a good night's sleep.

Eventually the morning buzzer sounded, and Leon unwrapped himself from the bedding. The cold air hit him like cascading ice water, and he gasped from the shock. He began to shiver and pulled his blanket around himself again as he sat on the edge of his cot, not wanting to lose its warmth. The night shift guards began their final round for roll call, so those who had homes to go to, could do so, and those who resided in the guards' quarters could retire. They were in no mood for dawdlers.

Leon jumped as a billy club banged into the open door of his cell.

"C'mon, 212. On your feet," Davis ordered. "It might be Sunday, but that don't mean you can spend all day in bed."

Leon nodded as he grumbled to himself, then got to his feet. He started to walk toward the open door, but he didn't make it. His legs morphed into wet noodles, and a ringing dizziness assaulted his head, as he collapsed to the floor of his cell. Through the spiraling blackness, he heard voices in the distance, calling out:

"C'mon Nash. Where are ya?"

Then, "Oh crap. Convict down! Cell number 12. Is the doc sober?"

***

When he awakened, he had no idea how much time had passed. He lay in a bed—not his bed, he wasn't in his cell; he was in an open room. His head hurt, and it felt like it was made of lead. He found it hard to breathe, and he was hot. He tried to move and was instantly assaulted by a coughing spasm that left him gasping for what little air he could draw into his lungs.

Doc Palin was over to his bed in an instant.

"Easy, young fella," his gruff voice actually sounded soothing as he helped Leon to settle back onto his pillow. He placed a craggy hand upon his patient's forehead and then to his cheeks.

Leon thought the doctor's hands felt unusually cold.

Doc sat back from his examination. "Hmm," he began, as usual. "You're still burning up. This is what you get for barely eating enough to keep a damned gopher alive."

Doc Palin disappeared for a few moments and then returned with a cup in his hand. He lifted his patient up to a partly sitting position and supported him there while pushing the cup to his lips.

"Drink this. It'll help you sleep."

Leon tried to comply, but his struggle to breathe came in short, shallow gasps and taking water into his throat made him feel like he was drowning. He panicked and tried to fight against the doctor's ministrations, but he was so weak, all he could do was choke and cough.

"I know," Palin encouraged him. "Take it easy, a little bit at a time. C'mon, you need to get this down."

And so it went. It probably took twenty minutes for Palin to get the full cup of fluids down Leon's throat. But, one sip at a time, between bouts of harsh coughing, finally got it done. Leon was exhausted. He felt like a landed fish fighting to survive, but the medication was fast-acting and he faded away, even before the doc had settled him back onto the pillow.

He heard a voice, off in the distance, "How is he, Doc?" It sounded like Kenny.

Leon didn't hear the response, just a rumbling that he knew was a voice, and then he was gone into oblivion again.

***

In the days that followed, Napoleon Nash was barely aware of himself. He thrashed and struggled with inner demons, while the fever took hold and ran its course. He dreamed about his sister. She was a young adult, and she called to him, asking him why . . . why . . .

"Why did you leave me, Kwinaa? You're my brother; you were supposed to protect me. Why did you run away?"

They were in the dark cell, but he could see her, and she was surrounded by a halo of bright light. She reached out to him, begging for help, and then her hair caught fire and she was surrounded by flames. The bright light around her expanded and radiated out from her glowing form. Leon tried to reach out to her, but he was belted in and his wrists and ankles were shackled. He couldn't get to her, and then the floor of the cell became like thick, rolling mud, and she began to sink into it.

"Help me, Kwinaa. Help me. Why did you run away?"

"Jenny! Nooo . . ."

He struggled and fought against his bonds and tried so hard to get to her, but to no avail.

She continued to burn and sink into the mire, until the blackness engulfed her, and the fire was snuffed out.

Leon was left alone in the pitch black, and he screamed.

Then coldness hit him like a shock. The black pitch swirled away, and suffocating pain hit his chest. He struggled up and out of the dark cell as he rose toward the light, like a swimmer who had dived too deep and now fought to reach the surface as his lungs burned for air.

Solid images came into focus as he regained consciousness. His breath came in short, shallow gasps, and he struggled in rising panic.

Then he felt the coldness again, and he noticed a hand, feminine but wrinkled with age, pressing a cool, damp cloth against his brow. A soft voice strove to ease his fears.

She appeared to be dressed in a gray suit, and his fevered eyes focused on the dangling gold cross around her neck.

It looks different though. What's different about it? Still, it's odd. What would a Godly woman be doing in the dark cell? Then, with an overwhelming sense of relief, another thought came to him.

Am I dead? Am I in heaven? Is the struggle over? Then he dismissed that thought with an inner snort. *Right, if I were dead, I wouldn't be fighting to breath. Unless this is Hell. That wouldn't surprise me. There's not much chance of me going to heaven.*

Then he was gone again—drifting.

And Jack was there, laughing at him.

"Ha, ha. You're in prison and I'm not. Serves you right, you arrogant bastard."

"No, Jack. No. I didn't mean to be. Come back, Come back. Don't leave me here."

"Come back. Come back," Jack mocked him. *"Why would I do that? All you ever did was put me down, tell me I was stupid. Why would I come back to that? I've got a life now . . a life now . . . a life . . ."*

Jack drifted away out of sight, out of reach. Leon thrashed and yelled and tried to follow him, but he was in the dark cell again and all was blackness. He became mired in the rolling mud, and it pulled him down, deeper to Hell.

He screamed again.

He awoke and gasped for air. But it came a bit easier this time, and the vice on his chest was looser.

Or was that just his imagination?

Dr. Palin sat over him, feeling his forehead, and checking his vitals.

"He's still feverish," the doctor said to someone Leon couldn't see "But I believe he has finally turned the corner. Your diligence just may have pulled him through this."

"Ohh, I do hope so," Doctor Mariam answered. "He's not a bad man . . . bad man . . ."

And Leon was gone again.

The next time he awakened, he lay on his side with his knees drawn up—his usual sleeping position these days. He felt as weak as a half-drowned hummingbird, but his mind was clear, and he could breathe. A man stood beside the bed. He touched Leon's shoulder and gave it a slight shake.

"Leon," came a familiar, gravelly voice, "you awake?"

"Taggard?" Even to Leon, his voice sounded weak and distant.

"Yeah," came the answer. The man turned and pulled a chair over. He sat down, placing himself in the patient's line of sight.

Leon looked at him, not completely convinced he was real. He reached out a trembling hand and touched his friend on his knee.

"Is that you?" he whispered. "Are you really here?"

Taggard smiled and took Leon's hand in his. Leon didn't pull away. "Yeah, Leon, I'm really here. Bein' an officer of the law gives me some privileges. You've had quite a rough go of it. We were afraid we were gonna lose ya."

Leon struggled with shortness of breath. He was fine until he tried to speak and then the air was sucked from his lungs and he gasped. Finally, he forced out two simple words. "How's Jack?"

Taggard smiled and shook his head. "Really Leon? You're just barely back in the land of the livin', and all you wanna know is, how's Jack?"

"Ya."

"Get some rest," Taggard told him. "We'll talk about Jack later."

"Taggard," another gasp, "don't . . . leave me . . . here." The effort to speak proved too much for his ailing lungs and he felt darkness overtake him again. "Please . . . .."

Taggard sat for a long time, holding his friend's hand and watched him struggling, even as he slept, to draw in air. That quiet but desperate plea cut him to the quick, especially since he knew there was absolutely nothing he could do about it. They were all trying, but Governor Warren wasn't giving an inch. It was going to be hard turning his back on his friend and leaving him in this place. Now, even more so after having seen him like this.

When Taggard first walked into the infirmary, he had noticed the prisoner lying on the bed, but Dr. Palin had to assure him that the prone man was indeed Napoleon Nash. Taggard would not have recognized him as the high-spirited outlaw leader whom he had known for so many years. If they had passed in the street, Taggard would have walked right by him.

It wasn't just the shaved head and the prison garb, nor was it the worn out and pale complexion from having been extremely ill for the past week. Maybe it was all those things put together, then combined with his weight loss, the sunken cheek bones and the shadows under the eyes that made him so unrecognizable. Whatever it was, Leon was a changed man, and it broke Taggard's heart to see him reduced to this in such a short time.

Then, to have to turn around and leave him here. Sometimes Taggard regretted putting on a sheriff's badge. Sometimes.

***

The next day, Leon was sitting up with the assistance of numerous pillows, and Mariam was helping him sip some broth. He felt silly, having to be spoon-fed, but he also knew he was still very weak and would have had a hard time doing it himself. He also liked the company, and if letting her spoon-feed him soup would keep her sitting and talking to him, well, he could make that sacrifice.

"Why are you here?" Leon asked her in a tone that still sounded distant. "How did you know I was ill?"

"On my last visit, I asked the warden to let me know if you ever needed anything," she explained. "So, when you became ill, he was good enough to contact me. Then you had mentioned Sheriff Murphy in your letters to me, so I took the liberty of contacting him."

"Oh." He tried to take in a lung full of air, but this only caused him to start coughing again.

Meriam put down the soup bowl and held a cloth to his mouth. He gagged and hacked until loosened phlegm rose to the surface and exited into the cloth.

Gasping for air, he fell back into his pillows. His brow was covered in sweat, but he felt chilled to the bone.

"Sorry."

"Don't be silly." Mariam tucked the blankets more snuggly around him. "It's good that you're coughing it up. It shows that you're getting better." She gazed at him for a moment, the wrinkles around her eyes creasing with concern. "Would you like me to leave you to rest?"

Leon shook his head and forced out a "No." He breathed in, more cautiously this time. "How long have you been here?"

"Five days," she answered, as she retrieved the soup bowl. "Once I got here, I couldn't leave you. You were very ill."

"Oh." He sipped at the offered spoonful of broth and managed to get it down. "I'm sorry." He forced it out again. "I've kept you from . . . your duties."

Mariam smiled at him. "Tending to the sick and less fortunate are part of my duties, Napoleon. The orphanage is in good hands with the Sisters. When Dr. Palin needs assistance here, I do try and accommodate."

Leon ghosted a smile. "Oh. I guess I never thought of myself in that category."

"Sick?"

He smiled again as he needed time to recover from his spoken words. He drew air in until he felt there was enough to continued. "Less fortunate."

Mariam dropped her smile and looked him in the eye. "I don't think of you in that category either, Napoleon."

She put down the bowl of soup and, picking up his hand in both of hers, she raised it to her mouth and kissed it. Leon felt his throat tighten; he wasn't used to such an open and honest display of affection.

"I don't care what you have done in your past," she said, "or what the law thinks you deserve. I only know you have a kind heart, because I have seen it, and from what Sheriff Murphy says, there are plenty of other people out there who agree with me. I know it is difficult, but don't give up hope."

Leon felt awkward; he couldn't think of anything to say.

Taggard approached the bed and saved the situation.

Leon smiled up at him. "Taggard."

"Leon. You're lookin' a little better today. But what the hell—oh, sorry, ma'am. Don't they feed ya in here?"

"It's not that the inmates don't get fed, Sheriff," Dr. Palin, who had overheard the comment, informed them. "There's not much we can do if the inmate refuses to eat."

Two reprimanding looks got sent Leon's way.

He shrugged, actually managing an innocent demeanor. "You know me, Taggard." Another hesitation and breath drawn in. "I never was one to eat much."

"Yeah, but ya usually eat enough to keep yourself alive," Taggard's tone carried a bit of heat. "You're not doing anybody any good if ya starve yourself ta death."

Leon looked away from their accusing stares, and though he made no comment, his thoughts were clearly written across his face.

Mariam gave his hand another squeeze. "It does matter, Napoleon. Your welfare matters to a lot of people. So, you start looking after yourself, all right?"

Leon breathed a smile. Is that a woman thing, being able to read a man's mind like that? Jean did it on a regular basis, and now the Preacher-lady appeared to be just as proficient with this ability.

"All right," he agreed. "I will."

"Good. Now, on that note, I will leave you two men to talk. I will return later to check on you."

She got up, took the bowl and left the men alone.

Taggard took over the chair and sat down beside his friend.

Leon looked his friend in the eyes. "So," he struggled, "how's Jack?"

Taggard sighed. He hoped to not have to jump right into that. Leon didn't look up to handling a whole bunch of bad news, but that seemed to be all the sheriff had to give him.

"I dunno, Leon. He's disappeared."

"Wa . . . what?" Leon sat up straighter and then was attacked by a brutal coughing spasm that must have lasted a good five minutes.

Palin was at his bedside in an instant, putting a cloth to his patient's mouth and helping him lean forward "Sheriff Murphy, perhaps you should leave him alone for now. Let him get some rest."

"No," Leon managed to gasp out between gagging. "No. I'll be fine."

Palin looked disapprovingly at his patient and the friend.

"Well, shit," he grumbled. "Fine. Don't listen to me, I'm just the fuckin' doctor. A few more minutes, that's all ya get. And for Christ's sakes take it easy. You don't need a relapse."

Leon nodded as he got his breath back and settled onto the pillows again. The coughing spasms left him exhausted, and, though sleep threatened to overtake him, he forced himself to stay focused. He needed to find out all he could about his nephew.

"What do you mean he's disappeared? When?"

"About a week after Christmas," Taggard said. "Apparently, he and Marsham had a blowout, and Marsham sent him packin'. Nobody's heard from 'im since."

Leon groaned holding a hand against his aching chest. "Why?"

"Jack has been drinkin' too much. And bein' abusive," Taggard explained. "I guess Marsham had finally had enough of it."

"What's going on?" Leon asked. "I got a letter from David sayin' the same . . .. Not like him, it's just—no," Leon stopped talking, a pensive look crossing over his face as he took advantage of his change of heart to draw in more air.

"What?" Taggard asked.

Leon looked at him, thinking about it for a moment.

"No, this is like him. This is how he was at Blessed Heart. He was so hurt and angry over what happened to our folks." He stopped again, replenishing his air supply. "But there was nothing he could do about it, so he lashed out."

"Yeah," Taggard thought about it, "that would make sense. He was very angry about the pardons. Almost told the governor to shove it, if it didn't include you as well."

Leon smiled. "Really?"

"Hmm. Mr. Granger and I had to really talk him into signin' them papers because it went against his grain, that's for sure."

Leon suddenly threw the blanket off himself and started to get out of bed.

"I . . . back to my cell," he insisted. "Gotta write David."

"Whoa! Whoa, you're not goin' anywhere, Leon." Taggard caught his friend under the arms just as Leon's knees buckled, and he began sliding to the floor.

Palin was there in an instant, and they both hoisted Leon back onto the bed, despite his many protests through more ragged coughing. Taggard couldn't believe how light he was. Even without the doctor's assistance, the sheriff would not have had any trouble getting Leon back in bed. The man was literally wasting away.

"No." Cough, cough. "I gotta write David." He protested even as the blanket was being pulled over him.

"Leon, relax," Taggard said. "Calm down. I'll bring ya some paper so you can write him a note from here. I'll make sure it gets to 'im. You just get better. And for God's sake, eat something.

"No. I have to . . ." Leon tried to fight the doctor in his efforts to get up, but his strength failed him, and between beads of sweat and another coughing fit, he collapsed into his pillows.

"No argument this time, Sheriff. Out you go," Palin insisted. "I'll give him a sedative to calm him down, and he'll sleep."

"Yeah, all right," Taggard agreed. He put a hand on Leon's shoulder. "Take it easy, Leon. I'll see you later, okay? Get some rest."

Leon could barely manage a nod, as the vice tightened upon his chest again.

CHAPTER SEVENTEEN
KENNY REECE

It hadn't been Kenny Reece's lifelong ambition to become a prison guard. That was hardly the first choice of a career for a young man growing up in a wealthy family in Tennessee. But, like with so many things, the war changed all his plans and set his life upon a path that was not of his choosing.

His family-owned large properties and raised fine riding and carriage horses for the other well-to-do citizens of the South. It was a good life, filled with social events and good friends, along with the status and respect that, as a young man, he had taken for granted would always be his. He would eventually inherit his family's business. He was courting, and completely expected to marry, one of the prettiest belles in the county. Life was good; he was a happy man.

Then the Civil War exploded in their faces. Though the speculation of war had been the talk among the young men of the county, none thought it would ever touch home. If they wanted to be a part of the battle, they would have to go to it.

Kenny, being young and foolish, thought it would be great fun to join up to help fight for the Confederate cause. Several of the well-to-do families bought commissions for their sons, so Kenny and his friends would be officers. It would not be fitting for the higher icon to get down and dirty with the regular folk. It would be an adventure.

It didn't take long for the adventure to become a nightmare. The viciousness and brutality of the war shattered Kenny's delusions of grandeur long before the first year of fighting had passed. Then the war didn't end. Long after everyone was ready to give it up and go home, the battles raged on. Predictions of a short and conclusive skirmish were soon buried under a never-ending pile of shattered lives.

Kenny lost everything dear to him. His mother died of the fever, his father was killed, trying to protect their property. All their finely bred and highly-strung horses were confiscated for the army's use, never to be seen again. Their opulent home was ransacked and burned to the ground. He lost count of how many people he saw blown up or maimed for life—many of them his friends. The world had gone mad, and Kenny struggled just to hold on to his own sanity.

When the war finally ended, he returned home to find nothing there for him. His family and home were gone. His fiancé had given up on him and married someone else. Someone who still had something to offer her. With only his severance pay to live on, he turned his horse around and headed west.

He worked his way along, taking jobs as they came up and living from hand to mouth for over a year. Still, it was better than what he had come from; here, at least, nobody was trying to shoot him. Usually.

He did find it worth his while to lose his Southern accent. The further West he went, the more people looked at him suspiciously and ask him where he was from? What side did he fight for? He studied the Western dialogue and worked hard at mastering the different sounds. It wasn't long before he could get by with just a slight twang, which usually only showed when he was angry or stressed. He survived.

He found work, mainly with the ranches that always seemed ready to hire drovers or wranglers. Not surprisingly, he showed an aptitude for breaking horses, so he often got hired for this type of work. Still, it was nothing like the lifestyle he had come from; he was used to being the man who did the hiring, not the man asking to be hired. It was a difficult transition.

For the first few years he kept drifting, following the herds and taking work where he could get it. He finally ended up in Montana, on one of the bigger ranches, and settled in as the permanent wrangler there. Then, what often happened when nature can take its own course; he met a young lady and took himself a wife.

Allowing nature to take its course again, the children started to arrive. Within five years, Kenny had three sons, and a career as a wrangler was beginning to look a little inadequate. He wanted to be able to offer opportunities to his children that a wrangler's pay would not accommodate. He kept his ears and eyes open for a career that could offer the stability and income he needed for his growing family.

Then he got word of the new penitentiary being built in Laramie, Wyoming, and that soon, guards would be needed. Kenny took the article home to discuss with his wife, and they reviewed the pros and cons together.

It was not a very prestigious job, and it could be dangerous, dealing with convicts. But then, breaking out half-wild mustangs was dangerous too, and Kenny wasn't getting any younger. If he could handle a wild three-year-old bronc, he was reasonably confident he could handle an uppity convict.

Plus, it was a government job, which meant stability, decent pay, which offered the possibility of saving enough to send the boys to college. There were prerequisites of course. No previous criminal record, able to read and write English, and those with military experience, especially officers, would be given priority.

It sounded like a perfect fit. So, Kenny kissed his wife goodbye and headed to Wyoming to see if there was a future for them there. As it happened, the prison officials also felt Kenny was a perfect fit, and he was hired on the spot. Since he didn't have any previous experience as a guard, he was not given the highest position, but seeing as how he had been an officer in the war, even if it was for the Confederacy, he was given a position of some seniority.

All that was left for him to do was find a place to live, move his family over and be ready to start work as soon as the prison opened.

When Napoleon Nash arrived at the prison, Kenny Reece had been working there for thirteen years., and had made his way up the ranks to a higher seniority, junior only to Carson and the warden, while taking over as senior guard when Carson was off-duty. His oldest son, Connor, was getting ready to go back East to study engineering. The two younger boys were still going to classes in Laramie, but also had aspirations of furthering their education.

A daughter had been added to the brood and instantly became the apple of her father's eye. Life was good for the Reece family, and for the most part, Kenny liked his job. He knew the rules and he knew what he had to do to enforce them.

But, just like with any job, there were aspects to working at the prison that he had a hard time justifying. He had seen more than enough brutality in the war and didn't much care to have to see any more. Unfortunately, the nature of his work made it impossible to avoid it altogether, so he learned how to cope and to deal out corporal punishment when it was called for.

Often, he found taking away privileges worked just as well, if not better than a physical reprimand, but there were still rules to be followed and hard men to be kept in line. He learned early that to allow a convict to know you were soft could be dangerous.

Kenny took the time to learn something about each of the new inmates, so he would have a better idea of what to expect from them. Carson's rule of thumb was simply to beat a man into submission; using physical and mental abuse to break his spirit and force him into compliance. This technique worked on many who passed through their doors, but occasionally it backfired. Then the guards ended up with an inmate who was seething inside and just waiting for the opportunity to strike back—consequences be damned.

Hank Boeman was one such individual. Built like a Brahma bull, and with the attitude to match, Boeman had no difficulty maintaining the alpha position over his fellow inmates. He even managed to intimidate the junior guards into keeping their distance. Kenny kept his eye on him, certain he was going to be trouble one day.

Napoleon Nash had the potential of being another, but with one significant difference; Napoleon Nash was intelligent. He learned the rules quickly, and once having learned them, figured out how to break them without getting caught, thereby avoiding punishment.

So, when Boeman showed up for supper that winter's evening, all battered and bruised, Kenny knew it wasn't from slipping on the steps.

No one had witnessed the incident, so there wasn't really anything that could be done about it, and Kenny wasn't so sure he wanted to. Boeman had been pushing Nash ever since the younger man had been incarcerated. It was only to be expected that, sooner or later, one of them would be knocked down a peg.

But Kenny also knew that Carson was betting on Boeman to come out on top. That guard never did like to see intelligence and charisma displayed by an inmate, and he'd try to crush it any time it came his way.

As previously stated, Kenny was just as quick to dole out punishment as any other guard, but he didn't like to see a man beaten into the ground, mentally or physically. There was no need for it, and often resulted in an inmate becoming even more vicious and unpredictable than he had been when he first arrived.

Once Kenny realized Carson had singled Nash out to be his new pet project, he did everything he could to counter the effect.

He made sure Nash received the mail and parcels that were

addressed to him. He also left a copy of the Cheyenne Gazette on his cot, so he would know his partner was safe. He also got him a break from the work floor by setting him up in the laundry room once a week. And, as is already known, he arranged for Nash to receive reading materials that were more on a level with his intellectual abilities.

Still, Kenny could tell that Nash was not adjusting to prison life. He did his work and stayed out of trouble, but he was depressed and sullen, and he wasn't eating enough to maintain his strength. So, Kenny wasn't really surprised when he started his shift, to discover that Nash had taken ill and was in the infirmary.

Nash's condition was touch and go for a while, and Kenny found himself relieved when he learned that the Preacher-Lady, who also ran the orphanage, had come over again, to help with the care of a particularly ill inmate. So often, the diligence shown by those ladies had made the difference between an inmate recovering or succumbing to his illness.

As Nash's fever finally broke, and he became more lucid, but still not well enough to return to the cell block, Kenny made a point, during his lunch break, of bringing over the letter and the book that the inmate had been reading before his collapse.

It was during this visit, while Nash was asleep, and Dr. Mariam was taking a much-needed break, that Dr. Palin called Kenny over for a conference.

"What's your opinion of Nash?" Palin asked. "Would you feel he is a candidate for Trustee?"

Kenny sent a speculative look over to the sleeping inmate.

"No," he finally stated. "Not yet, anyway."

"No?" Palin repeated, surprised at that answer. "What the hell do you mean, no? I have found him to be very courteous and polite when he comes over here to exchange medical journals. He is obviously bright. Shit, I've given him books that took me months to plow through and finally come to understand—he's returned them in a week. I thought, at first, he was just covering up, that he wasn't really reading them, so I tested him with a few random questions." Palin smiled and shook his head. "That bastard. He answered them all correctly, without hesitation, so he obviously retains what he reads."

Palin hesitated, and with a sigh of regret, glanced at the inmate. "It's a shame really; with a brain like that, he could have done anything he wanted, but he ended up choosin' a life that ultimately led him here.

A real damn waste."

"And that's the problem," Kenny answered. "He's too smart for his own good. You're right; he could have done anything with his life, but he chose to live outside the law.

"Don't ever forget who he is, Doc. Don't ever forget it. Napoleon Nash can be charming when it suits him, but he can be devious as well. He learned the rules here very quickly, then he learned how to manipulate them. Any of the other inmates do him wrong, he waits until the right opportunity presents itself, then he retaliates. He doesn't react right away, on the spot, because he knows he'll end up in the dark cell. He bides his time, until he gets the offender alone and then lets him have it.

"When Kelly and Kristiansen ended up with bloody noses and black eyes, I thought it odd that they both insisted they'd tripped or walked into something. Then I thought about it for a bit, and realized they both had, on different occasions, done something that had irritated Nash. I saw it in his eyes; just a flash of anger and then it was gone, so I thought nothing more of it. Until a week, maybe ten days later, they showed up injured. That got me paying more attention.

"Then, there was that work detail to clear snow from the yard. Carson is itching for a fight between Nash and Boeman, so of course, he puts the two of them out there, working together. I think, 'Well, let's just wait and see what happens.' Sure enough, Boeman pushes for a fight and Carson does nothing about it. I figure, give it a week, and see if Boeman shows up with some bruises.

"Wouldn't you know, it only took a couple of hours and, all of a sudden, Nash was looking pretty pleased with himself."

"So, you're sayin' Nash can't be trusted?"

"I'm saying, you have to watch him. As you've already noted, he's an intelligent man. A gifted man, even. If we can give him enough things to keep him occupied, he might just survive this place. But I caution you; don't forget he's in here for a reason. He has no respect for rules, and if he comes to feel slighted or hard done by, well, I don't know him well enough yet to judge how far he would go."

Palin smirked. "I'm already agreein' with ya to some degree. I think we need to give him somethin' more to do that is gonna challenge 'im intellectually, or he's gonna get himself into trouble. Since the fever broke, I've noticed the way he sleeps, and it worries me."

"What do you mean?"

"He sleeps curled up in a ball," Palin said. "That's no damn good. I see an inmate sleepin' like that, especially early on in their incarceration, it sets off warnin' bells. It tells me they ain't adjustin'. They're retreatin' deeper and deeper inside themselves, until one day they don't come back out. For a fella with his brains, it'd be a damn shame."

"Yeah," Kenny agreed. "I've seen that happen before. They often end up committing suicide."

"Exactly. Now, if we could just give him somethin' ta hold onto, somethin' that would give him a reason ta keep goin', well, maybe we could prevent that from happenin'."

"Hmm," was Kenny's response. "What did you have in mind?"

"Well, since that smart-ass Wickham got paroled, I'm findin' myself in need of another assistant. Even if it's just for one day a week. That would give him one day in the laundry room, one day over here helpin' me, and then only three days on the work floor. He'd have to be a Trustee though. We'll have ta get that jackass of a warden to agree to it. But if we can, we might just save this fella's life."

Kenny smiled at the Doc's opinion of their boss. Palin's dislike of Mitchell did not go unnoticed. He then reflected on what Doc was suggesting, and he shrugged his shoulders. "I dunno. There are a lot of tools over here that could be used as a weapon, not to mention the medications he could get into."

"Those things are always kept under lock and key."

Kenny smiled. "The locks you have on these cabinets aren't going to stop Napoleon Nash. Like I said; don't ever forget who he is." Kenny sighed. He leaned against the counter and folded his arms as he looked at the inmate. "On the other hand, if he recognizes it as a privilege, something he could look forward to doing, it might just be all he needs to help him adjust to life here."

"My thoughts exactly."

"Let me think on it a bit, Doc. I'll keep a close eye on him over the next week or two, and if things look good, I'll speak to the warden about it."

The two men locked eyes for a moment, and then they looked over at the sleeping man.

The seed of an idea had been planted.

***

The next day, Leon knew he was getting better only because Palin told him he was. When he had time in his misery to notice it, his fever was gone and he no longer suffered from the cold sweats, but otherwise, he was still sick as a dog. So much so that he preferred his friends not see him in such a retched state.

Palin stayed close with a cloth and spittoon as Leon's lungs fought to evict the thick, yellow phlegm that still strangled his breath.

"Bloody hell." Leon gasped as another coughing spasm sucked the strength from his body. "This is worse," gasp, "than being," gasp, "sick."

"That's only because you were so sick, you don't remember being sick," Palin grumbled as he held the spittoon in ready position. "For us who witnessed that, well, we're happier seeing you awake and suffering."

Leon groaned, his hands, as they clutched the spittoon, shook with weakness from the exertion.

"Dammit," Leon choked and hacked some more. "Give me somethin'," cough, cough, "to ease this." He gagged as more phlegm was forced up from his aching lungs.

"Nope." Palin wiped his patient's mouth. "You need to get this crap outta your chest. It's the only way you'll get better."

Leon sucked in a shallow gasp. He gagged again, but nothing came up. With a ragged sigh, he fell back onto his raised pillows.

Palin watched him for a moment, but as his patient quieted, he took the opportunity to go clean out the spittoon.

Leon felt chilled again, as the sweat from his exertions lost its heat. He pulled the blanket up around his shoulders and sat there, watching as the doctor walked away.

Breathing a little easier now, he took the time to look around his environment. He realized the room he was in wasn't quite as open as his first impression had made it. It wasn't even all that big. Long and narrow, the far wall consisted of bookshelves, locked cabinets and counter space. It did triple duty as infirmary, dentist office, and barber shop. But the barber only came once a week to shave heads, so the doctor here had to be a jack-of-all-trades . . . and the master of none, came the unbidden thought.

There was only the one entrance and it was kept locked most of the time. A second door led into a small office and supply room. That door was also kept locked if the doctor was not around. There was a private lavatory and bathroom, and next to it was another door which, apparently led to more private cells for women prisoners.

Leon hadn't seen any women inmates, so he assumed that there weren't any. But Dr. Mariam soon informed him otherwise. They were there, but they were quiet and kept sequestered. Apparently, they weren't even permitted time outside.

Leon sighed. It seems there were even worse situations than his own. Still, the infirmary was just as much a prison cell as his own sleeping accommodation was, and having a little more room didn't help him feel any less confined.

The door leading to the cell blocks opened, and Leon managed a weak smile.

"Taggard."

"Hey, Leon." Then Taggard caught Palin's eyes. "Is he up for a visit?"

Palin sighed. "Goddammit. All right, but just a short one. And don't go gettin' 'im all excited like ya did the last time. We've just gotten through a bad coughing spell, and he's gonna be tired."

Taggard nodded. He sat in the recently vacated chair and gazed upon his friend. Those dark brown eyes were still listless, exhaustion seeping through to redden the outer rims. A sadness was there, too; a sadness brought on by the realization of his situation.

Taggard smiled and touched Leon's arm, just for an instant then pulled it away. "I stopped in to say goodbye. I gotta be headin' home, soon. There's talk of another snow storm closin' in, so I better be makin' tracks before it hits."

"Yeah, I suppose," Leon managed a whisper, disappointment flitting across his features. He knew he would be going back to his cell soon. Back to the loneliness, back to the cold and the silence. He handed Taggard a sheet of paper. "Here." He swallowed and wheezed. "If you could send this to David, I'd appreciate it. I'll write him a longer letter after I'm finished reading the one he sent me. I hope this will give him something to go on."

Taggard nodded and took the sheet from him. Then it became quiet between them. Taggard didn't know what to say. He truly wished he could take Leon away from here; just take him home. But he couldn't. Leon knew it, and Taggard knew it too, but that didn't make things any easier.

"Hang in there, Leon," Taggard finally said. "We're all workin' at it, you know we are. But Governor Warren took so much criticism for givin' Jack his pardon, he doesn't dare do the same for you. We may have ta wait until a new governor comes into office and then start putting pressure on him."

"How long do you think that will be?"

"I dunno. There's been some talk that Warren is into some shady dealings, maybe he'll be ousted. Who knows? Just hang on, okay?"

"Yeah." Leon was tired of people telling him to hang on, to be patient, to not give up hope. His thoughts, now freed from the fever, returned to his nephew, but another spasm of coughing brought Palin's attention to him. Leon waved him away, knowing he had to get the words out. "I'm worried about Jack. I'm afraid of what he might do."

"Yeah," Taggard's concern switched to the other partner, "he's like a powder keg right now. I keep expectin' ta hear he's robbed a bank, or started shootin' up a town, or somethin'. It's like he's runnin' scared, and without you with him, who knows what he'll get up to. You always could keep him focused."

"I know." Leon rubbed his chest as he breathed. "But he did the same for me. He kept me grounded too." Leon managed a smile. "I'd get going on about some wild scheme, and he'd look at me with 'that look' and I'd know I was pushing the limit. He seems to know when something's not right; he kept me honest." He laughed, but that morphed into hacking, and he struggled to finish his joke. "If you can say that about a couple of crooks."

"Yeah, I know," Taggard chuckled, then sighed; it was time to leave. Besides, Dr. Palin was giving him the stink eye. "I'll make sure David gets your note and maybe it'll give him some ideas. Right now, all we can do is wait and hope that Jack shows up again and has enough common sense to not go and do something really stupid. Then, maybe, we can get this whole thing worked out."

Leon nodded.

Taggard stood, then put a hand on his friend's shoulder. "I'd best be goin', Leon. I'll keep you up to date as best I can, and in the meantime, eat somethin', will ya? You're wastin' away."

"Yeah, yeah. Okay." Leon agreed. "Keep in touch. Please."

Then Taggard was gone. Leon felt all alone, as though the world outside had again abandoned him. He tried to convince himself that this wasn't the truth, but he couldn't shake the feeling.

He caught Palin's eye and nodded to assure the doctor that he was all right. With a heavy sigh, he turned back to David's letter and continued to read where he had left off before his illness hit. Maybe there would be some clue where Jack had gone.

> *Christmas Eve Day,* David continued writing. *Trish and I had planned on meeting the Marshams at the church for the social where there was going to be carolers and the usual hot apple cider, fresh pies and warm cookies; all that stuff that comes with the holidays. I hoped Jack would be with them, since I suspected Christmas was going to be difficult for him to get through. Jean mentioned he had become increasingly moody as the big day approached, so I thought, if I could just talk to him a little . . .*

***

Arvada, Colorado

Jack didn't ride into town with the family that afternoon. There were some things he wanted to get done around the barn first, and then he would ride in on his own later and meet them there. Should be fun and being able to listen to Christmas carols sung by a choir on Christmas Eve, would be a real treat. Yup, it'll be real nice, spending Christmas with a family again.

A few hours after the Marshams left for town, Jack finished what he'd wanted to do, but he still hung back. For some reason, it didn't feel right, going into the church as one big family. Didn't feel right at all. He let a few more hours pass, making up chores to do as an excuse, until he felt enough time had elapsed. He then saddled Midnight and rode into town on his own.

He put his horse up at the livery and walked toward the town square with every intention of joining the family as soon as he could track them down. He knew it was important to the girls that he be there with them all. He knew that, and he had every intention of doing it.

But as he walked through the cold winter wonderland, and the enticing aromas of roasting chestnuts and hot apple cider invaded his senses, he felt a tightness come into his chest that had nothing to do with the chill in the air. People walked past him, all in gay, festive spirits; laughing and talking, and some, especially the children, were even singing carols as they danced along the boardwalk already caught up in the holiday fun.

Jack's pace slowed as the singing from the church reached his ears, and his expression went from pleasant expectation to anxious concern.

His feet stopped walking. He couldn't do this.

A conversation came to his mind, unbidden:

Then Christmas. Sure would be nice to spend Christmas with a family again.

Sure would.

A vice squeezed his chest, and his throat burned as he choked back the sob that threatened to break forth. He turned on his heels and headed for the saloon—he needed a drink.

***

As the evening's festivities quieted, and families dissipated, Cameron felt irritation. All three of his ladies were disappointed that Jack had not appeared. Penny, especially, had her heart set on their friend joining them for the family outing.

Well, there was still Christmas Day to look forward to, and everyone would be home for that.

David stayed out of it. He was concerned for Jack, and he knew Cameron was miffed and would probably be giving that man what for, as soon as they got home. But Jack was a big boy. He and Cameron were just going to have to work this out between them.

David let Jack know often enough that he was open to talk anytime Jack wanted to. But the offer had not been accepted, so David knew he had to back off. As hard as it was, he had to wait until his friend was ready to come to him. Or not.

So, with Penny, Caroline and Eli settled in under piles of blankets and pillows in the back seat of the buggy, the Marsham family said their goodnights to the Gibsons and headed for home.

Much to everyone's surprise, and Penny's further disappointment, when they arrived back at the ranch, Jack was nowhere to be found.

Cameron had given Sam some time off, so he could spend the holidays with his mother. Sam had been trying to convince that woman it was time to sell her little house and move to Arvada. She was getting older, and Sam would feel a lot better if she were closer to him.

He also wanted her to meet Maribelle, since that relationship had now become serious. Sam had a good sum of money in the bank, what with his own savings and his portion of the bounty for Leon and Jack, so he felt he could afford to look after his mother properly. All he had to do was convince her of this. It could turn out to be an interesting Christmas.

With Sam gone, Cameron sent his family into the house to warm up, while he set about unharnessing the team and putting them away for the night. It was then he discovered that Midnight was also absent from his stall. Karma, along with the other riding horses, nickered with relief at having a familiar human show up to feed them. They had been convinced they were never going to eat again.

Cameron grumbled as he went about getting the barnyard livestock fed and settled for the night, then returned to the house for a good stiff drink. He hoped Jack would at least have the courtesy to show up for the next day. And be sober. If he didn't, it was not going to be a merry time for anybody, and Jack would hear about it.

***

Five days later, when Cameron headed to the barns for the morning feed and turnout, he noticed the door to the one barn swinging open. The three dogs came out to greet him, wanting breakfast, so obviously nothing was amiss, or Rufus at least, would have been barking.

Cameron entered the barn to the nickerings of the numerous horses inside and noticed right off that Midnight was back in his stall. Odd thing was, the horse was still fully tacked up and the stall door, like the barn door, was wide open.

Cameron went down the aisle and, giving the big gelding a rub on the nose, looked inside the stall. Sure enough, there was Jack sprawled out in the straw, sound asleep.

Cameron took a deep breath and told himself to keep his anger in check, at least until he had a chance to talk to the man. He stepped forward and gave Jack a kick on the bottom of his boot.

"Hey, Jack, wake up." Another kick. "Wake up!"

Jack jerked awake, and his right hand went for his holster. He stopped himself in time and, looking up at Cameron, he yawned and stretched.

"Where the hell have you been?" Cameron demanded.

"In town," Jack mumbled.

313

"In town?" Cameron no longer tried to keep his anger in check. "Do you have any idea what you have put this family through?"

"Oh, sorry." Jack picked himself up and brushed straw from his hair. "I got busy."

"Busy?" Cameron was livid. "You knew the girls were looking forward to you being here for Christmas. What in the world could have been so important that you were willing to disappoint them like that?"

"I dunno," Jack shrugged, sending more straw bits to the floor. "I met some friends at the saloon, and we had some drinks and then—"

"Then you spent five days at the brothel," Cameron finished for him.

"And what if I did?" Jack's tone hardened. "You ain't my pa. I don't need your permission to—"

"No. I'm not your father," Cameron growled. "And I'd be damned disappointed in you if I was. Where the hell are you getting the money for all this?"

"None a your business," Jack yelled back. "God dammit! The way you and David keep naggin' at me, I may as well be in prison too. What the hell do I owe you, anyway?"

That did it. Cameron, who very rarely lost his temper, lost it big time right then and there. With one quick stride into the stall, he sent a vicious right upper-hook into Jack's jaw and sent him into the back wall.

Midnight jumped and started blowing.

Jack went down in a heap, but quick as a cat, was up on his feet again, steaming mad and ready for a fight.

But the look in Cameron's eye brought him up short and though still angry, and no way near ready to apologize, he had enough sense to back off and stay away from his peacemaker.

It was all Cameron could do to not take the advantage and beat the man to a pulp, fastest gun in the west be damned.

"I think you'd better leave, Jackson," Cameron said through clenched teeth. "Go to wherever it is you like to disappear to for days on end. Only this time, maybe you better think about what it is you really want, because I've about had it with who you are now."

With that, Cameron stormed out of the barn and headed back to the house before he did something he really might regret later. Halfway there, he intercepted his youngest daughter, as she dashed toward the barn. He reached out and grabbed her arm as she ran past him, swinging her around to a stop.

"No, Papa," she insisted. "I heard Mathew. I want to see him."

"No. Go back to the house."

"But Papa. Please—"

Cameron exploded. "You stay away from him. Do what I tell you and get back to the house!"

Penny's face screwed up with emotion, and she turned on her heels to ran back the way she had come. She charged up the porch steps and through the front door, passing Jean, who was getting Eli ready for breakfast. She hardly gave her surprised mother a glance as she stomped up the stairs to her room to have a hissy fit all on her own.

Jean watched with concern as her daughter disappeared up the stairs, then she turned to speak to her husband when she heard him enter through the front door.

One look at the expression on his face and she decided now was one of those few occasions when talking was not going to help. She watched, open-mouthed and silent, as he seethed past her and disappeared into the kitchen.

She went to the front door to close it and saw Mathew in the yard. She was just about to call out to him, when he mounted his horse, and, booting the animal into a tired gallop, took off down the road toward town.

Jean stood there for a few minutes, her mind trying to work out what exactly had just happened. She felt a chilling dread come over her and hoped that whatever had happened in the barn wasn't going to be irreparable; that this wasn't going to be the last time she would see Mathew.

Men! she thought with a flash of anger. Too prideful—the whole lot of them.

Then Eli reminded her that she was holding him out on the front porch and it really was cold out here.

***

Upstairs, Penny was into a full-fledged crying fit. She couldn't ever remember the last time she'd been this angry; it really had turned out to be the worst Christmas ever. She lay on her bed and cried into her pillow, until she heard galloping hooves coming from outside. She jumped up from her bed and ran to the window overlooking the yard, just in time to see Mathew heading away from the property.

Her first impulse was to run out of the house, saddle a horse and go after him. But even in her agitated state of mind, she knew that wasn't going to happen. For one thing, her papa would stop her, and then she'd really be in trouble. And for another, her mother's words came back to her, unbidden but sensible: Don't chase after him. Wait until he's ready to come to you.

Penny rested her chin on her arms upon the windowsill. She swallowed her hurt and wiped away her tears. She tried really hard to be sensible.

***

. . . so, for now, that is all I can tell you, Napoleon. We have no idea where he went. He's not in town, as I checked the saloon, the brothel, and even the opium den, but no one has seen him. I even checked the jail, but no luck there either. I have asked Sheriff Jacobs to let me know if he hears anything, and I also sent a telegram to Taggard Murphy to let him know what's happened. Maybe Jack headed back there. I hope he hasn't gone too far, as the weather has been nasty of late.

Cameron feels bad about it all now. The beginning of winter is not the best time to send someone packing, but he lost his temper and wasn't thinking. We're all hoping Jack has simply holed up somewhere safe until the weather improves, and then he'll send us word. And of course, I'll let you know as soon as we hear anything.

Your friend,
David Gibson.

CHAPTER EIGHTEEN
THE WAYWARD SON

Laramie, Wyoming
Winter 1886

Leon held her close, pushing his body into hers. She was soft and warm, her flesh yielding to his hardness with open invitation.

He loved her more than anyone he'd ever known.

She responded to him with a gentle sigh, her arms wrapped tightly around him, caressing him, holding him, her long auburn hair tickling his nose. He smiled with the pleasure of her, the pleasure they were giving each other. He softly nibbled on the lobe of her ear, then reached up and kissed her closed eyelids.

She moaned with a soft passion, arching her back and giving herself to him. She nipped gently on his chin and ran her tongue along the stubble of hair on his jaw line. When she reached his chin again, she gave it a sharper bite.

It hurt, but the pain only served to arouse him further, and he came down hard on her mouth and kissed her deeply and passionately, reflecting his lovemaking.

He came up for air, then nestled in again, nuzzling her neck, taking in her sweet scent.

"Gabriella," he whispered, "I love you. Don't leave me. Please don't leave me here alone."

Her answer was a soft breath caressing his ear.

"Ahh . . . Mr. Nash . . ."

Then . . . "Nash!" Bang. "Wake up!"

Leon awoke with a start. He lay on his stomach, a layer of sweat covering his body, and he clutched his pillow like a long-lost lover. A wave of overwhelming sadness washed over him, and then he groaned as he became aware of his current predicament.

His body had responded naturally to the stimulation of the dream, just as it would have done in reality. Now he was expected to get to his feet and go stand at the open door of his cell, in full view of the guards. Ohhh nooo. Maybe I can delay, give things a chance to settle down.

Then the billy club hit again—Bang—against the door of his cell.

"Nash," came Carson's voice. "What? Do ya think you're a gentleman of leisure now? Get outta bed. If you're not at yur cell door the next time I walk by, you'll lose your books for a month. Ya hear me?"

Leon closed his eyes and groaned. Obviously, there was nothing for it; he was going to have to get up. He swung his legs over the side of the cot and sat, thinking that maybe he could just keep his hands low, strategically placed to hide his situation.

But as he stood at the door of his cell, the first thing he saw was the smirk on Carson's face as the guard came back toward him. He knew it was too late.

"What's the matter Nash?" Carson chided him with a sneer. "Ya missin' your partner? Ha, ha . . . .."

And the guard walked past him, his annoying laughter echoing along the cold corridor of cells as he carried on with his morning roll call.

Leon gritted his teeth. Oh, how I hate that man.

***

Breakfast didn't help him feel any better about his life in general. Lumpy oatmeal and weak coffee. With everyone pestering him to eat more, the least they could do was offer him something that was edible.

Oh well, I'm not all that hungry anyway.

The only good thing about the day is that it was his turn in the laundry room, but then, that didn't turn out to be a fun time, either. It was late morning and he'd began to think that maybe he could stomach some lunch, when two of the younger guards sauntered into the room, their billy clubs in obvious attendance.

Leon looked up, tensing. He didn't like this, not one little bit.

Here he was again, caught between the rules. If he dared to ask what was going on, he would be punished for speaking out of turn. But the way those guards maneuvered themselves into position, one on either side of him, he had a feeling he was in for a beating anyway. He swallowed nervously as he tried to back away from in between them. All he succeeded in doing was backing himself into the wall.

Instantly, and in unison, the two guards pounced on him, each grabbing an arm. At this point, Leon figured he had nothing to lose and fought back, yelling his anger at them. But even just one of these bucks would have had little trouble holding Leon down, so two of them were just having fun. They pulled his arms back and held him snug.

Carson walked into the room, holding the billy club in his right hand and tapping the end of it against the palm of his left. He had a smug smile on his face.

Leon fought harder, but the guards held him tight, and pulled him upright to face their boss. Leon yelled in the hopes that someone would hear him, but then the billy club hit him full force in the gut, and his yell was cut short as he doubled over in pain.

The two guards pulled him back up again and then Carson got in his face. He grabbed Leon by his shirt front and came in close, sneering at him.

"I've seen the way you've been lookin' at me, Convict. You think I don't know what you done to Kelly and Kristiansen, and then Boeman, too?" He brought the billy club up and pushed it across Leon's throat applying pressure. "I know what you damn injuns are like; you ain't got the guts to face a man, you gotta come at 'im from behind. You may not look like a redskin, Nash, but you sure got the traits. You think you're gonna get back at me, the way you did those other fellas? Well think again. If I ever get a pricklin' on the back of my neck that you're comin' after me, I'll cripple ya. You hear me? I've done it before, and I don't mind doin' it again. You hear me, Convict?"

"Yea . . ." Leon gasped, as the vice returned to his damaged lungs.
"Good."

The club was removed from across his throat, but before he could take a breath, the business end of it came plowing into his gut, not once but twice, fast—in succession—bam, bam.

Oh God. Leon thought he was going to die, the pain was so bad. The two guards released him and amongst déjà vu images of Morrison beating him in the jail cell, he sank to the floor and, with knees drawn up and arms clutching his torso, passed out.

***

A short time later, Kenny was starting his usual morning rounds, and he stepped into the laundry room to make sure Nash was where he was supposed to be. The first thing he noticed was no Nash. The next thing he noticed was a pair of legs wearing stripes sticking out from behind the laundry table. Kenny was instantly on the alert, his billy club up and ready for anything.

He backed out of the room and did a quick scan of the hallway, until he spotted one of the guards coming in from the cell block.

"Murray."

Murray glanced up and spotted Reece. "Yeah?"

"Come here. Now."

Murray picked up on the urgency and was at the laundry room door in a couple of strides.

"Yeah, what's up?" he asked, then, "Oh, well isn't that interesting."

Reece had moved the table out of the way, but the convict was lying on his side with his back to the guards, so they couldn't see his face or his hands.

"Watch my back," Kenny said, "and be careful. Remember what happened to Hicks."

"Yeah," Murray answered with a nervous swallow.

Hicks was a young guard who had knelt beside what he thought was an unconscious inmate, only to have the convict suddenly roll over and plunge a pencil into his jugular. By the time help arrived, Hicks had bled to death.

Murray had his billy club ready and came around to stand by the convict's feet. Reece cautiously approached the prone man and gave his shoulder a nudge with the club.

"Nash, is that you? Can you hear me?"

A barely audible response. "Yeah."

"Roll over, onto your back," Kenny ordered him. "Slowly. Let me see your hands."

Leon tried to comply. He gradually straightened out his legs and slowly pushed himself onto his back. He had his hands out, so Kenny could see them, but the movement caused so much pain, his knees came up again and his arms hugged his torso.

Fortunately, Kenny had gotten a good enough look to know that Nash wasn't holding anything that could become a weapon. He lowered his club and moved in close. Murray was right behind him.

"It's all right, Nash," Kenny assured him. "What happened?"

"Nothing."

"Uh huh. Murray, go get the doc."

"You sure you're all right with him alone?"

"Yeah. He's not gonna do anything. Just go get Palin."

"Okay." Murray trotted off on his errand.

"All right, Nash, let me see." Kenny moved Leon's hands away from his torso and lifted the shirt. He sucked his teeth when he saw the bruising already starting to blossom. "Ouch. Nothin' happened, huh?"

Kenny sighed, and sitting down on the floor, they waited for Palin to arrive.

***

"Hmm," was Palin's only comment as he did a quick exam of the bruised area.

Leon tried to lie still; his eyes closed in an effort to absorb the pain. He'd already had to go through this once, why were the fates putting him through it again?

"This rib has been injured before, hasn't it?" Palin asked him.

"Yeah."

"How long ago?"

"Ah." Leon had to think about it. "Nine, ten months ago. When I was first arrested, in Arvada."

"Arvada?" Palin asked, surprised. "Arvada, Colorado?"

"Yeah," Leon confirmed. "A lawman there kicked me in the ribs."

"Not the deputy, I hope."

"Deputy?"

"Yeah. Ben Palin. He's my nephew, and I sure wouldn't wanna hear that he's treatin' prisoners like that."

"Oh." Leon thought back to that time and did recall a young deputy being there, but he couldn't for the life of him remember the kid's name. "No, it wasn't the local law. It was the marshal who arrested me."

"Hmm," Palin commented. "That's a relief. Still, that's no way for a lawman to treat a prisoner in his custody."

Leon made no comment but couldn't help thinking that it was no way for a guard to treat an inmate, either.

"Well, it's not broken this time," Palin announced. "But obviously, you've got some pretty bad bruising here. You'll have to take it easy for the next couple of days. Kenny, help me get him to his feet and back to his cell."

"Yeah, okay, Doc."

Once Leon was settled onto his cot for the rest of the day, Kenny joined Palin on the walk back to the infirmary as they discussed the incident.

"What does he say happened?"

"He won't say," Kenny answered. "You know how they get."

"Yeah. But it doesn't take a genius to guess."

"We can't know that for sure."

"C'mon, Kenny. I've seen enough bruising made by those damned billy clubs to know it when I'm looking at it again."

Kenny sighed. "Yeah, I suppose you're right."

"Are you gonna do anything about it?"

"There's not much I can do, Doc. Carson's my superior. I've complained to the warden before about his abusiveness, and I get shut down. The best I can do is keep an eye on things."

"That Carson is a fuckin' bastard," Doc grumbled, then sent Kenny a sideways glance. "It would help if we could keep an eye on Nash in the infirmary."

Kenny smiled. "Yeah, all right Doc. I'll speak to the warden about Nash coming over to help you there. After this, maybe he'll be willing to behave himself."

"Good."

***

Arvada, Colorado

Early evening found David and Tricia settled down in the living room to enjoy a relaxing cup of tea. Tricia was busy writing a letter to her cousin, Miranda, who lived in Idaho, while David read a letter that had arrived that day, from his colleague back East.

> *David, old man!*
>
> *How grand to hear from you. We were beginning to think the Wild West had swallowed you up. Heard you took a wife,*

probably the prettiest girl in town too, knowing you. Any little ones yet? Better get going on that you know. Time's a wasting.

Of course, we've all been following the trials of Kiefer and Nash! Even back here, we've heard about those two bandits. It never even occurred to us that you would be right in the thick of it, seeing as how you're in Colorado and they were on trial in Wyoming. I guess one territory is just like another, huh?

You should have heard all the chatter going on here about those trials, and then when pictures of the outlaws got circulated, WELL! You wouldn't have believed the giggling and swooning that was going on, and not just with the young, flighty maidens either! It doesn't take a genius to figure out what those old ladies were talking about during their Saturday socials! Don't be surprised if you start getting letters from some female acquaintances, wanting to know what they're REALLY like!! A shame about that Nash fella going to prison, though.

Anyway, down to the serious stuff now. As to your question regarding Mr. Kiefer and his unusual behavior, there really isn't much information available on that subject. I have heard of a few cases of soldiers coming back from the war displaying similar bouts of depression and temper.

Often these were people who had lost friends in battle, were perhaps the only one to survive out of their group and would return home with overwhelming feelings of guilt for having survived when no one else did. It's almost as though they think they themselves didn't deserve to live, when so many others died, and they begin to exhibit anti-social behavior to the point of sabotaging their own happiness.

Unfortunately, if they cannot find their way out of this type of thinking, often they end up, not only destroying their own lives, but the lives of those closest to them, as well.

The only thing I can suggest to help your patient is to get him to talk about what he feels and why. Not an easy thing, I know. And considering his own personal background, I would expect he is very guarded about what he says at the best of times. But I should tell you, often these cases have ended with the subjects taking their own lives. Those few who do get through it, have only done so because they've had support from friends and family, and they were willing to talk about it.

I know you already keep thorough records of your patients, David, but might I suggest you write down everything you can about this one. As I said, there is very little information available about this type of depression and you might consider publishing a paper on it, once your treatment is concluded, one way or another. I would also appreciate you keeping me informed of your progress. It would be a shame indeed if this young man, after having earned his pardon, ends up throwing it all away.

Friends for always, David. Keep in touch.

Michael Griffin.

David sat back with a sigh. He wasn't sure if this letter helped him or not. He had received a short note from Napoleon a couple of days ago, and it did offer some insight into Jack's behavior. The ongoing theme did seem to be feelings of anger and guilt. And the best way to deal with it all, was to get Jack to open up and talk about it. David snorted. At which point, Tricia looked up from her writing with a questioning arch to her eyebrows.

"Oh, it's just what Mike had to say about Jack Kiefer," David explained. "Even if I knew where Jack was, this isn't going to be an easy fix."

"Does he give any suggestions at all?" Tricia asked.

"Yes," David answered, feeling frustrated. "Get him to talk. But whenever I try to, Jack pushes me away."

David sat quietly, looking at the letter in his hands, his thoughts miles away. Tricia got up and poured herself and her husband more tea. Then, sitting down again, she put her own letter-writing aside for the time being and waited quietly for him to open the discussion.

Finally, David sighed and shrugged his shoulders, looking dejected.

"I don't know what to do. I can usually find the answers with a patient who's ill or injured, but with this, I don't even know where to start."

"Where do you usually start when a patient comes to you with a new problem?"

He paused, reflecting. "I suppose I keep it simple, ask them where it hurts."

"And if they're unconscious and can't answer you?"

"Then I do an examination. I feel my way along, very gently at first, until I know what I'm dealing with and then go deeper so I can get an idea of the extent of the injury."

Tricia nodded and smiled. "Sounds like a good place to start to me."

David looked up, meeting her eyes and smiling back at her. "You're wonderful, you know that?"

"Yes, I know," she smiled, a teasing glint in her eye. "Now, I better get back to this letter to Miranda, before we lose the candle-light altogether."

David sat back to drink his tea and reflect on his next course of action. Then there came a knocking on their front door.

David groaned. "Oh no. I hope Mrs. Wales hasn't gone into early labor. All I need tonight is a new mother-to-be in a panic—not to mention, the father. No, no, I'll get it," David got to his feet and went to answer the door.

"Oh. Carl. What can I do for you, this evening?"

"Yeah, howdy there, Doc," Sheriff Jacobs answered him, looking a little contrite. "Listen, that Kiefer fella is over at the saloon right now, tryin' to stir up trouble. He's drunk and pushin' for a fight and, well, me and my deputies could take him out, but we'd be riskin' a gun-fight, and I'd really rather not do that if we can help it. You asked me to let you know if he came around, so, I'm lettin' ya know. Seein' as how you're a friend a his, an' all, well, maybe you can talk 'im down."

David stood in the doorway, his mouth hanging open. He couldn't' quite believe the coincidence of this situation.

"Doc?"

"Oh. Yes, Carl, sorry," David collected himself. "Of course. Let me just get my coat, and I'll be right with you."

He turned to get his coat and scarf and found himself looking into Tricia's worried eyes.

"David? Are you sure?" she was obviously concerned, and rightly so.

He went to her and put a hand on her arm. "It's all right. Don't worry. I'll be careful. Umm, maybe you could see that the guest room is ready. We may have company tonight."

"Yes. All right."

***

Walking with the sheriff toward the saloon, David wished he had thought to grab his hat as well, since it had started snowing again. He briefly wondered where Jack had come from, since this was hardly traveling weather, but he pushed that thought away as being unimportant. He focused his mind on the problem at hand.

Walking into the bright lights and warmth of the saloon, it didn't take any time to appreciate the situation. There was Jack all right, standing at the bar with an empty bottle of whiskey in his hand.

He was busy shouting at Bill, the barkeep.

"'Ooo the 'ell are you ta tell me I've ha' 'nough ta drink? If I wanna buy ano'er bo'le, then I'll buy ano'er bo'le . . ."

There was a wide circle of empty space around Jack. Everybody in the saloon was doing their best to focus on something else, not wanting to get into a scuffle with the drunken gunman. Deputies Palin and Morgan were on either side of Jack, staying out of his reach, but still trying to keep some semblance of control over the situation.

As soon as the two men entered the saloon, Jacobs moved quietly into position behind Jack, so he could take the man down if needs be. But he wanted to give Gibson his chance to end the episode peaceably.

David took a deep breath and walked toward his friend.

"Jack," David called to him, but Jack was too busy yelling at Bill to hear him. "Jack!"

Still no response. David reached out and touched Jack on his shoulder.

The reaction was instantaneous.

Before David could even blink, Jack spun around and had that six-shooter in his hand and aimed at David before the empty whiskey bottle made it halfway to the floor. If the atmosphere in the saloon had been awkward and heavy before, now it was like a lead boat sinking to the bottom of the ocean.

Even with everything David had heard at the trial, he still couldn't believe the speed of the man, and that was him being drunk and with a stiff shoulder. David's hands went up instantly, but he didn't back down. With his heart pounding in his ears, he stared directly into those blue eyes—like death turned to ice. He saw it, and he shivered.

A voice, unbidden, came to him, '. . . if there ever comes a time when you get in between the Kansas Kid and something he wants . . .' But David still held his ground, and the fear he felt never made it to his voice.

"What are you going to do, Jack? Are you going to shoot me?"

Then something happened that had never happened to Jack Kiefer before, once he had drawn his gun—he hesitated. Suddenly, he was unsure.

"Wh . . . what?"

Out of the corner of his eye, David saw Jacobs slowly start to close in on Jack, but David stopped him with just a gesture. He stood still as a rock, his hands raised, pinning Jack with his eyes.

"Are you going to shoot me, Jack?"

"No. I . . ." Then the ice from the blue was gone, replaced by just a hint of indecision. Jack looked at the gun in his hand and it started to waver, then slowly, the muzzle dropped down. Jack looked up to his friend again, with eyes that were now clouded with pain and fear. "David," he whispered, "help me."

David moved in and, with one hand on his friend's left arm, he reached down with his other hand and took the gun out of Jack's grasp. He then handed it over to Sheriff Jacobs.

"It's all right, Jack," David assured him, both hands holding onto him now.

"What's the matter with me, David?" Jack's voice quivered. "What's wrong?"

"I don't know, Jack," David admitted. "But you coming to me and asking for help is a huge step toward us finding out together."

***

There was one big collective sigh of relief as David led Jack out of the saloon. The three lawmen followed behind until they got outside onto the boardwalk.

"Do you want me to take him from here, Doc?" Jacobs asked. "He can sleep it off in a cell for the night."

"No, that's all right, Carl. I'll take him home. I think he'll be okay now."

"Well, if you're sure. Thanks for comin' over. I sure didn't much wanna get into a showdown with 'im. But I think I'll just hang onto his gun until he's sober. He can come collect it tomorrow, or better yet, the day after."

"Probably a good idea," David agreed. "Goodnight, and thanks for coming to get me."

"Uh huh. You have a good night too there, Doc."

The group parted.

Walking down the quiet street toward David's house, the snow still fell through air that was cold and crisp. Now that the crisis was over, Jack returned to mumbling the way only a man who's had too much to drink can mumble.

"Ever'body'ss ma' a' me. Why eve' bod' s ma' a' me?"

"I think everyone has a right to be mad at you, Jack," David answered. "You've been behaving pretty selfishly lately."

"I 'av?"

"Uh huh."

"Ooo."

Back at the house, Tricia met them at the door, not wanting to go to bed until her husband came home safely.

"Oh David," she frowned with concern, "is he going to be all right?"

"Yeah, I think so. I'll get him settled. You go on to bed and I'll join you in a while."

"All right. There's still some hot water on the stove, if you want to make tea."

David gave her a quick hug and a kiss on her cheek. "Good night."

In the spare bedroom, David got Jack's coat off and sat him down on the bed to take his boots off.

Jack stated mumbling again.

"Cam' 'ates me."

"Cameron doesn't hate you."

"Ee sad . . . doon 'ike me."

"He doesn't like the way you've been behaving," David clarified. "It's not that he doesn't like you."

"Umm. Eve' 'Osey ma' a' me. She 'icked me out."

"Miss Jansen?" David asked. "She kicked you out? Is that where you've been, Jack?"

"Yah."

"Where have you been getting the money for all this?"

"Max."

328

David frowned. "Mr. Coburn?"

"Ya."

"Well, I doubt he meant for it to be used in this manner."

"Hmm."

"Okay," David said, once he had Jack stripped down to his long johns. "You get some sleep. We'll talk more about this in the morning."

"Yah, slee' . . ."

David swung Jack's legs onto the bed and got him lying down, then pulled the blankets over him and basically tucked him in.

"Good night, Jack."

The soft snore that came up from the pillow suggested that Jack was already taking the good doctor's advice. David let go a huge sigh, then picking up Jack's coat, empty holster and his boots, he took the lamp and left the room.

***

With the house now cooling down, David hurried to his bedroom and, putting the lamp down on the nightstand, he stuffed Jack's belongings under the bed. Then, turning out the lamp, he got undressed and, shivering in the night-time chill, slid into bed under the covers and snuggled in behind his wife.

Tricia stiffened.

"David! You're freezing."

"You're not. You're nice and warm."

Silence.

Then a suspicious, "David, what are you doing?"

"Nothing."

GASP! Arrgg! Your feet are like ice blocks."

"They're warming up fast," he replied as he began to kiss her on the back of her neck.

"Where's your hand going?"

"Nowhere."

More kisses.

Another gasp. "Your fingers are so cold."

"Hmm, but where they are, is so warm."

Tricia giggled. "You pest," she accused him as she rolled over to face him. "You always could get whatever you want."

He smiled, and returning his fingers to her cozy, warm nest, he pulled his wife into a long passionate kiss and warmed up considerably within her embrace.

***

The next morning the Gibsons were up early, as David had his rounds to do. The stove was lit with coffee on to perk and oatmeal simmering, while David got his medical bag ready to go.

"I should be back by lunch," he assured his wife while they sat over a quick meal. "Jack will probably sleep for a while yet, but if he wakes up before I get home, I don't think he'll be any trouble. In the meantime, I'll send a message to the Marshams to let them know the wayward son is home again."

"I'm sure they'll be relieved. I also expect he'll have such a hangover when he does wake up, he probably won't want to move anyway." Tricia brushed a loose strand of dark hair out of her face. "I'm sure we'll be fine."

***

A few hours later, Tricia sat at the kitchen table, continuing with her letter-writing, when she heard a door slowly creak open. She looked up to see a disheveled head peeking out from the spare bedroom.

"Good morning," she greeted him, trying to sound casual.

"Hmm. Mornin'," came the self-conscious reply. "David around?"

"He's gone on his rounds," Tricia informed him. "He'll be back soon."

"Oh. Do you know where my boots are?"

"Your boots?"

"Yeah."

"No."

"Oh."

She smiled at his discomfort. "Come on out. Come sit and have some coffee."

"Coffee?"

"Yes. It's right here and ready. Come, have a cup."

"Coffee. Yeah, good idea."

"Good," Tricia smiled. She got up and poured him a cup.

He came out to the kitchen, fully dressed minus his boots, and sat at the table.

Tricia set the coffee cup in front of him. "Would you like some oatmeal as well?"

"Ohh, not yet," he said as he hugged his cup.

He really did look a mess.

Tricia poured herself another coffee and stood leaning against the counter, watching him as he took a sip, then sat there with his eyes closed, savoring it for a moment.

He took another sip, then opened his eyes and blinked at her.

"You're Tricia," he ventured.

"That's right."

"David's wife."

"Yes," she confirmed and took a drink from her own cup.

"You've seen me naked."

Tricia spluttered and choked on her coffee.

Jack panicked.

"Oh! I'm sorry. Did I say that out loud?"

He got up from the table and looked like he was going to bolt back into his room, but Tricia held up a hand while she got her breath back.

"No, no, Mr. Kiefer, that's quite all right," then she laughed at the absurdity of it. "That was a necessity of your convalescence. I'm quite used to helping David with his patients' care. She sent him a reassuring smile. "Please, sit down again. Don't worry about it. Enjoy your coffee."

Jack relaxed, though he still felt embarrassed. "Yeah, okay. It's all right?"

"Yes. Please, sit down."

"Okay. Sorry."

"Here, let me give you a top up your coffee," she offered, and did just that. She spooned out some oatmeal into a bowl and put it on the table in front of him. "Try and eat a little bit, if you can," she encouraged him.

Jack nodded.

When David got home an hour later, it was to find his wife and his patient sitting at the kitchen table and having quite a good laugh over something.

"Oh David," Tricia greeted her husband as he came in. "Were your ears burning?"

***

After lunch, Tricia discretely went next door to visit with her friend Millie, so the two men could be alone to talk. David poured coffee for them both, then sat down at the table across from Jack. Silence settled between them.

"Do you want to talk, Jack?" David finally asked him.

Jack looked at him, then down at his coffee cup.

"Yeah and no."

"Why 'yeah'?" David asked.

Jack shuffled in his chair, like a misbehaving schoolboy. He was uncomfortable. Men didn't talk about this stuff. Even he and Leon would respect each other's privacy and not push. But now, David was pushing.

"'Cause, I wanna find out what's wrong with me," Jack finally mumbled.

"Okay. So, why 'no'?"

"'Cause," silence. Long silence. Then finally, "cause I'm afraid to find out what's wrong with me?" He said it as a question, feeling that it didn't make sense.

"Okay," David responded, "that's understandable."

Jack visibly relaxed.

David continued. "I want you to say whatever it is you're feeling. Even if you don't understand why you feel that way or if you think it's contradictory. Doesn't matter—just say it. I'm not just your doctor, Jack. I'm your friend as well, and I want to help you get to the bottom of this."

Jack nodded. "Cameron hates me," he said, obviously upset by this assumption, since it was the second time, he had commented on it.

"As I assured you last night, he doesn't hate you," David said. "We're all your friends, and we all want to help you, but you've been making it very difficult lately. Cameron feels bad about what happened last month. He's been worried about you. We all have."

"Cameron has the right to be mad at me," Jack admitted. "I know I disappointed them at Christmas."

"Yes. Why did you do that?"

Jack shook his head. "I really had a good time out there at Thanksgivin'."

"Well, that's good."

"No, it wasn't!" Jack exploded, slamming the palm of his hand onto the table. "I had no right—havin' a good time with the family like that—no right at all."

"Why are you angry, Jack?"

"'Cause, Leon shoulda been there. One of the last conversations we had together, I was talkin' about how good it would be ta spend the holidays with a family again. Then there I was, doin' it. I had meant for both of us—not just me. But Leon got thrown to the wolves so I could go free. So that I could have a life again—have a family again. And that ain't the way it was supposed ta be. It was supposed ta be both of us or neither of us—not one or the other. We're partners. Both of us or neither of us!"

"So, you feel that the governor betrayed you."

"Damn right, he betrayed us." Jack's anger seethed. "And if it was just gonna be one of us goin' ta prison, it shoulda been me."

"Why?"

"Because I—" and here Jack choked on his words, and he had to stop and take deep breaths before continuing. "Because I committed murder. I've killed, and Leon would never a done that, he'd a found another way. It ain't in 'im ta kill. Even those men that attacked our farms, I don't think Leon would a done what I did—well, he didn't, did he? I'm the one who had ta go after 'em, track 'em down, even murdering one of 'em in front a his own daughter."

Jack stopped talking and sat staring into space, clutching his coffee cup.

David thought he was going to start crying, which wouldn't have been a bad thing, really. But Jack fought back the tears, though his pain was still apparent.

Finally, he had control again, and taking a deep breath, he continued.

"I shouldn't have got off scott-free. I ain't earned the right ta be happy."

There was silence between them again for a moment. David thought back to the letter his friend had sent him, describing the symptoms of others experiencing this type of depression. He had gone into great detail about how the war veterans would experience feelings of overwhelming guilt and remorse, thereby sabotaging their own happiness. They truly believed they didn't deserve to have a good life, when so many people they knew had paid the ultimate price.

David sighed. It all fit. Jack had been hit hard, and he was foundering. He needed to get his self-confidence back, his self-respect back, before he would be able to do anything to help Napoleon.

Jack gave a deep sigh. "Besides that, Leon is smarter n I am," he said. "He'd have a much better chance a gettin' me outta prison, than I do a gettin' him out."

"Why would you think that?" asked David, surprised that Jack would feel this way.

"Cause those politicians talk circles around me," Jack thought this should be obvious. "Three hours later is when I think a what I should a said, and by then it's too late. But Leon, he can talk circles around their circles. He'd a had me outta there ages ago. But Me? Deal with those educated men? I don't even understand half the words they use, so why even bother tryin'?"

"So, you went out and got drunk instead," David commented.

Jack hung his head and did not respond.

David sighed and ran a hand through his hair. "You're not stupid Jack, far from it. Granted, Napoleon does have an edge."

"Yeah."

"On all of us. And not to the extent you think," David was quick to emphasize. "Napoleon is analytical and tends to think everything through. You're more intuitive and you go on your gut instinct."

Jack smirked and rolled his eyes.

"No," David continued. "I'm willing to bet, there have been plenty of times when you and Leon have butted heads because he was being logical, and you just felt that something was wrong. I'm also willing to bet that, more often than not, you ended up being right."

"Yeah . . . well."

"Yes," David again emphasized. "You're not stupid, Jack. You just need to find another way to solve the problem. If the fast-talking politicians run circles around you, then you come at them in a straight line."

"I don't know how," Jack admitted with a frustrated sigh.

"I have every confidence you will figure it out. You have a lot of people here who are willing to help you. Don't sell them short. Look what Penny and Caroline did to get you pardoned. They got that campaign going pretty much on their own. They did not let self-doubt get in the way; they knew what their goal was, and they aimed straight at it. With those two ladies on your side, you can move mountains."

Jack smiled. "Yeah, that was amazin', wasn't it?"

"It sure was," David agreed. "And with Mr. Coburn willing to help, and Miss Jansen . . . did she really kick you out?"

Jack looked sheepish. "No, not really. She just told me to smarten up and get my butt movin'. That Leon couldn't sit around in prison for ever, and I better start gettin' around to whatever it was I was gonna do ta get 'im out." Jack sighed. "So, between her naggin' at me, and Cameron givin' me what for, well, it finally sunk in that I better figure out what's wrong with me and do somethin' about it. You're the only one I could think of who was willin' ta leave that door open, so—here I am. Even at that, I couldn't just come and ask for your help, I had to go get drunk first."

David smiled. "It doesn't matter how you got here, I'm just glad you did. It would have been helpful if Miss Jansen had let us know you were with her, though. We were all very worried."

"Don't blame her, David." Jack said. "I told her you were all mad at me and didn't wanna hear from me. She was just goin' along with that."

"Well, I suppose," David accepted this, but it still bugged him.

"David?"

"Yes?"

"Where are my boots?"

"I hid them."

"Can I have 'em back?"

"No."

"Why not?"

"Because even though you sound positive right now, come tonight, when everything is quiet and you start mulling stuff over in your mind, you just might decide to take a walk. I don't want you doing that. Not by yourself—not yet."

"Well—when?"

"Just relax," David advised him. "You'll get them back."

At this point, the front door opened, and Tricia came home. It was getting on to supper time.

***

It was two fifteen in the morning.

David jerked awake from a sound sleep. He lay quiet for a few moments, his wife lying beside him, snoring softly. Then he got out of bed and quickly dressed, just as much for the warmth as for modesty.

Tricia stirred and briefly woke up. She couldn't see her husband, but she knew he was there, standing by the bed.

"What's the matter?" she mumbled. "Why are you up?"

"Jack's awake."

Tricia held her breath and lay there listening for a few seconds. "I don't hear anything. How can you tell?"

He shrugged his shoulders in the darkness.

"I dunno. Go back to sleep, Babe, I won't be long." Then added under his breath, "I hope."

CHAPTER NINETEEN
PARTNERS

As soon as David stepped out of his bedroom, he could see the low light coming from the kitchen. Wrapping his robe more snuggly around him, he made his way down the hallway and into that room. Jack was up and fully dressed, pacing around in his stocking feet. He was agitated, his lips moving in a silent argument with himself, and it was hard to tell who was winning.

"Jack?"

Jack spun round in a flash, his right hand dropping to the gun that wasn't there.

Then he saw David, and relaxed. "Damn it, David, don't sneak up on me like that."

"How are you doing?" David asked him, ignoring the warning. "Do you want to talk?"

"No," Jack answered flatly. "What I want is out. Let me out."

"No."

Jack suddenly came at him, his body hostile.

David fought the urge to step back; he held his ground and held his eye.

Jack stopped just short of grabbing David's shirt front and becoming violent.

"You've got no right to keep me here," Jack insisted, his voice getting louder and angrier.

David silently sent a plea to Tricia that she stay in the bedroom. He didn't want her involved in this.

"I have every right," David said. "It was either here or the jailhouse again, and I think you've had enough of the inside of that place."

Jack glared at him, then backed off and started to pace the kitchen again. He pushed his hands through his curls, looking like he was going to explode.

David came further into the kitchen and set about lighting the stove. He needed a moment to think. This agitation suggested withdrawal from a drug of some sort. But David wasn't going to make assumptions yet. This mood could also be indicative of his depression.

In any case, it was time for coffee.

"What are you feeling, Jack?"

"What?"

"How do you feel? Tell me."

"I dunno."

"Yes, you do," David insisted. "Think about it and then tell me."

"Arrggg." Jack couldn't have sounded more frustrated. "Restless," he finally stated. "Mad. I'm angry."

"Angry at what?"

"You. For not letting me out."

"No, that's not it," David insisted. "You woke up angry. Why?"

Jack stopped pacing and leaned against the far wall, his back to the doctor. He was misery personified.

"I dunno."

"Not good enough," David answered. "Why are you so angry, Jack?"

Jack turned away from the wall and sat down at the table before his legs gave out beneath him. His body had just turned to jelly and suddenly, he sobbed. He fought it, choking it back, trying to maintain control.

"No, Jack," David assured him. "It's all right. Let it out."

"No!" Jack continued to fight it, but the sobs attacked him and with one final, gasping, "No . . ." he succumbed, and his misery took him over.

David left the coffee to perk, and sitting down beside his friend, he put an arm across his shoulders and rubbed his back.

"It's all right, Jack. It's all right."

David caught movement in the corner of his eye and looked up to see Tricia standing in the hallway. He smiled quietly at her, assuring her that all was well, and she nodded and turned back to the bedroom.

It took a good fifteen minutes before the sobs started to ease off. By that time, the coffee was ready, and David got up to pour them both a cup.

"Here," he offered as he sat back down, "have some coffee. I made it extra strong."

"Yeah, thanks," came the strained response. He still struggled.

David rubbed his back again, helping him to relax.

"My ma," Jack began, still fighting emotion. "Ahh David, she was beautiful and kind. She was my best friend—I loved her so much. And those men, they just came and they . . . they raped her, over and over and over again. And I couldn't do anything. I couldn't protect her."

"I know. That was a terrible thing for you to witness. No child should have to see that."

Jack nodded. He sniffed and wiped his eyes, then took a good swallow of coffee. It was hot, and he could feel it burning his throat, but it felt good and it helped to calm him down a little bit more.

"Now Leon," he continued. "It was my job ta watch his back. I always told him; I would always be there ta watch his back." He stopped and wiped his eyes again. The sobs had eased off, but the tears still fell freely. "I didn't watch his back. He's my partner, and I didn't watch his back. I just—we walked right into that ambush. I should 'a been payin' more attention, but I let my guard down and . . . and now, he's stuck in that prison, and . . . and I don't know . . . if I'm gonna be able ta get 'im out."

"You can't be on alert all the time, Jack," David told him. "Napoleon doesn't blame you. He's worried about you."

Jack tried to laugh through his tears. "He's the one in prison and he's worried about me?"

"Yes," David confirmed. "He misses you and wants to see you."

Jack took a deep breath and sighed. "I just couldn't face 'im. I was sure he knew I had let 'im down—that he wouldn't wanna see me."

"No. You couldn't have been more wrong. The letter he sent me was filled with concern. He very much wants to see you."

Jack nodded and took another gulp of coffee.

"You okay now?" David asked him. "Think you can get some more sleep?"

Jack gave a huge cleansing sigh and then nodded again. "Yeah."

"Good. Tomorrow is . . . no, I should say, today is Saturday, and the Marsham's have invited us out to lunch, weather permitting. So, we can all sleep in a little bit and have an easy day. Sound good?"

"Yeah."

***

David slipped into the warm bed and nestled against his wife.

She shifted position and got comfortable with his arms around her.

"A lot more to him than just what the dime novels say," she commented.

"Umm hmmm," came the muffled reply.

Tricia smiled and gave her husband a gentle caress on his arm.

"You're a good man, David."

"Hmmm."

***

Later that morning, when Jack came out to the kitchen for more coffee, he spied his coat and boots waiting for him.

"Oh good. And my gun?"

"That's still at the sheriff's office," David informed him.

"Oh. And my hat?"

"Probably with your gun."

"Oh." A moment's silence while Jack sipped his coffee. Then, "Can I get them back?"

"No."

"But I feel naked going outside without my gun."

Then he looked embarrassed and sent Tricia a furtive glance.

Tricia smiled and went back to focusing on breakfast.

David frowned, wondering what that was all about, then he disregarded it and carried on. "I don't want you having a gun just yet. I don't think it's safe. I want to be sure you're in control again."

"I'm fine."

"Give it some time."

Jack sighed. David can be such a mother sometimes.

"I'll need a hat."

"You can borrow one of mine."

"David—"

"No."

Jack sighed again.

Tricia placed a pile of flapjacks on the table and started to dish out the bacon.

"Come on boys, stop your arguing. Sit down and eat breakfast."

David grabbed the coffee pot and took it over to the table to pour out three cups, then returned it to the stove, giving his wife a little peck on the cheek as he did so.

Jack sat down at the table and sulked.

But, by the time he'd had his second coffee and his first decent meal in days, Jack had resolved himself to the situation and was actually in a good mood. He felt a little nervous about going out to see the Marshams that afternoon, not too sure what Cameron's reaction was going to be, but he also wanted to go see them and apologize. Hopefully he hadn't burned his bridges there.

Later in the morning, Jack and David walked to the livery stable to get the horses ready for the trip to the Rocking M Ranch.

Eric, the livery owner, saw them coming and brought Rudy, David's little chestnut gelding out of his stall. He began to get him harnessed up for the buggy ride, while Jack carried on past them, down to where Midnight was stalled.

"Hey Middy, ole' man. How ya doin' this mornin'?"

Midnight had been done in after their ride from Denver, but fortunately, Jack had enough sense and regard for his horse to tend to the animal's needs. Under the watchful eye of the livery man, he made sure that Midnight was stabled and bedded down before going over to the saloon to have a drink, or two. Jack was relieved to see that this morning, his horse appeared bright eyed and eager for some exercise.

Jack grabbed his tack from the saddle racks and proceeded to get his gelding geared up and ready to go. Twenty minutes later, they were in front of the Gibson's house. Tricia came out to join her husband in the buggy and, with Jack riding Midnight along beside them, they headed out of town.

It turned out to be a cloudy day, but it didn't feel like it was going to snow again, so nobody anticipated any trouble getting to and from the ranch. Even the roads were in decent shape, despite numerous ruts and potholes developing over the winter. All-in-all, it was not a bad day, and everyone enjoyed the opportunity to get out for some fresh air and a long-awaited visit with friends.

Trotting down the lane leading to the ranch house, Jack spotted Karma in the field. She had a couple of other riding horses with her, but as soon as she spied her old friend, she whinnied to him and came trotting to the fence line.

Midnight greeted her, but knowing he was under saddle and

expected to do his human's bidding, he didn't stop or try to pull off the road. There would be time for a re-union soon.

They continued into the yard to the chorus of barking dogs. Sam came out of the barn to greet them and he grabbed hold of Rudy's bridle.

"Afternoon, Sam," David said.

"Howdy Doc, Mrs. Gibson," Sam answered. "How's the road?"

"Excellent," David told him. "No problems at all."

Sam smiled. "That's good to hear. Once I get your horses settled with some lunch, I'll be heading in to see Maribelle. Sure didn't want to have to deal with bad roads."

"You and Miss Willis seem to be getting serious, Sam," Tricia commented. "Is there going to be a wedding this summer?"

Sam blushed. "I dunno," he mumbled, shrugging his shoulders. "Maybe."

David rolled his eyes at his wife's teasing.

Jack dismounted and seeing that Sam had his hands full with the harness horse, he led Midnight into the barn and settled him into his usual stall. He grabbed some hay from the feed room and threw it over the wall for his horse. Then he headed back outside, nodding to Sam who was just bringing Rudy in for his own lunch.

As soon as Jack exited the barn, he got hit with a tingling of fear and guilt as he saw Cameron standing there talking to the Gibsons. Then the rancher turned and met Jacks eye. Jack dropped his gaze, suddenly feeling very much ashamed of himself.

Cameron smiled and extended his hand.

"C'mon Jack," he said, "welcome home."

Jack felt a wash of relief, and the two men shook hands.

"Thanks Cameron," he answered with an awkward smile. "I'm real sorry about . . . well . . ."

"Yeah, I know. Me too."

Then, much to Jack's surprise, and a mixture of embarrassment and pleasure, Cameron pulled him into a quick hug and a slap on the back.

"C'mon up to the house," Cameron invited them. "The ladies are all looking forward to seeing you."

Half way to the house, Caroline and Penny, unable to retain their lady-like patience, burst out the front door and into Jack's arms before he had a chance to feel embarrassed.

"Mathew! You're finally here." Penny hugged him, her face alight with pleasure.

"It's about time," Caroline came in on his other side. "We've missed you so much."

"Yeah, I missed you, too." Jack mumbled; his throat tight.

Then each young lady took one of his hands and hurried him forward.

"Come on. Mama's got lunch ready."

"Yeah, yeah. I'm comin'."

The greeting Jack received from Jean couldn't have been more welcoming. It was the warmest he'd had in ages, and he felt like he wanted to stay within that embrace for the rest of the afternoon.

"Welcome home, Mathew."

"Is it my home?" he asked her, still needing that confirmation.

Jean pulled back from the hug and looked up into his beseeching eyes. "Of course, it is." She smiled at him and gave his arm a squeeze. "It always will be. Now, sit. Lunch is ready."

The atmosphere around the table was relaxed and the conversation flowed easily, just as it should between good friends getting together. They talked about everything from the price of beef and the crop of new foals and calves expected that coming spring, to what the lumber market was up to. Then all the way to Mrs. Wales' expectant arrival, and the possibility of Sam and Maribelle tying the knot come summertime. This last comment was met with a snort of derision from Caroline which was quickly followed by a reprimanding look from her mother.

Throughout the conversation, Jack stayed relatively quiet. He knew he felt better after having bared his soul to David, but at the same time, he also felt embarrassed for blubbering like a baby in front of him. Here he was supposed to be this intimidating gunfighter who could squash men down into the floorboards with his icy stare, and David hadn't even back down. Far from being intimidated, the good doctor had taken the ex-outlaw by the hand and then quietly but firmly, brought him emotionally to his knees.

Even Leon had never done that. Of course, Leon had never tired. But then again, Leon was just as damaged as Jack was. It would have been like the blind leading the blind.

Jack sat there, watching his friend across the table, talking and laughing with the family, relaxed and animated with the conversation, and he felt a slight twinge of resentment.

It should be Leon sitting here with us. It should be Leon helping me get through this difficult time. Oh, but then, if it was Leon sitting there, then I wouldn't be having a difficult time.

Still, it didn't seem right that this man whom Jack had only known for about ten months, had reached such a level of trust, that Jack had allowed himself to show his vulnerability.

Geesh, I can only remember one time, after we were grown, when Leon and I cried together. And considerin' what had happened, it ain't surprisin'. But that was only because we trusted one another. This feels like a betrayal to his partner.

Then Jack shook his head and admonished himself for thinking such nonsense. *A person can have two close friends in their lives, for goodness sakes. My friendship with David don't take nothin' away from my friendship with Leon. And besides that, David's a doctor. He knows how ta get under somebody's skin and pull out their innermost secrets. Hmm, that man really needs to be watched. Ohh dammit. There I go again, getting all guarded and defensive.*

Why can't I simply accept the fact that David is my friend, too? I assured David of that very thing in Cheyenne, after Morrison had tried to undermine that relationship. According to Jean, even Leon had a high regard for the good doctor; respects and admires 'im for his intelligence and abilities displayed when he saved my life.

Hmm, wish I could'a been there ta see that. Well, I was there, but, oh, where was I? Oh yeah, Leon feeling an undying debt of gratitude toward David for that very thing. After all that, I doubt Leon would feel any resentment over David and me bein' friends.

Still, Jack felt guilty. Come to think of it, guilt seemed to be all Jack felt these days. What was that all about? Guilt over not being able to protect his mother. Guilt over shooting down that raider right in front of his young daughter. Guilt over blindly walking himself and Leon into that ambush. Guilt about yelling at Cameron. Guilt now about not sending Leon a letter all through the winter, not even at Christmas.

And oh—Christmas. Something else to feel guilty about. What he had put this family through after everything they had done for him and for Leon.

And that look Cameron had sent him, that day on the train, coming back from Cheyenne. It had almost been one of disgust and anger. What was that all about?

Is there something else I'm supposed ta feel guilty about? Oh brother.

Then, over afternoon drinks, the discussion, by natural selection, settled onto Leon. Jack was pulled away from his disturbing inner musings and began to listen with interest.

"So how is he doing, David?" Cameron asked. "Have you heard anything?"

"Yes," David admitted after a bite of pastry. "Sheriff Murphy sent me a quick note to assure me that he was feeling much better. The worst is apparently over."

"That's certainly good to hear," Jean spoke for them all.

"Yes. It got quite worrisome," David agreed. "Apparently, Napoleon hasn't been eating and that contributed to his illness being as bad as it was. He's lost a lot of weight, but he is being encouraged to eat, so I expect he's picking up."

Throughout this intercourse, Jack sat silently at the table, with mouth open and a slightly incredulous look on his face.

"What are you sayin'?" he finally asked. "Leon's been sick?"

"Yes, pneumonia," David told him. "It was quite bad for a while, and we were all very worried. Your friend, Sheriff Murphy braved the bad weather and made the trip to the prison to make sure he was being looked after properly."

"Why didn't anybody tell me?" Jack demanded to know.

"Well, for one thing, nobody knew where you were," Cameron threw back at him.

Jack's expression fell, and he looked contrite. "Oh, yeah," he mumbled. "But he's doin' okay now, right?"

"Yes," David assured him. "The doctor there seems to know what he's doing. Sheriff Murphy is impressed with him. So, with that in mind, I would think Napoleon had the best care he could have gotten anywhere."

"Oh good." Jack breathed a sigh of relief. "I mean, what if . . ." he couldn't quite finish that sentence.

"Then you would have had one more thing to feel guilty about," David answered bluntly. "Fortunately, it didn't come to that."

Jack didn't answer as he wondered if David could read minds as well. More and more he began to see what a fool he had been, and the damage that had been done, and could have been done, because of it. He felt a hand on his arm and looked into Penny's brown eyes and quiet smile, and he couldn't help but smile back at her. She really was very pretty.

"So, Mathew,' Jean began gently, "do you think you might feel like writing Peter a letter now?"

Jack looked at her and shook his head. "No," he answered, and a heavy silence surrounded the table. "I think it's time I went ta see 'im."

***

Jack took the train into Wyoming, the weather still being too cold and unpredictable to ride horseback or attempt the stage. He felt uneasy, taking this means of transportation, considering what his last train ride heading in this direction had been like. Of course, it brought back thoughts of Morrison and all the stuff that happened during those months of incarceration.

He thought guiltily of Gus Shaffer, knowing he never had inquired as to how that outlaw was doing. He tried to console himself by the assurance that if Gus had succumbed to that bullet wound, Jack would have heard about it, one way or another.

He wondered if getting in touch with members of his old gang would be in violation of his pardon and simply stir up more trouble than it was worth. He vetoed the idea. There was no need to dig up the past. Taggard would know what was going on with the gang and would pass on any information he thought relevant. Best to just leave it at that.

Still, there were a lot of reminders of his old life on this train ride.

The Elk Mountain Gang was still active in the area and everyone traveling by train or coach were very much aware of it. All the mothers kept their children within sight, and the men wore sidearms, with many carrying rifles as well.

Jack was glad they weren't stopping trains anymore; sooner or later, the next train robbery would have been their last. Some of the glances sent his way, made him suspicious that his identity might be known by the other passengers and, even though nobody made a point of it, this thought made him nervous.

Then a loud yell behind him, "Kansas Kid!" caused his right hand to do what it always does when he's startled.

Two exuberant youngsters ran past, both holding up toy guns and the first one repeated, "I'm the Kansas Kid. Bang! Bang!"

Jack felt his nerves jingle, as the playfulness continued. Boys could be so expressive with their sound effects.

"Well, I'm Napoleon Nash," the second boy shouted, as he waved his gun above his head, "and I'm the best bank robber there ever was."

"No, you're not," came the response from the first boy. "Napoleon Nash is in prison, so how could he be the best? The Kansas Kid is the best."

Then they were gone, off into the next car, being chased by an imaginary posse, as the rocking of the train threatened to dismount them.

The authentic Kansas Kid relaxed into his seat again and breathed a sigh of . . . something. He wasn't sure how he felt right about then. A certain amount of relief that he, himself, would hopefully never be chased by a posse again, and a little bit of pride that he was being thought of as 'the best'. But he also felt hurt that Leon was already considered a 'has-been'. That wasn't right.

Napoleon Nash was the best outlaw that had ever been or ever would be, as far as Jack was concerned. He felt like standing up and shouting it to the whole train. They couldn't just write him off like that. He was a legend. He was a genius—even if Leon did say so himself.

Jack wanted to grab those boys by the scruff of their necks and shake some respect into them. But all he did was sigh and look out the window at the partially snow-covered landscape passing by.

Spring was coming; it was just around the corner. It was almost a year ago, when Leon and Jack had run into Cameron in that town of the forgotten name, and he had talked the boys into coming to visit. It seemed like yesterday and an eternity ago. Almost a year since he had last seen his partner, not counting that very brief glimpse in Cheyenne. But that didn't really count.

Jack sat back and rubbed his right shoulder; it ached. He and David were going to have to get back after that, when he returned to Arvada.

Almost a year. Jack found himself still feeling that little bit of anxiety with the thought of seeing his friend again, under these circumstances. He was scared to see him caged up and in chains, like some wild animal, and he wasn't sure how he was going to handle that.

How would Leon look? Would he look like a convict now? Or would it be the same old Napoleon sitting there, the sheer force of his personality still shining through? Jack didn't think he could handle it if Leon was a broken man. And Jack would see it right away, even if Leon tried to hide it, Jack would see it. And then Jack would be a broken man too.

He sighed and tried to relax; this train ride was taking longer than he wanted it to.

***

Laramie, Wyoming

Saturday. Finally.

As was his usual routine on Saturdays, he took a cup of coffee and headed to his cell after lunch with the intentions of reading the afternoon away. The temperatures had noticeably warmed up inside the prison, even without the fireplaces burning all day. His cell had become a comparatively comfortable haven instead of the claustrophobic shoebox he had first described it as.

Therefore, it was irritating that only an hour after sitting on his cot, and settling in to read about how to treat damaged lungs, Pearson showed up at his door with the inevitable command;

"Convict. Follow me."

Leon groaned, but closed his book and allowed the guard to escort him to wherever he had to go. His irritation started to diminish as he recognized the routine of preparing for a visitor.

Murray met them in the anti-chamber again and Leon allowed himself to be pushed up against the wall, then searched and shackled once more. Not that he had much choice in the matter, but this time he didn't feel that same anxiety he had when he was first brought here to see Doctor Mariam. The only question in his mind was who had come to visit him?

Leon was taken through to the processing room, and Pearson got him seated at the table before leaving to carry on with his duties. Just like before, Murray stayed to stand guard, rifle at the ready just in case anybody got too riled up. Leon glanced back at him, then sighed and turned to face forward and await whoever it was coming to visit him.

When the door opened, and his visitor stepped self-consciously into the room, Leon forgot about protocol and was halfway to his feet before Murray had a chance to step forward.

Grabbing him by the belt, Murray hauled him back into his chair again.

"What do ya think you're doin' Nash? Sit down and stay there, or this visit's over—now."

Jack felt anger and resentment at that lackey treating Napoleon Nash in such a demeaning manner.

Murray saw the ice daggers headed his way and instantly brought the rifle up into a ready position. Was he going to have trouble with the visitor now?

"No, Jack, relax," Leon told him, his smile so deep the dimples took over his whole face. "Sit down. Oh God, it's good to see you. C'mon Jack, sit down."

"Leon," Jack greeted his friend while sending a nasty glare to the guard. Then he brought his gaze back to the inmate and really looked at Leon for the first time in ten months.

He couldn't hide the shock in his expression. Was that really his friend sitting there? He knew it was; the voice was him and there was no disguising the brown eyes and those dimples. But the shaved head, the sallowness showing through his dark complexion along with the weight loss did so much to otherwise change the appearance of his friend, that Jack found it hard to believe it was actually him.

Leon's smile softened, and he felt sadness at the shock and pity he saw—just for an instant—in Jack's eyes. Then it was gone, and Jack smiled back at him as he sat down at the table, opposite.

"Do I really look that different, Jack?" Leon asked.

"I dunno, Leon," Jack shrugged. "I guess, I just . . .wow, they shaved off all your hair."

"Yeah. Maybe next winter Caroline can knit me a hat. I really feel the cold now."

"Well, it might help if ya ate somethin'," Jack reprimanded him. Any anxiety he had been feeling about seeing his friend again, had disappeared, and he naturally fell into the same old rhythm of their relationship. "David said you weren't eatin' and you've been real sick too. By the look of ya, I'd say he was right."

Leon scowled. "David talks too much. I'm fine."

"Ya don't look fine, Leon. Ya look like shit."

"You're a fine one to talk," Leon threw back at him. "Taggard says you've been drinking—a lot. Hanging out at the brothel every night. What the hell was that all about?"

"Nothin'," Jack mumbled, looking shame-faced. "Taggard talks too much."

Leon settled into his chair, giving his friend a discerning look.

"Yeah, well. You doing better now?"

"Yeah. You?"

Leon shrugged. "I guess." He smiled again. "Sure is good to see you, Jack."

Jack smiled back; relief evident in his eyes. "Yeah. It's good ta see you too. I'm sorry it took so long for me ta get in touch. I just . . ." He shrugged.

"I know, Jack," Leon assured him. "David kept me up on what was going on with you."

"Oh." Jack looked embarrassed, but he supposed he shouldn't be surprised, since David had mentioned that he and Leon were exchanging letters. Jack shuffled in his chair. "Listen, I wanted ta talk to ya about that day we got hit."

"Oh yeah?" Leon frowned. "What about it?"

"I let my guard down," Jack insisted. "Bein' with the Marshams like that, I just let myself relax too much. I lead us right inta that ambush. This is all my fault."

"Aww Jack, I told you before, this wasn't your doing. I don't blame you for this. Never did."

"Yeah . . . well," Jack mumbled. "We're doin' everything we can to get you outta here, ya know. You'd be amazed at what Penny and Caroline have accomplished. And Josey too. And, 'a course, Taggard. Oh, and Max. You should'a seen him at the trial, Leon. He had everyone runnin' for cover." Jack laughed at the memory of it.

"Yeah?" Leon smiled. "I can just imagine. Good ole' Max."

Jack turned serious again. "We'll get ya outta here, Leon. Just hang in there."

"I know," Leon answered, though he didn't sound optimistic.

Jack lowered his voice, still aware of Murray standing by the door.

"What's it like, Leon? Is it as bad as we thought it would be?"

Leon swallowed, his dark complexion paling even more. "It's worse."

"Worse? How could it be worse?"

"I don't know," Leon shrugged. "Maybe it's just because it's real now. It's always cold, and the food is terrible—so you'd have a real hard time in here. I'm always having to watch my back, because there's always somebody wanting to challenge me or teach me a new 'rule'. You know they don't even tell you the rules until you break what is apparently a rule, and then they whacked you with those damn billy clubs all the guards carry. So that's how you learn what a rule is, because you get hit for breaking it.

"Then some of the guards try to set you up so you inadvertently break a rule, just so they can punish you. I swear, those fellas like to hurt you." He hesitated and glanced back at the guard. "Oh, but not you Mr. Murray. You're always fair."

Murray cocked a brow at him, knowing a line of bull when he heard it, but willing to let the matter lie.

Leon turned back to face Jack and lowered his voice. "One of them, unfortunately he's the senior guard, well, he's worse than Morrison."

"Really?" Then Jack looked at Murray, concerned that Leon might be pushing his luck. This was odd, since Leon was normally cautious with his words where the law was concerned.

"Yeah," Leon continued. "There always seems to be one in a group. I'm still carrying some bruises from him, and I hadn't even done anything. He just suspected I was thinking about doing something."

"And were ya?"

"Yeah, but that's beside the point. But then, there's this other guard, Kenny Reece, he's an okay guy. So, if you ever need to talk to one of the guards, he's the one to see. Though he's given me a few bruises too, for fighting or for mouthing off."

"Really? You, mouthin' off? I can't imagine."

"Yeah. And then they have this place called 'the dark cell'. Oh, you don't want to end up in there, Jack. It's terrible. It's pitch-black and no light or sound can get into it. They'll lock you up for days at a time and it just about drives you mad and I'm sure there are spiders in there and goodness knows what else. No, you definitely don't want to end up in there. Gives me the shivers just thinking about it.

"Still, I suppose it's not all bad. There is a library here, as such, though it didn't take me long to read most of the books, so then I asked the doc for some medical journals because after seeing what David did to save your life, well, that kind of got me interested in that stuff, so, I've been reading a lot of those. Now I get to go over to the infirmary one day a week and help there, mostly just cleaning stuff and maybe helping the doc with stitching up a cut or something, but it's still a break from the warehouse.

And Doc Palin, he's a pretty good guy, considering what he's got to put up with, though he drinks a bit, but you can hardly blame him for that, working every day in this place, and, oh, Mariam Soames came by to see me."

"Doctor Mariam? Really?"

"Yeah. It was sweet of her. Apparently, she set up an orphanage here in town and there's some Catholic nuns helping out with it."

Jack's expression hardened. "Oh yeah?"

Leon sighed and nodded. "I know. I thought bad thoughts, too. But maybe with someone like Mariam running things, it's changed for the better. I can't see her allowing the kind of treatment we got."

"Yeah, I suppose." But Jack still didn't appear convinced.

"They do more than just run the orphanage, too," Leon continued. "The Sisters help here when they're needed, and Mariam really did a lot when I got sick, and then there's chapel every Sunday. I didn't want to go at first, but it was either that or the dark cell, so . . . now, it's kind of a nice break, you know, kind of makes you feel a bit better, even if it's just for a little while."

"I never saw you as a church goin' man, Leon."

"No. I'm not, generally. But Mariam is one of the preachers who come to give the sermons, so that makes it worthwhile to go and listen to her preach. It's kind of nice, hearing a woman's voice in this God-forsaken place."

"Really? They let a woman do that?"

"Yeah."

"Is she good?"

"Well, she's different. But, you know, she never was the 'fire and brimstone' type."

"Yeah, I know, Leon. But people can change once they think they're doin' 'God's work'. Maybe she ain't the person we thought she was."

"No, she's the same person. She truly cares about the people here and puts a lot of effort into her sermons. She really does make a difference here on Sunday mornings, such a pleasant voice too, and she really can throw it, so even if you're sitting way back behind everybody else, you can still hear what she's saying. Her message is nothing like what we got at Blessed Heart. It's really kind stuff—almost makes you want to believe it's true."

"Oh. So . . . she's good at it?"

"Well, yes actually, she is. At least it's a little bit of a diversion from this hell hole, and a man can fantasize, can't he? At least that's one thing they can't take away from us in here." He hesitated, his focus turning inward. "I've been having strange dreams lately."

"Yeah. Tell me about it."

"I don't know where they're coming from. I never used to have dreams like that, and they really seem real, you know? They've gotten me into trouble a few times, waking up and thinking it's all real, then you get someone like Carson, who just loves to get you at a disadvantage."

"Carson?"

"The head guard. Come on, Jack, keep up."

"Sorry."

"Yeah, Carson has got me good a few times because of dreams I think are real. It's bad enough trying to deal with things that are real, without having to deal with things that aren't real, and you just think they're real. It gets real confusing sometimes.

"Oh! I forgot to mention the really big rule. I've been whacked quite a few times for breaking this one, mainly because it just doesn't make any sense. You know they don't allow you to talk in here? Not at all. Not unless a guard asks you a direct question and then you can only answer in one word, 'yes' or 'no', that kind of thing. Can you imagine, not being able to talk at all!?"

"No talkin'?"

"Yeah."

"Oh. Well that explains a lot."

"What?"

"Nothin'."

"Hmm. Oh, and now that winter is finally starting to fade away, we actually get some time outside on the weekends. Of course, we go outside to walk back and forth to the warehouse, but that's different; it's not for leisure, anyway, I was out in the yard this morning for a little while and it sure felt good to get some fresh air again. It was a little too cold for me though, considering I'm still kind of getting my strength back from being ill, but it was nice to get outside for a while.

"Then on the weekends, like now, when we're not in service, or have visitors, I can go and read in my cell and have some time to myself. That's kind of nice; don't have to watch my back so much in there. One of the other inmates thinks he's the big rooster here—like that's supposed to amount to anything, and he keeps thinking I want to take over, so he's always lying in wait for me, trying to get me into a fight—I got him good awhile back." He smiled with the memory. "So, hopefully he got the hint to leave me alone. Still, I think there's going to be trouble with him yet—I can just feel it in my bones, you know?" Leon sighed, then frowned. "So, you're being awfully quiet. What's going on at home?"

"Oh. Ah, let me think." Jack was caught off guard. "Oh, Cameron wanted me to ask if it'd be all right for him ta breed Karma this spring. He said he'd like ta get some new blood into his breedin' program, and he thinks he could get a real nice stud colt, if he could breed her to the right stallion."

"I gave Karma to him," Leon answered. "It's up to him what he does with her. Though I would appreciate it, if he doesn't sell her."

"He ain't gonna sell her, Leon. Besides, he never took you serious about you givin' her to him. He knows you said that just 'cause you were desperate ta keep her safe. As far as Cameron's concerned, he has Karma on loan, and she's yours, just as soon as we can get ya outta here."

"Hmm," was Leon's noncommittal response. "How is she doing?"

"Good. Fat and shaggy," Jack smiled as fondness seeped into his eyes. "Penny has really taken to her and rides her whenever weather permits. So, she's doin' good. Still, I see her sometimes, gazin' off to the horizon, and I know she's lookin' for you. But she likes Penny too, so she's all right."

"Yeah, that's good." Leon looked a little sad, missing his mare and the wild gallops they used to share and enjoy so much. Oh well.

"You haven't answered my question, Leon."

"Hmm? What was that?"

"Is it all right with you if Cameron breeds her this spring?"

"Oh, sure," Leon agreed, then smiled, becoming reflective. "Might do her some good. Maybe being a mother will help her to develop some common sense."

"Yeah, well just remember you said that, Leon—not me."

Leon nodded. "So, how are the girls doing?"

"Fine," Jack answered, then brightened up. "Oh. Caroline and Sam are courtin'."

"What?" Suddenly Leon was half out of his chair again. "What do you mean, Caroline and Sam are courting?"

"Settle, Nash," came Murray's warning from behind him. "Sit down."

Leon sent a furtive but resentful glance back at the guard, then did as he was told. He lowered his voice to a quiet but angry whisper.

"What do you mean, they're courting?"

"Well, what?" asked Jack, confused. "What . . .? Oh. No! Not each other."

Leon sat back in his chair, his whole body relaxing in a relieved sigh.

"Oh, thank goodness. For a minute there I thought I was going to have to break out of here and go shake some sense into that girl."

This statement was met by an incredulous snort from Murray.

"Fat chance 'a that," Jack commented. "Her courtin' Sam, that is. She never did let him forget his part in all this."

"That's my girl."

"Damn it, Leon. You and Caroline; two peas in a pod. Neither one of ya is big on lettin' bygones be, are ya? I tell ya, if you can forgive Carlyle, then ya ought'a be able ta forgive Sam. He's not a bad kid, he just made a mistake. He's sorry for it now."

"Yeah, well. When you're going down for the third time, it's kind of hard to forgive the person who threw you off the boat in the first place."

Jack thought this was an odd analogy for Leon to use.

"You readin' Moby Dick again?"

"What's that got to do with anything?"

"Well, I've noticed in the past that often the book ya happen ta be readin' at the time, influences the way ya say things."

"Oh."

Silence.

"Well, are ya?"

"Well, yeah," Leon admitted. "Don't see that it matters." Then he brightened up and went back to the original topic. "So, Caroline's courting somebody?"

"Oh yeah," Jack came back on track. "Steven Granger."

Leon frowned. "The lawyer?"

"Yeah. Steven's gettin' ready ta move his practice ta Denver, and then Caroline is gonna go and work for 'im as his assistant. She's gonna live at a boarding house for ladies until other arrangements can be made. Josey will be keepin' an eye on her, too."

"Oh," Leon remarked. "Yeah, Josey mentioned something about that. So, this is what was behind Granger coming to the ranch for

Thanksgiving—to get this organized?"

"Yeah."

Leon nodded. "Yeah, that's good. I think they'll be good together. Get Caroline away from that idea of 'law enforcement'." He smiled and gave Jack a wicked look. "Josey also mentioned that Penny is kind'a sweet on you. Of course, I knew that before, but it's nice to have it confirmed."

Jack looked embarrassed. "Dagnabbit. Josey talks too much."

"It's about time you settled down and took yourself a wife," Leon teased him. "You're kind of running out of options, you know."

"Yeah, but she's so young."

"Hmm. I suppose the longer you wait, the older she'll get." Leon shrugged. "But still, a lot of men take wives who are a lot younger than they are. Especially when they get started late, like us. Come on, Jack. You've always wanted a family; now's your chance. What are you waiting for?"

"I'm ain't ready," Jack mumbled. "Not yet."

The two friends locked eyes and understanding passed between them.

"Well, don't hang on too long, Jack. Don't let life pass you by."

"You're not gonna be the one payin' for my happiness, Leon," Jack said. "You got a right to a good life, too. You've earned it. I'm gonna get you outta here, 'cause for one thing—well, we seem ta do better when we can watch each other's back."

"Yeah, I know."

"Not only did I mess up Christmas for everyone, but I missed your birthday as well," Jack said. "I didn't even bring ya a present."

"Yeah, ya did," Leon smiled at him. "You brought me the best birthday present I've ever had."

They locked eyes and Jack's smile joined Leon's.

"Yeah, okay," Jack agreed. "Likewise, I guess. Happy Birthday, Leon."

"Happy Birthday, Jack."

Jack sighed. "It's gonna be Eli's first birthday in a couple 'a weeks," Jack mentioned. "That little fella is growin' like a spring calf. You should see 'im. He's gonna be a real scrapper."

"I suppose," Leon mumbled, feeling like he was losing out on all the fun stuff.

"We'll get ya out, Leon," Jack said. "You'll see 'im soon. Just

356

hang in there,"

Leon brightened, more for Jack's sake than his own optimism.

"I know, Jack. I'll hang in. Not much choice, really."

Murray pushed himself off the wall and came toward them.

"Hour's up," he announced, "Time to shut it down."

"Oh," Leon was disappointed, "already?"

"Oh," Jack seconded. Now that he had gotten himself here, he didn't want to leave. He found it hard to say 'goodbye' to his friend, then turn around and walk away.

The two men looked at each other, neither one wanting to break contact.

"C'mon, break it up," Murray ordered. "Let's go."

"Yeah, I guess you better go, Jack," said Leon, who was more accustomed to following the guards' orders than Jack was.

Jack nodded. "Okay," and got to his feet, preparing to leave. "I'll try ta get here every month. Gee, an hour a month. That's not very much, is it?"

"It's better than nothing," Leon pointed out. "Thanks for coming, Jack. And if you can get out here once a month, that would be great. I'll look forward to seeing you. Say 'hello' to everybody back home for me, will ya?"

"Yeah, I will." Then he just stood there for a moment, looking down at his friend. He had thought coming here was hard but leaving was proving to be much more difficult. Finally, he forced himself to break away. "I'll see ya later, Leon," and he walked over to the door and opened it, preparing to leave.

"Jack?" Leon called after him.

Jack stopped and looked back. "Yeah?"

"Partners?"

Jack smiled. "Yeah, Leon. Partners."

CHAPTER TWENTY
HINDSIGHT

Laramie
Winter 1886

Leon felt better. His appetite returned and even though he never was one to go back for seconds, he did now tend to clean up what was given him. It cannot be said that the weight piled back onto him, but he did at least stop losing it. The sallow hollowness of his features filled out some, and the color returned to his complexion.

It was still chilly with snow lingering, but he managed to spend more time outdoors again, and the fresh air worked wonders on, not only his health, but also his attitude. It didn't hurt in helping him to sleep better as well.

A new prisoner, by the name of Carl Harris, arrived, and Boeman decided it was in his best interests to leave Nash alone for the time being, and turn his focus onto the new wolf in the pack.

Leon couldn't have been happier with this transference. With Boeman otherwise occupied, Leon only had Carson to worry about. So, for the time being, he could drop his vigilance to some degree, and if he knew where Carson was, he felt safer regarding his back.

His time in the infirmary also helped to make life in the prison a little more bearable. He finally had a job to do that could challenge his intellect, and he found Dr. Palin to be an interesting and co-operative teacher. Whenever a prisoner or guard was brought in with some injury or another, Leon was always right there, assisting where he could and constantly asking questions. What do you do when a lung gets punctured? How do you stop excessive bleeding? What's the best way to set a broken bone?

Many of these procedures, Leon had performed himself, when they were riding the outlaw trail, but it was always by the skin of his teeth— trial and error. Nobody really knew what they were doing. It was more like; 'Well, it worked last time, so let's try it again.'

Much of what Leon learned from Palin excited him and made him want to dig deeper and learn more. But there were other times when the information he gathered depressed him, and he would return to his cell in the evening, sullen and moody.

He would be filled with remorse and regret during these times, thinking back to friends long buried, whose lives could have been saved if only Leon had known that simple procedure that Palin had just shown him.

He felt things too deeply, Leon did. Always the uncle, the outlaw leader, the one with the brains, the one everybody looked to, to make things right. Take charge, be in command, always have the right answer. Then someone in his gang, someone he was responsible for, would die, because he hadn't known about that simple procedure that Palin had just shown him.

On those occasions, he regressed back to old habits and just picked at his supper before retiring to his cell. He would stare at a ceiling he couldn't see until the early morning hours finally wore him down, and he fell asleep.

On the most part, though, his time in the infirmary was a positive influence in his life. Just as Kenny hoped, Leon recognized it as a privilege and something he valued and cherished, therefore it was something to be protected. He stopped lying in wait for any inmate who may have ticked him off. He decided that retaliation wasn't worth the risk of losing that one precious day a week, when he was allowed to feel human again.

Dr. Palin also found the time with Leon to be just as stimulating and rewarding as Leon did himself. Palin was pleased to have his impressions of Leon be justified tenfold.

The convict did have a brilliant mind and was able to grasp the strange words and difficult procedures with hardly any effort at all. Indeed, there were occasions when Palin felt a slight twinge of jealousy at the ease in which Leon picked up techniques that Palin himself had struggled with before finally conquering them.

Fortunately, those feelings did not linger and for the most part, Dr. Palin enjoyed his student and was pleased with the man's progress. It should also be noted, for better or for worse, that Palin inadvertently ignored Kenny's advice and did forget who Leon was. The two men gradually slid into a friendship.

One afternoon, after a particularly busy day of treating minor injuries incurred on the work floor, Palin pulled out his bottle of whiskey and invited Leon to join him for a drink.

Leon smiled; quite tempted by the invite, but hesitant over the legitimacy of it. He was getting too used to following the rules.

"Are you sure that's okay, Doc?" he asked while watching Palin pour out two shot glasses.

"Hmm. If you promise not to tell, I'll do the same."

Leon's smile deepened, and he joined Palin at the table. Sitting down, he lifted the glass and took a swig. It attacked his senses, burning into his throat and his nasal passage and almost setting his eyes to watering. It was far from top shelf, but it was the best thing Leon had tasted in many a long month.

"There ya go, son, one for the road," Doc toasted him.

"Thank you," was Leon's heartfelt response. Then, whether it was the whiskey making him braver or just that he had become comfortable in the doctor's presence, Leon decided to ask a more personal question. "So, Doc, how is it you ended up with such a cushy job like this?"

Palin rolled his eyes. "Ohh, long story, son, long story."

Dimples pitted Leon's cheeks, and the mischievous twinkle came into his eye; the perfect example of the charismatic conman.

"I don't see any patients needing attention and it's at least an hour until supper," Leon observed, the twinkle intensifying.

"Hmm," Palin responded while he refilled their glasses, "well, there's really not much ta tell. I learned doctorin' while growin' up in the logging camps in Washington, up there by the Canadian border. Never went ta school, except for the school 'a hard knocks, and I tell ya, there's nothin' like seein' a man chop his own damn foot off ta teach ya fast how ta stop a fella from bleedin' ta death."

"Ahh, yeah," Leon agreed. "I can see the incentive."

"Hmm," the doc nodded his agreement, "then the war broke out, and a bunch of us roughnecks decided ta make some extra money by smugglin' supplies across the border and 'escortin' them down south to help with the effort. That took us a few months of hard travelin', then wouldn't ya know, we only got paid about half what we were promised."

"Ah huh," Leon commented as he downed another glass, "thieves all over the place."

"That's for sure," Palin agreed. "So, once we got down to where the fightin' was happening, well we didn't have enough money to go back, so we stuck around and decided to join in." Palin emptied his glass and poured another round. "The powers that be found out I had some doctorin' experience, so they pressed me into service in that capacity."

"More on the job training?" Leon asked with a slurry smirk.

"Damn right. Jesus!" Doc exclaimed. "And they wonder why I drink."

"I thought it was 'cause of the won'erful job ya got here."

"Hell no. I was drinkin' long 'fore I ended up in this backwater cesspool. Christ. War fin'lly over an' I can't f . . . find a job worth crap. An' why? 'Cause I ain't got no licens'sense. Nev'r wen' 'ta school." Another round of drinks was poured. "I'm better doc'or than those big Eastern trained big shots, an' I en' up here, treatin' a bunch a' filthy con'its."

"Yea," Leon agreed as he downed another glass. "Lowlif's thieves—ever one 'a 'em. Ya deserve better en' 'at, Doc."

"Yea! I'll drink ta 'at."

"Me too."

"Hmm, I wasss sure there wasss another bottle 'round here somewhere—ohh, hier it iss."

"Ssso, ya never married, Doc?" Leon asked, followed by another drink.

"Hell no. No wife—no kids. The war kind'a took care a' that. My brother now, he done the resect . . . spetable thing." Palin squinted at Leon and waved a finger and a half empty shot glass under his nose. "He came sou' wi' me on that ill-fated sssup . . . y run, but then he gone an' got hisself a decent job afta tha' war. Up an' got married and ssset'led down. Ats ma' nephew there in Colorada—Bennie. Good lad. No kids ma'self tho'. Nope. No kids."

Leon went quiet for a moment. He had been about to agree with Palin in saying that he didn't have any 'kids' either, but it stuck in his craw and he couldn't get it out. Then he swallowed it down with another shot of whiskey—and he changed the subject.

"How long you been here, Doc?" he asked.

"Oh crap. Since forever." He laughed. "An' only an eternity left ta go . . ."

"Yeah! Me too."

The two men started laughing together as though it were the best joke they'd heard all day.

"Sooo . . ." Leon started again, trying to get his sentence formulated. "Wha' 'bout the guards? Yu known 'em a long time?"

"Ahh, yea," Palin admitted with a sneer. "'At Carson. Wha' a fuckin' asshole. Wha' a prick. Kenny, now ee's a good guy. Ya ee's a good ung fella."

Leon smiled at Palin referring to Kenny as 'young' since he was at least fifteen years older than Leon himself. Still, it was all relative, he supposed.

"Ya?" Leon said. "Ee married?"

"Kenny?"

"Ya."

"Oo ya," Doc nodded, causing his head to spin. He grabbed the edge of the table to steady himself. "Go' hisself a fine lady an' four young'uns."

"Four?"

"Ya. Three boys an' a girl. Cute-isss' littl' 'ing ya ever seen."

"Aww, 'ats nice," Leon mumbled. "Nothin' like a daugh'er."

A curse from the entrance interrupted their conversation.

"What the hell? Aww Doc. You getting your trustee drunk—again?"

"Aaaa Kenny. We wa' jus' talkin' 'bout yu' . . ."

Leon groaned and dropped his forehead onto his arms that were resting on the table. He was in for it, now.

"Come on Nash, on your feet," Kenny ordered him, as he grabbed one of Leon's arms and started to pull him up. "If you can, that is."

Palin tried to wave him away. "Aww, we wa' jus' havin' a frien'ly drink, 'enny,"

"Yeah, I know, Doc," Kenny answered as he draped Leon's arm over his shoulders and dragged him toward the exit. "You best get some coffee into ya, before you head back to your quarters. And for christ sake, don't let the warden see ya, or you'll be out of a job for sure."

"Wher' we goin'?" Leon asked, suddenly worried he was headed for the dark cell and doing his best to put on the brakes. He wasn't having much luck.

"Don't worry about it, Nash. I'm just taking you back to your cell."

"Oo, okay."

"And keep your mouth shut, will you?" Kenny instructed him. "You're damn lucky Carson's gone home for the evening, or this would be the last time you'd be helping Palin in the infirmary."

"Ahh, no. It's okay."

"No, it's not okay. I catch you drunk again . . ." Kenny left it at that and shook his head with an exasperated sigh.

Palin was an all right guy and a decent doctor, at least compared to what prisons usually end up with, so Kenny tried to cut him some slack. But this was pushing it. If he wanted to get drunk on his own time, that was his business. But when he decides to include his trustee in on the imbibing, that could get everybody into trouble.

Fortunately for everyone involved, most of the guards and other inmates were in the common room for the evening meal, so the trip to Leon's cell went unhindered. Those few who did noticed them, took no notice and assumed that Kenny knew what he was about. Maybe Nash had gotten sick again. In any case, Kenny got Leon settled onto his cot and prepared to head for home himself. He just had one final errand to conduct.

"I'll bring you some coffee," Kenny told him. "You hungry at all? I'll bring you dinner too, if you want it."

"No, not hungry," Leon mumbled.

"What a surprise," Kenny commented dryly. "I'll get you your coffee. Then you stay put Nash, you hear me? You don't step out of this cell until morning. You get that?"

"Ya."

"Good!"

Kenny turned on his heels and stomped out of the cell, muttering obscenities as he went.

***

Leon didn't know how he got through that night and when the morning buzzer sounded, he thought his head was going to explode. He groaned as he rolled onto his side and swung his legs off the cot. It took him a few more seconds to convince his torso to follow and come up into a sitting position. He moaned and held his head. He couldn't believe the headache he had, but at least it was laundry day, and he could keep to himself.

He managed to convince his legs to take him down to breakfast and, over a bowl of lumpy oatmeal and warm coffee, he sort'a, kind'a, got himself back to the land of the living. That was the last time he was going to join Dr. Palin for a simple drink. Holy Cow. Whatever that stuff was made of, it sure packed one hell of a whollop.

After picking his way through breakfast, he joined the herd heading out through the prison proper, but once onto the main floor, he branched off and headed for the laundry room. He didn't even make it to the door, when he noticed a pair of feet standing on the floor in front of him. He slowly pulled his aching eyes up the legs of a guard's uniform, passed the belt buckle, could even kind'a count the buttons on the shirt, noticed a small smile playing about the lips and then looked into the light gray eyes of Kenny Reece.

"Convict," Reece said, "follow me," and he turned and walked in the opposite direction of the laundry room.

Leon groaned. Oh no. He was in for it now. Seeing no way out of the situation, he turned and followed the guard to wherever it was, Kenny had decided to take him.

Half an hour later, standing outside in a downpour of cold rain, Kenny had obtained a hat, a coat and a rifle. Leon had obtained a shovel, a hammer and a bag of nails.

Later, upon reflection, Leon insisted that day proved to be the longest, most miserable day he had ever put in, working at the prison. Every piddley little job Reece could find for the convict to do in the yard, was handed over to him.

The steps needed clearing, the drains needed unclogging, and the wooden railings needed repairing. Lunch? What lunch? And the rain did not let up. Within thirty minutes, Leon was soaked to the skin. Before the morning was half over, even with the physical work, he was shivering, and his hands were numb with the cold. His head would not stop pounding. More than once, despite the ever-ready rifle in Kenny's hands, Leon made a run for a corner and heaved up whatever he had left in his stomach. He was in absolute misery, and his only consolation was that Kenny had to be out there with him.

Finally, the invisible sun neared the end of its decline and the light in the yard faded. Kenny stood up from the bench under the awning, where he had been watching Leon shovel mud off the walkways and motioned to the convict.

"All right, Nash," he said, not using the usual 'convict', "that's enough, head back in."

Leon released a huge sigh and leaned against the shovel for a moment. He did his best to gather up what was left of his consciousness and convince his legs to move toward the entrance.

"C'mon, convict," Kenny pushed, reverting to the norm, "pick up your tools, let's go."

***

Back in his cell, Leon stood just inside his door, dripping pools of water onto the floor. He didn't want to sit down on his cot. He was soaked through and through and didn't want to get the blanket wet. He was already cold enough, why add to his misery for later?

Vaguely, Leon became aware of another inmate approaching Kenny and handing him a clean set of prison garb and long johns. Leon assumed this was the inmate who had taken over his laundry duties for the day, and the ex-outlaw leader snarled at him.

The man wisely avoided eye contact and moved away.

Kenny plunked the fresh clothing down on Leon's cot, then turned to him and stood there with his arms crossed. His intense gaze bored into the exhausted convict.

"Get yourself changed into some dry cloths and then head down for supper."

"Uugh."

"And if I ever catch you drunk again, you'll be spending three days in the dark cell, and all your privileges will be revoked. Do you understand me?"

Another groan.

"Good."

***

It is fair to say that Leon slept like the dead that night, and breakfast actually tasted pretty good. It was Saturday, but not surprisingly, he opted out of his time in the yard and chose instead to spend the morning nursing some coffee and reading *Les Miserables*. He was still tired in body and mind, but for the most part, was feeling much better and promised himself that he was never going to do that again.

An hour after lunch, Leon found himself in the visitor's room, pleased as punch to be in his partner's company.

"Sure is good to see you again, Jack," Leon said for the umpteenth time, with the smile refusing to leave his face. "With all the rain we've had lately, I wasn't sure you were going to make it."

"Aw, rain ain't gonna stop me from comin'," Jack assured him. "A blizzard, yeah—but not rain. You look a lot better 'n the last time I saw ya. You back ta eatin' again?"

"Yeah, for the most part, so, you can tell Taggard and David to stop nagging at me, okay? Please."

Jack smiled. "Yeah, I'll tell them." He turned serious again. "You sure you're doin' okay, Leon? Ya look a little, I dunno, sorta low key."

Leon looked down at the table, feeling embarrassed. "Yeah," he answered. "Me and the doc got a little drunk the other day, and then Kenny worked me into the ground in the pouring rain, while I still had a hangover, to let me know I had broken another rule."

"Really?" Jack sympathized. "I thought you said Kenny was one of the good guards."

"He is."

"You're kiddin'."

"No. If it had been Carson, you'd be taking me home in a pine box, instead of sitting here chatting with me."

"Aww, Leon." Jack looked ashamed of himself.

Leon furrowed his brow, wondering where that came from.

"This ain't right," Jack continued, "I'm the one who should be in here, not you."

Leon sat back in his chair and sighed. He looked around the room, trying to collect his thoughts.

"By rights, I suppose both of us should be in here," he finally pointed out, "but I'm glad you're not. I need you out there to get me out of here."

"But that's just it, Leon," Jack complained. "You're the one with the brains. You'd know how ta deal with them politicians. I'm totally lost."

Leon sat quietly for a moment and studied his friend.

"You're not stupid, Jack," he commented, echoing David's sentiment from earlier on. "You're just used to letting me do all the thinking." He smiled with a mischievous twinkle. "Now it's your time to shine."

Jack rolled his eyes and hardly looked convinced.

"That's what everyone keeps sayin'," Jack declared, feeling frustrated. "David says I'm 'intuitive'. Like that's gonna help. If I was so intuitive, I would 'a known about that ambush and we wouldn't 'a walked right into it."

"Are we onto that again?" Leon snapped. "I thought this was settled. Come on, Jack. That was almost a year ago. Leave it be." He sighed and then sat for a moment and studied his friend. "How's your shoulder doing? Has David helped you get it back again?"

"Yeah. We're back ta doin' them stretches an' stuff ta get it workin' again. It aches a lot, especially when it's wet and cold, like this. It's been kind'a sore these last couple 'a days, so I'll probably have David look at it when I get home. But other than that, it's doin' better."

"Good," Leon nodded. "You back at the Marsham's place now? You and Cameron still getting on okay?"

"No, I'm still stayin' with David, but Cameron and I are gettin' on fine. Often go out ta help at the ranch during the daytime, but both Cameron and David insist that I stay at David's at night. And David won't let me go out on my own after supper."

Leon frowned. "What do you mean, 'David won't let you'?"

"The only time he lets me have my gun and boots and coat is when I'm headin' out to the Marsham's, or comin' to see you," Jack grumbled. "The rest of the time he keeps 'em hidden, so I can't go out on my own."

"What?" Leon was incredulous. "Why?"

"I dunno," Jack mumbled, breaking eye contact. "He keeps sayin' that I ain't 'all right' yet—whatever that means. If'n I ain't back at his place by a certain time, he practically sends a posse out lookin' for me. Thinks I'm gonna sneak off at night and do somethin' stupid."

"Why would he think that?"

"I dunno," Jack mumbled again, shrugging his shoulders. "He seems ta think it's all right for me ta come and see you all on my lonesome, but not spend the evenin' in Arvada, havin' a few drinks. I tell ya Leon, it's downright embarrassin'."

"Why do you put up with it?" Leon asked. "Why don't you just leave? It's not like you have to go back to Arvada now. Why don't you go stay with Taggard for a while?"

Jack sat quiet for a moment. "Well, it's just that, well . . ."

Leon sighed. "What, Jack?"

"Well, I kind'a agreed to it."

Leon frowned again. "Why?"

"Well, ya know," Jack said, feeling awkward. "I weren't behavin' normal. I know that. But I couldn't stop myself. Then Cameron threw me out, and Josey started layin' inta me, and I knew somethin' was wrong, but I don't know what." Jack took a deep breath and almost got angry with himself. "I know if I was ever gonna get you outta here, well, I had ta get better, so I asked David ta help me. He told me I had to agree ta this and accept whatever restrictions he put on me, or it was no go. And Taggard and Cameron both know about it, so," Jack shrugged. "Still, I am doin' better. It's like he just don't trust me. It's frustratin'."

"There must be more to it than that," Leon insisted. "Have you talked to him?"

"Sure, I've talked to him," Jack shot back, then; "I dunno." He looked down at the table again, struggling with what was on his mind.

Leon sat back and waited, knowing more was coming, and also knowing that Jack probably had a good idea why he wasn't allowed out at night. He just didn't want to admit it.

"I was talkin' ta Cameron about it the other day while we were out ridin' the north pasture," Jack said. "I complained about what a pest David was bein' and that he wouldn't leave me be. Cameron commented it was because David still felt responsible for what happened the last night in Cheyenne."

"Oh," said Leon. "What happened?"

"I dunno," Jack insisted. "That's what I asked Cameron, and he just looked at me, kind'a funny and then asked me what I remembered."

"Well, what do you remember?"

Jack sighed, and his expression became reflective.

"That last night in town, Max hosted a real nice dinner party for all of us," Jack reminisced and didn't notice Leon's disappointment. "Everything was real good, and the girls were funny, gettin' their first taste of champagne an' all. They got real giggly." He smiled at the memory, but then he turned serious again. "Everybody was bein' real supportive, but I couldn't enjoy myself very much, knowin' you were stuck in here and everything. It didn't feel right."

Leon smiled. "Really?"

"Yeah. I couldn't have a good time. In fact, I was real angry about the way the whole thing worked out. It weren't fair."

"Hmm," was Leon's only comment. Medical knowledge wasn't

the only thing he was picking up from Dr. Palin.

"And I remember David bein' a real pest—again. He wouldn't leave me alone." Jack got angry just thinking about it. "Finally, I yelled at him; told him to back off 'a me, ya know? He just wouldn't leave me alone."

"Hmm," Leon commented again. "And did he then? Leave you alone?"

"Yeah, finally. Good thing too, I was gettin' real angry. I felt like I was gonna strangle him if'n he didn't back off."

"Hmm, that can be irritating," Leon agreed, though his expression showed doubt, and he wondered if David had good reason for hovering. "What happened next?"

"Shortly after midnight, the party started ta wind down. I headed back ta my hotel room." Then Jack laughed. "Man, I must 'a been really drunk. That champagne sure has a kick to it, ya know? 'Cause I don't even remember goin' ta bed, and I sure don't remember gettin' on the train the next mornin'. But I must 'a done, 'cause that's where I was when I woke up; on the train."

"Hmm," Leon said again, "and that's all you remember?"

"Yeah. Well, except . . ." Jack hesitated, looking confused.

"What?"

"On the train. I was havin' a real bad nightmare. David woke me up, but I glanced at Cameron, and he had this strange look on his face. Like he was mad at me or somethin' . . . I dunno. And after that, everybody sort'a started treatin' me different. Like I was gonna explode on 'em or somethin'. It was real weird, and it made me mad."

"Oh yeah?" Leon asked. "So, is that when you had the fight with Cameron and disappeared for a month?"

"Well, that was kind'a the beginnin' of it," Jack admitted sheepishly. "I guess I was drinkin' too much durin' that time."

"Hmm," said Leon again.

"Will you stop that?" Jack growled at him. "It makes it sound like ya know somethin' I don't."

"Oh, sorry."

"Do ya?"

"What?"

"Know somethin' I don't?"

"No, no," Leon assured him. "At least not on this topic."

Jack looked at his friend suspiciously, not sure if there was an insult in there or not.

"So," Leon continued, shifting position in his chair and straightening up, "you don't remember anything else about that last night in Cheyenne?"

"What else is there to remember?" Jack demanded. "I went ta sleep."

"Drunk on champagne."

"Yeah."

"Hmm."

"Stop that. You're beginnin' ta sound like Makua."

"Well," Leon became defensive. "I'm just trying to work things out."

"There's nothin' ta work out, Leon. I'm fine."

"All right, all right," Leon relented. "So, you're staying at David's place for now?"

"Yeah."

"Have you been able to talk to him about stuff?" Leon asked tentatively. "You know, about . . . the things that happened . . . in Kansas?"

Jack hesitated, then admitted, "Yeah. A bit." He shifted. "It ain't easy, talkin' about that stuff. But he's so relentless; he just keeps pushin' and pushin'. Geez Leon, I've told 'im stuff you and me never even talked about. That don't seem right somehow."

"Well that's all right," Leon assured him. "He's a doctor after all. And a friend too, right?"

"Yeah, I suppose. So, you're all right with that?"

"Sure, if it helps."

Jack shrugged. "I guess."

A flash of pain crossed through Leon's eyes, and he cleared his throat, trying to find a way to put his disappointment into words without sounding preachy.

"I wish you had told me about that other stuff though," he finally commented.

"What other stuff?" Jack asked, concerned that he had missed something.

Hesitation. Silence. It was Leon's turn to shift uncomfortably. Then resolve set in. Just spit it out.

"Well, what happened when you . . . when we split up."

"Oh. Yeah." Then Jack looked hurt as well. He knew he had

disappointed his friend "I'm sorry, Leon. I just . . . I didn't wanna lay that onta you. And I was so sickened by it, myself, I guess I just hoped it would go away if I didn't talk about it. And I knew how you felt about killin' 'an all. So . . ."

"They'd done just as bad to my family, as they did to yours, Jack," Leon pointed out. "And if I hadn't 'a blocked out the worst of what they did, I just might have joined you on that venture."

Hurting blue eyes looked up to meet hurting brown.

"I wish I could'a blocked it out," Jack finally stated.

"No, ya don't, Jack," Leon assured him. "That was one of the worst moments of my life, suddenly remembering it all in that way. You don't want to go through that."

"Yeah, that's what David said," Jack admitted. "Still, it's weird. How could you have forgotten that?" Jack realized he had cut Leon to the core with that comment, and he backstepped. "Oh, no, Leon. I didn't mean that as a judgment on you, just, in general; how can it be that our minds can block out somethin' like that, just as though it never happened? That's weird."

Leon nodded, accepting the apology. "I dunno, Jack," he admitted and then smiled. "But Jenny is really making up for lost time here, I'll tell ya. I've had some really strange dreams about her," he turned reflective again. "I kind'a envy you, having David to talk to. There's nobody here who gives a damn."

"What about Doctor Mariam?"

Leon grimaced. "I don't want to tell her my deep, dark, secrets. She might try to use it against me, later on."

"I thought you said she weren't like that."

"No, not so far. It is nice to have her here, but she's still . . ."

"Yeah, okay. What about David? You could always write to 'im. Tell 'im about your dreams in a letter. Might help."

"Yeah," Leon considered that. "It certainly wouldn't hurt." He smiled. "Enough of this doom and gloom. How are the girls?"

Jack smiled as well and brightened up. "Caroline is so excited about moving to Denver. It's still a month away, and she's already packin'. And now there's fightin' over who's gonna get her room, Penny or Eli! It's turnin' inta quite a circus."

Leon laughed. "I bet. Yeah, the girls are growing up." Then Leon lost his smile and turned reflective again.

Jack noticed the shift. "You'll see them again soon. I know I was sounding doubtful, but we are gonna get ya outta here. It just might take some time."

"I know, Jack." Leon sighed and changed the subject again. "How's Jean doing? I hear from the girls regularly, but just quick notes from Jean at Christmas and then for my birthday."

"She's fine. She's busy with Eli, and now, with Caroline gettin' ready ta move out on her own. You are on her mind, a lot. She's always askin' after ya, wants ta know everythin' we talk about after my visits here."

Leon smiled. "Everything?"

"Well, I edit it some."

"That's good. Send her my love."

"Yeah, a' course."

Leon smiled, a twinkle coming into his eye. Jack knew something was coming.

"So, how are things with Penny?"

"Aww Leon," Jack grumbled, "we're friends, you know that. I've always liked Penny, but . . . that's it."

"Uh huh."

"She's been ridin' out with me sometimes, when I go check on the stock, just ta give Karma some exercise, you understand."

"Uh huh."

"She sure is an excellent horsewoman," Jack continued, and smiled reflectively. "And she sure do look fetchin' in that ridin' habit."

"Hmm."

"No, I mean . . . she's really growin' up. It's just; she's not a little girl anymore," then Jack became angry. "She's always been pretty, you know that . . . she's just nice ta talk to . . . we're just friends, Leon."

"Fine," Leon answered innocently. "What are you getting so defensive about?"

"Nothin'," Jack mumbled. "It's just, you're insinuatin'."

"What?"

"Nothin'."

Leon smiled; his eyes playful.

"That's all right," he said, "there's nothing wrong with you and Penny just being friends

"Yeah."

"Give her my love."

"I will. They all miss you and with everythin' else goin' on, they're still workin' on the governor."

Leon smiled. They were going to win yet.

Then there came a discreet cough from Pearson, who had been standing unobtrusively behind them.

Both ex-outlaws groaned, together.

"Aww, no."

"What—already?"

"Dang it," Jack groused. "I feel like we were just gettin' started."

"Yeah, I know," Leon agreed. "It was good to see ya again though. I guess you better go. Say 'hi' to everyone for me and try not to get too frustrated with David. He is just trying to help."

"Yeah, I know. I just wish I knew where he was goin' with it, that's all."

"Time will tell."

"Right." Jack stood up. "Take care of yourself, Uncle. Try not to get into any more trouble, all right? I'll see ya next month."

"Yeah, I will. See you next month."

***

While Pearson escorted Leon back to his cell, the inmate reflected upon the conversation with his nephew. He would write David a letter, and certainly not just about the dreams he'd been having of late. There was something missing in Jack's narrative concerning that last night in Cheyenne. He couldn't have gotten that drunk by drinking champagne at a dinner party. Something else happened that Jack wasn't admitting to, or—and Leon knew this was quite possible—had blocked out of his conscious memory.

David knew there was more to come; that's why he was keeping Jack on such a short leash. It wasn't over yet, and Leon felt for his partner, knowing what he would go through once he remembered whatever it was he didn't want to remember.

Once back to his cell and left alone again, Leon intended to start the letter to David right away, but then he noticed that he had a letter waiting for him, sitting on the pillow on his cot. He sat down, leaned against the wall and, drawing his knees up, he took the letter to see who it was from.

All it had as a return address was two words; Toronto, Ontario. Leon frowned. *Who would be writing to me from Canada?*

Suddenly he felt his blood turn cold, and his heart jumped to his throat. The writing; he recognized the writing. It had been so long, but he was sure of it. His extremities went numb, as so many emotions ran through him.

Did he want to open it, or simply burn it, unread? Anger and hurt hit him first, and his throat tightened against a sob he could not, would not allow to surface.

Then, taking in a deep, steadying breath, he opened the envelope.

Mr. Nash,

If you're reading these words then it seems you are willing to hear from me, even if it is simply morbid curiosity. I know I hurt you, and you have every right to be angry. I had to do it; you must be able to see that by now. Neither of us is to blame, or, perhaps, both of us are. I knew better, but I allowed you to convince me we could do it. Now, all we have between us is anger and heartbreak.

I didn't get news of your trial and subsequence imprisonment until just recently. I was stunned by the details. This is not justice, this is revenge. Even during our time together, when you were active in your profession, you didn't deserve so harsh a sentence.

I believe your claim that you and Jack had an arrangement with the Territorial Governor, not only because you claim it to be so, but you have been noticeably absent from articles reporting outlaw activity. It is shameful what the current governor has done to you, and is trying to do to Jack.

I have resources, Mr. Nash. You know I do, and I assure that every course that is legal will be followed until we succeed in getting your sentence is rescinded.

You may scoff at me now, but I do still care for you. I have never stopped loving you. It doesn't take much to bring you to mind: a certain scent on the wind, a train whistling. A particular expression or gesture sent my way with twinkling, dark eyes and a dimpled smile. All of these things and more bring both overwhelming love and devastating heartbreak.

I will never forget you, and nor will I abandon you. When you get out, you can finally be the man you want to be, indeed, the man you should have been. Try to think of this as a diversion on your journey, however appalling, and know that your friends will assist you toward a better life.

Stay brave and try not to lose hope. The good times will be yours again.

With all my love

Gabriella.

Leon sat and stared at the letter for a long time. Then read it over again.

He wasn't sure which emotion had precedence. Part of him had been disappointed that he hadn't heard from her during his trial, but then the logical part took over.

Why would she contact me? Besides, being in Canada, she likely didn't even know about it until it was all over with. It doesn't matter anyway; what we'd had is over. I could never trust her again, and she knows it. What does she mean: 'When you get out . . .'? How dare she talk to me as though we have a future together!

She destroyed that future when she . . .

His anger flared and he scrunched up the letter and threw it against the far wall. He sat and fumed; his lips tight with burning betrayal. He could never trust her again. How could she even suggest that there could be anything left between them?

But then . . . His stance softened, and he glanced at the forlorn ball of paper sitting on the floor. *. . . there is something between us, something invaluable . . . Yes, but she took it away from me, didn't she?* His anger rose again as he bared his teeth against the love he felt; the love he could never be rid of. *She took it away from me. I never want to see her again . . .*

He sighed. *Still, if seeing her again meant . . . well . . . that might be worth it. And Gabriella is resourceful. She knows people and knows how to work the underground. It might be better to have her on my side.* He frowned, then got up and retrieved the letter. He set it on his small table and flattened it out, trying to soften the creases. *Nothing says I have to trust her, but maybe, I can use her. It would be no different from how she used me. Maybe this is a good thing. Maybe . . .*

When I write to David, I'll include a message for Jack to get in touch with her. But where? Toronto is a big city, and she hadn't included any real contact information. Jack could track her down if he wanted to, but maybe she doesn't want to hear from either of us. She cut us both out of her life, and her reasons for doing so were pretty damn clear.

He chewed his lip, considering his options.

But she says she would add her name to the list of those helping. Did that mean she was going to get in contact with Jack anyway? Has she already? But if she has, wouldn't Jack have mentioned it? Maybe Jack thinks I don't want to hear from her, too much hurt there. Yeah, isn't that the truth!

She hadn't needed to be that brutal. It's not like we had to get married in a church or anything. We talked about it and maybe I wanted it, but then, that happened. It's probably a good thing we didn't marry in the legal sense; it would never have worked out. But . . . why did she have to cut me off so completely? Why did she have to disappear as though there was nothing between us?

Deep in his heart, Leon knew why. She wasn't willing to live her life or raise a family with an outlaw. Jack had come up against the same thing with Haley, a young woman who'd once had designs on him. Both had tried to force them into a choice, and both men had baulked at it.

And now, here was Gabriella, talking about helping him, about being there for him in his time of need.

"When you get out . . .". Yeah, right. She's dangling our past love under my nose as incentive to hang on, but then what? Once I get out, or more likely, if I ever get out, would she still be there for me? Or would she hop the next train and leave me heart-broken all over again.?

He snorted. *Well, if she gets in touch with Jack and really is serious about helping, that would be a good thing. Nothing says I ever have to lay eyes on her.*

He folded the paper and slipped it back into its envelope, then set it inside the cookie tin with his other valued letters.

CHAPTER TWENTY-ONE
REVELATIONS

Arvada, Colorado

When Jack stepped off the train in Arvada, it was a nice spring day; the sun shone, and though not exactly warm, it was pleasant and gave a gentle promise of things to come.

More out of habit than expecting anything, Jack headed to the telegraph office, dodging around the numerous puddles and rain ruts left over from the previous day's downpour.

He smiled as he went, seeing some of the local boys playing and jumping in the water, sending splashes shooting into the air, and the youngsters screaming with laughter whenever one of them got a dousing in the face.

He trotted up the steps to the door of the office, his thoughts gently touching on his own childhood memories of playing in those self-same puddles and coming home soaking wet. Then suddenly, he was jolted back to the present and backstepped, then tipped his hat to a young woman coming out of the door he had just been about to enter.

"Ma'am."

"Mr. Kiefer," the young lady acknowledged him with a smile.

Most of the local people accepted him now, as one of their own, at least for the time being. He had shown himself to be mild mannered and very polite after the initial episodes of drunkenness and disorderly behavior. Most of them now, including Sheriff Jacobs, were willing to cut him some slack.

Jack smiled and allowed the lady to pass, then he stepped into the office.

"Afternoon, Clayt," Jack greeted the telegrapher, "anything for anybody today?"

"Oh, Mr. Kiefer. Yes." Clayt turned to snatch up the small envelope and hand it over to him. "No telegram, but a letter came for you."

"For me?" Jack was surprised as he took the envelope.

"You're Jack Kiefer, ain't ya?"

Jack sent him a narrow-eyed snark then took the letter. "Yeah, thanks. Anything else?"

"Nope."

Jack nodded then left the office and started walking toward David's place. He ripped open the envelope and read the message as he carried on down the boardwalk. Then his gait slowed and ultimately came to a halt, as his mouth fell open in surprise. He had to read the words again, just to be sure;

Jack: I know you and Napoleon have no reason to want to hear from me, but I could not stay silent any longer. You both know my background and my abilities, and I am offering assistance to right this terrible wrong. If you are willing, you can reach me at the address below. Gabriella Tanguay. St George Ward, Toronto, Ontario, Canada.

Jack read the short note three or four times before he remembered to close his mouth. He folded the piece of paper and put it in his pocket, then made the conscious effort to start walking again. He still couldn't quite believe it. Gabi getting in touch? He wondered what Leon thought about that. Why hadn't he mentioned it? But then, Jack reasoned, a letter coming all the way from Ontario in the winter, more than likely it was delayed en-route. Leon may not have received it yet, or it may have gotten lost. That certainly wasn't unheard of.

Jack thought about this for a bit. Well, if Leon don't mention it next time I'm out ta visit, I risk upsettin' 'im, and ask. This is important.

He walked into the house, his mind still miles away, and absently removed his coat and gun belt, he hung them off a chair in the kitchen where David would see them. He then sat down and started to pull off his boots.

Tricia came out of the living room and smiled.

"Jack. Nice timing; supper will be ready in about 15 minutes."

Jack returned the smile but didn't say anything.

"How is your friend doing?" Tricia continued.

"Better," Jack answered. "He's still havin' trouble adjustin', but at least he's eatin' again, and he's helpin' out in the infirmary. That's givin' him somethin' a little more challengin' ta do."

"Good. Hopefully he'll settle soon. Would you like some coffee?"

"No thanks. Is David home?"

"Yes. He's just finished with his last patient of the day and is in his office."

"Oh," Jack hesitated. "Maybe I shouldn't bother him, then."

"No, it's all right, Jack. Go ahead."

"Yeah? Okay."

Tricia smiled again as she watched Jack pad his way in his stocking feet, down the hall to the door of David's office. When he wasn't drunk or recovering from one of his numerous nightmares, Jack Kiefer was a polite and unassuming man. Just as with Jean before her, Tricia found it difficult to find the balance between Jack Kiefer, the man, and the Kansas Kid; infamous gunslinger. He was a hard one to figure out, but her husband considered him a friend, so Tricia was willing to hold judgment until their guest had found his footing, and his true personality had a chance to shine through.

Jack knocked quietly on the door and then responded to the 'come in' that was David's voice.

"Oh, hi Jack," was the doctor's response, as he looked up from the paperwork. "How is Napoleon doing?"

"Better."

"That's good to hear. Is he eating?"

"Yeah. Though he still could stand to put on a few pounds." Then Jack smiled. "But then, he always was kind'a scrawny, so . . ."

"I noticed," David admitted, the pot calling the kettle black. "As long as he's stopped losing. We can't have him getting sick every winter. This one time was bad enough."

"Naw, he's doin' better, David. He did mention havin' bad dreams though, so I suggested he write ta you about 'em. I don't know what you can suggest in a letter, but still, it might help."

"That's a good idea," David agreed. "Just the act of writing them out will help to cope with them better. Did he say what they were usually about?"

"Yeah. His baby sister."

"Oh. Well yes, that's not surprising. He probably still feels a certain amount of guilt over the situation. Not just that he left her behind, but that he then blocked it from his memory. That will take him some time to get over."

"I still think that's weird," Jack said. "That a person's mind can just block out a memory like that."

David sat back and scrutinized his friend.

"Yes," he agreed. "And the person doesn't even realize they're doing it."

"Yeah. Like I said; weird." Jack sighed. "Anyway, my shoulder's been real sore for the last couple 'a days. I was wonderin' if you could take a look at it."

"Oh. Yes, of course." David stood up and gestured for Jack to sit down by the examination table. "Take off your shirts and we'll have a look. Is it a deep pain, from inside?"

"No," Jack answered as he pulled off his shirt and undershirt. "It's just under the surface, and its burnin'. It feels like there's a boil or somethin' there, on the shoulder blade. I dunno, maybe it has nothin' to do with the injury. Maybe it's somethin' new."

David stepped around behind Jack to examine the area.

"Oh yes," he announced. "It's an abscess. This is good."

"It's good?" Jack wasn't convinced.

"Yes," David gathered together some supplies. "Remember I told you that you had bone chips floating around in there, and if we were lucky, they would simply work their way out on their own? Otherwise, we might have to go in and dig them out."

"Oh yeah," Jack agreed. "I had forgotten about that. But now ya mention it . . ."

"Well, this is what's happening," David dabbed some disinfectant on the red swollen area. "They're starting to work their way out. This might hurt a little bit."

Jack leapt to his feet with a yelp and spun around to send an accusing glare to his doctor.

"You cut me!"

David stood there, looking innocent, but the small scalpel he held in his right hand, supported Jack's accusation.

"Yes," David admitted.

"Damn it, David, you're always hurtin' me! That's the last time I come to you for help. Damn it. Why do I trust you? I swear, that's the last time, David."

"No, it's not."

"Just you wait," Jack promised, "you'll see. Why would you think I'd keep comin' back when ya always hurt me?"

"Because, if you'd calm down and stop blustering, you'd realize that your shoulder doesn't hurt so much anymore."

Jack's countenance softened, and his focus turned inward.

"Oh yeah," he muttered. "You're right; it don't hurt nearly as much."

"Yes. That's because the pain was caused by pressure building up under the skin. I opened the abscess, so it could drain and release the pressure. The bone chips will come out with the fluids."

"Oh. Oh, all right."

"Now, sit back down here, so I can clean it up and put some gauze over it. It'll be a little tender for a while, but it'll heal up fine."

"Yeah, okay," Jack sat back down and let David continue with his treatment. "A little warning next time would be nice."

"I did warn you—a little."

"Ha, yeah," was Jack's reply. "Is that it? Are the bone chips all out?"

"Oh no. It's not that easy. This will probably happen once or twice a year for the next few years, but gradually, they should all work their way out and it'll stop. Meantime, you know what it is now, so the next time an abscess develops, you'll get in here to let me take care of it. Won't you?"

Jack sighed. "Yeah, okay. How come you're always right, David?"

David laughed. "You haven't spoken to Trish lately, have you?"

***

Jack was dreaming.

It started out as a good dream; such a relief from all those nightmares he'd been having.

This was pleasant.

Jack and Penny rode the north pasture, looking at all the new foals. It was a warm, beautiful summer's day and the grass was long and green and swaying in the gentle breeze. There were flies buzzing around them and the young foals ran and played together. They bucked and flapped their tails, flinging their heads about as they squealed with enjoyment of the bright day.

Jack and Penny stopped their horses under a widespread tree down by the creek, and, dismounting, they took out their lunches from the saddle bags. Penny spread a blanket over the soft grass, while Jack unsaddled the two horses and allowed them to roam loose to graze.

When he returned to the blanket, Penny had laid out sandwiches and fruit, and they settled into their respite. They talked and laughed over the antics of the playful foals, enjoying one another's company.

Jack couldn't take his eyes off her; she was so beautiful; young and lively, sparkling with sexuality. He wanted her; he could no longer deny it. She was all he ever thought about, all he ever dreamt of. Her figure filled out the skirt of her riding habit in a way that set his heart to thumping.

She looked at him with a mischievous sparkle in her warm brown eyes, and her tongue slid out and licked her lips, teasingly. Jack groaned and, leaning in, he kissed her gently on the mouth. Her arms went around his neck, returning the kiss and pulling him in, letting him know she was hungry for more.

He laid her back on the blanket and, showing some measure of self-restrain, he took her gently, softly; not wanting to hurt her in a way that might frighten her off.

She responded willingly and, far from being frightened, she responded as a woman would—a woman who knew the way; a woman who knew what she wanted.

Jack felt a shiver go through him; this was no maiden. She'd had a man before—many men before, by the way she came after him. She was experienced, she was aggressive. Jack felt anger rise in him. She had tricked him. She had lied to him, pretending to be innocent. She was nothing more than a wonton bawdy girl.

He pulled away from her and suddenly, it wasn't Penny anymore. She could almost be Penny, with the long blonde hair and the smoking brown eyes. But this woman was older, and her eyes and face were painted; her lips red with color. The fetching riding habit had turned into a tight corset and black stockings. She smelled of cheap perfume.

Jack became enraged. He'd been played for a fool, and he wasn't going to put up with that. No woman was going to get away with tricking a man that way. He was still lying on top of her, holding her down, and his left hand grasped her throat while his right turned into a fist, and he began to hit her over and over again. Her nose broke and started to bleed, and her lip split. Then suddenly it was Penny again, her innocent brown eyes filled with terror and confusion, pleading with him to stop.

But he couldn't stop. He kept beating her. He started yelling at the top of his lungs, roaring out his rage and his frustration, and then he was scrambling, pushing himself up and gasping for air . . .

He was surrounded by darkness, and he was cold, yet sweating. Every fiber of him shook in terror, and he continued to yell. Grabbing the blanket to his chest, he sat up in his bed and pushed himself into the corner of the wall.

He could see a light approaching, just a sliver at first, then his bedroom door opened, and the light shone brightly in, hurting his eyes, blinding him. But someone was there, some dark, menacing shadow lurked in the doorway, towering over him. He pulled the blanket more tightly around himself, as his shaking increased, and he gasped for air. He was terrified.

"Jack! Jack. You're all right."

Jack squinted through the blinding light, trying to get some definition of that cloaked and threatening figure hovering over him.

"Jack, it's me, David. It's all right. Calm down. You were having another nightmare."

He felt a hand touch him on the shoulder and he shrank away from it, still gasping to breathe. His teeth chattered, as his mind and body refused to let go of the night fears.

"Jack, it's over. Try to relax."

Gradually Jack calmed down. His eyes adjusted to the light from the lamp, and he could make David out now, standing over him, with his own blanket draped over his shoulders to keep out the early morning chill. His breathing and heart rate started to come down, but he was still shaking. He was freezing cold, and his teeth wouldn't stop chattering.

"Oh God, David . . ." He barely got the words out.

"Yes, it's me." The relief in David's voice was evident. "You're all right. It was just another nightmare."

"Oh my God. Oh God. Where the hell did that some from?"

"Bad one?"

"Oh God. It was awful. That was the worst one yet."

"You want to talk about it?"

"No!"

"Okay. Let me light the stove and put some coffee on. You want some coffee?"

"Yeah."

David reached for the lamp to go out to the kitchen, but Jack grabbed his hand, stopping him.

"Don't take the light. Don't leave me in the dark."

"Okay," David assured him, and left the lamp on the side table. "Don't go anywhere. I'll be right back."

Jack nodded. "Yeah."

David disappeared into the darkness, and Jack could hear him feeling his way around the kitchen. Another light flared up and spread out, chasing away the shadows and the night fears.

Jack remained hunched up on his bed, leaning against the wall with his blanket tugged snugly around him, while he tried to warm up and calm down.

It didn't take long for David to get the stove lit, as he had gotten into the habit of leaving paper, tinder and kindling in the basket beside the stove before heading off to bed each night. It only took him a moment to transfer the fuel into the belly and set it alight. Once that was done, and the coffee set to go, he returned to the bedroom, bringing with him a cup which he handed to Jack.

"Here, drink this. It'll help."

"What is it?"

"A couple of shots of brandy," David told him as he pulled up a chair and sat down. "Believe me, you'll feel better for it."

"I thought you didn't want me drinkin'."

David smiled. "This is medicinal, so it's all right."

"Oh," echoed out from the cup, as Jack held it up to his mouth and downed it in one go.

"Feeling a little better now?"

"Yeah. You're right, it's helpin'."

"Good." David stretched out his long legs and yawned. He smiled sheepishly at the look Jack gave him. "Sorry."

"Don't let me keep ya up, David."

David ran his hands through his tussled hair and scratched his scalp, then yawned again before he could stop himself. "No, it's all right. I don't mind."

"Ya sure?" Jack grumbled. "I wouldn't wanna impose."

"Jack, it's fine," David insisted. "I'm still just waking up, that's all."

"Well, okay. So long as you're sure."

"Hmm. You feel up to talking about it now?"

"No."

"It'll help."

"David!"

David smiled. "Yeah, okay. I'll stop pushing. Did you get in to see Sheriff Murphy on your way to the prison?"

"Yeah," Jack answered, more relaxed now that David wasn't going to keep pushing him about the nightmare. "There's not too much happenin' there. He's tried ta get in ta see Governor Warren, but he keeps gettin' blocked out, so he's gonna leave it alone for a while." Jack sighed, running his hands through his curls and rubbing his eyes. Then it was his turn to yawn. "I got a letter today from an old friend 'a ours. I was surprised ta hear from her, 'cause she and Leon were . . . well . . . once close, and well . . . it's complicated."

"Yup," David commented. "It always is."

"Yeah," Jack agreed. "Anyway, she's quite a resourceful lady, and she's offered to help any way she can. Maybe comin' at it from a different direction might get some results. Like you said; a straight line rather than runnin' in circles."

"It's worth a try," David responded, hoping to keep Jack talking.

"Penny has been busy makin' up fliers ta send around ta places they didn't get the first time. Once Caroline gets settled in Denver, she and Steven have some plans from there."

"That sounds promising."

Jack nodded. "I'll have ta get in touch with Steven soon, and find out what he has in mind. Here I've been assurin' Leon that we're gonna get him out of there, and I've hardly done anything to that end."

"You're had a lot on your plate lately, Jack," David reminded him. "Get yourself better first and then you can go full force into this campaign, along with your friends."

"I am better," Jack commented, almost in a huff.

"Then why are you still having nightmares?" David pointed out.

Jack rubbed his eyes again and groaned. "Ohh, I don't know. I just wish they'd stop. I don't know where this last one came from—it was brutal."

"New one, was it?" David asked. "Never had it before?"

"No, never." Jack sighed. "And I never want it again."

"Hmm. Coffee's ready." David stood up. "I'll bring it in here. You just stay there and keep warm."

David nipped out to the kitchen, poured two coffees, then came straight back into the guest room, to find his friend staring off into space, his expression taut and anxious.

The doctor sat down and scrutinized the man sitting across from him.

"Jack?" he said, quietly.

Jack jumped and popped back to the present.

David smiled and handed him the mug. "Here's your coffee."

"Ah, thanks." He took it and downed half the cup in one gulp.

David cringed, knowing it must have burned. Jack appeared not to have noticed.

"You all right?" David asked.

"Yeah."

"What were you thinking about just then?"

Jack turned sad eyes toward him, a worried, almost frightened expression floating across his features.

"It's just, that dream," he answered quietly, almost in a whisper. "I don't understand where it came from. It was, it was so . . . brutal."

"Was it about Napoleon again?"

"No, no. Those ones are bad too, but at least I understand where they're comin' from. But this one . . ." Jack shook his head, again running his hands through his curls. "This one came outta nowhere. Penny was in it—at first.". He creased his forehead, confused. "Then it wasn't Penny—then it was again."

David took a sip of coffee. "When it wasn't Penny, who was it?"

"I don't know," Jack felt fear rise in him again, and he couldn't understand why. "It was a prostitute. She looked like Penny, but it weren't her."

David shivered slightly. He took another sip of coffee to calm his own nerves. He knew he had to tread carefully here, gently; this was dangerous ground.

"What was she doing?" he asked.

The question got met with silence. Jack broke eye contact and stared into space again. He locked up.

David back stepped. "When the dream started, you were with Penny?"

"Yeah."

388

"Was it pleasant?"

Jack took another sip of coffee, then looked at David and nodded.

"Yeah, it was nice," he murmured. "We went ridin' together, like we often do, ya know?" David nodded. "I was thinkin' how good it was to be havin' a pleasant dream rather than them awful nightmares. I was actually thinkin' that while dreamin'—isn't that weird?"

"Yeah."

Jack sighed. "We stopped under a tree to have lunch, and it was sunny and warm; a real nice day. I felt good. Penny was . . . beautiful."

"Penny is beautiful," David agreed. "She was happy? You were having a good time?"

"Yeah," Jack whispered. "Then we . . . well, we started to make love." He was embarrassed at first, then his expression morphed to one of anxiety and confusion. "That's when she changed; she wasn't Penny anymore."

"She became the prostitute?"

"Yeah. I felt betrayed. I got angry. Real angry."

Silence again, and Jack looked back into his dream, his eyes darting back and forth as he watched the events unfold through his mind's vision. Then suddenly, he was shaking and broke out into another cold sweat.

David watched him intently, and then he saw it; the light in Jack's eyes changed, and suddenly they were filled with terror and revulsion. David knew that what Jack recalled now was no longer the dream, but the reality of that last night in Cheyenne.

Jack's coffee cup clattered to the floor, splattering its contents in every direction. He pushed himself back, deeper and deeper into the corner of the wall.

"No!" he gasped. "No, no, no. No. What is that? I couldn't have done that. No! Please. David tell me I didn't do that." He gasped for air, grabbing at the blanket. Then he was crying, sobbing wildly, desperately begging for absolution. "Please tell me David. Tell me I didn't do that—"

David was on his feet in an instant, his own coffee cup forgotten on the floor. He reached out for his friend, trying to calm him down, trying to bring him back to reason.

"Jack, it's all right. Settle down. It's all right."

"No—!"

Jack lunged forward, a crazed gleam in his eye. He shoved David hard, pushing his friend away from him.

David went back, falling over his own chair and landing with a crash and clatter onto the floor, cracking his head against the far wall.

Jack came to his feet and ran. He didn't know where he was going or why—he just knew he had to run, had to get away from that despicable reality that was himself.

TO BE CONTINUED

Cast of Characters: Volume Two

- Bains, Joan: Witness at Leon's trial
- Betsy: Waitress, Cheyenne, Wyoming
- Bill: Bartender, Arvada, Colorado
- Bill: Deputy, Cheyenne, Wyoming
- Boeman, Hank: Alpha inmate, U.S. Penitentiary at Laramie City.
- Carlyle, Frank: Rocky Mountain detective
- Carson, Floyd: Senior guard, U.S. Penitentiary at Laramie City.
- Charles, Brian: Witness at Leon's trial. Fellow orphan
- Clayt: Telegrapher in Arvada, Colorado
- Cobb, Malachi: Gus Shaffer's partner. Member of the Elk Mountain Gang
- Coburn, Maxwell (Max): Texas rancher. Friend of Leon and Jack
- DeFord, Harold: Lawyer for the prosecution
- Fred: Prisoner in the Cheyenne jail
- George: Prisoner in the Cheyenne jail
- Gibson, David: Doctor in Arvada, Colorado
- Gibson, Tricia: nee Baxter: David's wife
- Granger, Steven: Lawyer for the defence
- Griffin, Michael: David's friend from back East
- Hamlin, Clive; Medical assistant, Cheyenne, Wyoming
- Harris, Carl: Inmate. Buddies up with Boeman
- Higgins: Assistant to the Governor, Wyoming
- Jacobs, Carl: Sheriff, Arvada, Wyoming
- Jansen, Josephine (Josey): Childhood friend to Jack and Leon
- Jaxton, Edward: Witness at Jack's trial. Described the day when Jack shot Quincy Bartlett
- Jefferies, Merle: Sam's mother
- Jefferies, Sam: Hired hand at the Rocking M
- Jefferies, Tom: Sam's father
- Johnston: Inmate
- Jones: Doctor in Rawlins, Wyoming
- Kelly: Inmate
- Kiefer, Jackson (Jack. The Kansas Kid). Alias: Mathew White.

Ex-outlaw
- Konachy, Harvey: Young inmate who committed suicide
- Kristiansen: Inmate
- Lacey, John: Chief Justice, Wyoming Territorial Court. 1884 - 1886
- Layton, Richard (Rick): Rancher, part-time deputy, Rawlins, Wyoming
- Lindy: Leon's first sexual encounter
- Lobo: Member of the Elk Mountain Gang, Wyoming
- Shaffer, Gus: Current leader of the Elk Mountain Gang, Wyoming
- Marsham, Cameron: Friend to Leon and Jack. Rancher, Rocking M Ranch, schoolteacher. Arvada, Colorado
- Marsham, Caroline: Eldest child of Cameron and Jean
- Marsham, Elijah (Eli): Youngest child of Cameron and Jean
- Marsham, Jean: Cameron's wife
- Marsham, Penelope (Penny): Middle child of Cameron and Jean
- McEnroe, Henry: Judge, New Mexico. Knows Leon and Jack. Friends
- McPhee, Fedamire (Fingers): Con man. Leon and Jack's benefactor during the early years
- Millie: Tricia's next-door neighbor
- Mitchell, Mason: Warden, U.S. Penitentiary at Laramie City.
- Morrison, Tom: Sheriff. Rawlins, Wyoming
- Murdock, Rolland (Rolly): Witness at Leon's trial. Early acquaintance of Leon's
- Murphy, Taggard: Ex-outlaw. Former Elk Mountain gang member. Sheriff. Medicine Bow, Wyoming
- Murray: Guard
- Nash, Antoinette: Leon's half-sister
- Nash, Edward: Leon's father
- Nash, Frederick: Leon's half-brother
- Nash, Jenny. Leon's full sister
- Nash, Louisa: Leon's half-sister. Jack's mother
- Nash, Napoleon (Leon). Alias: Peter Black. Ex-outlaw, former leader of the Elk Mountain Gang, Wyoming
- Palin, Ben: Deputy, Arvada, Colorado
- Palin, Walter (Doc): Doctor, Wyoming U.S. Penitentiary at

Laramie City.

- Pearson: Guard. Wyoming U.S. Penitentiary at Laramie City.
- Redekopp, Jonathan (Red): Con man
- Reece, Connor: Eldest son of Kenny and Sarah
- Reece, Kenny: Senior guard, Wyoming U.S. Penitentiary at Laramie City.
- Roberts, Kenneth: Witness at Leon's trial
- Ross, Clyde: One of the raiders who attacked the Nash/Kiefer farms
- Schulmeyer, Eric: Livery man. Arvada, Wyoming.
- Shields, Charlie: Member of the Elk Mountain Gang, Wyoming
- Shoemacher, Mike: Deputy, Rawlins, Wyoming
- Snodgrass, Nigel: Witness at Leon's trial
- Soames, Mariam: Degrees in theology and philosophy. A friend to Jack and Leon, assistant to Dr. Palin, and runs the local orphanage. Laramie, Wyoming.
- Stanton, Julia: Witness at Jack's trial. Describes how Jack murdered her father
- Strode, Alex: Deputy. Rawlins, Wyoming
- Taff: Doctor in Cheyenne, Wyoming
- Tanguay, Gabriella: Actress, former undercover agent, Leon's ex-lover
- Turner: Sheriff, Cheyenne, Wyoming
- Wilkens, Lilly: one of their marks
- Wilkinson, Hank: Member of the Elk Mountain Gang
- Willis, Maribelle: Sam's girlfriend
- Wissen, Cal: Julia Stanton's father

WYOMING GOVERNORS

In order of term

- Hoyt, John Wesley: 1878 – 1882
- Hale, William: 1882 – 1885
- Morgan, Elliot: 1885.
- Warren, Frances: 1885 – 1886
- Baxter, George: 1886
- Morgan, Elliot: 1886 – 1887
- Moonlight, Thomas: 1887 – 1889
- Warren, Frances: 1889 – 1890
- Barber, Amos: 1890 – 1893
- Osborn, John: 1893 – 1895
- Richards, William: 1895 - 1899
- Richards, DeForrest: 1899 – 1903

Volume Three: Dangerous Games

Leon groaned audibly and ran his hands over his scalp. He hadn't done himself any favors with his 'over reaction'. Kenny was mad at him, he could tell, and the last thing he wanted to do was push the patience of that particular guard. Carson could send him to the dark cell, but Kenny, by withdrawing his support, could send him to the insane asylum.

Then a thought came to Leon's mind. He frowned and turned still as stone while the thought took hold and spread out, slowly becoming a plan. It was a dangerous plan, as he would very likely be hurt and, almost certainly, be spending time in the dark cell. That thought sent fear shivering through him, and he almost backed off the whole idea. But it wouldn't go away, and he knew that he just might have to accept that punishment if he was going to play games with the warden and the other inmates, and still manage to keep himself alive.

Yes, the plan took hold, and the more Leon thought about it, the more he was convinced that it would work. It is safe to say that anyone who knew Napoleon Nash well, would have shivered at the smile that played about his lips.

About the Author

I have always been a cowgirl at heart even though I have lived my whole life either on the West Coast of Canada and the USA., but our road trips always draw us east and south. Montana, Wyoming, Colorado; these are places where my imagination runs wild.

I've been an artist/writer all my life, painting and writing about my first passion; the West. I also found a nitch with painting pet portraits and animal studies. Now that I am retired, I can indulge in the things I love the most; my husband, my animals, my art and my writing. I'm busier now than I have ever been before, and I wouldn't have it any other way.

www.TwoBlazesArtworks.com